RESCUE CHECKLIST

RESCUE CHECKLIST

A. P. SHEFFIELD

Rescue Checklist
Ready to Answer So Others May Live

Cover design by Miblart.

Trade Paperback ISBN: 979-8-89109-560-1
Hardcover ISBN: 979-8-89109-780-3
eBook ISBN: 979-8-89109-561-8
Library of Congress Cataloging-in-Publication Data number: 2023921740

Published in the United States by Be Ready LLC, Blairsville, Georgia.

Subjects: Adventure and adventurers-Fiction, Teen and Young Adult Action and Adventure, Suspense, Military, Coast Guard, Disaster, Allegory

Printed in USA
1st Edition 2023

CONTENTS

PROLOGUE

"We do this job because every once in a while
someone is out there without hope,
desperately praying for their life, and we got to be the answer."
–Mario Vittone, USCG Aviation Survival Technician (Retired)

"We're always ready for the call,
We place our trust in Thee.
Through surf and storm and howling gale,
High shall our purpose be.
"Semper Paratus" is our guide,
Our fame, our glory too.
To fight to save or fight and die,
Aye! Coast Guard we are for you!"
--Semper Paratus, The United States Coast Guard Marching Song, 1927

PART I

FOLLOW ME OR DIE ALONE

Chapter 1

HELP IS ON THE WAY

The scariest place in the entire universe is alone in a stormy vast ocean, desperate for rescue. Joshua swung back and forth in a sea of desperation. Disparaged eyes of people searched for him to wrench them out of the sea of chaos that threatened to engulf them all. Fear drug them all down below the surface of survival. Their despondent futures endangered their souls.

Where would their help come from, he thought.

Joshua Mansoul persevered over his fears as he roamed through a sea of unfamiliar faces in his high school cafeteria. The school cafeteria was often a place that provoked fear. He pressed forward to find an open location to sit. He needed to find respite from the hurricane that raged outside and the storm of emotions within him. He white-knuckled his tray. He tried to remain calm and remembered to breathe as his dark brown eyes swung back and forth over the sea of anxious people. This wasn't his familiar sight of obnoxious high school students. The cafeteria was filled with evacuees who'd probably lost everything in Hurricane Ike. They were more desperate for rescue than desperate for attention. They represented every age and nationality and part of humanity.

He thought, *This could be the largest segment of humankind ever to have arrived in our Red Cross Shelter.*

The tumultuous storm birthed misery and covered Joshua's Gulf Coast hometown of Galveston, Texas. They all wanted to survive it.

"Rescue me," they all seemed to say to him with sad looks of misery.

Joshua aspired to thrive in it.

He thought, *I gotta find one willing soul to look up.*

The lunch period was renowned for its tough crowds on a regular school day. It was a challenge to discover a free seat on a typical day. However, things were way more intense than the hangry (hungry and angry) teens and their excessive high school dramas that wrote the script for their principal's demise. The devastation Hurricane Ike had caused outside threatened his school's inside-controlled chaos. Displaced people who spoke several dialects from across coastal Texas were packed inside the building for want of shelter and food.

I have a decision to make.

I am a survivor of storms, not a victim of them.

Joshua continued to shuffle forward as his eyes roamed back and forth. Baffled children, teenagers, young adults, parents, and some elderly cowered under their weighty and bedraggled exteriors. Their interior lives had been strained to the breaking point.

I know how the recent storm has torn apart your lives...mine was, too.

Joshua's compassion recognized their desperation that the storm already could have claimed their every possession and perhaps their souls. He let out a long sigh and realized he had stopped moving forward. He threw back his shoulders, drew himself up to his full 16-year-old height of 5'9", and looked for someone who needed his rescue. He scanned the crowd and saw a younger person who looked like himself at 13, the year he was rescued. The boy with coal-black hair, dark-tanned skin, and a mournful look caught his eye. The look tore at Joshua's heart, mind, and soul.

This guy needs rescue, just like I was, thought Joshua.

"Ayúdame (help me)," he whispered to his unseen papa.

He did not have to imagine a rescue. He'd lived through one, and he wanted to pay it forward. He remembered his rescue from the sludge of Hurricane Katrina three years earlier. He remembered the nasty, muddy flood waters that rose around him then, and today, it was a flood of gloomy and miserable faces. He wanted to find someone else to experience freedom as he had been given it.

Just one person at a time, he thought.

Joshua crossed the room to a Hispanic family that looked just like his. They reminded him of his own, and he stood motionless. The boisterous children who climbed on their mama seemed oblivious to him and their mother. She stared blankly at the wall behind them in shock at all that had happened to them in the past day. Two miserable teenagers sat across from her, who looked woeful when he approached and then rolled their eyes when he waited.

Ugh, I won't take it personally.

He courageously dared to show his crooked teeth and pasted on a smile. He hoped they at least appreciated his effort.

He hoped that his vulnerability would give them something else to think about.

Sometimes, having teeth like mine at least gives me pity points.

He asked, "May I have this seat?" again in Spanish, "Puedo tener este asiento?"

I'm so relieved my voice didn't crack as it stubbornly has the last couple of years.

Each one looked at him with a bit of confusion for different reasons. Why he addressed their hurricane of a family with kindness, in a familial manner, and courtesy, they could not fathom. The mother nodded her acknowledgment and shrugged towards him as if to say, "You look safe enough," with a weary gaze of indifference. The teens just lowered their eyes in self-consciousness. The new smiling face enthralled the kids, and they eyed his tray full of goodies. They were the eye of the storm, a joyful moment that only Joshua could see.

He sat, closed his eyes, and murmured something under his breath that the family could not quite recognize. He recognized his thanks for his food, such as it was, while he nervously gripped the sides of his tray and tried to think of a way to break the ice.

He said, "Gracias."

His eyes popped wide open, and he smiled widely when he realized he'd caught them openly staring at him. He laughed out loud since he'd surprised them, and the children laughed noisily with him.

The teenage girls are probably used to being more fashionable than their current state in old sweatshirts, messy buns, and no make-up; he had tried not to notice.

Their cheeks had turned bright pink, and they suddenly became more interested in their dirty fingernails than him, or so they tried to make him think.

The children clamored to his side and begged for the chips and snack cake on his tray, "Tapas por favor."

Their mother snapped out of her daze and urged them to knock it off, but Joshua just chuckled since he understood their hunger.

Joshua asked the kids, "Who will sit still for chips, cake, and a story?"

His parents had done the same to him and his brothers at the same age as these kids. His stomach growled when he remembered the delicious food his mother made as his father told them ancient, fantastic, adventuresome stories.

The dark-eyed children, a small boy and a girl shushed, leaned towards him, and settled on their mother's lap. Joshua peaceably fed them his food and rescue account while the storm raged around them.

"First, let me introduce myself. I am called Joshua. A couple of years ago, I was caught in another hurricane, Katrina, a lot like this one," he began.

The entire family grew silent. Even the teenage girls, who had tried to look bored, gave him their attention.

"My family and I were just one family of the 60,000 people stranded in New Orleans," he continued, "That is a beautiful city far from here. It is in a soggy place near the Gulf of Mexico. Fortunately, the USCG, the United States Coast Guard, rescued over 33,500 *souls.*"

He placed his fist over his heart and paused for emphasis. He looked around the long table that now had 16 souls that sat around him with rapt attentiveness. He realized he had the attention of more than just the immediate family closest to him. The mother unconsciously reached up and touched her necklace with a gold crucifix around her neck as the words registered with her.

"I promised and you've done what I asked," he said.

He opened the snack cake package for the children, who had been good listeners. He broke each in half, raised them, glanced upwards, and then handed each side to the open-handed children. They were giddy with appreciation, raised their halves, and mimicked him to everyone's amusement.

One of the teenage girls asked, "So, how old were you when Katrina hit? I think I remember that happening, like forever ago."

"I was 13 and am the oldest chico in my family," he said.

Forever was hardly three years ago, but maybe it had been for this girl.

Joshua was almost lost in his thoughts.

It seems like yesterday to me.

He continued, "My two brothers, Jimmy and Jude, were still small. We heard about a storm far away for a couple of days, but then my parents told me they became more concerned because we had no car to leave New Orleans. My dad had his building tools and went to look for boards to cover the windows since we had nowhere else to go. When he returned with what he could carry, he also said we should sleep upstairs that night. The wind and rain were so loud. We begged him to return downstairs, but he knew to keep us as high as possible."

Joshua paused momentarily as the group listened to the intensifying winds and rain that pounded the rooftop. The eerie effect was that he shared a ghost story, but they were all inside under the white luminescent lighting. The mama wanted the rescue story to continue, so she urged him on.

She asked, "So then what happened?"

"On the morning of August 29th, we had to stand in water up to our waists inside the upstairs of our house," he continued. "My Dad kept reminding us that help was on the way; we just had to believe in him. It was the most scared I'd ever been before. When we saw the water rise to the top stairs on the second floor, we knew we'd lost everything we owned down there. We were miserable as we realized how much we were losing, but we were thankful we had each other. And we had hope."

Joshua looked at the kids on their mother's lap, who clung to one another.

"My little brothers were not so brave as you two munchkins. We had to take turns holding them on our backs all night because there was nowhere to put them down. The water rose to our ankles and then our knees. All I wanted to do was find a place to sit down and fall asleep. I was thirsty, too! So much water and nothing we could drink!"

Joshua paused and took a long gulp of water from the bottle on his tray.

I see everyone else is thirsty, too, now; Joshua noticed as others unconsciously did the same.

He began again, "Eventually, my parents decided to go out on the rooftop once the rain stopped falling. My mom wanted to try to figure out how to get help, but dad just knew help was on the way."

An older gentleman with crazy hair and round spectacles had approached the table, and some other strangers of various ages stood behind and listened intently.

Joshua knew, *If I raise my voice a little more, I can try to rescue a few more from their despair with my story of hope.*

The smallest boy said, "Mama, his neighborhood was like ours before we came here..." Then he turned back to Joshua and demanded, as kids do, "What happened next?"

Joshua re-engaged, "We were finally sitting on the rooftop in disbelief at our neighborhood underwater. The next thing I remembered was sounds that thumped and rumbled so loud my heart thudded in my chest. I realized it had a thundering rhythm, and we saw helicopter blades swooshing over us. I'd never seen anything so powerful in my life. A big guy in orange came down from the helo on a cable like a samurai warrior and held an axe like a sword."

Joshua held his arm as if he were holding an axe and shouted, "Ándale! Ándale!"

Everyone burst out with laughter after his dramatic shout. The children on their mother's lap had leaned so far forward on every word of Joshua's that one slid off. When the warrior arrived, the other had crawled on the table to be closer and clapped her hands. Joshua leaned towards her and her brother and relished the innocence and rapt attention of the children.

They are listening and believing in my hope-filled story!

He sipped his water and continued with sweeping gestures as storytellers do, "The rescuer first tried talking to my parents, but they couldn't hear over the tremendous noise of the helicopter. He just motioned upwards, and then an orange and silver basket big enough for me to jump inside was lowered down from the helicopter. I went running into the basket first. I was so excited! I went willingly, but my brothers, not so much. Jimmy, well, he was terrified. My Dad danced on that roof and said, 'Keep looking up, niños! I held open my arms to Jimmy, and since we were scrawny, the orange warrior angel helped put him across from me, too. He faced me in disbelief. I held onto my brother to save him from crawling out because he was afraid to leave Mama and Papa."

Joshua said, "The leap of faith we must all take, to trust our rescuer."

Joshua looked up and continued with arms over his head. "Up we went; I saw my neighborhood and then my city underwater. I was so happy to fly up in that basket and wave at my parents below. My mom and Jude came together next. We learned later my papa refused to leave. He hugged the warrior angel and gestured he would search for and rescue our neighbors.... My mama said the last thing he told her was, 'See? Help was on the way. I'll meet up with you soon.'"

Joshua took a deep breath, looked down at his empty tray, and collected his rolling emotions. The silence was heavy in the room, but it seemed out of reverence, not sadness. The fear, sense of loss, and bewilderment over the past three years still felt weighty. However, his dad's last words hung over him like a comforter on a cold night, 'I'll meet up with you soon.' Joshua finally cleared his throat to check his emotions and pulled his eyes towards the mother who sat nearby. He saw her tired, dark eyes brimmed with tears, so he pressed on to bring her the good news of the rescue.

He continued, "Jimmy said that he saved me from falling out of the basket because I cheered and danced as we went soaring up to the angels in orange. Some people create angels that look like blonde Barbies with white wings. Nope, I've seen what angels look like myself. The ones I saw wore orange and were as tough as can be."

Joshua flexed his arm next to his head to reveal a big bicep for a thin young man. He grinned his biggest grin yet. The small crowd laughed at the thought of him being a robust and muscular angel. Joshua glanced at his tray to refocus and saw that the kids had mainly eaten the food before him.

I can eat later, Joshua admitted as his stomach grumbled, *I hope.*

"The big letters, USCG, painted on the bottom of the white and orange helicopter, was the most welcome sight I'd ever had. I still dream about those letters. It was the rescue we'd never imagined but had hoped for so badly. I can't remember much after that. I think I immediately fell asleep; I was so exhausted. I'd been rescued from that icky, chaotic water, and that was all the peace I needed."

Joshua asked the young kids, "Was your neighborhood's flood water icky when you left?"

"It was so gross," the little boy said. "At first, we thought it was cool, like a huge swimming pool took over, but Mama said not to touch it because, yuck, snakes!"

One of the teenagers asked quietly, "What happened to your dad?"

Joshua paused before he answered, "I am still waiting to see my dad again. He went on to rescue many of our neighbors and helped them get on top of their roofs for the Coast Guard to find. I'm at peace with him giving his all to rescue our neighbors."

The other teenager said, "Awe, that's tough," as her eyes spilled over with tears.

The rest of the group fell silent in respect.

Joshua replied with his head held high, "When I try to fall asleep at night, I focus on the good news, and I still envision those big letters, USCG. I remember my dad's courage and the courage of the men and women in the Coast Guard. Now I know they stand for the United States Coast Guard. I dream of that wonderful, amazing sound of thundering blades. I'm so grateful for their mission to rescue every man, woman, and child who will follow, answer, and remember them. They even grabbed some people's dogs and cats. I want to be a rescuer, too, to honor them. What about you?"

They nodded their heads in appreciation, but none spoke up. The perspective of the gathering had changed with the undeniable and profoundly personal story Joshua had shared. Instead of the misery he had found them in, they were then thoughtful. In a silent reverie, they considered his hopeful words as though they had a choice to make themselves and sat with contemplation instead of desolation.

Mission accomplished, thanks, Papa, thought Joshua.

He glanced at the ceiling over him, then returned his gaze to the now large crowd gathered around him.

"Congress recognized the Coast Guard's response with an official entry in the Congressional Record. That's just an impressive way to say it was a big deal. I know they are out there today in the storm, making more rescues as we sit here in safety. So, my story of rescue is like one of many others rescued. Today may be your day to rescue someone. You and I should never forget what it feels like to ask, Rescue me, and then follow."

The mother said, "What is your name?"

"Joshua Mansoul, there you are!"

An exasperated middle-aged woman from across the room wove herself through the crowd. She wore a pained smile and a worn Red Cross apron with a nametag that read *Maria.*

The group laughed nervously for him at the well-timed interruption.

Uh, oh. both names...

The petite woman had dark hair pinned back with gray roots that framed her round face. She bustled to Joshua's side and admonished him. Surprised by the crowd of onlookers around him, she asked,

"Where have you been?" she added, "Have you eaten?"

Joshua looked around and blushed at the group that surrounded him. There were additional kids and their parents, maybe grandparents, from nearby tables who now stood behind the others. They had all listened in to his story of saving grace.

He gestured to them and replied, "I've been doing what Papa asked me to do."

A look of confusion swept over the woman, who everyone now realized was his mother.

She hugged him from the side and asked, "And that would be?"

One of the younger kids from the rag-tag gathering piped up, "Getting warrior angels for the next mission!" he proudly flexed both arms on either side of his head.

Everyone then burst into laughter, a welcome sound in that sad place. Maria had a confused look. Joshua fist-bumped the kids first, and even the pink-cheeked girls grinned at him openly. His brown eyes sparkled with wisdom and joy. He glanced up at his mother and stood in obedience at her expression of dismay.

He cleared his throat and added, "Please excuse me; mi Madre has found something for me to do."

As they walked away, another ominous gust of wind shook the building.

Maria realized that as she had cleaned and cooked, she had depended, maybe too much, on Joshua's assistance.

"I thought it was entirely up to us to keep the crowds fed and as comfortable as we could make them," she added, "but I couldn't find you!"

She still had her arm around his waist while he stood a few inches over her. She wiped her brow and, with exhaustion that made her voice tremble, turned to gaze up at him.

"You're too thin. You're never going to grow giving your food away, muchacho."

Joshua squeezed her tightly and redirected their steps toward a place for uninterrupted conversation. She squeezed him back and exhaled deeply.

"Do you remember, niño?"

He summoned his courage to address what he thought his mom was concerned about that day.

Was now really the time to discuss this? In the middle of my high school, now turned into a refugee center.

He embraced her and muttered, "Of course, Mama. It's like our experience on replay, isn't it?"

For almost everyone he knew, high school was the storm of daily life. He looked around and noticed how crazy it was that it had become a shelter in the hurricane. Kids tried to play made-up games; some adults attempted to sleep, and others sat dazed. He had offered hope.

Mission accomplished.

He looked down and saw the deep lines of pain and concern emblazoned across her forehead. He knew people were watching them. Maria steered them from the gawking crowd to a storage room, away from nosy people, outside the cafeteria. When they were inside, she burst into tears. Joshua then fought back tears of his own.

He said, "Mama, I know it's hard to relive what happened to Dad that day. This storm, Ike, and every named hurricane or terrible storm should bring us to our knees. What did Dad say to us over and over? 'Help is on the way!' We must continue to cling to that. You and I keep hope alive by being the rescuers for others. We want to be like the warriors that rescue more families like ours, one soul at a time."

Joshua's mother went limp into his arms. He caught her and slid them down the wall behind them. He held onto her a long time as she wept before he whispered into her ear.

"You and Papa have told me this since I was a child, 'In this storm and every day, you and I must decide. Will we answer with hope or despair?'"

She felt like a sword had pierced her soul as she grieved the desperateness of those around her who had been without hope. She remembered how her losses had torn apart her heart, her beloved husband and father to her three amazing boys, for the pain of the past and continued struggle afterward. She also cried for the people who would grieve without hope of rescue while the storm raged around them and later from their tragic losses.

Later, as they huddled together on the floor, she pulled her sixteen-year-old child closer and cried joyfully. She sobbed an ugly cry, full of gratitude, for a son who would comfort her in her grief with wisdom she did not yet possess.

She wiped her face with her food-stained apron and said, "My Joshua has grown up so soon, too soon."

It was he, she realized, as she relaxed in his embrace and sighed deeply, *that now held her instead of the other way around.*

She touched his face and added, "And not just in stature but with such wisdom. Te amo. I love you, niño."

She thought, *He shouldn't have had to bear these burdens, but he has done so graciously.*

He put his head down on hers and breathed in her rosemary, olive oil, and grease scent.

Joshua wondered: *How long will I be able to hold onto her?*

How many more storms will find us?

With some reluctance, Joshua realized, *From now on, I will protect her more than she can save me.*

I think I'm adulting now.

Joshua looked up at the ceiling in hopefulness, *Rescue Me.*

He shivered, and then the future excited him for some unknown reason.

Follow Me.

He closed his eyes and focused his imagination on the USCG bold letters. He recalled the feeling of the helicopter's rotor blades' resonance as it washed over and through him. How long they sat on that hard floor in the sea of vast uncertainty, they did not know. However, they were comforted by hope and memory of his papa's words "Help is on the way."

Chapter 2

LOOK UP

Two years later...

"Joshua Mansoul, please report to the office immediately."

"Ohhh, you've done it this time, Joshie!" derisive laughter broke out amongst his peers.

Joshua gathered and shoved his things in his backpack on his way out of the World Civilizations classroom door. The intercom had been a rude interruption to his teacher's lecture but a welcome reprieve. The laughter was shut out as the door closed behind him in the quiet hallway. As he walked to the principal's office, he wondered what on earth he could be in trouble for. A senior in High School, he had good enough grades, volunteered at the Red Cross (mainly for the free food), worked as a lifeguard regularly, and was as kind to everyone as he knew how to be.

He thought, *Maybe I did poorly on a paper, and the swim team coach is mad.*

I can almost taste graduation; please, don't let this be about not graduating...

Joshua looked through the office's large windows and saw the secretary, another student, the principal, and an older white-haired man who sat slumped as if he had waited for a bus to arrive.

The petite secretary said, "Welcome, you've been expected."

If that was meant to put him at ease, he wasn't sure it did. Another student, slighter than he was, stood nearby, signing out for the day.

With a nasal voice, the stocky teen whined, "I don't want to go to the orthodontist's office again for my stupid braces to be adjusted. It hurts every time afterward. I'll still have to do the classwork, too."

He looked at Joshua for empathy. Joshua's back stiffened. He would have given a lot to have the opportunity to get braces for his crooked teeth. Joshua smiled obnoxiously big, which he rarely did, at this kid to see if he had a brain. When the groveling teenager unexpectedly saw Joshua's crooked and toothy smile, he took a step back in disgust. He was struck by the misshapenness of some of his teeth and the awkward way it made him feel. The freshman felt for the door behind him, turned around, and yanked it open to escape.

Joshua thought, *Some entitled kids I will never understand.*

It bothered Joshua how some people complained about what they were given and lacked general gratitude. His mom worked so hard in town. She also volunteered so much at the American Red Cross that they finally gave in and hired her there. The pay wasn't what she was worth, but he knew she must have felt closer to his dad when she was helping other people in her unassuming way. The pay was extra food for her three hungry sons.

The annoyed secretary turned back to her desk. She shook her head in disapproval of the far too many students she had endured who whined. She remembered Joshua still stood quietly and had taken in the whole scenario. She came around the desk and knocked politely on the principal's door.

"Joshua Mansoul is here to see you now."

Joshua shifted from one foot to the other as he realized the ancient man regarded him closely, *too close*. With his prominent thin mustache, Principal Blanchard introduced Joshua to Mr. Jones, the older man who struggled to his feet. They obviously wanted to talk with him, and the principal turned abruptly into his office and offered chairs to each of them across from his desk. They each sat, although it was hard to watch the stiff man try to get up and down after he waved off their assistance.

Principal Blanchard said, "Well, let me get straight to it, Josh."

This hardly bothered Joshua, but no one who knew him called him that nickname. It was forgivable, though, since he'd never stepped foot in the principal's office, and for good reasons. Mr. B, as the students referred to him commonly, let his eyes rest on Joshua momentarily as if unsure how to proceed. Ever conscious of his crooked teeth, Joshua smiled with a lift of the corner of his mouth to encourage the principal to go on and not frighten him.

Joshua thought, *Let's get this over with, please.*

Joshua curiously glanced at the older gentleman to his right. He seemed somewhat familiar, but he couldn't place him. He didn't want to stare openly, so he returned to face Mr. B. and leaned backward in his chair to wait.

Where have I seen him? That white bushy unibrow?

"It came to my attention that you were recently given an award for saving a life at the beach last summer while on lifeguard duty. Is that right?"

Joshua, surprised that the subject of his job at Stewart Beach was what brought him to the principal's office, nodded. Joshua still felt relieved that he had been able to pull the child to shore after a rogue sneaker wave filled with sand, rocks, and debris had pulled her far out in the Gulf. He had felt like he had to tread on the water; it was so thick that day. He had begun CPR just before more help arrived.

"The paramedics had saved the girl's life," Joshua always told people, "because I was just part of the lifeguard crew."

His job was to fish them out of trouble while the medics were on their way. The medics were not willing to be overpowered by the wall of water, though. The local newspaper had recorded his heroic swim that no other lifeguard was ready to initiate. Water had the potential to become a fundamental threat to human life. Watery chaos had threatened life since the beginning of existence on Earth. Particularly for the innocent, unassuming, disrespectful, and unprepared, it was all too often fatal. His humility about the scenario was not lost on Mr. B. nor the man beside him, who suddenly leaned forward and cut in.

Mr. Jones said, "I'm here to offer you an opportunity of a lifetime. I read about your rescue in the paper months ago. I had to get some help to track you down when I saw your record-breaking swim times for this school last month."

The timeworn man pointed, "Your principal here," glancing cautiously towards Mr. B. "Didn't think an old man ought to butt into a high schooler's life he didn't know, but I wore him down. I also promised donuts."

Perfectly timed, the school secretary carried a tray of donuts, coffee, and milk. She set the tray right in front of Joshua and gestured to him his choice of a small mountain of various donuts. Joshua's stomach rumbled at the sight and smell. His mother worked shifts for years and volunteered at the American Red Cross ever since his dad was... well, gone. The boys were always welcome there and probably enjoyed the free donuts more than they should have. That community became like an extended family. She did her best to provide well for her three growing sons, but they were always still hungry. As the oldest teenager,

Joshua was already the biggest, so he insisted that the younger boys take the first and more generous portions. He found volunteering at the Red Cross when he could make up for a few missed meals during the week. The boys quickly learned that making themselves helpful was rewarded with food. In that way, the whole family was paid.

During swim season, his clothes practically fell off him. He burned so much energy, and he was so hungry. Some of his buddies often included them in their big weekend meals. Joshua did not hesitate long to pick up a chocolate éclair, and he waved off the coffee at first for a carton or two of milk. The men watched with animation as he inhaled the first and second donuts. Mr. Jones cleared his throat and smiled knowingly at the secretary as she watched in part disbelief and amusement at the scene. She excused herself then, and Mr. Jones began with the story he had come to share while Mr. B poured himself a cup of coffee and added some milk.

Jones put his finger in the air and theatrically impersonated Abraham Lincoln's address, saying, "'Four score and twenty years ago,' that's a school joke, right?" he snorted a bit as he directed his comments to the principal. Then he sobered and directed his gaze right at Joshua.

He said, "I was part of an elite group of guys who decided it would be a good idea to hop out of a perfectly good plane we called the Albatross that landed on the ocean to rescue survivors in the water. The problem was that most people weren't in trouble on days with calm seas and light and variable winds. While we sorted out how to rescue people in the US Coast Guard, our team grew into what you may now know of...."

At the mention of the USCG, Joshua's dark eyes widened in disbelief.

Was he in the USCG?

"Don't look so surprised, young man. Do you think I walked like this 50 years ago? It's probably because of the crazy stuff I did back then that I walk like this."

He laughed about himself and loud enough for the secretary to hear in the next room. A swimmer's back was the weakest link on a hoist. After far-to-many unexpected waves and heavy survivors, Jones' back had been pulled unexpectedly in calm and heavy seas during his service time. Mr. Jones didn't complain about his obvious suffering, but the trauma to his body was evident. Joshua appreciated that about him, swallowed his last bite, and wiped his chin to brush off the crumbs and icing. Mr. B. drummed the desk with his fingers, mildly amused at the senior citizen.

Joshua spoke with hesitation for the first time, "Sorry, sir, and this has what to do with me?"

As he regarded him straight on, he noticed the big bushy eyebrows that were wildly unkept, and recognition hit him at last.

Then Mr. Jones laughed and exclaimed, "It has everything to do with you. I met you two years ago when Hurricane Ike came and thrashed our town. We were in this very school when it was a shelter. You remember? You were there, no? You told me you wanted to be a rescuer. I still see that in you and think you may have what it takes. I'm here to ensure you have every opportunity to live your dream... and mine."

He pulled two things from his shirt pocket then. One set of round glasses confirmed what Joshua had earlier missed. This was one of the men who sat at the table while he told the children his story during Hurricane Ike. Secondly, the man pulled out a crumpled red, white, and blue ribbon attached to a medal that was suspended beneath it. The award was a bronze four-bladed propeller superimposed on the form of a cross that was suspended beneath it. His hands shook ever so slightly as he handed the medal to Joshua and gestured for him to hold it and examine it more closely. Joshua received it cautiously like the heirloom that it was to Mr. Jones.

Mr. Jones said, "I got this Distinguished Flying Cross long ago before you were born. I entered the Coast Guard when I was about your age. I mostly enjoyed the 30 years I spent responsible for some crazy rescues. My family and I were stationed all over the U.S., mostly in the Middle Atlantic. The medal and my wallet were the only two things I grabbed before I left my house, right before Hurricane Ike took it all. I'm old and have been in some consideration of my life, like older men do. I carry this cross in my pocket ever since, and...," he sobered some and wiped a tear that swelled in the corner of his eye, "I think I need to pass on the legacy."

He hesitated and collected his raw emotions about what Joshua had no idea. Mr. B. chose that moment to offer Jones a cup of coffee. He nodded yes, and then, as if by rote, he offered some to Joshua as well. Joshua accepted, which surprised even himself.

I have never tried coffee, but between the seriousness of the conversation and the sweetness overpowering my mouth, he thought, *it seems like as good a time as ever to try it.*

Joshua handed the medal back to him with care, eagerly accepted coffee, and refused the milk. The bitter coffee had a pungent odor but warmed his senses in what he felt must be a masculine way.

What is this conversation about? A men's discussion about the past, the present, and now what? My future?

Mr. Jones continued, "I was in after high school in the 60s."

He threw up his two fingers in the peace sign and smirked.

"I suppose I helped shape the swimmer program before it became what it is today. Back then, the CG had to sort it out and separate it from the Navy's in the 70s. It was no joke, and men had died."

While they all sipped coffee in companionable silence, Joshua wondered how different this must be from other office visits the principal had. He again reached for another one of the donuts. The silence was broken only by the tick-tock from the clock on the wall. Indeed, time waited for no man. Mr. Jones stared at the treasured medal for a long while. Both men watched him as he humbled himself and allowed a moment to carefully regard the award that shook in his hands. He had visualized the courageous cost of his effort to save others. No one could any longer see the bravery, but the cross had marked him for life. He then sniffed, carefully folded it, and deeply stuffed it in his pocket. He patted it once more for safety. Joshua wisely observed the mindset of a rescue swimmer up close for the second time, others first always.

"If you think you can hack it, meet me at the CG recruiter's office to sign on before you've graduated. Think about it."

Joshua nearly spit the donut in his mouth across the room.

"What?"

Mr. Jones repeated slowly, "I said," loudly for dramatic effect, "You might not think I'm a prophet, but you should follow me down to the recruiter's office downtown unless you're hard of hearing. With swim times like yours, you must be in good health. Well, besides your hearing," he added with a wink.

"Your man here," he thumbed toward Mr. B. "He said you've got the grades to pass the ASVAB (Armed Services Vocational Aptitude Battery Test) and enlist immediately. From there, you get to boot camp, work your tail off, and maybe by fall, you enter Aviation Survival Technician School (AST) for only the most elite and mentally and physically challenging *opportunity* this great nation offers. Start today to get prepared. There will be a checklist or three."

Jones laughed at his private joke, but no one else understood it. Joshua barely swallowed the donut lodged in his throat. Part of him wanted to jump out of his chair. He envisioned his dash down the hall to pull the fire alarm as he went to get away. The other part of him loved a challenge; perhaps this was *the challenge* of a lifetime. Unsure of what to do or say, he was stunned.

Look up, he thought.

Joshua looked at the room's ceiling and closed his eyes. He saw the bold black letters USCG form in front of him. He gripped the coffee cup tightly so as not to drop it as he pondered his response.

What he heard was, "Follow me."

The orange-suited CG warrior dude mouthed that to him when he was thirteen on the rooftop in the middle of Katrina, but he just now heard the exact words that echoed around in his head.

Who said that? This man was another rescue swimmer who asked him to follow. Again? He's not the same warrior angel with his unsheathed weapon visible, or is he?

Of course, someone trained to leave their helicopter also had learned to rescue people off waves and rooftops. The swimmer wasn't in the water that day he rescued Joshua and his family, but he had laid it all on the line to save people in misery. Joshua and his family had been the survivors. Joshua didn't understand then; he instinctively trusted his dad and did what he and the swimmer told him to do. Now, the choice was his.

Would he follow?

Mr. Jones sensed the hesitation, cleared his throat again this time, and spoke unusually softly.

"After my medal was awarded to me for 'heroism while participating in an aerial flight,' I wondered if I would ever suffer. I found out soon afterward I'd suffer for what was right. I still do. We're better off to suffer for what's good. Truthfully, I became frightened of what could've gone wrong and would've happened to me, hell, what could've happened to everyone, including my crews."

He realized his foul language and looked apologetically at Mr. B. and then back to an attentive Joshua.

"I kinda showed off in my arrogance, and many fellas do. Even stars fall sometimes, and I did. My leadership gave me a second chance, and I am forever grateful. I was surely humbled. I told you this beforehand, so you know it won't be all sunshine and rainbows. Your life will be hung by a thread of steel. And your soul," he pounded his chest, "will get squeezed until you feel emptied. Kid, I see something fierce and faithful in you, meek and humble. It's past time for me to hand the mission over to you. A young man with a clear conscience, body, heart, and soul so that others may live. People who will die alone or live and follow you are out there."

Taking one last swig of his coffee, Mr. Jones then stood haltingly. Joshua offered the man his arm to pull himself up on. Mr. Jones grabbed his bicep in a surprisingly firm grip. He placed his free hand firmly on his shoulder and squeezed.

He told Joshua, "I get along well with a little help, and so will you. It's been a pleasure to be with you face to face, young man."

He turned to Mr. B and said with a wink and a coy grin, "Thanks for the confessional, Father."

All the men shook hands, and Jones lumbered away from the fresh young face of what he saw in himself as a young man. Mr. Jones turned with a slow movement towards them once more.

He said to Joshua, "Help is on the way."

Chapter 3

Semper Paratus, Always Ready

Several months later, in preparation...

"Mansoul, you want half my sandwich, too?" whispered Jordan Roi.

She secreted half her sandwich to Joshua off her galley tray onto his. There wasn't time nor the allowance of leisure of conversation at chow each day. Generosity was another thing, though. It's hard to make a rule against too much of that. Joshua knew that because he'd been the one to give away his food most of his life. For the first time, he was regularly at the reception of shared food.

Jordan Roi quickly became a steadfast and informative confidante. As a tall 6'0" dark-haired teenager, she needed the same caloric intake as her peers. However, she loved to share everything, and it was her excuse to say something. The hardest part of 'boot' (CG boot camp) had been the lack of conversation for her. She'd created a journal to record her observations of people and events. She counted down the days until an honest dialogue could be had, especially with the people who most intrigued her, like Joshua Mansoul.

Ben, from the Midwest mitt of Michigan, flanked Joshua on the other side and murmured while chewing, "Here, let's see how many he can finish in one setting..." and handed another half sandwich over to Joshua as well.

Ben, nicknamed "the mitt," quickly became the class clown of 'boot.' He consistently demonstrated he was from Michigan by lifting his right hand, shaped like a mitten, to point to his hometown in Traverse City, Michigan. He found a way to make even the most brutal drill instructor crack a smile, even if in disbelief. One morning, there had been an inspection that hadn't gone well. When demanded to answer for it, he piped up, "The Ben-spection passed, sir!" The whole company of recruits laughed out loud and then regretted it after the Company Commander gave them miles of running afterward for having guffawed.

Caleb was a big red-headed guy and wanted the sandwich himself. He knew better than to stack his other half on top but did so with a stifled laugh.

He thought, *You're going to make yourself so sick, Joshua, ...or fall asleep in class.*

With more sandwiches to eat, Joshua smiled as he chewed. He knew it was joy and satisfaction to eat guilt-free for the first time in his entire life.

Finally, I'm not costing my mother a nickel.

His buddies in 'boot' knew he was almost always ravenously hungry.

Later that afternoon, the lecture hall was warmer than expected, and the trainers continued to speak more than he remembered.

Maybe those last three sandwiches weren't such a good idea after all, thought Joshua as he tried to stifle a yawn.

When his head bobbed on his chest and sleep overcame him, he felt a nudge from Caleb. Grateful for the nudge, he knew Caleb had just saved him from a significant punishment had he been caught asleep. Caleb just had something different about him that made life more adventuresome and better for being around him. Caleb was a giant of a man, and at 6'3", he stood over Jordan and rested his elbow on Joshua's shoulder. When they sat down in class, it put them more on eye level.

Joshua thought, *I shouldn't eat so much at lunch.*

Caleb was renowned for his courageous spirit and teamwork, which was a huge encouragement. He had a glimmer in his blue eyes and gave Joshua the name 'Yeshua.' He informed Joshua that they'd surely be good friends.

"Mansoul, our friendship will make history," Caleb said.

Joshua replied, "Yeah, right, amigo."

It wasn't long before Caleb's slight elbow nudge rescued Joshua and became part of their storied history. Joshua was forever in Caleb's debt for having saved his skin. He'd be sure to remember his kindness. While the barracks were cleaned that night, Ben, who also happened to be his bunkmate, teased Joshua unmercifully about his new three-strike sandwich rule.

He threw his arms out sideways like an umpire and hollered, "Three sandwiches, and he's out!"

Ben was the gregarious one of the three, but the faithful friend he was came from a background like his, and they could relate on a whole different level words didn't convey. Around week six of 'boot,' Ben had shared that he'd also lost a close loved one when he grew up. His gratitude for life was an endearment most people their age didn't convey or understand. Their shared compassion for humanity drew them together.

The best part of 'boot', Joshua realized, was a close tie between the newly formed friendships and the large quantities of food. He knew he had both at once. The great friendships developed, like Joshua's stature with the additional food. They formed when they cleaned at night just before they fell into a deep slumber, only to be awoken way too early to start the strict regimen again. However, he got all the food he could eat, although rapidly, three times a day. At chow time, some in 'boot' bemoaned the food provided. He had never seen anything like the abundance; unlike school, this was provided without limits. They even expected you to drink and eat so much to be successful. He gained weight while his fellow trainees lost some pounds. He became more muscular and filled his frame for the first time.

Joshua thought every day, *I'm so thankful not to worry someone else isn't going to get what they need if I ask for more.*

He slept so well during training for that reason alone. The eight weeks of 'boot' at Cape May, New Jersey, may have been horrendous for most, but Joshua seemed to thrive on the regimen, camaraderie, and calories. He grew an inch and gained 10 pounds. His arms rippled with new muscles, and he had never felt stronger or more thankful. Boot tended to grow up all the attendees. People from every background and culture merged to become machines of readiness and good order. It was an eye-opener for all; that was the purpose. Some were shocked, but others electrified. The ethos was Honor, Respect, and Devotion to Duty.

Some attendees found the horrific schedule, rushed duties, and the demeanor of the drill sergeants was their humiliation. They almost passed out in their bunks each night, but every day seemed more exhilarating than the previous one to Joshua. However, for some, like Joshua, it was impossible not to have made friends with other teenagers from all over the country. They huddled over checklists, manuals, and protocols and tested each other on every chapter and section they had to memorize. It strengthened their knowledge, wisdom, and discipline. While at Cape May in New Jersey, he was grateful for those moments that pulled them through and built them into a unified mission.

Eventually, everyone learned the Carolina girl, Jordan Roi, liked to talk non-stop. That was whenever she could, which was rare before lights out in separate quarters, but they had heard she was a real talker. She had thick, curly dark hair, dark skin, and perfect white teeth that could reflect the sunshine. Her hair pulled out of every restraint she tried in the hot, humid environment and left her as an obvious girlie girl amongst the men. The guys couldn't help but discuss her at nighttime.

"She must have a lot of words to use...," said Caleb.

"After 'boot,' she can use them with me," teased Ben.

She was one of a small group of women at 'boot.' She was one of the most knowledgeable and helped Joshua pass some ridiculously hard tests. Her quick wit and understanding often helped him with the academic assessments and procedures. Although her verbosity was intense, it was helpful. Once, his mind locked up on an exam, and he could barely remember his name. Joshua didn't want to be tempted to cheat. He stared hard at the ceiling and then closed his eyes. He tried to summon the imaginary black letters of the USCG painted on the underbelly of the helicopter to calm himself down. He took several deep breaths and considered how grateful he was, which relaxed his nerves. His mom had taught him that trick. He remembered their laughter in disbelief as Jordan sang about the history of the USCG to the tune of 'She'll be coming round the mountain when she comes.' Her words struck him in the nick of time. He remembered an essential point on the test just when he needed it with her crafted song. Her love of wisdom spurred those around her to score higher than they would have without her.

Joshua spoke to her after the final exam, "Jordan, you are dangerous. You can still be my wingman anytime."

She returned the old *Top Gun* quote around on him and said, "No, you can be my wingman," and flashed him a brilliant smile.

Since his first coffee with Mr. Jones, Joshua had tasted the fruit of the possibility of preparation for an active part of the rescue mission in the CG. In retrospect, he realized he had wanted to be on a mission and become a rescuer badly for most of his life. He later discovered his family and friends were not as surprised about his recruitment as he was. Of course, it hit his family hard once he left for roughly eight weeks of 'boot' camp just days after High School graduation. It was his first big move away from home and further divided his nuclear family. He left his inconsolable mother in the hands of his brothers, Jude and Jimmy. They weren't as conscientious about her moods as he was, so he did his best to contact her when he could.

He texted: I'm well. Exhausted but full.

Maria replied: My heart is full to hear from you, thank you, niño.

Remarkably, Mr. Jones had taken a keen interest in the welfare of his family and not just Joshua's future. It was as if he knew Joshua's success depended on whether his mother was well cared for. He knew he needed to be clear-headed during 'boot' and hopefully followed later by his 31-week Aviation Survival Technician (AST) program. In several letters from home, he had been informed Jones' veterans' group had begun to help his mom make some financial ends meet. They pitched in and did some home repairs even Joshua hadn't known lacked attention. He was thankful his mom and brothers wouldn't lose their home due to financial strain until he could help provide for them from his salary.

Mr. Jones wrote, “It feels good to roll up my sleeves again for the sake of the CG” and “maybe I’m not too old yet to be of help.”

Joshua was relieved the assistance was going both ways for all involved. His littlest brother, Jimmy, was the smarty pants in the family and wanted to go to college. It only made Joshua strive harder to get the extra flight pay, earn all he could, and give all he could.

He texted his brothers: Hermanos, keep up those grades!

Jimmy replied: U keepin up the push-ups?

Jude replied: Run, Joshua, run....

Jimmy replied: U touched the Ocean yet? Or the sky? U Coastie ;)

Joshua was grateful for the friends he made in the formative weeks of his CG career. When they graduated, he looked forward to their intersection of paths someday at a future duty station. Some would head to ‘A’ school (specific career training schools), later to ‘C’ school (advanced specialty training), or some direct to the fleet wherever needed. They all went to separate billets (jobs) for follow-up training while they awaited orders to ‘A’ schools. Some went to schools of their choice if they won them by placement on their order of merit list. With few exceptions, everyone enjoyed the camaraderie of the CG community and the individual parts that made up the whole.

Joshua knew he had made the right decision while he learned more and more about the mission of the CG. The strict protocol established by the CG was the order and process of conformity to the singular image of the Guardian. The rules were for everyone who found themselves in need. They were agents of hope amidst the chaos. He liked obedience to a mission beyond himself, his family, neighbors, and the world. They brought rule and peace against the agents of chaos that threatened their own. Guardians knew any job in the CG would have had benefits and given them careers to have been proud of to make the mission a success. No assignment or task was too small or too unimportant. The hierarchy established every Guardian was part of an outstretched arm of the mighty forces of good in the world.

One trainer said, “If you don’t know what to do, DO the dishes!”

Another yelled, “You got time to lean, you got time to clean!”

He quickly discovered Coast Guard positions came in all sizes and particular skill sets. Joshua appreciated the Storekeepers, Yeoman, and especially the Culinary Specialists who kept him well-fed. They anticipated the travel with their jobs and further education about their new *Semper Paratus* community. *Semper Paratus* meant Always Ready and was the CG’s proud motto. They were all expectant for their first duty assignments, even if it meant dish duty.

Joshua found out at graduation from ‘boot’ that the CG needed him in sunny Destin, Florida. As a non-rate, having yet to attend a formal training program, he was thrilled to see some action at a highly coveted billet, Coast Guard Station Destin. Headquartered in New Orleans, the 8th Coast Guard District was responsible for U.S. Coast Guard operations spanning 26 states, including the Gulf of Mexico coastline from Florida to Mexico, the adjacent offshore waters and outer continental shelf, as well as the inland waterways of the Mississippi, Ohio, Missouri, Illinois, and Tennessee River systems. Joshua was the lowest-ranked person at Station Destin. Since he was brand new to the unit, he had much to soak in besides the sunshine.

“Yo, Mansoul. You know how to clean?” was heard every day for weeks.

“Aye, aye.”

Joshua thought, *my mother's expectations for cleanliness were something, but the CG took it to a whole new level.*

He had hoped some of that would have lessened after 'boot.' However, being the youngest and least experienced, he got the brunt of the least desired duties. Service of others came more naturally to Joshua than to some he learned. He did his best to make it a game to keep his morale up. Dish duty would've been preferred to what he was told to scrub.

"Yo mama don't live here!" hollered a Guardian to Joshua when the senior ranking person left a sink of dirty dishes for him to clean and an entire mess hall.

Obviously, or you'd know better than to leave them for me..., he thought.

Joshua picked up a dish rag and went to work. His towel became part of his uniform over the next several weeks. The senior grades left for an emergent call while their food was again left behind on the table in the chow room. Joshua's role quickly became clean up after the others as they ran ahead of him to fulfill their duties. It was order and protocol, but Joshua thought to himself in the weeks of sanitation.

Perhaps they needed to remember what they had learned about the importance of service within the unit and to others outside.

The ethos of honor, respect, and devotion to duty were tested at units when various members forgot they served each other and the community at large. Some Guardians fell prey to the idea that their way was better than *the way.* When a Guardian lost sight of the scope of the mission, they quickly became attracted to the life of misery and misery loved company. That person promoted the trickle-down of misery, mainly to try to place it upon anyone of lower rank. Joshua had borne the weight of his brothers, but to do so for strangers was a new experience. As the lowest-ranked person, he resolved to keep to the ethos and follow it regardless of rank.

Joshua mumbled to himself, "My Command sees everything. When it comes to my turn to lead, things will be different. Lead me away from those trials."

Joshua lived for the days spent out of the crystal-clear water on the 29' small response boats. As a unit member, he progressed and was one of many personnel who performed tow training. He arrived just days before Labor Day weekend and assisted with plenty of tows during and afterward. Their various duties kept them on patrol year-round, but August was the hottest month. Some days were more memorable than he wanted.

"Hey, fellas," shouted an inebriated and mostly naked person on a party barge near the Destin Pass in the famous Crab Island area. "Come on and join us over here! Woohoo!"

Loud music blared from several directions, and the water's surface had become a club-like atmosphere with dancing, floating parties, and games between and on top of boats.

"Gracious," said Helmsman Morris, "Some of these people barely have any self-control."

Morris was irritated at once again being called out as though he, too, was out partying. He was in uniform and at the helm of the CG rescue vessel. They both had to tear their eyes from the revelers who beckoned to distract them. Joshua was uncomfortable and tried to change the subject. Temptation was everywhere, yet they were called to rescue people in the middle of their self-induced dangers.

"Since the water's waist deep in some places, I guess most everyone gets way too comfortable in the water," said Joshua.

"Yes, we rescued a swamped boat, lost kids, swimmers caught in the strong currents headed out the pass, inexperienced boaters, drownings, and loads of drunken boaters...just this week," said Boatswain Moshe with exasperation.

"Do you feel as though you've wrestled alligators? I mean, all these hordes of people having "fun" makes your job endless, doesn't it?" asked Joshua.

"Yes, a good way of putting it, Seaman Recruit Mansoul; let's just hope the 'alligators' don't bite us while we try to rescue them. Be on the lookout for sharks, too."

Joshua considered how that day on the water was like his days as a lifeguard on shore, *with lots of watch and wait and seconds of excitement that may be more like terror for onlookers.*

"HELP!"

"Somebody, help us!"

Joshua and Moshe swung themselves in the small boat towards the cacophony of voices they heard just over the roar of the music and laughter.

Moshe picked up a bullhorn and said, "State your emergency."

"He just dove in and came up like this...HELP him! PLEASE!" a panicked woman's voice screamed.

After their boat's siren sounded, the music quieted, and the crowd silenced. The friends of a teenager who was seemingly lifeless in the water were frantic. The blue lights came up on board, and radio calls were made for advanced life support to be met on shore immediately for further aid. A small crowd had gathered around the vacationers, but the sea of people began to part, boats were moved, and games ceased so the CG vessel could get closer and render aid. A man who looked the same age as Joshua, someone's teenager out for a good time, was loaded into the vessel on a backboard. Joshua was bereaved to acknowledge this young man's soul did not also join them after they rushed him to shore and the awaited medical services that met them there.

That does bite, and hard, contemplated Joshua for days and weeks afterward.

Moshe counseled him, "My Father-in-law gave me some good advice, 'We're not alone out there for a reason. You'll burn out if you don't share the load of whatever the Commander tells us to do.'"

Joshua replied, "It should be common sense not to do some of this stuff. What they do is crazy."

Boatswain Moshe replied, "Our job is to teach the rules and instructions, to show them how to live, what to do. Believe me; we only get the hard cases, and there's no such thing as common anymore."

Since ancient times, every vessel has reported "souls on board" while on the water. Joshua's career in the rescue of the souls of humanity began with tragedies and triumphs. It was not long before his eyes were opened, and sadly, the harshness of reality became an hourly way of life. The vacationers, fishers, and revelers would flow in and out of Florida. There were so many people, each with souls, to rescue. That was the CG mission 24-7, *Semper Paratus*. The mission never took a holiday.

The Destin Station had an open house with the CG Auxiliary one toasty hot weekend before the summer was over. There were planned to be search and rescue operations, heaving line throw, Florida Wildlife officers, CG mascots Sammy and Coastie, a 47' motor lifeboat (MLB) tour, as well as the off-duty 29' small response boat most frequently used in the shallow waters off Florida coastlines. The other CG members nominated Joshua, the non-rate, to be dressed up as Sammy the Sea Otter. The role of the enormous mascot was to encourage children to keep waterways clean, wear a life vest, and swim with others.

The mascot outfit came to him and smelled of horrible body odor. After several hours inside a furry human-sized sea otter costume in the Florida sun, Joshua wished for any other Coast Guard assignment. He longed to go and clean anything, preferably if it was in the shade.

Perspective, Joshua thought, *on my cleanliness operations*.

Finally, Petty Officer Moshe gave Joshua a reprieve after he had done a great job interacting with their youngest visitors.

He asked, “Mansoul, you want to go and collect more drinks since we’ve run out early?”

Before Joshua could comment, he added, “I have another CG member who needs a little time in the suit since he nominated you in the first place.”

Since the sun was past its hot apex, Joshua trotted in his big furry brown suit as fast as he could to shed it. Once he was out of the children’s sight and changed, he inhaled and exhaled with sweet relief. The traffic on the connected barrier islands at that time of day was always atrocious. He welcomed the solace of the air conditioning, salty sea breeze through the windows (yes, with the AC blasting), and some serious hydration of himself as he inched along Highway 98. Joshua enjoyed his collection of juices, water bottles, ice pops, and colas he could find and hurried back to provide them to the open house guests.

“Hey, the best stuff just got put out last,” said one kiddo as he slurped on a grape pop.

The gleeful comment wasn’t lost on Petty Officer Moshe, who looked at Joshua.

“Is that what I sent you for?”

“My treat,” said Joshua, “Please, don’t send me back to Sammy the Sea Otter.”

They shared a good laugh and began to clean up the mess left after the event. Joshua hoped that was the last he'd see of the sea otter for a very long time.

Joshua was focused on one part of the mission he primarily vowed to attain: Aviation Survival Technician (AST), the distinguished job known informally as a rescue swimmer or swimmer for short. What was personal to Joshua was he had lost his dad in the hurricane's aftereffects. He knew the CG swimmer had saved what his dad held most dear: his beloved family and respect. He, too, wanted to rescue anyone who would call out to him. He desired to do the same as the angelic orange sky rulers had done for him. They were the representatives of the delegated authority that ruled. Thanks to them, not the fictional winged angels, but the heroic transcendent ones for the breath in his lungs, the strength to look up daily, and obey. He knew he was never alone.

I need the mission as much as the mission needs me.

Moshe continued to pour wisdom into Joshua, "In saving others, your salvation is worked out. Work the checklists, Mansoul: prep, hoist, get home."

Joshua was grateful to have been a part of some extraordinary rescues and even more preparation scenarios in Destin. As a first duty station, he could not have been more excited and appreciative of those experiences. He waited daily for a lifetime opportunity to enter AST 'A' School. In the meantime, he ran and ran some more. He improved his run times and kept at his ability to do the pull-ups and push-ups. The local Mid-Bay Bridge run was a 3.6-mile trek in each direction with one big hill in the middle. The bridge spread over the middle of the Choctawhatchee Bay. Even on the hard concrete, it felt so good for him to "get away" from the demands of non-rate status.

Out here, I can run across the water away from the absurdity on shore and the chaos on Crab Island.

Joshua's free time was spent on the beach with buddies and a volleyball if he wasn't physically or mentally in preparation. It wasn't hard to find something great to do near the white sandy beaches of Northwest Florida. The water was shallow along the shore and was warm in the summertime and well into the fall. He became a snorkeler and enjoyed the dolphins, sea turtles, and occasional sharks. He was always grateful the meals were hot and ready when he arrived at the galley. He had to admit the hours were limited, and the environment was much less robust at the small boat station than in 'boot.' He had to learn to cook for himself since the galley wasn't always open. He chose not to spend his paycheck eating out like some fellas. After a few loud smoke alarms and visits from the fire department, he got a handle on his burnt meals. The unit sure hoped so.

"You should've been a Fireman, Mansoul," said Moshe.

"I'll clean it up, Petty Officer, as per the checklist," said Joshua.

Joshua had been part of the USCG for almost a year. It had already been full of rewards. He was sorry to leave such a beautiful location but had met his goal. At last, he entered AST 'A' School in Elizabeth City, North Carolina. It was known affectionately as ECity to the locals and Guardians alike. When he arrived, he realized it was the farthest he had ever been stationed from his home in Texas. He heard their leader's caution of a mindset of preparation for what was sure to come. Rescue Swimmers trained Rescue Swimmers. Men and women who knew what would be imminent took turns to warn them and remind them of what kinds of torment they would face. It was not a threat, nor was it personal to Joshua. He knew he represented every person that would come behind him. Joshua was introduced to a physically, mentally, and spiritually toilsome experience. From the onset of the class, they ran the checklist repeatedly as a matter of life and death. While a marathoner and in the best shape of his life, he thought he was prepared. However, he learned he was still unprepared for the physical preparation he would need to keep up his entire rescue swimmer career to be operational.

My land PT (physical training) is good, but my swimming under these threats...

They were trained to swim blindfolded, with bricks back and forth underwater, and learned how to assist pretend combative people about to drown in the water. His lifeguard days long ago were like lessons in how to walk, and now he was expected to dance. He swam laps and had to sprint down and back until he collapsed, then get up and run, followed by a reward of workouts to include push-ups, pull-ups, and flutter kicks. The instructors worked them into a frenzy. Joshua learned to control his breath and remind himself it was not their will to let him die.

Even when I think they're trying to kill me.

A Senior Chief hollered from the poolside on a typical day, "I don't see gills yet! Another mile, this time with a survivor under your arm!"

Another added, "The drills will continue until morale improves."

One instructor, a salty and boisterous Chief who was most feared, repeatedly reminded them to believe in the mission. To be *always prepared* meant to check everything frequently.

"We're not making pizza here!" he hollered.

"You do it wrong; your friends die!" his voice grew more insistent.

The call was to understand and obey the mission unswervingly.

“You can’t say no. Otherwise, it’s all your fault,” the trainers made it painfully clear.

Joshua remembered his lifeguard experience on Stewart Beach years before. The looks on the other lifeguards’ faces were fearful and reticent. He alone had been the one to go out no matter the cost that day.

No, I’m not interested in a lifetime of making pizza, resolved Joshua.

Some guys and the few girls present complained about their new taskmasters, and some sadly walked away and tapped out. When they rang the bell of defeat, his back would stiffen when he heard it, and his resolve to finish grew. Some thought the tests and constant irritation were personal to them, and they were being pushed out on purpose. It was not even the actual tests some gave up on but the near-constant test of their wills.

“At ‘boot’ we learned honor, respect, devotion to duty, but this is cruel,” said a trainee.

They were in the men’s locker room and expected to return to the pool within minutes after having been for a long run.

“Not cruel, just fuel,” replied another trainee.

In frustration, the angry trainee slammed a locker door closed and threw his towel down. Joshua picked up the towel left behind and added it to his devotion to duty to keep the room clean.

I want to rescue the rescuers...

Joshua wanted to save his ‘A’ school comrades from the precipice of resignation. His heart and mind burned with their departures, but he knew they would fulfill other parts of the boundless mission if they chose obedience where their abilities conformed best.

Each ‘A’ school trainee’s conscience had to be shaped, equipped, and tested, never to give up so that others may live. The mental fatigue was enormous, but that was the point. Crews and survivors depended upon the rigid standardization of ASTs. Some left the school, and it wasn't easy on anyone. Ultimately, it was never up to Joshua or the disciplined swimmer program whether everyone passed the school. The checklists had to be followed for the mission to be successful. Those commands were given from the highest level of the Coast Guard.

AST 'A' School was, by far and away, the hardest thing Joshua had ever done. The rate at which people had eventually trickled out of the program was nearly 85%. Great swimmers, strong people, and dedicated individuals mostly fell short for many reasons. The rough process was, at times, just too much, and the refinement process too rigorous for everyone. The mission of the CG was inviting to all, but the AST demands were for those only refined in the fire. The worst part of the school environment was the fear. Joshua embarked upon the "water confidence" course, and one day, he would shiver in terror and another in an adrenaline rush. On the side of the pool they trained in hung an ominous sign,

So Others May Live.

The Rescue Swimmer motto was the code they all agreed to live and die by. No matter what it took, he decided from that point on he was all in for some stranger he may never see again.

A frequent lecture from leadership was, "Do not fear what they fear."

The days wore on and on, and he realized his greatest temptation to quit the rigorous exercise tempo, exhaustion, lack of sleep, and academic instruction was himself. He had to overcome himself to keep his mind, body, and soul focused on the outcome he wanted most. It wasn't what was most comfortable at the moment at all. It was his determined attitude when he "entered the water."

Their instructors repeated, "The only difference between the rescuer and the rescued was the attitude in which they entered the water."

He would be prepared to do his part and hope they would do theirs. He could never control them but completely controlled his reactions and emotions. His fear could not overcome him in the middle of a rescue. It could harm either the survivor or his crew and was unacceptable. Therefore, the instructors gave him and his fellow trainees plenty of opportunities to overcome their fears.

Do I put my confidence entirely in myself? No.

Joshua knew he would have a competent crew to rely upon when he questioned his judgment. They, too, had been trained and re-trained annually to be faithful to the procedures outlined for them from decades, if not longer, of experience and tradition. He would only fear the loss of the spiritual connection from the body, not the circumstances of chaos that surrounded him. Nor would he fear those who could only destroy his body but not his soul.

One day, an instructor hollered at him, "You gonna make your daddy proud or disappointed in you, Mansoul? Just say the word, and you're out of this."

It had been an incredibly strenuous day in the water, and words couldn't be spoken over the repetitive drown-proofing drills they performed. Joshua could only take the hidden pain of his desperate desire to make his daddy proud and try to use it redemptively. He knew the mental pressure was used to strengthen him for the journey, but he struggled to breathe through it. The voices in his head were agents of chaos. Joshua surfaced and gasped for air, literally and figuratively.

The instructor couldn't have known his dad's whereabouts but added, "Where is your daddy now? You want to call him and tell him you couldn't take it?"

Joshua plummeted again under the water's surface in a chokehold role-played by the instructor, who taunted him and pulled him under.

"If you've seen me, you've seen my father," spoke Joshua at the end of his trial, exhausted and emboldened.

The elite Rescue Swimmer designation was what Joshua yearned for more than whatever life offered. Rescue swimmers were a tiny percentage of the CG. He relished the education about how the different members of the units worked together to make a rescue a success. The CG trained their members to understand each part of the mission. They could synchronize their duty with any other CG crew member wherever they were used for a mission. His anticipation of being dropped into the ocean was just the tip of the spear for a well-run machine of highly technically trained and motivated individuals. They all performed nuanced tasks to make a successful mission. Some of the Guardians he would never see, let alone meet face to face, but his life depended upon them.

The swimmer was the only rating in the CG who acted completely alone once unhooked and unrestricted in the ocean. They were each isolated in the chaos and turmoil that necessitated a survival technician. ASTs were expected to perform the same duties, whether male or female. They had to prove they had what it took to do the required tasks, regardless of gender. However, once they proved their ability, he or she was surrounded by an immeasurable force of people, power, and resources to do supernatural rescues. Joshua badly wanted to participate in the divine nature of rescue. Preparedness was vital to his own life and the survivors' lives. He hungered for it. He wanted the "So Others May Live" badge so much he could taste and see it just before him: for his family, strangers, and all those who walked the earth.

Joshua knew, *It will be good. It will all be worth it. But what will it take?*

Chapter 4

NO EXCUSES, CHIEF

Elizabeth City, North Carolina

After a long day of AST education, Joshua felt overwhelmed. He had a brutal lesson on helicopter emergency flotation systems he would be responsible for soon enough. ASTs were trained to inspect, service, maintain, troubleshoot, and repair cargo aerial delivery systems, drag parachute systems, aircraft oxygen systems, helicopter emergency flotation systems, portable dewatering pumps, air/sea rescue kits, and special-purpose protective clothing. Further responsibilities included the storage and handling of aviation ordnance and pyrotechnic devices. The trainees were drained after weeks of relentless physical exertion and mental application.

Joshua and his peers agreed, "I'd rather run a mile than rerun through these questions."

The next day, a test was planned everyone dreaded. As the airmen filed out of the classroom, mentally and physically exhausted, the instructor, Chief Simon, commented like an old-timey schoolteacher,

"You all get plenty of beauty rest and show up when you're all prepared for your exam, Sweeties. Nightie night."

The derisiveness did not help motivate the students in the least. Like the rest, Joshua stayed up later than they wanted to so they would have the test material memorized. Unfortunately, Joshua's three roommates had already quit AST due to the rigors of their A-school class. He had felt increasingly isolated as each one packed their bags and left. They all grieved their missed chance at the sometimes-coveted AST badge. They had stayed up late many nights, cramming and eventually snoring in their textbooks. Some had taken to the study methods of standing up or on their backs in flutter kicks to strengthen their abs and brains while they remained awake. He dreamt of the days when he had at least one who would stay awake with him at that late hour. That night, Joshua faded faster than before since he was all alone.

He thought to himself in his exhaustion; *I think I'd do better on the test if I'd slept a whole night's sleep. I think I will begin at 0800 (military time) instead of at regular roll call at 0600. It seems to me that Chief finally understands we have our limits.*

His head swam each day and all night with all the knowledge he had to know and demonstrate, from lifesaving skills to maintenance, troubleshooting, making, and repairing parachutes for life rafts, dewatering pumps, medicine, spare parts, etc. These things were dropped to survivors, but he had to know how to use and maintain dewatering pumps for stranded boats. How to use protective clothes and gear for land and ocean rescues was vital. The knowledge base grew daily for what they expected to understand, repair, and perform. When Joshua awoke refreshed, he noticed how quiet the dorm seemed.

Hmmmm, too much quiet. I sound like Mama.

He dressed as rapidly as possible and went to the schoolhouse at 0745 to be early. He sharply realized he was alone.

Joshua quoted from *Top Gun* to himself, "This is not good, Mav."

He crossed the street to the Aviation Technical Training Center (ATTC) facility. He squared his shoulders, took a deep breath, and opened the door. He followed the long, silent hallway to his classroom and tried not to sound as loud as his boot heels did when they echoed off the walls around him. His firm and courageous knock on the door of a classroom full of trainees already busily taking their tests was almost his destruction.

He was late, *no*, he thought, *I am inexplicably late*, for the first time in his life.

Every head in the room turned to the uninvited interruption. Then, his instructor, Chief Simon O'Riley, who did not always show restraint, walked briskly to the door. The superior made Joshua's heart thud in his chest with every step. He'd have swum a million miles instead of on the other side of the door with everyone's attention on the showdown.

His instructor thundered, "Airman Mansoul, WHERE HAVE YOU BEEN?"

When the echo reverberated down the hall from his instructor's question about where he had been, Joshua was still too stunned to reply. Beads of sweat that had formed on his brow began to drop down the side of his face. He focused 1,000 feet in front of him.

He promptly gave one of five taught responses to a superior, "I have no excuses, Chief."

He wanted to scream; *You told us to get some rest!*

That, of course, did not pass his lips. Nervous grimaces broke out among his peers, but they did not dare make a sound. They all waited for the stern discipline that would surely come at any moment.

Joshua thought, *Being tardy was unacceptable, but an hour late for an exam of this importance was grounds for being what...? Tossed out? Publicly humiliated and sent back to retrain elsewhere? Losing my opportunity to become a Rescue Swimmer? I'm catastrophizing.*

Joshua forced himself to breathe and remembered his checklist.

My attitude is the only thing that separates me from a survivor. Do not fear what they fear.

His lost future flashed before his eyes for the second time in Joshua's life. Everything he held dear for his career and his sense of self was in the hands of his instructor, who he, with great dread, realized had an hour to wait in anticipation to confront Joshua on his delay. Not being prepared was breaking a fundamental rule in the CG. Quite naïvely and publicly, he had just done it. Joshua probably appeared to him as an immature, unfit, lazy trainee.

Is my life over?

A single bead of sweat dropped onto his shirt and wrecked his impeccable uniform. It was always ready for inspection, but his situation further deteriorated since it had become blemished. The class members collectively held their breath with him while the instructor debated his next response. Simon enjoyed the significance of his response. Joshua, at last, could barely hold his rigid stance at attention a moment longer. Drops of sweat continued to pour down his brow. All he would allow was one flash look at the ceiling to see the USCG letters in his imagination and force himself to remember that help was on the way.

Unexpectedly, a soft whistling sound grew louder and louder down the hall. Joshua stood frozen. He listened as did his classmates until most of the room understood the cheery, upbeat tune to the CG song. Everyone present knew the words since their first days of basic training, whether months, years, or decades ago; "Semper Paratus is our guide, our fame and glory too..." The man and his whistled tune came to an abrupt halt just feet from the confrontation in the hallway. It only added to the awkward conflict with the wide-open door. His song ended poetically on a long note with the mutually understood upbeat charge, "Aye! Coast Guard, we are for you!" Since the words had all been recited in their heads, the anticipation of the next moment was palatable for all.

Chief O'Riley turned with a pinched face towards the elder and senior ranking man and addressed him, "Good morning, Master Chief Samuel. We're training today and testing. What can I do for you, Master Chief?" The salty, grizzled, and highly revered Air Survival Technician Master Chief (ASTCM) Samuel adeptly sensed the tension in the air.

He said calmly to both the men, one who stood at rigid attention while he sweat profusely and the other who seemed annoyed at his unplanned interruption, "What is the preparation for today, Chief O'Riley?"

Taken aback by the follow-up question, the instructor replied, "Systems failures in a Jayhawk, Master Chief."

Master Chief Samuel replied quietly for only the two men closest to him to hear, "Why then is your student producing a puddle on the floor outside your classroom?"

Joshua wanted to escape this moment. Any amount of training in the pool nearby would be welcomed over this experience. Instead, at that moment, he stood in a pool of sweat as the Master Chief of the entire aviation technical center had so astutely pointed out. Unnerved by the question, the Chief pondered his response. He usually preferred a sarcastic retort, but he realized that was what had gotten himself and Airman Mansoul into the situation in the first place. Never had Mansoul missed any training nor been late that he was aware of in the entire 'A' school schedule. His impeccable record made the Chief relish the thought of discipline for the teenager.

Chief O'Riley grasped at his best response, humor, and said with sarcasm, "Seems he's wet himself, has he!"

The joke fell flat on the whole room, and Mansoul dropped his shoulders just slightly enough at the dig that he gained the sympathy of the entire classroom.

Master Chief Samuel pushed his way forward to the head of the class and said to no one in particular, "Follow me." He picked up one of the exams on the empty desk where presumably Joshua should have been. The instructor and Joshua followed the Master Chief inside to take their places. Joshua exhaled for the first time in minutes and felt his cheeks were aflame in embarrassment. He was relieved not to be passed out from fright.

That may have immediately caused my dismissal from the course, he thought.

Joshua held on to his composure and considered; *I thought the drown-proof training in the pool was rough.*

All attention in the room was on the Master Chief, and he began to read the test questions randomly for students to answer out loud. Though highly unusual, the instructor had little to say in how the Master Chief conducted the test.

How will I grade it after this? Simon ruminated with frustration.

Distracted by that fact, Chief Simon O'Riley almost missed the Master Chief, who waited patiently for the class to answer a most difficult and technical question that was not supposed to be on the exam. No one raised their hands to answer. Chief O'Riley began to perspire himself when he realized it may have reflected poorly on himself as the instructor if not *one* student knew or even attempted to answer. As a long and awkward silence ensued, he shifted his weight back and forth with his arms folded in front of his barrel chest. It was then

Simon O'Riley began to understand the Master Chief had also put him to the test.

Did I adequately prepare my students to answer when they don't know the answer?

Semper Paratus was essential to the mission, so to answer respectfully was important whether one was "Always Ready" with the correct answer or not. The lone bead of sweat trickled down Simon O'Riley's neck as he dropped his arms in resentment to either side and balled his fists. He knew he did not like the hot seat he now found himself on.

"Not one of you knows what the nut on top of the main rotor to the mast that holds the entire Jayhawk helicopter together is?" said Master Chief Samuel.

He tested their responsiveness more than their knowledge. Students shifted nervously in their seats, and at the front, already in disbelief at the morning's goings-on, Joshua courageously lifted his hand.

Joshua thought, *I've followed this far, may as well go all the way.*

The entire class was shocked at his willingness to guess due to what he had just endured. Why would he endure more scorn, now on their behalf, they could barely comprehend. He demonstrated courage was not the absence of fear but the accommodation for it. He had considered the higher cause of respect of the authority they sat under. The Master Chief was owed an answer to his question. Joshua humbled himself further to answer the question called by his superior's superior and face the consequences. He feared the authority figure more than the possible consequences of his actions. In this way, he completely entrusted himself to the Master Chief's supremacy over his future. Master Chief Samuel nodded for him to begin.

"Master Chief, the Jesus nut."

There was an audible gasp from the class throughout the room. Master Chief Samuel broke into a wide grin.

Samuel demanded, "What did you just call me?"

The whole class erupted, some into nervous laughter and some with disbelief at how the tension had escalated for the last few minutes. Even the annoyed Simon O'Riley had to give it to the Master Chief for how he'd pulled a fast one on the whole class and taught them all with humor, something they'd need to know. More important than an exam question was the test of audacity to respond with an answer to authority when asked.

Chief Simon O'Riley contemplated, *How in the world did that kid, Mansoul, know the slang term for the retaining nut already?*

The Master Chief left the exam purposefully face down on Joshua's desk before him and patted his damp shoulder. He demonstrated he valued the pressure Mansoul had endured on all his classmate's behalf. He strode to the back of the room and paused slightly next to the instructor. He leaned towards him so only the Chief could hear him.

He gently whispered, "That's how I show humor, Chief. Let's use it to redeem, not ridicule. What you meant and what you said were evidently two different things, and no laughing matter. Remember, when we train these men and women, every word could mean life or death for their survivors or for them. Affirmative responses are the strength of our mission. Don't you think Mansoul passed the test we gave him?"

"Aye, Aye, Master Chief," was Chief O'Riley's reply.

"Good, we don't need the DCCS (Senior Chief Damage Controlman) called to the training unit," he said with a wink.

Like many work environments, there was a healthy banter between jobs in the CG. Joshua and his peers witnessed and participated in the playful mockery between the "surface" CG and the "rotor heads" of the CG. Parody had its limits; like most families, there was a distinct limit to the jokes allowed from outside. This class wanted soon to be a distinctive part of the rotor heads. The mission depended upon them their utmost respect and gentleness for success. *Semper Paratus,* Always Ready, meant the most important part was their exemplary actions that necessitated their seamless work together. The mindset that they were all on the same team was critical to everyone's success. They put their lives in one another's hands every single day. Joshua had never known it to be more authentic than that day. His classmates learned the lesson vicariously. Master Chief Samuel patted his hand on the Chief's shoulder as a sign of camaraderie and then proceeded down the hall and whistled the CG song again. He picked up on the refrain, "High shall our purpose be."

Joshua resolved to push himself harder and with more discipline than he thought many of his peers were willing to do. However, he admittedly did not have the distractions of family nearby. Since he'd never known life without hard times, the new environment seemed like life in abundance. The hard times became more brutal in a different way. When others complained about correction and being rebuked, it stiffened his spine to anticipate what they could come up with next. He did his best to encourage his peers, but he admitted to his mama in his weekly phone conversation the expectations were almost unbearable some days.

"Surely, Mama, I've seen the worst of the CG," he said.

"Oh, my boy, you must do your best, and the rest will be taken care of," Maria replied.

"Mama, where else can I turn?" he asked.

"Niño, your Father has done great things for me and you. Persevere for us all," Maria answered.

Eventually, 'A' school was behind him. It had been nearly a year, but the transformation was remarkable. He was strong in every sense of the word, yet he had an extraordinary meekness and humility shown through how he greeted his family. He was still the same self-sacrificing young man and always stayed in touch, asking more about them and their lives than sharing his trials and victories.

Jimmy said, "So, you're finally our "big" brother."

Jude added, "Took you long enough."

They were humbled. They did not want to admit it but they finally recognized he had remained thin to share his food with them. They had even matured enough to realize he had slept on the couch throughout high school, so they didn't have to. He had become well-built, and they marveled even more at his self-sacrifice for their sakes and resolved to do more of the same for one another. As Joshua progressed towards officially becoming a swimmer, his leadership increased significantly in the eyes of his family and those who surrounded him day to day. It had become evident he had done what most people only dreamed of. His brothers wondered if they had what it took.

Joshua considered, *Would they desire to become part of this mission now that they had memories of being up close and personal to his calling into the mission?*

His brothers inquired about his friends, some who had passed and become swimmers and some who had not but went on to other significant CG careers.

Joshua regaled them with the recent conversation with his buddy Ben.

"Ben told anyone in earshot, 'I dare you all to run the ECity Marathon in mid-March. I'll buy the fastest marathoner lunch'."

"Our girl, Jordan, said, 'I hope to finish the half-marathon at a faster pace instead, but I'll be there to cheer you all across the finish line.'"

Joshua smiled and relayed to his brothers, "Challenge accepted. The future already looks brighter. Anything for a free lunch. You guys want to join us?"

In one second, both his brothers replied simultaneously, "Para Nada."

Just a few weeks before the end of 'A' School, the CG assigned him a permanent change of station (PCS), which would become his first actual unit and duty assignment as a swimmer. He was surprised to have been assigned to Air Station ECity, North Carolina, and glad to make it his new home. He was thrilled Jordan and Caleb would make ECity their home for the next four years. He had heard in the lives of service members that home was wherever your orders sent you. He and Caleb decided to move off base and get a small apartment together since they shared so much in common. They loved to exercise, local history, travel, and the beaches of the Outer Banks. Their education about the sacrifices and the storied mission of the CG had begun. It was a great thing not to go it alone. They both knew and appreciated.

They were sad to learn their good friend, Ben, got a different assignment to Humboldt Bay, California. They decided to celebrate their respective transfers across town or the continent. Everyone promised to stay in touch and learn from one another's adventures on opposite Coasts. They decided to run the marathon together as a celebratory sendoff. Not all of them had especially trained well for the marathon. At about the halfway point, where Jordan had finished, Ben also decided to quit and opted for an early lunch.

Caleb said, "I vow never to let Ben live the early finish down," while he and Joshua pushed one another the final 13 miles.

They decided, with the encouragement of one another and with renewed purpose, to race one another to the finish. They were glad Jordan caught them as they crossed the line together for proof with a photo finish.

After they finished together, Joshua remarked, "For Ben! We're going to hold him to his agreement to a free lunch!"

Teamwork was essential. They had learned that in the CG and the brutal footrace. While they recovered from the long competition, Caleb sauntered over to the registration tent.

He asked, "My buddy only finished a half-marathon instead of the full. Can I get a half-marathon medal for my friend, Ben, instead of the full?"

To his surprise, Ben's friends ceremonially gave him a half-marathon medal and a good dose of humility.

Ben laughed at himself and said, "I promise to train while I'm in hilly California. At our next reunion, I will chase you down!"

Caleb hung the marathon medal around Joshua's neck with gratitude. In turn, Joshua did the same for Caleb.

Joshua told Ben, "Now, since we finished simultaneously, we will all go to lunch, and you're buying us *both* meals!"

Ben smiled and shrugged, "Okay, as long as I get your pickles..."

They all cracked up at Ben's comebacks.

From there, they all headed to their favorite spot at the town park along the river and enjoyed their Cookout lunch while Ben enjoyed his provision of lunches and shakes. He relished their friendship before he had to set out alone on his new assignment. They decided it was the best meal they'd enjoyed in ECity. Jordan determined to write about their lives later. She took some photos to savor their time's sweet and sour moments.

Joshua's mother was stunned when Joshua appeared up close after AST 'A' School graduation. She wasn't the only one. His extensive instruction regimen had transformed Joshua further in stature. He graduated near the top of his class, which was unusual for such a young trainee. It was due partly because he was under 21, which kept him from some of the shenanigans that tempted other trainees. Joshua knew his young and naïve status did have its issues. He had learned the hard way about sarcasm. Some graduates had bravado, which made them act and operate like gods. All these swimmers were good guys, and Joshua loved their sense of adventure and tenacity. The problems only arose when they desired to put themselves in place of the authority of the Commandant or left the protocols.

Joshua observed their mannerisms and wondered, *Does their drive to succeed make them feel invincible, or perhaps it's some "on top of the world" emotionalism?*

Mr. Jones had also made the trip to see Joshua graduate and to congratulate him.

"Ah, my young protégé, you have finished the course. Now your life as a rescuer begins!"

Joshua replied, "It was even tougher than you said it would be, Master Chief Jones."

"Ah, Mansoul, you're gonna do great stuff one day. Give a lot of people a fresh start."

"Thanks again, Jones, you've been such an inspiration and have become like family. I mentioned I knew you once around the schoolhouse, and they couldn't believe it until I showed them a photo of us together."

"Too funny; I did the same thing this week at the barbershop. Make me proud, AST Mansoul."

"Pride doesn't seem to be in short supply around here, Master Chief."

"Hmmm. Do you remember what I said about that, Mansoul, at our first meeting for coffee? You inhaled donuts like nobody I'd ever seen."

Joshua turned red while Jones reminded him of their donut meet-up.

He answered him, "Not quite."

"Never forget, Mansoul, the mission is in the hands of a crew. You and all those big-headed, muscular swimmers don't get anywhere, let alone home, without your crews."

"Roger, Master Chief," said Joshua.

"You don't need to inhale arrogance like you did the donuts. There's gonna be enough trouble of its own every day. You don't need to go ask for it."

"The qualifications just keep pounding away at me, Master Chief. Soon, I gotta go away to EMT school and afterward gain proficiencies on my airframe. The waves keep coming higher and higher."

"Ah, the baptism that every swimmer must submit to. Be glad your initiation is this year while you're still young. You made the distinct choice to turn from any person's life to the sold-out focus of an AST. Every time you enter the water, you," he thrust his hand shakily out to place it on top of Joshua's head, "You...whether you're out water-skiing or about to rescue a survivor, you remember your baptism as an AST. You've dedicated your life 'so others may live.' Remember your induction to this priceless duty and be grateful."

Jones pulled Joshua closer until he bear-hugged the sinewy Joshua into a fierce embrace. Joshua felt their friendship thicken into a familial hold while he hugged the frail man back. A heavy tear splashed across Joshua's impeccable uniform sleeve, and a few more fell on his arm from Jones' overwhelmed emotional state.

Joshua replied, "I am grateful. I want to be like you."

He patted the man's back.

He thought, *The uniform will not last, but our bond will.*

Jones stiffened and held Joshua back at arm's length while he carefully regarded him.

He spoke again, "Young Mansoul, persevere until the wings are upon you," he tapped the spot where the distinctive rescue swimmer wings would one day be upon his chest.

Joshua looked down at his uniform and smiled knowingly towards Jones. They both envisioned the shiny, unfurled wings that would surround the central crossed fins. The emblem of flight and swiftness in the water that the hundreds of swimmers ahead of him had worn. There was still more to be done to earn the honor and privilege to sacrifice his entire life.

Joshua replied, "And that's where they'll stay."

The two men hugged again and laughed as they heartily slapped one another's backs. The past and the future were entangled in joy.

After graduation, there was a small reception. Chief Simon O'Riley warmly shook AST Mansoul's hand.

Chief said, "I wish you well, Mansoul."

In a moment of gratitude, Joshua pulled the Chief O'Riley a little closer in the handshake.

He whispered, "Chief, my buddy, AMT3 Jordan Roi, gave me the entire Flight Mechanic 'A' school exam on our marathon training runs. If I asked her to talk the whole time we ran, I could keep up with her a little longer. The Jesus nut was the most memorable exam question she shared," he added with a large grin.

Simon O'Riley nodded approvingly, "Mansoul, I had wondered."

O'Riley walked away and shook his head deep in thought, *That poor kid's teeth...*

ECity was where Joshua had done his preparation for swimmer status. The ECity Air Station unit was where he would fulfill the syllabus and get his first six flights with an instructor until he was fully qualified. It was a great consolation not to learn a new city, although ECity seemed more like a small town. It was a quaint historic place where the ocean voyagers had come upstream to meet the train a hundred years ago or more. The fields of NC met the Pasquotank River as it wound its way from the Great Dismal Swamp and emptied into the Atlantic Ocean. It was part of the Intercoastal Waterway and was also a significant mode of travel 100 years ago. By Joshua's time, it became used mainly by tourists. The tiny strip of land called the Outer Banks separated it from the mighty Atlantic Ocean. From the air, he loved to watch the ground formations hit the sea. He enjoyed spectacular sights almost daily, like wild horses, beautiful lighthouses, and gorgeous beaches unencumbered with high-rise buildings found farther north into Virginia.

Joshua trusted those who set his course, and his purpose was extraordinary. Each day, he awoke with the anticipation of where his next mission would be.

Where will I first be tested with "To fight to save or fight and die"?

Joshua's respect for the mission of the USCG grew daily as his training continued at his new unit. From the Culinary Specialists (CS), his beloved food preparations people, to the Boatswain's Mate (BM), the most versatile member of the operational team and a master of seamanship, he was continuously impressed. After graduation, he was assigned to Emergency Medical Technician (EMT) school, followed by six months of more training as a part of his qualifications on his exact airframe and its systems.

Joshua took to the consumption of lots of coffee and made friends with peers as dedicated to the mission as he was throughout. Joshua was thrilled when he rejoined the rescue swimmer program again to fulfill another syllabus to become a journeyman. He began to anticipate the day when he would earn his Aircrew wings after he'd qualified on his airframe, the MH60T Jayhawk. That all stood for Military Helicopter, T being the model number, and the proud 60 mechanics called it the "Big Iron." Just as warriors of old took great care of their steeds, he too was proud to take great care of his mechanical instrument of deliverance. He wanted to be on-call as the duty rescue swimmer without anyone who looked over his shoulder. The exceptions were his Chief and the chain of command all the way up to the CG Commandant, who ultimately bore responsibility. His first-day solo was on the horizon.

The exhaustive preparation still came in waves as part of the rigorous CG strategy to be Always Ready. The Rescue Checklists 1-3 were part of him by then.

1) Preparation
2) On scene

3) Completion

Joshua's career, he knew, was still in Rescue Checklist 1: Preparation. He remembered his previous harsh lesson about the importance of timeliness. He was grateful to be out of the classroom and into the shop. He took captive every task, the most random mechanical information, and devoured the workings of the Jayhawk airframe assigned to him. Joshua took every lesson to heart as he knew the machine would be an extension of his life-saving skills one day. He was thrilled to be in the shadow of the duty swimmer and jumped at the opportunity to carry the nearly 75 lbs. of gear to the helo for him.

"Mansoul, you piece of dirt, get over here with my gear!"

"Aye, aye, Chief!"

"What's with those teeth, Mansoul?"

"Chief, not enough hockey in Texas to knock them out properly."

"Won't find a girl with those things; you'd better take up hockey soon."

He was not qualified yet, but the brash sound of the Search and Rescue (SAR) alarm excited him, and his blood pulsed through his veins. He anticipated the Rescue Swimmer wings after his operational RS syllabus was complete, and he would become part of the crew to "turn the plane" and assist in life-saving missions.

He began to sing or hum the CG song to himself absentmindedly,

"We're always ready for the call,
We place our trust in Thee.
Through surf and storm and howling gale,
High shall our purpose be.
"Semper Paratus" is our guide,
Our fame, our glory too.

To fight to save or fight and die,
Aye! Coast Guard we are for you!"

Joshua had a lot drilled into him throughout the years of instruction he had received. CG protocols seemed to be endless. He and others lived by "the checklists." It was no ordinary life. He was motivated to be the best version of himself physically, mentally, emotionally, and spiritually. He allowed himself more sleep now than at any other point in his course. The trainees conferred with one another, and each thought they no longer took a fire hose to the face each day. He could stay awake just long enough to reflect on his family; his last thoughts were of his dad.

Have I made you proud, Papa? Maybe even Jones may be pleased?

Joshua realized he had not persevered for the fame of completing the AST requirements, the glory of a splendid uniform, and more pay, but to fight through the pain... to follow unconditionally.

If I follow you, I will never face the unescapable alone.

He soon would wear the heavy orange samurai warrior dry suit to protect him from the frigid elements of land and sea. His specific role had been planned for years.

Do I have what it takes to be a rescue warrior?

Joshua's best memory of his papa would always be as the ultimate warrior. All he had on was a wet, nasty, old t-shirt and jeans. He had pointed him and his family to be rescued, and his last words to him were, "Look up." Joshua now understood what made the helicopter blades roar and the rotor's power that washed over him so many years ago. Then, it was a surprise answer to hope-filled prayers. Joshua had learned it was the coordinated efforts of those who had unselfishly gone before him, prepared for his nightmare of Katrina and saved him. From then on, the engines' power and the crews' dedication would carry him to "unreachable" people. The big, bold, black USCG letters swam in front of his eyes every night. Not only was he about to rescue others, but Joshua was also part of the CG's mission to bring them all home alive and more than alive for their participation.

Joshua, at last, completed the initiation requirements and wore the AST badge of wings and fins with honor. The spread wings on his uniform reminded him and the crews he served with of the powerful gift Jones had spoken of earlier. The ritual to become an AST was handed to him by others like Jones, the current Master Chief, and Chief Simon, who had also fought the good fight. He reminded himself his new AST status symbolized his preparation for every new day. It was paramount to retain his necessary proficiencies and interdependence upon the crews he interacted with each mission. Joshua knew his baptism hadn't come through only fire but through the water, too. He was rescued by the water for the water.

From thereon in his career, Joshua could solo as the crew's swimmer, but that did not mean he was ever entirely alone. He understood he had along with him the unfathomable power and the boundless comfort of the mission's existence to enhance life. They danced between their highspeed operations and their compassionate vigilance. The CG aviator's annual dunker training in the pool was a constant reminder of their mortality and that they had to plan and prepare to escape certain death themselves while always in preparation to save others. Their success depended entirely on their interconnectedness to search for and save the lost and hurt and those close to the jaws of death.

Chapter 5

JUST ONE AT A TIME

Kitty Hawk, North Carolina

Joshua sat on a CG picnic table outside the hangar, still in his dry suit, and nibbled on a granola bar. He gazed up at the circling seagulls, frustrated and annoyed at the circumstances and himself from the previous SAR (Search and Rescue) case. The seagulls, who flapped their wings erratically while the winds whipped, knew the drill was someone had probably fed them from the table, and eventually, they would get scraps. When the birds of the air needed food, they had it.

How could this have happened on my watch?

It had been an average SAR case; bad weather, missing surfers, a motor lifeboat (MLB) was launched and on scene. The waves had gotten more significant, though, and the overhead search had been initiated. When the waves reached 10 feet or more, the SAR had gotten noteworthy, like level 8 spicy on his tongue. Checklist 1 had been initiated, and Joshua was on duty.

I'm finally wearing my wings, and the rescue was all mine.

Joshua chomped hard on the granola bar in his hand and ground it in his teeth.

He remembered then that it was the perfect protocol for Checklist 2 when the two surfers were spotted. Time the waves, insert the swimmer, and fish the two guys out expeditiously. Joshua landed in the water perfectly on schedule, thanks to his capable crew. He was prepared and ready. He reached the surfers after he swam over the waves that towered between them. He asked them to follow him and was stunned when they denied his help.

Who in the world refuses to be rescued?

Joshua was still baffled. He opened another granola bar and chewed with gusto.

I've trained for combative, confused, and inebriated survivors, but not for this. Did I miss a training day on "thanks but no, thanks"?

The CG had strict protocols and demanded a strict account for every action, especially the unusual ones. Joshua knew there would be an explanation expected for having left the scene of a SAR with the survivors still in the chaotic waves and wind. He was alone in his interactions with them. There would be a reckoning, which wasn't enjoyable for anyone involved. The MLB crew had also staged nearby and offered to help after he left the scene, but they were refused.

What else could I have done or said to convince them of my willingness to rescue them from imminent destruction?

The SAR alarm just next to him screeched and made him startle for the first time in a long while. He'd been so lost in his thoughts he laughed out loud at his reaction.

Geez, Louise, I gotta pull myself together to go on another SAR case, especially in these terrible conditions.

He hustled inside and swallowed the tiny bit of food he had left to chew as he strode through the door. He wished he'd eaten better if he knew he'd be gone again.

I need a bathroom; it could be a while this time.

Captain Samuel Nissi met the crew gathered in the ready room. They took in the directions from the CG watchstander and Operations Officer of the Day (Ops Boss). They had gotten reports from District 5 about one of the same surfers now without boards who had frantically waved in distress to a passing vessel. It had dropped a life ring but had turned away from the rescue due to fear of getting overturned itself. The small circles required to rescue the people in the massive sea conditions made it possible it would be swamped or capsized. Joshua looked at the large clock on the wall. The red numbers, like a scoreboard, taunted him. Time was rarely on a rescuer's side; he had eventually decided over his months as an official AST. It'd been hours since they had been on the scene. The Ops Boss informed them the lifeboat, out of Oregon Inlet nearby, which had been on the scene, had responded to a different SAR case on the other side of Hatteras as far south as they were west. In a helicopter in these conditions, they could likely make better time. Time was what the surfers did not have; it seemed to everyone involved.

Captain Nissi said, "Listen, you all, I'm sending you right back out there. Bring those boys back to me this time. My orders."

He added, "Their names are reportedly Nic and Christian."

The whole crew nodded their assent and stealthily snuck a look at Joshua. Joshua stood dumbfounded.

Joshua said, "Sir, with all due respect, my CG training says I am not to impose my will on survivors who can make decisions of their own free will. How can I forcibly bring them back to you?"

"Mansoul," Nissi stepped toward him and put a firm hand on his shoulder, "I've handed over my authority to you. You go out with everything you have and bring them to us. Do what I'm telling you to do. You will have obeyed me if you have done this."

Nissi nodded at each crew member who gapped at him in stunned silence. They knew what he implied in his instructive words. It had been the storied history of the combined Life Saving Service and the USCG to be required to go out to save, but not necessarily to come back. They looked at one another for a morale boost. They would collectively put Petty Officer Mansoul back into the snarling Atlantic Ocean for salvation's sake. One by one, they looked at Mansoul, who stood at his full height, still inches below them. His eyes were focused on Nissi alone, and he drew his shoulders back with resolve.

"To fight to save or fight and die, Aye... Coast Guard ...we are for you," said Joshua.

He led the way with his pilots and mech, who bravely followed him toward the Jayhawk. Even their walk through the violent wind was problematic, and he was about to swim through it. The aircraft commander lifted the Jayhawk off the tarmac into the wind. They were cloud riders, after all.

He said, "Perhaps this time, the winds of change will be in our favor..."

Joshua replied, "We never know where it comes from or where it will go."

Christian never heard the thunderous reverberations over his head. His entire body was sucked and submerged in the torrential waves. His head again rose above the surface of the chaotic water as it churned and endlessly pushed him under. He repeatedly tumbled as though he was in a clothes washer machine. Saltwater slapped him conscious as he fell down the front of a wave. He momentarily regarded the hazy summer skyline and noticed it faded to a cobalt blue. His eyes stung, and he tried to pry them open one last time when a flash of orange appeared in his periphery. He plunged underwater and gagged on more water, then resurfaced to gasp for air.

Was the sun moving?

I'm losing my mind now.

This is what it's like to die slowly. I don't want to...

Christian, a lanky high school teenager with short black hair, could not hear the roar of helicopter blades as they knifed through the air above him. He was the quintessential surfer dude with a new tattoo, board shorts, and no concern for a flotation device. Wave after wave of salty, putrid sea water tried to drown him constantly. It slapped him like a wet rag, and he choked on it repeatedly.

I'm hopeless.

Forced repeatedly under the surface for how long he had lost track. He was about to drown, and he knew it. His body and mind, overwhelmed and exhausted, barely broke the water's surface. Suddenly, just feet in front of him was a long cable with a hook on the end that held a sky ruler in orange who descended from heaven. Christian desperately wanted to bridge the gap of his inadequacy to get to the ribbon of steel dropped close to him.

Help me... Is there any hope for me?

He was too weak even to lift both of his arms to acknowledge it. A 15-foot wave washed over him yet again. The sky ruler lost sight of him momentarily but, due to practice, knew where to expect him to surface, and he did. Christian's body throbbed with hypothermia exhaustion, and then he realized his heart hurt, too.

Why do I feel my heart right now about to burst?

I cannot get to the line or him. He's gonna leave me again...

His misery intensified as he desperately understood he could not do what someone else must do for him. Rescue had already been offered earlier in the day when Christian could have freely offered himself up, but he had rejected the submission earlier. Hours later, Christian was cleansed of his pride and wanted help in the worst way. His conscience had been cleansed of his self-sufficiency. His only hope was for someone to accomplish what he could not possibly do for himself.

Please, how long do I stay in this ocean of misery?

Another wave pushed him under. He lost sight of the rescuer and all hope.

In his despair, Christian realized, *I can't do it. I'll die, but he was so close...*

Suddenly, an unfamiliar but flawless, gruff voice shouted in his ear over the mayhem of helicopter noise, wind, and water in his ears. The teenage boy gasped in surprise and swallowed yet another salty mouthful of water.

Did he come for me again?

Another 15-foot wave pulled them up and then threw them both down together. He blinked wildly and turned slightly toward the strong-arm hold that held him fast. They popped to the surface and gasped for breath. He was nose to nose with goggles and a snorkel, and behind those were the kindest eyes he'd ever beheld.

Could it be? he thought.

The longest second in his life happened when he recognized *someone* was nose to nose with him and had materialized out of "nowhere."

The CG Rescue Swimmer yelled again, "Did you order a pizza?"

He had the biggest grin Christian had ever seen, complete with crazy crooked teeth. His funny question snaped Christian out of his disbelief. His rescuer, Joshua, locked eyes with Christian.

He shouted, "I'm a Coast Guard Rescue Swimmer."

Then, with a flicker in his eye and another grin of deep satisfaction, he extended his arm and yelled, "We've come for you; follow me, please."

Christian saw the rescuer wait for him to answer again. Christian nodded slowly with the last bit of energy he had left and realized his teeth chattered wildly, either from hypothermia or fear. He was not sure, maybe both. Another vicious wave pulled them up into the air. Then, it pushed them beneath its surface and threatened to pull them apart. Christian felt the tight embrace of the rescuer and angel of mercy.

He gasped as they resurfaced, summoned his last ounce of strength, and murmured from his soul, "Rescue me."

He closed his eyes, surrendered, and went limp in his rescuer's strong arms. Too exhausted to speak anymore, he sent a thought heavenward.

Why did you come back for me?

Joshua held fast to the survivor, Christian, as the next wave pummeled them. Once they resurfaced, he acknowledged the surrender and expeditiously pulled him by a seatbelt grip through the water that broke over their heads from the rotor wash. The rescue swimmer swam for both of them and attached them to a rescue sling. The swimmer gave the ready signal. Christian, who was utterly incapacitated, immediately relaxed into the notion he did not have to *do* anything, say anything, or even identify himself.

Am I still going to be rescued?

Christian jerked toward Joshua as they were abruptly pulled straight upwards. They were painfully crushed as their torsos smashed together. As the ocean gave up their bodies enmeshed together, limbs splayed, the awkwardness of the position was somehow a comfort to Christian momentarily. The pain in his armpits from the sling took

Christian's breath away, but the freedom from the ocean's death grip was exhilaration. The baptism of pain in the past hours of suffering had released its clutch on Christian, only to be raised momentarily into a new and wondrous experience. The weight of the lostness, the misery of abandonment, adrift and unknown, and the torment of anger and guilt gave way to liberty. Christian went limp in wide-eyed fear as their twisted bodies spun through the air.

Am I going to fall back to my grave?

"I've got you," said Mansoul.

Joshua squeezed Christian harder when he felt him go limp. Christian trusted this stranger more than he trusted himself. Joshua knew his survivor was about to be welcomed into the assurance of safety in the cabin of their deliverance. Almost as suddenly as the ride began, it ended abruptly at the helicopter's side. Christian was pulled backward through the surreal cabin door as Joshua dangled the last few seconds over the Atlantic Ocean, which snarled below them. They had escaped the death trap but without Nic. Christian's stomach revolted against the thought of his lost friend. He spewed salt water and whatever else was in his stomach into the ocean. The chaotic and unfathomable depths below them had already consumed Nic.

Unable to move if he wanted to, Christian showed no resistance and ultimately succumbed to the crew's will. The unspoken welcome of being linked to and then brought into the cabin with the rest of the crew in the CG helicopter was the best relief and welcome Christian had ever experienced. He was barely conscious but aware of the forces at play. He was a survivor, barely, though not of his own accomplishment.

"Swimmer is in the cabin," snapped Jordan.

The next face Christian saw was the helmeted Flight Mechanic, Jordan, who had a tremendously big smile that reached from ear to ear. She had already begun Rescue Checklist number three.

"Survivor is in the cabin," said Jordan.

She mouthed to Christian, "You made it!" She yelled to her crew, "Boo yah and a hallelujah!"

Christian fell backward into Joshua's lap in delirium.

He muttered, "Mercy."

Huge smiles spread across the faces of each of the crew as they moved into forward flight. They had hovered over the tumultuous, deep abyss long enough. Eyes continued to roam for Nic, though. No matter the joy, the apparent loss of the other survivor would never leave them.

Joshua disconnected from the locking hoist hook. He belted them both with certainty into the helicopter for the ride back to Air Station ECity. He worked down Rescue Checklist Part 3 for forward flight. However, in his mind, he flashed back to the other lost teen and the decisions they could have made earlier in the day.

Joshua wondered, "Why didn't the other surfer, lost to the ocean's waves, respond as this one finally did?"

An affirmative nod, a willingness to be rescued, would have made all the difference. Where was he now?

Nevertheless, this child of someone was already asleep at his feet.

Joshua remembered, *He had even whispered, "please", when we were nose to nose.*

Joshua saw him mouth the words, and the look in his eyes was all it took. The difference was an eager submission, not Nic's boastful tone with him hours earlier.

Joshua thought, *Why couldn't both those guys surrender their pride and arrogance? You thought you were good enough to paddle back to shore.*

The sinking feeling came over Joshua when he finally caught his breath inside the cabin.

There will be a reckoning sooner than I'd like.

There was always a debrief or hotwash among his crew and officers at the Air Station. Hands down, the roughest part of his job was the constant replay of what could've gone better for just one more survivor to be brought home quicker, in better condition, or at all. The hotwash was when all the mission participants discussed what went right and wrong. It would cement the loss in Joshua's mind and soul.

Why, Nic, Christian, did you reject my offer of help?

What it costs us you could never understand.

Joshua shook his head; he desperately tried to tamp down his resentment and anger. Instead, he focused on the joy of the moment with the teenager who shivered uncontrollably in his sleep right before him. Joshua gently nudged him to awaken; letting him sleep too much wasn't good. He didn't even know which teen it was, Nic or Christian.

"Wake up, you sleeper, arise from the dead," he thought.

He tried to nudge the teen again to keep him awake, but it seemed futile; he was too exhausted.

Thank you, we get to take one more home.

"Yeehaw," said one of the pilots.

Joshua couldn't help but look out the window for the other lost soul.

Chapter 6

WHAT WAS HIS ANSWER?

At Air Station Elizabeth City in North Carolina, Joshua, Jordan, and the rest of the crew spilled out of their H-60 Jayhawk helicopter and stretched their limbs, glad to be back on solid ground. Relieved to assist the teenage boy who still shivered and staggered in his walk into the hangar, Joshua scanned the onlookers. His fellow Guardians worked around the clock to maintain the aircraft and rescue equipment. They glanced up from their individual tasks and smiled at another successful rescue. This inspired and gave them all a sense of pride in their respective jobs related to the CG mission, "*Semper Paratus*, Always Ready."

Out of his peripheral vision, he spotted a civilian woman who rushed toward them. She broke free from the restraint of the CG Commander and other leadership who had contacted her earlier and escorted her onto base.

She ran unashamedly toward them and cried out, "Christian!"

Is that his name?

He assisted someone's son by the arm. The teenager noticed her and tugged backward, unsure of the reception by what Joshua could now only presume was his mother. She stopped abruptly before them both, burst into tears, and grasped her son in a bear hug. A moment later, she gathered Joshua, too, both cold and wet, into her arms.

She shouted, "Oh, thank you, God!"

Joshua felt his heart squeeze and knew Nic was the name of the lost one. He looked over the woman's shoulder to see another parent and sucked in a breath of guilt, sadness, and remorse as another mother slowly turned away from them. The guys were startled by Christian's mother's declaration and affection but relaxed into her tight embrace to enjoy the awkward homecoming celebration after a long, hard-fought battle of wills and physical strength. Both of their matches were different and yet the same. They persevered in the most demanding times and suffered for a good outcome. Joshua had decided it was all worth it when he joined the mission of the CG "to fight to save or fight and die."

Joshua wondered, *What had distinguished Nic from Christian when they fought the madness they had swum into?*

Christian and his mother, Eliana, as she identified herself, made their way toward an ambulance to transport survivors for evaluation in the local emergency department. They had turned and walked away in exhaustion. They clung to one another for emotional and physical support. She, however, stopped abruptly mid-stride and turned and led her son back up to Joshua. She looked up at Joshua, and with tears that still streamed down her cheeks, she spoke unashamedly.

She said, "Thank you, whoever you are. You, too, are someone else's son, and what you did for me, for us... well, I vow not to let your gift of mercy be forgotten."

She sniffled and entirely regarded Joshua and then her son, who stood inches over her. She wiped her arm across her face to catch the rivers of water that cascaded down her front. She carefully turned them around with her arms around his middle. She supported him as he staggered away barefoot, barely able to stand and walk without another word. Joshua pondered the significance of her words. He slowly turned back opposite them toward the rest of the crew. They all made their way toward the ready crew facilities for rest and cleanliness. He nodded toward their leadership in appreciation. They nodded back with consent for what the crew hoped for: hot coffee, food, and some warmth. After the stressful day's events, they agreed to meet thirty minutes later for the hotwash (an after-action discussion).

Joshua rehearsed in his memory, as he got cleaned up and fed himself, the strict CG protocols he had abided by. It was only by the collective wisdom and study the CG could maintain, and by sheer determination, the survivors, Nic and Christian, with hours-long exposure to the cold and open water, could have survived. Joshua reminded himself of the mission.

It was the contribution of the years of experience, research, and training by the people of the US Coast Guard, who made all rescue attempts at sea or land possible. More specifically, the Rescue Swimmer, more commonly known as swimmers, made it their motto, "So others may live." The crew brought the swimmer to the scene and individually deployed her or him into the fray for the rescue attempt. Swimmers prepared daily to be *Semper Paratus*, Always Ready for the call. The all-volunteer US service branch's experience, reason, and tradition were proven to locate and eventually bring survivors home effectively.

Joshua had finally completed the RS syllabus and earned his RS wings the previous winter. He had been part of several fantastic rescues of individuals. The virtue of the USCG was known far and wide as a community that put total strangers above their welfare to save the lost. Joshua finally admitted to himself he was nervous then, not in the ocean. He had trained for his work in the water and on land. The hotwashes in front of his Commanders, he hadn't so much.

Would the same virtue be seen in my actions, by default, the rest of my crew, in this hotwash?

The pilots, flight mechanic, and rescue swimmer took their favorite chairs at a long table in a stuffy conference room. The Air Station Commander, Captain Samuel Nissi, was also included in the late-night hotwash. A pleasant man of few words, he got right to the point.

Nissi said, "What happened out there today?"

Exhaustion strained the faces of the crew as they looked from one to another to try and explain the devastation of losing a victim to the ravages of the cold Atlantic Ocean. Conscious the pilots did their jobs expertly, the flight mechanic, Jordan Roi, began to relay her experiences. She was Joshua's dark, curly-haired friend from their earlier days and served with him as the mech. She had explained his responses to more than one person before. Joshua sat back in his chair, relieved again for her presence. As a flight mechanic, she was responsible for the hoists, precise directions for the crew, and cabin management, along with assistance to the swimmer when needed. Jordan was still a chatty woman in her early twenties by this time. She was a tall, power-packed lady who did her job with precision and punctuation. She loved being the authority on most subjects, and the other men in the room grinned sheepishly. They knew she would likely talk all night until she was interrupted. However, she made up for her verbosity in knowledge and expertise. The others were glad to let her tell her version of the story until they needed to clarify or express what had happened. She grinned quickly, and her even pearly white teeth flashed and lifted spirits around the room. Jordan began animatedly to tell the whole scenario from her perspective.

"After a long hour of searching for two surfer friends, Nic and Christian, off the coast of Kitty Hawk, we began to call off the helicopter search due to the deterioration of the weather. The cloud ceiling had dropped just feet off the cold waters of the Atlantic, and the sea swells had only worsened with the approaching storm. This storm was probably why the surfers chose to "chance it" and surf the larger built-up waves the storm pushed in. It seemed like a terrible way to be left behind, to know the crew had to be so close to the victims as to be heard yet not seen. We were frustrated that there wasn't a better location than off the coast around mile marker 6, Kill Devil Hills."

The mile marker system on the Outer Banks was unique. The road runs north and south, with the Atlantic Ocean's narrow beach on one side and the sound on the other. Businesses and beaches are noted as miles from the Wright Memorial Bridge on the north, and the numbers grow as they head south toward Hatteras Island.

Jordan exhaled and said, "A CG small boat had arrived on the scene to search but was also forced back after terrible conditions proved insurmountable. Most had given up hope, but we persevered. The search continued with the help of first responders, some family, and friends. The search was from above by a Herc (C-130 *Hercules*, cargo plane), which circled in a pattern. From shore, the search was conducted by brave persons who watched the beach from Kitty Hawk to Nags Head and hoped to find the two teenage surfers who were overdue by then for hours."

Jordan relayed the SAR's details like a court procedure witness. The crew and Captain Nissi were impressed.

She finally concluded, "Those are my observations from the back of the helo."

She closed her statement with her big, even smile again. She looked encouragingly toward Joshua first and then around the room to cheer them all up. She was on her second cup of coffee and took a long sip. An uncomfortable, awkward silence followed as if someone had fallen asleep in her exhaustive commentary on the day's events, or perhaps no one wanted to follow her. When the rest of the crew began to fear Jordan may break into the USCG song's strong refrain, "We're always ready for the call."

Joshua interrupted the silence, "Ahem, well..."

He paused for a moment, unsure whether to begin. He felt some raw emotions about the devastation caused by the senseless loss of the teenager.

Why am I not prepared for this part?

Joshua swallowed the lump in his throat.

The teen with whom I had spoken directly, disbelievingly as he later learned, *was named Nic.*

"Nic, the first teen, said to me, 'I'm good, man!' ...Increíble!"

Joshua slapped his forehead for his Spanish exclamatory phrase and repeated instead, "Incredible!"

Joshua had not meant to say something in his native Spanish as he relayed the incident. It only made them lean in as he began and reminded them how, at the appointed time, he had dropped the 30 feet into the churning waves off the coast of Kill Devil Hills, where the two surfers had been reportedly washed out to sea by a powerful rip current. Too far for the local lifeguards to reach, the USCG had been dispatched. Due to time restraints and already being in the air nearby, they were the best asset to divert for the rescue attempt. The SAR operation happened while they were airborne and saved time. The Jayhawk rescue helicopter and crew were on the scene in minutes. The surfers were spotted quickly enough with their brightly colored boards.

"I expected them to swim toward me and clamor excitedly for a lift. Instead, I was met with nearly unmatched bravado and the quintessential surfer mentality of "let it rip" toward the waves that pounded us all."

Joshua recapped for the crew what they had expected him to relay.

"I informed them I was a USCG Rescue Swimmer....

I invited them to follow me, and I would put them into a rescue basket, hoist them individually, and we would be back to shore in minutes. I told them, follow me, or die alone."

Weighty silence filled the room like an ugly, uninvited guest. It became uncomfortably hot for everyone. A dark presence seemed to lurk in the shadows. There was a long pause in Joshua's delivery of the course of events from his perspective. He silently deliberated what he did wrong when he invited them to follow him to safety. While sweat dripped down his neck, he paused longer than he wanted. He had to control the many emotions the day's exhaustion threatened to undo him in front of these fellow Guardians. Joshua worked his jaw against the emotion that threatened to work its way out of his right eye.

The pilot asked the inevitable, "What was his *answer*?"

Again, Joshua attempted to speak, and his voice cracked, "Nic, the bolder teenager, said, 'No, we're okay, man, leave us alone.'"

Joshua remembered how much earlier in the day the young surfers relished their epic waves, not unlike most surfers. They underestimated the power of nature and the human condition. His raw emotion turned to a pit in his stomach, and he felt the frustration return from earlier when he was in flight. He retold them what had replayed over in his mind.

I replied, "You're not good enough to swim back to shore in this storm in these conditions.

I turned my attention directly onto the other teen, who we now know was Christian, and implored him to follow me out of there! It was then Nic yelled at Christian."

Joshua added, "Nic said, 'We will not leave our boards! We've got each other to look out for in this epic storm and get back in on our own!'"

Joshua knew the conditions; the mighty wind and waves threatened them all.

"I was shocked they said no! Nic was determined they would swim their way back with no help.

They had not prepared for the worst-case scenario and trusted only in themselves," Joshua said, "What else could I do?"

"I told them it was asking for death if they wouldn't trust and follow me."

Joshua struggled to form the words, "It only seemed to fuel their crazed adrenaline high status...

We are trained not to force ourselves upon them. We don't go out there to condemn them but to save them. People make their own choices for life or death."

Jordan wrote furiously in the tiny notebook she always carried. She recorded something important, it seemed to everyone else.

Was it something I said? thought Joshua.

"Are you in public affairs, Roi?" said a pilot.

Jordan stopped her scribbles and put her pen down respectfully.

She said, "No, just passionate about the truth. It sets us free."

The silence after her statement was substantial.

Joshua thought, *There may be more reasons for these briefs than I realized,*

Joshua silently recalled the swim back to the hoist cable and the long, nauseated ride up to the cabin's safety. Joshua had made the "ready" hand signal to be hoisted, arm extended thumb up. Jordan had recalled all this already and shared it. He had been retrieved from the violent storm alone. He relayed how, once secured, they leaned outside the cabin door on their bellies.

"I was next to Jordan, and we considered the valley of death to see if they might come to me one last time. But by then, we knew they would already be out of sight."

Joshua stated the obvious to break the silence.

"Why ignore my offer of hope?"

Joshua sat back in his conference room chair, exhausted at his delivery of the previous events. The tension was palatable, and everyone, even Jordan, waited to speak.

"I'm finished," Joshua said.

He knew he wasn't. The hunger to rescue just one more drove him day and night to continuously prepare for the worst and expect the best outcomes. It was in moments like these when the results were the worst, he reminded himself,

I come to save the lost, not condemn them to die.

It was their choice, not mine. If they don't trust me, then they're already lost.

The crew all felt dismayed and turned to Captain Nissi, who stood confidently.

He said, "Take a brief break and then report back in 10 for a debrief of the second SAR case."

As they shuffled out for fresh air, Jordan paused long enough beside Joshua to say something she hoped would console him.

"They were given the truth.... It could have saved them both."

The pilot and commander turned toward one another to discuss what they could have done differently, if anything at all. They all pondered in the back of their minds what answers they, or perhaps their children, would have given in the same dangerous situation.

Joshua headed outside to clear his mind for a few minutes. He could not help but go over why he was there in the first place again. The discipline to become a rescue swimmer had been as daunting as the day's missions. His grueling preparation with the temptation to quit every day lasted for weeks. His time in AST School had tested his limits hourly and had been part school and part dance with the devil. The students were pushed past their extreme discomfort, and maximum effort was the expectation. Each trainee had to know their breaking point and survive the day. All they had to do was tap out, but Joshua didn't want to tap out now.

Joshua swung open a door and filled his lungs with a cold blast of air. He recalled those long days of preparation and those of his teammates and the crew and what it took to do his job to bring hope to the hopeless. The crew operated by strict procedures so they could perform on any team on any given day by the book. These were survivors, souls in perilous situations, not instructors in role-play mode.

He thought, *Today, a survivor died on my duty.*

It was up to swimmers to leave the crew for seconds, minutes, or hours to save individuals. Those heavy burdens weighed on Joshua as he looked up at the star-filled sky and took deep breaths. The price he paid wasn't just exhaustion and physical exertion. His psyche was battered; he knew people praised him when he made a save or cursed him when he didn't. There was real pain when questions went unanswered, or even worse, his anticipation and everything he lived for were rejected. Joshua drew an uneasy breath as he realized several cases hadn't gone as planned. He might be asked to go in for some "reeducation." There would likely be guidance that Captain Nissi would issue Joshua's command. Discipline was a challenge in more than one way.

Discipline will be a harsh word to hear, let alone bear.

Joshua was disciplined to do his job, but to receive it for doing his duty would be the most significant challenge he'd ever faced.

Certainly not a change to my flight status, please, not that...

He looked up and gazed into the heavens; *a rescue swimmer is who I am.*

"Captain on deck!"

At his appearance, Captain Nissi allowed the room to be brought to attention after their short break. He dismissed them to sit again. He congratulated the crew on the successful rescue of a teenager they now knew as Christian. He had been informed the second SAR case was more problematic due to the storm's terrible interference. The same helicopter crew had been scrambled again to be launched for the same survivors. When they found one, Christian, it was remarkable.

"I am," Captain Nissi cleared his throat and continued, "pleased. It isn't a routine procedure for the same survivor to be offered a rescue twice on the same day; good work, you brought him home."

He jested, "I guess that's why they pay me the big bucks to make those decisions. However, it keeps me up at all hours. I never sleep anymore."

He looked at his watch absentmindedly. The unspoken thought around the table was somebody must've been looking out for the young man to have survived several hours in those conditions. They also knew the teens had some faithful friends who never gave up their search for them. The parents had been thrilled to know one of the boys had been found, but the terror of not knowing which boy had cost them years of their lives and had also taken its toll on the command while they waited to find out.

"I'm going to quote from my favorite book about the historic US Life Saving Service,

> 'Often rescues began with a surfman rushing into the station from patrol. ...But whatever had to be done, it was the Keeper's responsibility to decide how to respond. People's lives, including those of his crew, depended upon his decisions. His career also rode on his decisions.'"

Captain Nissi knew he had become the "Keeper" of the United States Life Saving Service (USLSS) while on his watch. It worked out well in that SAR case, especially since the first go around didn't. The finality of the resolution rode on his shoulders, and he needed his crews always to remember, as much as he did, his authority to fulfill the mission. They were symbols of his superior power to lead, as was shared with him from the Commandant. He agreed to send the crew back into the terrible storm with hope for them and both teens. With curiosity if they had not already met their demise. He knew the mission had to continue despite the physical and emotional difficulties. He also knew he was responsible for directly sending the crew into harm's way to save those lost young men. They were his outstretched arm. The crews went by his word.

The USLSS existed to help mariners lost at sea who couldn't get to shore on their own accord. The U.S. decided hundreds of years ago to watch ships break up offshore and leave men, women, and children to die was unacceptable. Before the USCG was a dream in anyone's mind, there were established Life Saving Services (LSS) up and down the coasts of America. Nissi stood in an ambitious tradition and mission to rescue the lost and perilous. Whether the tragedies were of their own making in transportation, wars, pirate activity, or storm-related, the LSS went in. Many men who volunteered for this service never returned from the surf alive. This was the weight born on the shoulders of the Captain who sent them toward the foe.

In a brief hesitation in his address, Captain Nissi paused to gather his thoughts because there was a lot to negotiate in the wee hours of the long night. A voice lilted from the other end of the table. It was Jordan Roi, the pesky mech who never really knew when to shut her mouth.

She said, “Sir, with all due respect, those guys maybe had the very worst days of their lives, but the rescue swimmer,” she gestured toward Joshua, “you know he was having the time of his life. I don’t think it would’ve mattered if Joshua had been asked to go back for that kid 99 times.”

Nods of agreement impulsively passed between the pilot and copilot as they acknowledged they both affirmed Jordan’s comments.

Captain Nissi took back over the conversation and directed his eyes at Jordan.

“Nevertheless, AMT3 (3rd Class) Roi, we should not be unaware there will likely be bad press about this case, again, due to the nature of not having rescued both teens.”

He addressed the room, “I have suggested CISM (Critical Incident Stress Management) for Petty Officer Mansoul and... for the rest of this crew.”

Joshua’s heart sank. He heard his rank and last name from Captain Nissi and felt worse than when he heard his mother call his name when he’d displeased her as a child. His mind drifted to his mother briefly. His beloved mother raised him and his brothers on her own.

She did everything she could and miraculously more to get them what they needed.

My mother, he thought, *how I miss her embrace and meals, even if the food is better here.*

She could calm his fears, he hoped, no matter what the Captain's input would be about his future in the swimmer program. Joshua's mind wandered to his mother when suddenly he returned to the conversation about him. He realized he'd been told he was being sent to Kodiak to backfill temporarily for another swimmer injured in the line of duty.

Joshua uncharacteristically exclaimed with wide eyes, "Wait, what? Kodiak, like, in Alaska?"

The whole room burst out incredulous at his disbelief. The pilots also cast nervous glances at one another. They were surprised to recognize his orders so soon in such a remote and hostile environment for a swimmer in his first tour. Nissi smiled slowly and knowingly; he deflected the terrible press, guilt, and residual disgrace from the day's earlier loss of Nic.

Nissi said, "Pack your bags, Mansoul, as commanded."

"Aye, aye, Sir!" Joshua replied in shock.

Joshua was grateful not to have been reprimanded nor sidelined from active flight AST status. There was a minor impression he'd be carefully observed.

Maybe by even more people inside and outside of my unit.

The crew and command filed out of the conference room after the hotwash, to everyone's relief. After the long day, the decompression was coming soon, and the crew anticipated the reprieve of a long, hard rest before they could stand duty again. Unfortunately, or maybe fortunately for Joshua, he realized he had to pack immediately, clean up his place, and find a ride to the airport very soon. He pushed the door open to the cool night air, and the crew made their way to their vehicles. The mile-long drive wound to CG ECity Air Base's front gate and helped Joshua unwind from the day's drama.

Traffic halted suddenly, and a sea of bright lights and flashbulbs began outside the gate's entrance and exit. He realized reporters' vans and community members shouted at the vehicles as they attempted to pass. They practically blocked the gate. Momentarily, he was surprised at the late hour; so many people would come to congratulate them on their mission. Rarely did any CG member even get a thank you for a mission. Joshua had gotten a thanks from the woman, the mother of his survivor, several hours ago.

What was her name? hmmm...Eliana? I wonder what it means...

All those waterworks were over the son she thought she had lost and then was given back. When the vehicles slowly rolled past the mob, he realized their yells were hateful and cruel. Their faces were distorted with anger and some with rage. Reporters videoed the crowd as their obscenities filled the air instead of thanks.

Joshua thought, *they weren't here to ask what happened and not to thank us for what we tried to do... I offered rescue and life!*

They were "reporting" how they or he specifically, seemingly fell short, again. Joshua's heart was crushed for Nic, Nic's family, and the world, who only saw what they wanted to see. Then he felt his spine stiffen, and he ground his teeth. He was disrespected, and so was the mission of the USCG, Always Ready. He pushed down the gas and rolled through and past the gate. His knuckles were white on the wheel as he steered away. He stared into the blackness of the night ahead of his car's lights. "*Semper Paratus* is our guide, our fame, our glory too."

Really, where was the fame and glory tonight?

He began to mutter, "For you, I do it for you, Papa."

Undone by the day's tragic events, for himself and them, he knew he had to get away to find solace before he could find rest. Somewhere down the dark road, he realized he was sweating and gripped the wheel as if his life depended on it, and the silence became too much. He pulled off near the waterfront, parked, and turned off the ignition. He finally laid his head on the wheel and submitted his turmoil over the world's despair.

He moaned, "Why?"

The mission's reach was as vast as the ocean and as chaotic as the waves had been even on shore.

How would those spiteful strangers have answered him? On the open abyss of an ocean, his arms outstretched, calling to them, "Follow me..."

CHAPTER 7

PRACTICE

Joshua awakened with a start and didn't know if he was again in a recurrent nightmare until he heard the SAR alarm scream and saw the lights flash in the ECity ready room. It had been months since the awful SAR case when he lost Nic. Joshua had been to Kodiak, Alaska, and back since then. He had decided to list Air Station Kodiak first on his next dream sheet: jaw-drop scenery, harsh conditions for a rescue operations unit, and a small-town atmosphere certainly had intrigued him. The "rusted buckets" served as a fishing fleet at times in the North Pacific and had kept the CG busy for a long while. He had tasted the thrill of adventure and wanted more.

No joke, my only good dreams these days are full of Alaskan adventures. Why do I have the same nightmare again and again?

He threw back the rough wool blanket provided in the base's ready barracks for all those on flight duty. As he and the other fellow's feet hit the floor, they ran toward their gear to prep for a pre-flight brief. It would take just a minute to discover what would come at them. He pulled on more clothes as he went.

What a terrible way to awaken, thought Joshua, *at least this time, I can do something about it.*

He still had these recurrent nightmares about a survivor who refused his rescue. Others would refuse to come to him, too. In his follow-up critical incident stress training, he had been warned to deal with these. Nic's scornful face was the hardest to shake.

How am I going to let him go?

He had already made other remarkable rescues with the crews he served with at ECity. However, the tragic ones stuck with him the most. The particular scenario of Nic's flat refusal was like a hound dog who returned to him daily and reminded him of his humanity and the need for reassurance.

When can I put the mission and lost survivor to rest?

Nevertheless, he craved the thrill of the shrill alarm at the same time. He followed his dad's encouragement and the crews he now trusted with his life. His chain of command would not fail him, nor would the crew assembled around him, who also shook sleep from their heads and downed hot black coffee. At this time of night, in the pre-dawn hours, the coffee was well-burnt. The smell tickled his nose, the familiarity calmed his nerves, and the caffeine gave him a shot of energy.

Some of his peers who weren't on flight status went for the terrible energy drinks; some were banned entirely from use in aviation. Though cool for a minute, they soon were caught in an addiction. Sometimes, his buddies had to get help from medical to get off their use or were tossed from the CG altogether for their behaviors. Misery crouched at everyone's door and waited to devour them unexpectedly. It was often the youngest and inexperienced who suffered from the slightest offer of a "reprieve." It would get them snatched away from the mission like a lion on its prey. He had already lost buddies to innocent recreational activities that took themselves out. He wanted the mildest stimulant and simultaneously not destroy his self-control or self-respect.

"Ah, black sludge," said the Ops Boss to the crew.

"Bean juice, thanks," said a bleary-eyed pilot.

Others retorted, "What, no frappes for us, Boss?"

Joshua wondered silently, *I wonder if a spoonful of sugar would make this tar go down better.*

The CG watch stander and Operations Officer of the Day had been getting reports from District 5 and the update from a cruise ship about a Medevac (Medical Evacuation Medevac) case.

"An elderly person needs help on a cruise ship over 100 miles away. They're off the coast of Cape Hatteras."

Cruise ships regularly sailed from North to South or vice versa and had to make a wide berth around the dangerous shoals near the Outer Banks of coastal NC. There was a good reason it was called the Graveyard of the Atlantic. It was not an uncommon call for medical assistance and transport of a stricken cruise passenger to a higher level of care than the cruise ship could provide. The difficulty was whether the case needed the support of a CG Flight Surgeon (FS) or if the Swimmer could provide the required care. The crew prepared for a flight out before dawn, about an hour away. Joshua lingered for information and hoped for a flight surgeon (Doc) if the elderly individual was in terrible condition. He was not the physician people expected at times.

Will Doc get to the helicopter in the pre-dawn hour?

Joshua entered the back of the H-60 Jayhawk's cabin in total darkness and began his preflight rescue checklist while the rest of the crew did theirs. Within a few minutes, the inky blackness turned to pre-dawn blue, and a bright pink sky stretched across the horizon. The helicopter crew had completed their checklists and prepared to lift off the runway as planned.

Joshua realized, *I need to be back "in the saddle again," or is it my overwhelming passion as a swimmer?*

The memories since the last unfortunate and fortunate rescues seemed to taunt him in his sleep and even in his wakeful hours. This was what he wanted to be: a swimmer back on a rescue mission.

One question still nagged at him: *will my patient want my help? Why wouldn't he? Why am I even asking this question?* He ground his teeth.

How pleased Joshua was when, at the very last minute, "Doc," the Flight Surgeon, jumped inside the cabin. Doc laughed and waved across his forehead.

He spoke, "Maybe I cut it too close."

"Thanks for gracing us with your presence, Doc," said the aircraft commander.

"My pleasure," he replied.

Joshua flashed Doc the biggest grin he could and gave him a thumbs up.

The helo directly went into forward motion to lift off. It was also a lift for Joshua to not only share the burden of the rescue scenario, more than he'd admit, but also for a particular medical expert to perform lifesaving measures Joshua only knew of in a tiny way. Doc had a unique and humble personality for someone so brilliant and intuitive to serve with the difficulty of rendering aid in what felt like a third-world ambulance: very little light, chucked all around, and nauseousness for crew and patient alike. CPR in the back of a helo was excruciating at best, like a ride in a dump truck on your knees for an hour of chest compressions while trying to save a soul for another day.

The orange sun was spotted as they gained altitude and made for the giant cruise ship, which would appear as a speck in the distance soon enough. Since the sunrise was spectacular and the ride smooth and peaceful, the talk over the intercom was almost reverent yet dutiful. The tweet (Avionics Electrical Technician, AET) also sat near him and would be responsible for the duties in the back of the cabin while he cared for the patient. He had become friends with this tweet, Theo Lukas, after they'd been on several missions together. Every time he put his life in Lukas' hands, his trust grew. It happened when a swimmer was put down or hoisted from below.

How could I not want fellowship with these incredible individuals who also dared their lives for the same purposes?

The competence, confidence, and teamwork made the crew a cohesive force to be reckoned with, whether in the protection of boundaries, deterrence of disorder, or lifesaving measures. They all knew the situation they flew into was tragic, but that was the point of the CG. Redemption of a destructive or chaotic circumstance with life or limb rescuing hope. Help was on the way.

It had been several months since the terrible day Nic had been lost to the Atlantic. When they flew occasionally, Joshua's mind drifted back to what he could have done differently (if anything) to have changed the outcome. Joshua meditated on his CG career in the quietness of the long ride. He savored being on a SAR case or a MEDEVAC. He knew he was built to be a rescuer and couldn't imagine doing anything else. He enjoyed his TDY in Kodiak more than he could say. Going back was a front-runner on his "dream sheet" for his next tour of duty. More recently, rescues had happened up and down the Coastal Carolinas, into Virginia, and far out to sea. He'd had his remarkable moments and some unfavorable ones, but none stood out so much as Nic's loss. When Joshua looked down on the surfers headed out, it was like he rewatched a memorial to what could have been if Nic had answered yes and followed. Joshua did his best to refocus his mental state when he saw the kites. Those colorful wind-driven markers danced in the air as beacons of hope. For the souls of those who would want to be rescued in times of trial, he persevered on the CG mission. He relished these views, even more so as his last season in ECity ended. He would not serve the CG from ECity much longer as he was due to PCS again soon. He wanted to be able to leave Nic's memory here. He dreaded Nic's pride and unwillingness to follow him would plague his mission always.

How can I convince them all to come with me?

Distrustful people have always afflicted the historic Life Saving Service, the modern CG, and other helper agencies worldwide. Instead of deciding to trust the CG's long-standing faithful goodness and service to the world, some people wanted to trust in themselves more. They no longer saw the goodwill and did not fear life without the Guardian's assistance. Joshua had learned the truth in conversations with other Guardians. Survivors sometimes acted out of what they could only suppose, was fatigue, pride, or fear. Instead of trust and obedience, they decided what was good and evil in their lives, even amid their peril. They had chosen to wait, swim, float, or climb away from those who could rescue them in times of desperation. Even to their detriment and to those they said were loved ones, they sometimes brought the death sentence upon themselves.

The Guardians chose every time, regardless of how the victims got into their desperate circumstances (poor judgment, accident, or flagrant violation of the laws of man or nature), to pull them out one by one. Throughout the ages, those who gave themselves to rescuers were drawn into a more profound commonality and a more joyous life with a renewed perspective. Each soul was a treasured possession believed collectively by the U.S. to expend significant resources to preserve life and limb. At great personal risk, Guardians had tried to save everyone from those dreadful occasions for centuries. It had become all too obvious to Joshua and others on his missions their real enemy was not the wind nor the waves but the power struggle of a dark and chaotic world. They often spoke of their clashes with cosmic rebels on behalf of humanity.

Was it only more recently people, whether in fear or a distorted violation of self, believed a lie that Guardians would give them a misdirected end?

By aligning their will with our lifesaving services, their future was more assured and abundant.

Joshua said, "Live to surf another day."

"What, Mansoul?" asked the co-pilot.

"Oh, sorry, guys, I was lost in my thoughts and spoke out loud," Joshua said.

His face turned red, and he tried vainly to look out the aircraft's window to cover his embarrassment. Doc heard and regarded Joshua's comment and humiliation. He cocked his helmeted head toward Joshua as if he invited him to say more. Then he glanced at Lukas, who also regarded his friend closely.

"Hmmm. You guys know I'm always available to chat when you want to, eh?" said Doc.

"Not going to happen over the mic, Doc; thanks for the welcome mat," said the co-pilot.

Doc replied, "I didn't mean now, exactly, but you do have my undivided attention presently."

The aircraft commander said, "Well, since you asked, my kid's got diaper rash; what do you recommend?"

Laughter filled the headsets.

Some days, Joshua had swum into a struggle that wasn't with flesh and blood. Joshua had full recognition there was something more sinister at work against him than the natural elements. The Guardians would again prove faithful to their higher call no matter the storm; they would bridge the gap to "fight to save or fight and die." While they flew over the depths of the Atlantic, he knew he would again walk into a conflict with an unseen enemy who wielded an invisible sword of death.

If the survivor can still speak, will he choose life or darkness, follow or flee?

The gigantic cruise ship was miniscule against an unfathomable Atlantic Ocean. Rescue Checklist 1 had begun, and once the ship was spotted, the crew readied the aircraft for the deployment of Joshua. He would assess the patient's situation on the vessel and report on what was needed. The crew did not yet know if the patient was conscious or needed oxygen, a backboard, or a basket for a hoist directly into the helicopter on a litter. Rarely would the Doc hit the deck himself; the swimmer was trained to be the intercessor between the patient and rescue crew. He would be boots on the ship and make life-saving decisions. He could ask the crew for their opinions, but it took precious time they didn't have while they circled over the ocean. Timely life and death decisions would be made, not just for the survivor but for his fellow crew as well. Their lives were all at risk, with nowhere to land for miles and miles. They orbited nearby and waited for the patient, perhaps a family member, and swimmer to depart the scene before bingo. They were often left with just enough gas, "bingo," to return to the mainland to deliver the patient to higher care and fuel to get them all safely home. There was no option for a mechanical issue, crew fatigue, or misjudgment. The five helicopter crew members were also attended by a C-130 higher in the atmosphere, like a watchtower in the sky over them all. It communicated with Air Station ECity and District 5 Headquarters in Norfolk, Virginia.

Rescue Checklist 1 was complete, and the crew was clear about who was about to do what. The Flight Mechanic, Lukas, slapped Joshua's back. Joshua pushed himself out the cabin door.

Tweet Lukas announced, "Swimmer is outside of the cabin."

Joshua slowly descended via a cable until his feet pounded the small space previously made by the cruise ship employees. They now huddled against the side of the deck between piled-up deck chairs. The ferocity of the downdraft winds from the helicopter was even more prominent as it ricocheted off the gigantic cruise ship. Conversation was impossible, so Joshua undid the locking hoist hook, which connected him to the aircraft, and gave a thumbs up for the tweet to retrieve the cable. The helicopter backed away to give him time to assess the patient and speak to the staff, let alone not blow people and things overboard. Joshua was in a hurry to perform checklist two with the helicopter in the sky, so he half trotted through the doorway to get inside the cruise ship. When he passed inside, it became suddenly eerily quiet.

Is that elevator music in the hallway I hear?

Elsewhere on the ship were people who anxiously expected the CG. They desperately needed each other. Joshua's job was to locate them and make his assessment on behalf of the CG. Joshua followed a ship's staff member at a jog through the ship until he found himself out of breath.

This ship is even bigger than I thought.

Finally, the staff member stopped abruptly, and they both took a deep breath. Overhead a doorway it read 'Medical'. Inside was a room full of fretful people: an overworked Doctor of foreign origin, a harried native English-speaking nurse, an unconscious patient, and the frightened family of the survivor. The brusque cruise ship employee, Stephen, who had escorted him to the medical unit, stepped inside first and then aside for Joshua to enter. Joshua, who felt like an intruder, followed him inside.

"This is, umm... the Coast Guard," Stephen gestured to Joshua.

He did not know how to introduce the orange-clad angelic messenger before them properly, so he stammered and read his name off his uniform, "Mr. Mansoul."

Joshua thought, *not exactly a Mr., but thanks for the effort of a formal introduction.*

Joshua nodded and said, "Petty Officer 3rd Class Mansoul."

I didn't practice this enough at A school either... how to enter a cruise ship medical facility. Note to self: ask about this later.

Joshua looked for the doctor and nurse among the people and took in the room. The cramped quarters were high-tech, but the patient had become way worse than anyone had desired. The shallow breaths, even with oxygen and the white translucent skin, told him this patient would not likely survive a transfer to the helicopter via a long hoist. The Doctor, who had coordinated with the CG, approached the ship staff representative, Stephen, and Joshua to explain again how the patient would pass away without much higher care than the ship could provide in the next 24 hours. It appeared to Joshua he or his uniform intimidated the doctor.

High-pressure situation. However, he does look exhausted himself.

The ship's doctor admitted, "Sir, there is not one more thing we can do... the CG must take him now."

The ship could not make a port within 24 hours to get the man into an Intensive Care Unit (ICU). The nurse looked at Stephen with pleading eyes, and the family threw him and Joshua begging glances worse than a five-year-old holding a puppy. Stephen assured them he was doing all he could to get the CG to take him as quickly as possible. Joshua motioned for Stephen to follow him outside the medical room.

When Stephen and Joshua met face to face, it was a surreal conversation for them both. Strangers, and yet they were to discern the outcome of so much in such a short period. Joshua knew his decision was literally and figuratively putting this man's life in his hands. On the one hand, Stephen recounted no one on the ship wanted to observe the patient die without every measure pursued. On the other,

Joshua explained, "The CG "ride" will be more traumatic than any of you can understand. It could perhaps end the patient's life in his transportation."

Joshua anticipated they wouldn't want to put their loved one in that position if they completely understood what they had asked of them all. He asked for a moment to convey his assessment to the crew via radio to the District 5 CG response coordinator. That also included C-130 Hercules and his helo, who waited impatiently and orbited with less fuel for them on board every second. Their lives also hung in this balance. He got the flight surgeon on the radio.

"Doc, I'm afraid he won't survive long on the ride, but since we're here, we can't leave them with the request to save him," Joshua radioed.

"Roger, Mansoul. We will send down the litter. Advise them of the risks involved. Room for one family member, nothing else."

Joshua exhaled loudly enough for the cruise ship employee to hear him. He turned back to Stephen, the ship's Doc, and the family. Their eyes all pleaded with him.

Joshua said, "I need four strong men to get him out onto the deck now!"

He heard a collective gasp as the family threw their arms around one another in relief and gratitude. The decision had finally been made after hours of disparagement. One family member was chosen to accompany the patient to advocate for him at the Regional Medical Center, where they would seek urgent care closest to them. Strong ship crew members hastily went onto the deck into brilliant sunshine while they carried the incoherent patient. They all tasted the salt in the breeze while family members tasted their salty tears.

Joshua knew more than anyone on deck the small likelihood that the end would justify the means for this herculean coordinated effort. The CG would only object to the attempt to save a life if the means would jeopardize the lives of an entire crew.

The man likely will not survive. On my watch, every effort will be made.

To bolster his confidence, he looked up. The helicopter with USCG on the underbelly had attracted the audience of hundreds of cruise ship vacationers for the free reality show. Joshua did not like the sensation of being watched, but his orange dry suit, made for visibility out in the sea, certainly made him the focus of their attention by standing out on deck. The litter was lowered first, and then men cautiously placed the patient-turned-survivor in the metal litter. Joshua strapped him in to be hoisted on his back to the cabin that hovered above them. He patted the man twice, and the man's son kissed his cheek while his tears fell on his father. There would be a minute as he transitioned from the deck to the helicopter; he would be without care, just the oxygen bottle tucked in tightly beside him. It was a fearsome hoist for a healthy person, let alone this fragile human.

It's probably good he's already unconscious, Joshua thought.

Joshua made the thumbs-up sign to his crew for them to hoist. Joshua held the trail line, waved the family member over, and prepared him to be ready to climb into the basket lowered next. When the patient was pulled into the cabin and secured, Joshua stood, gazed up, and expected the basket to be lowered. Instead, the trail line was dropped, and the door was suddenly closed. The helicopter transitioned into forward flight for shore.

No...

Joshua heard the whumping sound of the Jayhawk as it retreated from view and the increased sound of his heart as it pounded in his chest. Evidently, the survivor's heart had stopped on the ride up, just as Joshua feared. Joshua's shoulders and chin dropped with sadness. He had lost another survivor.

Now, it is up to Doc and the tweet to do CPR all the way to the hospital. The long trip will be the most physical and emotional experience I could imagine. I'm supposed to be there for that marathon.

"Godspeed," he whispered.

The crew had decided there was no time to collect the family member and swimmer. Joshua stood and stared up at his crew that flew away and left him in disbelief onboard the deck of a cruise ship. He began to coil the line in his hand and noticed they shook.

Another soul has slid through my fingers like this slippery rope.

Sadly, it was the same disbelief for the rest of the souls on board the vessels on the water and in the sky. It felt as if time had stopped, but the long arm of the CG moved on without them. For Joshua, the mission was over, but not for the crew.

And the protocol for me is what?

Joshua dreaded the reaction of the patient's son, whom he had planned to help hoist into the Jayhawk helicopter. Joshua stood just a few inches taller and knew hundreds of people watched their interaction. Joshua looked up from the empty line. He still had his helmet on, but he raised his visor. He visualized the big, bold black USCG that the crowd had seen on the underside of his helicopter and hoped the rescue encouraged them. The exception may have been the family member right next to him. Joshua's heart fell for all involved in this MEDEVAC rescue.

He thought, *When will it ever get easier?*

As the thwap of the rotor blades' sound died off, Joshua unsnapped his helmet and removed it. This was his non-verbal communication to all. He was unexpectedly the newest cruise ship passenger.

I am confident that joining a ship on the open Atlantic is infrequent.

Suddenly, he heard from the District flight coordinator on his radio, "Survivor is in sudden cardiac arrest and en route to Norfolk General. Swimmer left on the scene, await transportation."

I hope it's not a three-day sail to the next port since I've got nothing but my bright orange alien-looking suit to tromp around in on what I can tell is a state-of-the-art cruise ship.

A hand rested on his forearm from the man next to him and caused Joshua to jolt. He flushed, and beads of sweat ran down his neck. He remembered it was the son who had probably just lost his dad. He turned toward him from his gaze out over the ocean behind his helo. The middle-aged man's tears streamed down his cheeks unabashedly when Joshua met his eyes. He smiled, threw himself into Joshua, and hugged him as hard and the best he could around the dry suit and helmet tucked under his arm. Joshua smiled then, knew the son had little to say and felt no ill will. The son had no words to genuinely show his appreciation for the support of the family who had advocated for their father, grandfather, and spouse. Some people spoke their thanks and praise, others he learned, just cried. Joshua hugged him back and understood what the stranger couldn't know. He, too, was another son who had lost his dad when he had instead unknowingly flown away for the last time. They stood in a silent embrace for how long Joshua didn't care.

Minutes later, the cruise ship employee who had already run him to the Medical room, Stephen, shook hands with Joshua on deck. Stephen was a wiry middle-aged Phillipino man. His dark hair grayed at the temples and gave him a distinguished look. He was dressed impeccably and had a no-nonsense air.

He said, "Well, this is a first. We don't normally pick up passengers mid-cruise, but the captain said to make an exception for the CG."

He smiled wryly, turned abruptly, then, with a wave of his hand by his ear as if to order 'follow me,' he set out quickly toward the door he had exited earlier. Joshua had never dreamed he would re-enter the spectacle of a ship like this. Down the corridors, he went as he followed the staff member at a surprisingly fast pace. He was aware of people who openly stared at him as if they witnessed an alien who passed them in bright orange with neon yellow arms and a blue helmet. He carefully carried his helmet to his side to become more human and try to put others at ease.

Do I smile or not? Where are we headed?

At one point, he realized people had photographed him as he clunked down the stairs of a beautiful central lobby.

So much for the look of a samurai rescue warrior, he bemused.

Joshua laughed to himself and carried on a conversation in his head.

Has a swimmer ever been left aboard a cruise ship? I guess I'm about to find out. I may never live to hear it down, either. How will I get off? Who will come back for me? The hotwash for this will be odd. Poor Doc, he should get a cruise after what he's going through.

Inside the atrium, Joshua spied floor after floor of ballrooms, themed floors, entertainment venues, eateries, leisure of every kind, exercise equipment, etc. He had glanced around the deck before they entered the first door, and he had seen pools of every size, recreational experiences for every age, and people everywhere, only some who visibly gawked at him. His presence became more evident as people stood and stared as he followed Stephen. He hoped wherever they were headed, it was out of sight of the masses who followed his every move. He touched the rubber gasket around his neck and grimaced. The tight seals kept the ocean out of his suit and, though great for survival, were uncomfortable. He asked to stop and remove the top portion. After it was zipped off, it revealed the black base layer underneath, and Stephen grimaced. A dry suit and its warm underlayer at 76 degrees were bearable for only a few minutes. He continued with an awkward gait after the top portion was tied around his waist; it made the rest sag humorously as he walked to follow his leader. They turned inside a lovely banquet room and a breakfast buffet stretched fifty feet inside the vast banquet hall. The smell made his stomach grumble loudly.

So much for not being conspicuous.

How on earth could they prepare this excellent food all before 7 a.m.?

"We serve food 24 hours a day," answered Stephen to the nonverbal question stamped on Joshua's face.

An ice sculpture, linen napkins, and real silverware were on the tables. Stephen headed toward the head table and motioned for Joshua to sit when he pulled the chair out for him. Joshua was used to orders and obeyed in awkward astonishment.

Stephen said, "Your steward will be along quite soon, and the captain wishes to join you directly."

He leaned into his ear and quietly said, "On this ship, at his table, you don't eat until the Captain does."

Joshua replied as the steward appeared beside him, "I understand; I know not to do anything until the vessel's Captain says so."

Stephen said, "We don't know if you're his guest or his staff at the moment!"

Joshua smirked at Stephen, who vanished behind some hidden wall of mirrors. He observed the ant-like behavior of the many staff members who graciously served every guest and made it look effortless.

Joshua wished he had asked the steward, *"May I just eat with the behind-the-scenes staff? I am out of my league here. I would be out of my league with them, too."*

Smiling coyly as if she was about to be entertained, a pretty female steward approached and asked for his drink order.

Joshua said, "Coffee, black. Oh, and a pitcher of water, please."

He nervously wiped the sweat from his brow, unsure if it was the young woman's presence or his dry suit this time.

She answered shyly, "Por supuesto, of course," and vanished quickly.

Joshua carefully placed his helmet under his chair and waited nervously while his stomach growled ravenously.

So much for not being obvious, he grimaced as he regarded the luxurious room in awe.

The cruise ship captain was very good-natured and did his best to put Joshua, quite self-conscious, at ease in the elegant dining room. Joshua had never eaten with a Captain of any vessel. The barrel-chested man stood over Joshua as they shook hands before they sat next to one another. His bald head reflected the lights above him and looked somehow angelic.

Joshua wondered, *Is the lighting planned to shine around him and his gleaming uniform?*

The captain thanked him for the risks he assumed over the sea to come to their aid while Joshua's stomach rumbled. It had been hours since his hot coffee before dawn, and sumptuous food was tempting him, but he had no idea where to begin with all the cutlery and glass wear in front of him. The captain praised the abilities of his ship and the staff. They discussed the increased subject of older adults who enjoyed their days at sea with the support of what he determined was a very high level of health care. When the talkative captain finally put food into his mouth, Joshua's stomach rumbled, and they laughed. After the captain began to eat, Joshua knew he could finally dig into the savory food that awaited him. The steward poured him hot black coffee and offered to pour him cream and sugar. Joshua had never imagined someone waiting on him like this. He smiled sheepishly as if he'd been caught unprepared at the young woman.

"Just black, muchas gracias," he said.

He noticed she looked disappointed somehow, as though she had wanted to rescue him from plain coffee.

Is this a standard cruise service member or someone who loves her job in service as much as I do? he pondered.

Joshua understood wanting to serve. He couldn't imagine fulfillment in this extreme "relaxation" business. He already knew he would only be contented to serve where life and death mattered. As if, in hindsight, the captain at last came forth with what Joshua needed to know.

"Your return to your home base of operation has been decided by CG 5th District operations center. We will return you to your unit once we enter the Port of Charleston in one day. You will be picked up by the local CG shuttle, then offered a taxi to your home station."

"Aye, aye, Sir."

The captain asked surreptitiously, "Where is that, may I ask?"

The astute captain was not accustomed to being unaware of important details.

Joshua swallowed a lump in his throat.

"Elizabeth City, North Carolina," he replied.

As the captain looked around the banquet facility with evident pleasure, he mentally tried to place Elizabeth City on the map.

"Ah, yes, closer to Kitty Hawk as the crow flies, or should I say the Jayhawk?" he said.

Joshua nodded his agreement. They both knew it would be a long cab ride and unbearably hot in a dry suit over a day or more from now. Joshua summoned his courage and finally cleared his throat.

He asked in disbelief, "Sir, they really said a taxi? Like a yellow one from New York City?"

The captain almost spit out his coffee.

He gapped, "Have you never ridden in a taxi, young man?"

Joshua turned red.

"No, sir."

He had never been in a taxi before. He did not have money or a change of clothes. He pondered while he carefully sipped his coffee and tried to hide his shame.

How much more awkward could this situation become?

The captain replied, "A taxi from Charleston to Elizabeth City is a long ride.... It seems to me there may be a better solution, but who am I to question the CG District?"

The Captain leaned toward Joshua with a slow grin and a perfectly white set of teeth. He enjoyed the conversation very much.

He's enjoying this too much.

Joshua began to realize he had contributed to the set-up of a joke and was about to hear the punchline.

His pearly white teeth also gleam in the light...

The captain revealed, "Your "taxi" is a CG Hercules (C-130 Cargo support aircraft)."

They both laughed heartily, and Joshua's cheeks flushed at his naïveté.

The CG acted as a big family to step up and help one another in almost every situation. He knew to get himself home from such a long distance away wouldn't come out of his paycheck. He recognized he may have dined in style today, but he was much more like the steward on the cruise line. He was there to serve. The CG could not afford to fly nor put an entire crew's life in danger over the Atlantic for a simple ride home.

Maybe I could get to the ship's store for some real clothes, but would the CG authorize those for transport on a cruise ship?

Oh, he realized, *I have no cash, I.D., or wallet on me to buy anything.*

He brightened at his next thought, *Hey, I'm grateful for the big meal and the experience!*

Joshua's job had surprised him in just the few years he'd been in. He decided he had to laugh and keep looking up. In all his CG service, he'd remember the day he became a cruise ship passenger on a lavish ship while he intended to do the life-saving measures expected of his crew who worked "overtime" just then. He knew there was no overtime in the CG, but the mission had to be accomplished.

Joshua needed a different gracious rescue for when the captain departed. Joshua looked at his watch and read 0830 or 8:30 a.m. He had no idea what the protocol was to follow, and for the first time in a long while, he wasn't *Semper Paratus.* He sat and pondered his next move but felt like a kid who'd skipped school without a plan.

Stephen appeared again out of the blue at his elbow as soon as his last bite of food was finished. The captain stood, and so did Joshua immediately. The CG had taught him military etiquette, what some called manners. He could not have fathomed what it would be like to eat with a ship's captain when the alarm went off hours ago. He still couldn't grasp a dinner with a CG Captain. After farewells, the captain shook his hand and departed, trusting Joshua into Stephen's care. Stephen turned on his heel again, strode from the lavish banquet room, and beckoned Joshua to follow. He nearly forgot his helmet, but after he retrieved it, he rushed to catch up and tried to look normal, although he knew he would be anything but ordinary in his orange dry suit.

Joshua wished he had such command as Stephen did over the people he rescued. When Stephen moved, passengers would follow undoubtedly.

Why is that?

Joshua surmised it was because they had voluntarily joined the cruise to be taken care of and, therefore, surrendered their will and comforts to his disposal. They need not ask questions nor hesitate. They had already entrusted themselves to him and expected him to make their dreams come true, comfort at a high cost, and protection from the unknown. These things Joshua could offer, too, but people had previously not entrusted themselves to the mission of the CG. Therefore, he sometimes had to wait with long-suffering for victims of circumstance to make life-and-death decisions to trust him in the "heat of the" moment. Ironically, it was sometimes undeniably the coldest moments they'd ever spent.

Joshua represented what the CG was with everyone he met on board this vessel, on shore, and anywhere he walked in uniform. He moved around in their midst, and they made decisions with or without their acknowledgment of care or concern toward their rescuers. Joshua was grateful the family of the stricken man had appreciated the Coast Guard's responsibility to them. He knew the whole ship staff would know about his existence and acknowledge his presence there, even if the passengers seemed ambiguous. As the two men continued their "parade" through hallways filled with "elevator" music, people rubbernecked, teenagers flipped out cell phones to take videos, and children pointed and shrieked. Joshua only waved at the kids.

Some people certainly aren't ambiguous. I prefer to get good attention and not create drama.

Will these gawkers around me sleep better tonight since they know that not only was the CG Always Ready, but "Help was on the way," and would be for them?

Gracious, I'm right here in their presence.

At one hallway juncture, Joshua heard a tiny boy's voice say, "Look, Mom, an astronaut!"

Stephen threw a look of disbelief over his shoulder and rolled his eyes. Joshua could hardly contain his laughter at the call and response of those around him. Their pace sped up, and Joshua lengthened his strides so he wouldn't lose his guide. Stephen only quickened his pace the further they got inside the ship, and almost at a jog, Stephen stopped short. He abruptly turned toward Joshua.

He said, "I was about to take you to a remote place on deck, but I believe a wardrobe change may be necessary. People may ask for your photo and autograph as if we have a special character or vacationing astronaut on board. You wouldn't believe how I've seen people parade around here to get attention, but this emergency orange and yellow does top it all. We certainly can't hide you, and I imagine it would be sizzling hot in there by afternoon."

It already is. I should've tried iced coffee.

After the hot coffee, big meal, and jog through the length of the ship, Joshua had already begun to sweat badly in his "suit of armor." Stephen nodded with sympathy and took off again with purpose in the direction they'd just come from. Down a deck and around six corners, he stopped. At a nondescript door, Stephen paused and raised a hand to shield his mouth as he spoke.

He said, "What you are about to see, tell no one about."

He met Joshua's gaze with an even and somewhat threatened stare. Joshua sized him up and gathered he had tried to get him worked up about nothing like the captain. Joshua burst out in laughter. Stephen narrowed his eyes in an *I'm not kidding* look. Joshua stifled the outburst immediately.

What else could be "behind the scenes" on a lavish cruise ship to surprise him?

Stephen waved a card on his lanyard across the lock and swung the door open to reveal a simple, tidy lounge. He made way for Joshua to step inside. On a rack on the far side of the room were dozens of staff uniforms that matched Stephen's and everyone else's on the service side of the cruise. A couple of staff members watched TV or were on devices. They looked up and seemed mildly interested in his alien form, which had invaded their universe.

It was then Joshua realized he had been rescued. He'd woken up as the rescuer, and now Stephen was the "swimmer" who got him food, clothes, a place to relax while he waited, and every bit of it was free. Oh, it was not entirely free because, collectively, there was a high price to pay for such extravagances. It had already been paid for.

A good thing to remember, just like my CG service.

Stephen motioned him forward with an "I haven't got all day" look and revealed a storage closet full of lost or left behind items to include clothing, hats, suitcases, shoes, etc.

He said, "Take your pick from these leftovers, and please make yourself blend in for the duration of your *stay* with us. Try to get incognito if you can and come back here at 7 for dinner, or is it 1900, sailor?"

Joshua replied, "Wow. Yes, I don't know what to say, but thanks. A lot. A whole lot."

Stephen smiled saintly and promptly disappeared again as Joshua regarded the piles of brand-name clothes and designer stuff lost or discarded. Joshua was now part of the tour as a servant and a guest. He experienced the mercy he had tried to offer to the family of the sick cruise passenger. It became an odd awareness. Joshua was completely penniless and reliant upon the good graces of the captain, Stephen, and the rest of the crew.

Joshua knelt and began to rummage through the articles of clothing. It reminded him of being a kid and thrift shopping with his family. Three boys to feed and clothe was a lot of money. His mom was wise and had gotten good used clothes for them. Somehow, his mom felt nearer just by reenacting this old rummage routine. He smiled and knew this would be a great story to share one day. He needed clothes to fit in around the deck and for comfort, so he picked a blue polo shirt and some nice golf shorts he figured would fit. At the bottom were dozens of pairs of sunglasses. Some of the nicest brands available had been just chucked inside, so he didn't think twice and pulled a pair aside for later out on deck.

Joshua was deep in thought, *What am I to do with my dry suit...*

"The polo shirt doesn't quite match those shorts. Plus, you'll need pants for the captain's table, *and* you may as well take a hat. The sun is brutal on the sundeck, and you don't strike me as a casino guy, nor into the games room," said a cute young brunette woman across the room.

Joshua flushed when he realized she'd studied his choices. This had never happened when he shopped, so he had no idea how to respond. The girl jumped to her feet and crossed the small room to his side. She pulled a different, brighter-colored shirt from the bin.

She said, "Here, take this as well."

She searched for his size, pulled a pair of slacks from the staff hangars, and flashed a huge grin at him. The young woman had been frustrated. She had reread the same page three times while he was in her presence. She was drawn to him for some reason and gave up to assist him as well as she knew how.

She added casually, "Just return these here before you deboard tomorrow."

Joshua was struck speechless.

He realized, *I've never really gone shopping alone.*

Joshua's mom had always given him enough to get by and sent things periodically for his birthday or Christmas. Since he entered CG service, he had not needed more than his old clothes and what had been issued to him for Physical Training (PT), his uniforms, and gear. He had added some shirts from marathons and runs here and there, too.

Why am I suddenly embarrassed?

He was annoyed this woman had not offered her assistance but just took over. She knowingly and patiently waited as he thought over his response.

She inclined her head toward him and said frankly, "You're the same size as my brother, Laz, and he needs all the help I can give him."

Conscious he'd likely never see her again, he swallowed his pride and took the clothes offered. He looked as bewildered as he felt, and for the second time that morning, he felt his face flush red.

"Thank you."

"Take a suitcase for your uniform, sailor..." she laughed at his expense and pointed toward the men's room.

He did the only thing he could think to do since he didn't know what to do. He practiced what he wanted others to do when he offered help. He gladly took it, and they turned away from one another. He had never had a sister, but he would have wanted one like this if he had.

“Gracias.”

She replied, “No hay problema mi amigo,” over her shoulder.

She picked up her book and tried to read it again. As painfully shy as he seemed. she was surprised he was a tough rescuer. He was humble and appreciative, which was admirable, even if he wasn’t an admiral like her daddy.

Chapter 8

FOLLOW ME

Joshua had enjoyed his 24 hours on a luxury cruise liner, returned the clothes needed, and strolled off incognito with the most excellent used suitcase he ever had. His dry suit and helmet were tucked safely inside. He walked down the gangway like a regular voyager, whatever he thought they would be when they arrived in port. He was picked up by some CG members who spared no time to tease him over his situation. Though they had never previously met, the disbelief of the case had them all in fits of laughter. Joshua got in on the amusement when he tipped his new to-him hat toward them.

He said, "Uber me to the base and pronto!"

The CG shuttle van from the nearby Charleston unit took him from the cruise ship area of the port of Charleston across town to Joint Base Charleston. They gave him a windshield tour through the historic American city.

"We have a bottle of water and a dumpy old van for our VIP. I hope the Air Force will let us through the gate. Maybe we should put Mansoul in the front seat. They'll probably recognize him and roll out the red carpet," they razzed him about his misadventure endlessly.

Joshua was in awe of the giant Air Force C-17s that made his C-130 ride home look like a four-seater Piper Cub airplane in comparison.

Once again, he was teased mercilessly by the ECity Hercules crew after he boarded about his reception of the best collateral duty the CG had ever offered. After takeoff, they wanted to know if he'd brought them some extravagant ship food. He just had to laugh in disbelief with them as he regaled them with his stories. One crew member even opened a viral video of Joshua on his phone. To Joshua's dismay, it showed him the previous day as he tromped across the cruise ship deck with his helmet under one arm like an alien encounter. He'd quickly become a CG sensation. He sincerely hoped he wouldn't become an outrageous meme. Joshua wanted the conversation to change course. He hesitated and then asked about the patient. They all shook their heads sadly.

"Doc tried to save him the whole flight back," said the navigator.

Joshua felt guilty for his luxurious experiences. He made a mental note to drop by the clinic one day to thank Doc and seek out the mech to do the same. He wanted to encourage Doc to accompany them whenever he could. He knew the power of gratitude no matter the outcome. A simple thank you went a long way in the CG community and furthered the mission.

A few weeks later, the hot sand burned Joshua's feet as he climbed up the sand dunes of Jockey's Ridge State Park on the Outer Banks of North Carolina. It wasn't far as a crow or Jayhawk helicopter would fly from Air Station Elizabeth City. It was an hour or so drive, but it seemed like a world away when he needed time apart from his work world. He sought solace by himself for several reasons his whole life, but this weekend, he needed it even more. He tried to focus on his apartment's cleanliness, shined boots, and ironed uniforms, but it grew dull quickly. He lived in a small place, so there wasn't much more time he could have spent there. The walls had closed in, and his thoughts raced about his future as a rescue swimmer. He knew the end of his duration at the Air Station in ECity was soon to close, too. Some of his peers had already left the CG for other jobs after one tour or for other units in other cities.

Will I continue in the mission, 'So Others May Live,' or be tempted away by a less complicated lifestyle that offers comforts I've never known?

He continued to climb upwards on the dunes, past families with small children and their tired legs. Many whined about the weather, the hot sand, and their thirst.

Geez, I'm trying to escape the turmoil and found it here. I'm rather enjoying everything they're complaining about. Although, I thirst for something different...

Joshua was always prepared and opened his Nalgene for a long, refreshing drink once out of sight from the thirsty around him. He trudged upward and passed some people who tried to hang glide down the front of the giant dunes towards the Atlantic Ocean. Once he crested the hill, he could see miles and miles in every direction.

It is almost unfathomable the Wright Brothers had stood so close by near here 100-plus years ago.

They had discovered their ingenious machine could fly into the consistently stiff winds of the Outer Banks. He faced the winds and reminded himself the stiff winds of adversity were what he had and would face, too. He had chosen to be part of the USCG and positioned himself into the winds of adversity to fly.

Joshua saw colorful kites flown down by the beach. A giant marketplace of whirligigs and towered flight apparatus caught his attention.

He thought, *That might be a good investment for a few hours of fun and maybe a good souvenir from my ECity Tour before I'm reassigned either by my will or the CG's.*

Focusing on where the shore met the dunes, Joshua let gravity pull him toward the cool ocean that beckoned below. A sprint down the dunes enticed him, and after a few awkward steps, he just let himself fall, with massive steps, down the dune face. It was exhilarating and just what he needed to release some pent-up angst from his thoughts about the previous events of the year and his uncertain future.

The sun was even more scorching hot as Joshua pulled the door open to 'Kitty Hawk Kites.' He nearly ran into a familiar face. He jumped backward and fortunately remembered to pull the door with him to cover his shock.

So much for Semper Paratus, Joshua thought.

He hoped he wasn't recognized, but the look on Christian's face was of first dismay and then complete shock. Christian stood open-mouthed and stared at Joshua like he saw a ghost. Christian's mother gently laid a hand on his arm and then guided him outside. They gathered themselves next to Joshua. Joshua continued to hold the door for a few other patrons who entered. Joshua took a few deep breaths.

Where is my instruction manual for "when you run into a survivor at the store..."

He sensed their need for a private conversation. Joshua backed up onto a sidewalk under a large, shaded canopy. It provided just a bit of respite from the heat that blistered up off the pavement around them and the fiery sun. Paradoxically, now they were together as uncomfortably hot as they were once uncomfortably cold.

The three stood together, shifted their weight from foot to foot, and wondered who should begin. Joshua practiced what he knew and looked up. Christian and his mother followed his gaze, and they each saw the kites on display that danced in the wind all around them.

Eliana was her name, thought Joshua suddenly, *and Christian. Face to face again.*

He remembered she had thanked him immediately after the rescue. He appreciated the memory more than ever. Surprisingly, very few people, if any, ever thanked a swimmer or the rescue crew, let alone the technicians, cooks, and storekeepers who kept the CG mission alive and healthy night and day 24/7. She had done so, and he could do the same.

He regarded both Eliana and Christian, who stood mute. Joshua spoke first.

"I appreciated you coming to say thank you and introduce yourselves. I'm sorry for your loss, though. I mean our loss."

The emotional dam burst, and it was Christian who, evidently forgot they stood outside a kite store in public, grabbed Joshua in a bear hug as if his life still depended upon him.

"You came back for me! Thank you!"

Eliana stood there and openly wept again with a massive grin.

Joshua thought, *that means they are "happy tears," as Mama told me.*

She dug in her purse for a tissue. Joshua slapped Christian's back three times in good guy fashion, gently pulled the teenager away, and had to back up himself. Christian wiped his nose with his shirt sleeve and apologized for his emotional state. Joshua waved his hands as if to say, *no problem, it's understandable.* He wanted them to change the subject, so Joshua gestured to the kite store.

Joshua asked, "What are you up to here?"

Eliana held a bag with a large colorful kite inside and a stand in her other hand.

She spoke reverently, "We needed a way to honor Nic's life."

For an awkward moment, Joshua wondered if they assumed he was complicit in the death of the young man's friend. They both looked at the kite in sadness and not at Joshua for responsibility. Joshua was still at a loss for words and held his tongue as his mother would have said when he was little. A salty breeze blew over them from the ocean, and Christian lifted his head and stood straighter. He lifted his gaze to Joshua's face and squared his shoulders towards him. He studied the features of his face and looked deeper into his eyes for answers. It was uncomfortable for Joshua to be so carefully regarded. Joshua glanced toward Eliana for an explanation.

She smiled encouragingly and said, "Christian, tell him what you've thought."

He took a giant breath and held it since he was uncertain he wanted to continue.

Then he said, "I've been trying to remember your face exactly, but I couldn't."

Christian added, "I want what you have."

Christian exhaled then as though it had been an enormous effort to pronounce the words out loud. He waited for what Joshua could only presume was some answer, a blessing or a curse he did not know. Joshua was more thankful than ever for the shade as he began to sweat under the pressure of a young man's desire thrown out before him in a show of transparent appeal. He pondered how a young man so close to his age regarded him as a leader worthy to follow. He was humbled and yet pleased by the redirection of the conversation from an apology to appreciation to emulation. Joshua broke into a huge smile and was willing to bare his teeth and soul to encourage Christian, just as his papa had done for him.

"Follow me."

Chapter 9

FOLLOW US

"Watch out!" shouted a nearby kid.

A beach ball bounced over the beach blanket the Mansoul family had occupied. Virginia Beach, Virginia, was a gorgeous place to relax under the early September sun. It was only an hour or so from his home station of ECity, but it was worlds away from his day-to-day job of constant preparation and planning for rescues. Joshua rested on the blanket and closed his eyes to relax and meditate. It had been several weeks since his last trip to the beach when he ran into Christian and Eliana. They met up for coffee and donuts at Joshua's invitation a week ago. Like his first meeting with Mr. Jones, Joshua relayed his experiences with the CG and the mission's expectations. They enjoyed the donuts, and the young man passed the black coffee up for a frappuccino on Joshua. Joshua noticed he liked the donuts just as much as he had years ago when he shared them with Jones.

Joshua thought, *I've never had a frap-a-what-no. Looks like a sugar rush to me, especially on top of the donuts. He'll learn to like real coffee one day...*

Christian's first-hand experience, much like Joshua's rescue as a young teen, gave them a mutual appreciation and respect for the organization. They discussed Christian's future hopes and dreams.

Whether or not they included the Coast Guard's mission was still to be determined. Christian was a great swimmer and an average student. The question remained: Would he have the physical ability, mental determination, and passion to become a rescue swimmer?

If Christian joined, it would be glorious to pass on the torch, and it would be a real highlight of my ECity tour. However, the decision is up to someone else. Revelations always seem to come in their own precise time.

Joshua looked at his family and was pleased his mother and brothers had returned to visit him. They looked relaxed and at peace. It wasn't a memory he had. The vacations were only around town in his childhood. This time, they came to share the holiday before he got new orders to where the Personnel Service Center (PSC) only knew where. He had been stationed in Elizabeth City for two and a half years. His family could not afford trips to see him, but he had saved up to fly them to him. It was Labor Day weekend, and for the first time, he understood the importance of taking a break from labor. He renewed his perspective and was grateful for it and to share it.

Mama's smile sure does wonders for my soul and hers ... She has never had much of a break. I'm glad to have her here and maybe put her mind at ease.

Because he shared a tiny two-bedroom apartment in town, he had to locate places for them to stay from other friends who lived off base. His family was welcomed to stay with friends who were also part of another mission at a local place he enjoyed called Towne South. Sprawled out on the sand, he enjoyed the warm, salty breeze that brushed over them. The scent of tanning oil and sunscreen tickled his nose. It took him back to his younger, carefree days as a lifeguard. He was amazed at the crowds around him. He had seen the vast numbers of people on the beaches from the air many times when they flew up and down the coast in the back of the crowded helicopter. Sandwiched on the beach was an altogether different and comical situation. The brothers had played ball, swam in the surf, and teased Joshua about shark bites. They had nearly gotten impaled by a beach umbrella as it narrowly missed them while they were distracted by pretty teenage girls. They had to admit life was good on the beach without a care.

Joshua's leisure was broken by a ding on his phone, which he retrieved nonchalantly. The voicemail's number was familiar, and he supposed he needed to check it. He was slightly annoyed since he had just enjoyed the first two days of paid leave in several months. Joshua immediately heard Senior Chief Simon's voice on the voice message and instinctively sat up at attention. This drew the ire of his brothers and his mother's concern by the look she gave him.

"Ugh, he's always on call," complained Jimmy.

Joshua then tried to relax his posture while he listened intently. What he heard disappointed and distressed him, but he could not say why.

"Petty Officer 2nd Class Mansoul, whazup? You will report to the headquarters building at 1400 tomorrow, Friday, 3 Sept, in Bravo uniform. There will be a brief with Captain Nissi...and Mansoul; make sure you're on time," quipped the newly promoted Senior Chief Simon O'Riley.

Due to his unexpected orders, Joshua stepped onto the sizzling pavement the next day. A mist steamed from it after a light rain had just fallen. A pungent scent wafted in the air from the dampness of the hot tar on the runway nearby and the parking lot he crossed.

Joshua thought, *I'm thankful the rain is over and won't spoil my pressed uniform and shoes I just polished again.*

Joshua made his way carefully to the Command Headquarters. Joshua was way more nervous than he cared to admit. He was uncomfortable, although he did not think he had violated CG policy or procedure.

Why I am being called to Command on a Friday afternoon on a holiday weekend, he supposed, *cannot be good.*

He was determined to breathe easily and not sweat out his uniform before he even entered Headquarters. He couldn't remember the last time he had been in the building in months or years, maybe since his graduation. He looked around as he cornered the sidewalk, careful not to scuff his shoes.

He noticed an unfamiliar CG jet aircraft that sat on the runway not far away. He double-checked his reflection in a mirror just inside the door to ensure his uniform was complete again. He was glad he had taken the time to get a fresh haircut, shave carefully, press and iron the uniform, shine, and buff his shoes to have the correct uniform requirements for whatever was about to happen. He preferred the standard flight suit uniform, which was almost washed and worn daily. It was every CG member's duty to be prepared to wear the Bravo uniform. Joshua remembered with a smirk how his mama spoke to him as he left.

"You look so dashing," Maria said.

"Mama, I'm going to be late."

"Oops, I left a little lipstick on you."

"Mama, Geesh!"

His mother asked him to take photos and to send her the pictures of him and the two of them while he was in it. He was glad to have an opportunity to put it on once again. However, he finally admitted to himself he dreaded what was to come.

This is the first time I've been so nervous about going to command—so much for not sweating it out.

Joshua knew he had to use almost an entire day of leave to be back in the proper uniform and was sorely disappointed. However, it did give his family an up-close look at how he now belonged to a new family he had to put first. They had decided to go without him and see some of the great lighthouses up and down the coast of the Outer Banks. He had seen them all from the air. They stood tall and now uninhabited, but his brothers would likely get to amuse him with stories from inside. Jimmy had given him a tough time about him not going. Joshua quit his explanation after he realized he'd have to lead by example and not with a lecture about devotion to duty. After he'd passed Jude a couple of $20 bills for his patience and willingness to provide a lovely experience for their mother, Jimmy got quieter.

"Be a good brother and treat the family like I would, please, Jude," he tousled his hair.

Jude beamed his appreciation and threw his arm around Jimmy's neck.

He replied, "C'mon, Jimmy, I won't let you stumble on all those steps up the lighthouse, but I'll probably beat you to the top!"

Jimmy murmured, "Okay," and sheepishly left in better spirits. He knew his older brother was more like a father than he wanted to recognize.

The Mansoul family learned about the storied history of the lighthouse services and the pre-CG US Lifesaving Service (USLSS) traditions. Joshua had visited the old USLSS units strewn along the coast. He admired the strong testimonies of adventures and heroism the vacant lighthouses and stations demonstrated. A USLSS member took the Wright Brothers' photo of their first flight. Joshua wished he could be just about anywhere else in the CG but at command for an unknown reason. Nevertheless, the strange event ahead also intrigued him. He stepped cautiously down the long hall; his polished shoes echoed and announced his early arrival.

Senior Chief Simon O'Riley acknowledged Joshua with a curt "Mansoul."

He directed him to the middle of a boardroom table. Soon after, two more guardians arrived, and they looked like they were even more apprehensive of what was to come. They were directed to sit across from him. Joshua watched the clock and heard its distinctive menacing click towards doomsday. With 15 minutes to use before the end of the world as they each pondered it, Joshua decided to try to put them all at whatever ease he could muster. Their last names were evident on their uniforms, but he did not recognize them from the air station.

Joshua thought, *What could be of more comfort than to call someone by name?*

He spoke softly to them, "I'm Joshua, and you are?"

They looked at him in terror as though he was a zombie speaking to them. Then they softened as he smiled and waited patiently while the clock ticked impatiently. They eyed one another until the silence was unbearable.

The first spoke just above a whisper, "I'm Megan."

She reflexively pulled at her hair, which was swept into a big bun at the back of her head by regulations.

"I'm Stephanie," said the other teenager. She breathed a sigh of relief and smiled beautifully, then giggled nervously.

Joshua broke his wall of apprehension and chanced a big goofy grin towards each of them as a sign of brotherhood and encouragement. They sat then in companionable and nervous silence. He wondered if they were thinking about his crooked teeth now.

At least I took their minds off the present and the annoyance of the tick-tock of the clock. It seems like I try to rescue people everywhere I go.

Megan said, “I’m so nervous I think I’m gonna puke.”

Stephanie giggled louder and covered her mouth. Her neck began to turn red.

Joshua glanced at Senior Chief, who rubbed his eyes in disbelief.

Joshua tried to distract them from the awkwardness, “What’s your favorite thing to do?”

Megan remained silent as she clamped her mouth shut so absolutely nothing would come out.

Stephanie was by then in a fit of uncontrolled giggles and replied, “Softball.”

“Oh, do they call you Slugger Steph?”

“How did you know?” she replied.

“What’s your favorite posit...”

Senior Chief O’Riley shouted, “Attention on Deck.”

Captain Nissi entered the room per CG’s regulation. They all jumped to attention and then sat again after a nod from the Captain. Only Nissi relaxed at the head of the table. Nissi’s mischievous smile unnerved them and gave them all a sense of wonder instead of dread.

Joshua thought, *A full Captain is at the table with us and waits on someone else, too? What is happening?*

Megan’s face turned so red she was almost purple. Joshua’s sweat ran down his neck and back. He wanted to assist her and looked up. Next, but not last, entered his excellent friend, Jordan Roi, the same flight mech he had befriended in ‘boot’ and flown with many times. She was flushed as much as he had been but smiled brightly when she recognized Joshua was also present for this oddity. The people and their senior statuses surprised her, and she gasped.

She said, “My Word!”

The humidity made her already naturally curly hair stand up, even though it was evident she had tried in vain to contain it. Jordan's gorgeous smile diverted the focus from flawed hair.

She said, "Never early, never late."

I hope Command gets to see the smile, whatever happens.

Jordan made her way to his side of the table. She nodded her respects to her two superiors before she sat.

She looked at Joshua and had a question in her eyes: *Why are we here?*

Jordan communicated her thoughts in one look to Joshua. *Today, there could be a reckoning for them from the tragic loss in the previous year.*

Joshua's future flashed before him, and his shoulders dropped. He stole another glance her way for courage and forced himself to smile.

We were together on the fateful SAR, and I am thankful for her witness to my story. She saw more than any other Guardian what I did and went through. It is such a balm to my soul to have been seen and understood.

Joshua knew it wasn't just her job for Jordan to support him as a swimmer but the essence of who she was.

"A friend loves at all times," she had told him once before.

He wasn't exactly sure if she meant he loved her or if she loved him, but it was true either way. Her witness to his life somehow made it all seem worthwhile. His mom and brothers were supportive, but she had been there with him. She had a supernatural ability to understand him.

Joshua thought, *But why are these other women here?*

Joshua was torn between the apprehension the younger Petty Officers across from him exuded and the peaceful state of his Air Station Commander. In walked the Base ECity Command Master Chief, and Megan's timid smile faltered considerably more. He was the senior enlisted person on base and could strike fear and respect out of anyone who glanced his way. He sat and then gave Megan and Stephanie a sincere look of reassurance. Megan looked a shade of green. Jordan quietly handed her a lemon drop across the table. Megan looked unsure, but Jordan nodded for her to take it. The irreverent act coincidently put Stephanie into another uncontrolled fit of giggles. Jordan looked at the younger woman and smiled sympathetically.

She said, "Girlfriend, bite the side of your tongue to keep the laugh in check for the next few minutes. Ya got it? Then we'll have a good laugh later together."

Jordan, at last, looked at Joshua, who smiled his most appreciative sly smile.

She's a talker, but she's wise beyond her years.

Authority had an excessive way to intimidate people, but only sometimes was it for their best interests. Joshua knew with wisdom beside him he had been entrusted with the power he had only begun to recognize. He wanted it displayed for the younger guardians who were almost overcome with their fears about their future. In the room sat messengers of delegated authority *for* them, not against them.

I cannot fear them; only what is outside this room seeks to devour us and thwart our mission. They are my crew, at least for the next hour.

As a great leader, Captain Nissi knew his people and had earned their respect. He did his best to put them at ease and called them each by name. He thanked them for their presence with him. Thanks were unnecessary, as they were not protocol due to his rank and position, but the meekness (humility combined with power) he exuded in his rank drew others to him.

Joshua's perplexity was heightened, and he sensed they all awaited someone else, but he didn't put it together until after the Senior Chief barked loudly.

"Attention on deck!"

They all simultaneously leaped to their feet. They stared directly ahead. Joshua could not have imagined who could have walked through the door.

Whose presence would make even the Air Station Commander and Command Master Chief jump so high?

"At ease," a voice soothed from the doorframe.

They were in awe as each Guardian slowly took in the form that filled the doorway. He exuded both in stature and respect the authority due him. They had never personally laid eyes on the Vice Commandant of the CG. Half of the junior enlisted people in the room had no earthly idea they would ever have had the opportunity to meet him personally. Sweat immediately began to trickle uncomfortably down the backs of the junior enlisted. Joshua glanced at Megan as she swayed back and forth. Stephanie gnawed at her bottom lip. He glanced sideways at Jordan. She wore a sly smile. It played in anticipation at the corner of her mouth through her strong stance at attention.

Admiral Eleazar took in the gathered CG personnel before him. Some were terrified, others pleasantly surprised. The clock over his head ticked again loudly in the silence as they stood and waited for his next word.

Will it be a rebuke or recognition? Condemnation or curiosity?

Eleazar opened his arms and announced, "It's me!"

After a hearty laugh, he said to them, "At ease."

The Admiral made eye contact and shook hands with each of them one by one around the room as a move of reassurance of his goodwill. After he took his seat at the head of the long table, he paused and motioned for them to be seated as well. In their shock, they had stood beside the chairs and some beside themselves with apprehension. He welcomed them each by name and job title as a quick introduction to all present. They were astonished he knew they existed, let alone their names and occupations. He launched into his purpose for the brief with smooth articulation and an endearment they each heard in their unique way, as if he had called the meeting for them alone.

The youngest, Storekeeper Third Class, listened in astonishment.

The Admiral relayed Stephanie had been exemplary in the minute details of her monotonous job as storekeeper (SK).

He said, "You saved the CG an immense amount of money towards the previous fiscal year's budget."

She beamed her appreciation his way, and then she suddenly realized everyone regarded her. She giggled even as a tear of relief and silent gratitude for the acknowledgment of her unseen and humble job worked involuntarily down her cheek.

Megan dared to look at the Admiral as he recounted his gratification at her willingness to go above and beyond her duties as an electrician's mate on the small boat's electrical systems.

As he held her eyes, he added with a coy grin, "I also know about how you fixed all the outdated electricity to the laundry machines throughout the dorms. Much appreciated by all, I'm certain."

At this, Megan turned nearly beat red from the realization he knew of something she had done unrequested and what she thought had gone entirely unnoticed. She knew they needed to be fixed and just took care of it. She preferred to serve without anyone noticing. Purple blotches started to form from her neck up from all the attention directed at her.

Please don't pass out on us, Megan..., thought Joshua.

Master Chief did not know about that bit of trivia and looked back and forth from Nissi to Eleazar, stunned something had happened he was unaware of under his watch.

He wondered, a bit disarmed, *What else did the Admiral know he did not?*

It was another humble moment for the Chief, who prided himself on his awareness of everyone under his command. He reminded himself he was but one of many who stood as a council of authority under Admiral Eleazar. Eleazar took in the Chief's changed countenance and paused. It was as if he studied the man and read his thoughts simultaneously.

The Vice Commandant, Admiral Eleazar, said to the Master Chief, "You run a tight ship, and we appreciate your loyalty and your growth as a leader. Humility is a key indication of true authority."

The Master Chief's mouth inadvertently dropped open in surprise. Humility was not his best virtue. As Eleazar commented to the rest of those gathered, he continued to be a keen watcher.

I suppose I'd better work on it, the Master Chief contemplated, unsure if it was a compliment or an order.

The Admiral gazed around the room with a grin like a grandparent with his beloved grandchildren. Everyone relaxed in their mindset and expressions. The clock had almost stopped its march of doom tick in everyone's ears. Even if the youngest Guardians still sat in an uncomfortable and stiff position in their chairs, they hung on his every word. His eyes finally took in Jordan and Joshua, and they changed from a crinkled smile to a long, flattened expression of concern. The air became heavy as he studied them as if he had awaited this profound exchange for some time. Lumps formed in both aircrew members' throats until he finally broke the silence. The Vice Commandant leaned in their direction and placed his folded hands on the conference room table. When he spoke, his voice was choked with emotion neither of them expected from such a man of power and esteem. The clock suddenly ticked much louder than it had before.

Eleazar said, "I am sorry the decisions of others have far-reaching consequences on those nearest them and those who are incidental to their actions. As Guardians, our mission is to offer rescue. We must not force it, nor will we under my command, nor those who share in my authority. The responsibility for their sad conclusions falls upon my shoulders, not yours. We are a unified team, and we have come to say thank you for the role you played in our mission, no matter how difficult the outcome. I ask you to persevere in your faithfulness to meet this mission despite the tragedies. Spread the good news amongst your peers and all who will hear my assertions. We rejoice with those rescued and mourn those the darkness has taken, but our mission will not waver."

Jordan sat in stunned silence for the first time in Joshua's memory. So did the rest gathered there. She clearly understood she was not only being consoled but also sustained and commended for her participation in the loss and gains of the CG's mission. Ever the optimist, she smiled eagerly to uplift the Admiral's Spirit. Throughout the intense proceedings, her frizzy curls had become somewhat of a halo around her head.

She replied quietly, with what she knew to be true in the familiar CG tune, "Through surf and storm and howling gale, High shall our purpose be."

Everyone in the room took a deep breath and glared at Joshua as the last to speak. He did not frequently demonstrate the shiny optimism of his friend or a quick and witty response. He took a deep breath, gazed at Jordan, and then forced himself to look back directly at Admiral Eleazar.

Joshua spoke, "I'll follow you wherever I'm led, Sir, so that others may live...

We go where people need us because you entrust us as messengers of your authority and fulfill our mission. I'm your right-hand man."

The Admiral expected his people, each in their unique way, to have followed his commands. However, Joshua touched Eleazar deeply because he was one of the most recent Guardians who looked the other full in the face and was rejected. Obedience was not easy. The truth was evident to everyone who served: adherence to the CG protocols and leadership was costly.

Eleazar regarded him with tenderness and replied, "Son, this pleases me most. Can you be joyful in this alone?"

Joshua replied, "Aye, aye, Sir!"

"To hold the crew blameless. I am always in your service."

Joshua never expected to be personally acknowledged and respected by an Admiral. From the depths of his being, he realized it was the most desired response to the demands of a CG member's life. Admiral Eleazar knew him by name and was pleased with him.

He called me... son. I can't remember the last time I heard that from a man...

Eleazar had rescued Joshua. Joshua was thrilled to be called out and reassured to continue the treacherous mission he lived for. Checklist 3 for his participation in the loss of Nic was finally complete, he hoped. At that moment, he was thrilled and could have walked on water.

Captain Samuel Nissi, the ECity Air Station Commander, had called the brief with a cross-section of CG Base ECity representatives at the personal request of Admiral Eleazar while he was on Station. Base Elizabeth City housed several tenant units of the CG. All the bells and whistles had to be pulled, whether it was a long four-day weekend, holiday schedule, or not for such a high-ranking official. The CG never had a day "off." The whole point of being *Semper Paratus* was always to be ready for any event, crisis, or need sent their way. They trained when the days were smooth sailing and activated when they were fraught with disaster for any man, woman, or child. There were no distinguished factors, just a mission to rescue all. Everyone had trials; would they follow or try to flee them?

Joshua recognized the Admiral had made the guests feel like people in his household. His Admiral, Eleazar, exuded gentleness and respect. He was also keenly aware of the goings-on of their combined mission. Rightly so, because he was so highly regarded, his personnel wanted to obey his every word for the most part. There were exceptions, but even those who wavered in their duties and sought redemption were handled by Eleazar with the exacting precision of a surgeon who restored wholeness and restoration. Those who chose misconduct and threw away their honor did so to the heartbreak of the Commandant, Vice Commandant Admiral Eleazar, and the rest of the Guardians. Because people talked, Joshua knew some had disappointed the Admiral... but the Admiral took the high road always and wanted, if possible, to restore them to the mission.

There was no such dishonor to be dealt with today, much to Captain Nissi's obvious enjoyment and relief. Joshua noticed Captain Nissi had observed the personally invited guests from an arm's length. Nissi's job was to stand in the gap between his Airmen, crews, and stalwart mission to save people and report to the Admiral. The past year's record was nearly spotless, and with a glad sentiment, he had reorganized his records for the brief with Admiral Eleazar, which had happened within the hour.

Joshua and everyone present appreciated though the tragic loss of the teenager had come up, the Admiral's noble nature had not allowed it to become a point of strife. Nissi had complete confidence that, instead, it had promoted restoration for Mansoul, the crew on the fateful mission, and the good of the Air Station as a whole. Perhaps what had been required was a total concession of what had happened for the whole matter to be dropped into the depths of the sea forever.

Admiral Eleazar led the way and exuded leadership. Nissi also contributed to keep the mission alive and well. The Vice Commandant had an all-hands for all personnel on base later. With gratitude, he presented his coin in a handshake publicly to Joshua and the others he had met with privately earlier.

The total sum of the parts made the CG one of the world's renowned redemptive forces. However, the entire responsibility fell at the feet of the Commandant, and everyone grasped it. Each rescue, successful or not, as seen by the eyes of the media, insiders, and crew members on the scene, was due to the accountability of the top leader. Every job was done with precision by a guide. The procedures had to be followed. The duty standers in every job could be put down anywhere they were assigned and fulfill their duties with any other Guardian. Across cultures, crises, and typical duties, the people of the CG were reassigned strategically, promoted meritoriously, and designated with more and more leadership as their careers progressed. It was a natural leadership development as personnel demonstrated increased leadership, maturity, increased skill sets, and exhibited work ethic. No two Guardians possessed the same spirit, but they all had been allowed to hone their traits and capabilities for further service in the mission. They were fully committed and wanted to emulate the best leaders before them. In this manner, they became effective in the mission to be Always Ready.

The people chosen for the brief had been some of the service members the Command Master Chief and Captain had carefully observed under their watchful eyes for the previous year. The Guardians' leadership knew they wanted more than anything to see them develop and grow individually and corporately to strengthen their mission, *Semper Paratus*: Always Ready, and specifically for the rescue swimmers, *So Others May Live.*

Joshua stood rigid still, somewhat amazed by the turn of the day's events, as Admiral Eleazar approached him when he took his leave.

Eleazar put his hand on Joshua's shoulder and whispered low enough for only him to hear, "You've been an excellent messenger, son."

Then, he abruptly turned to Nissi and spoke encouragingly as they departed the building together.

"You, Nissi, have brought order and good discipline to the unit here and units elsewhere you have been in command of. You have faithfully kept the watch; keep up the exceptional work, Skipper."

Nissi replied, "As some of the Academy cadets recently shared with me, *Deo Juvante,* With God's help."

They shared a long look of mutual respect.

Joshua opened the door wide for the departure of the Admiral, known for mischievous inside jokes. Outside, the two Guardians, known to one another as cloud riders, headed toward the airplane that awaited Eleazar.

Joshua remembered, *That's the Admiral's airplane. I should've known he'd be here earlier.*

He observed from the doorway, the Captain, who snapped to a full salute, offered his quick response, "Thank you, Sir!"

Eleazar's laugh resounded over the whine of the airplane engine as it started. Vice Commandant Admiral Eleazar returned the salute.

He shouted, "Samuel Nissi, in this time of trials, we need the mission more every hour. We represent the CG's preeminence and the complex mission of our relationship on land, sea, and sky. May the whole world follow us!"

Joshua thought, *The whole world? Will they?*

Jordan ribbed him with her elbow. She nodded slowly at Joshua as though she clearly understood Eleazar's words.

She thought, *Should I hide from him what we're about to do? Or spill it?*

Jordan held her tongue, and Joshua was now at a loss for words. The men and women around him never ceased to amaze him. His observations from their afternoon began to open up more questions than give conclusions.

Jordan finally spoke, "Let's just watch and wait."

The two of them turned their stares from each other towards the official's retreat. The Admiral's plane was readied for departure, and Captain Nissi escorted him to the lowered airstair. At the bottom of the stairs, the Admiral turned to Nissi and spoke to one another out of earshot. Joshua wondered with pleasure about the kind of mutual relationship the people had who shouldered the responsibility of the mission to rescue them all.

Minutes later, Joshua and Jordan stood under a beachside pavilion not a quarter mile away on the Pasquotank River, the base's eastern boundary. A slight salty air breeze blew over them. Their sweat eventually subsided once the Admiral was out of sight.

Thank you for that, thought Joshua, *I think.*

They had gotten cold water bottles from a nearby vending machine and gulped them eagerly. They gazed out over the river that flowed directly in front of them. The river was a mile and a half wide and brown with tannins from the nearby Dismal Swamp. Nevertheless, it looked inviting since they were both still sticky and hot from the intensity of the brief and the humidity in which they stood. They were together to decompress from the afternoon's events. Hotwashes had become their way of life, and they enjoyed the companionable time together in contemplation. There was little conversation in the late afternoon from Jordan.

Joshua thought, *What a pleasant surprise.*

They both needed time to reflect on the surprise visit from the Vice Commandant.

"You're unusually quiet, Roi," prompted Joshua eventually.

The Admiral's CG jet took off behind them while Jordan voraciously wrote in her journal about everything said and what had transpired.

"Mansoul, I've got to get this all down while it's fresh on my mind," Jordan responded matter-of-factly.

The only sound was her pen as it scratched over her journal. Joshua contemplated how important the Admiral's commendation about how the rescue, which had robbed him of sleep and unfocused energy, was not to hang over his head any longer. It had finally given him the closure he badly needed.

Or has it? I am finally free to move on from E City and the shame.

"Has he forgiven us?" Joshua spoke the words to no one in particular.

"Yep, yep."

Jordan ribbed him again for the second time and said, "Deo Juvante, Mansoul."

His first CG tour was complete, and he bravely and respectfully looked up.

He thought, *I did it, Papa.*

He thought of his papa's face, which summoned him to look up. The VC, who wasn't on earth just then and had called him "Son," had done the same. His heart was whole and peaceful, like the river that flowed unstoppably in front of him. Its flow calmed his mind and soul like an aspirin on an unseen ache. He let out a sigh he had held onto for years. He had found his place in the world.

Jordan laughed out loud and regarded him closely. Still speechless, she went back to her journal and wrote more furiously.

"What are you writing about?" he asked, "me?"

Jordan read, "You're blessed when you are content with just who you are, no more, no less. That's when you find yourselves proud owners of everything you can never buy."

Joshua said, "Not me?"

She winked in return.

He knew he would stay as a part of the sky rulers' mission he had loved all his life. He loved the shared responsibility of fighting to save. The commendation of the Admiral seemed to him to add to his bright future—the sea of uncertainty he swam in since the days of his childhood had parted. As a man on a mission, he grew into his stature and became more knowledgeable and wiser. Due to the community, tradition, and command, he had given himself. He realized now with clarity the past hurricanes had been opportunities in disguise. After the storms of life, rainbows of promise and assurance had come. One person at a time, he would be there on a mission to bridge the divide between life and death for each of them. When Joshua had a survivor's attention, he knew the decision to follow or die alone was up to them, but he had fulfilled his life's purpose.

In the distance came a gentle and familiar sound. The hum of a Jayhawk helicopter began in the distance and eventually overcame the scribe sounds of Jordan's pen until the helicopter thundered overhead. It flew over the river towards them and presented those bold and beautiful USCG letters on its underbelly.

"It's a sort of exclamation mark on our experiences today ...maybe on this whole tour," Joshua marveled.

Jordan grinned at him, and he couldn't help but give her a full-blown, audacious, crooked, toothy smile as the helo hovered 100 yards behind them above the airstrip.

With emphasis on every word, Jordan said, "We've only just begun, friend."

He felt the reverberations of the helo, and her words echoed in his body and soul. He turned his gaze from the cloudless sky to the flight line. The helicopter lingered in a hover, and he looked up to see the bold black letters USCG and the mission beckoned to him.

...where you lead me, I will follow, but will they?

PART 2

ANSWER ME OR PERISH

Chapter 10

REMOTE

Kodiak, Alaska

Joshua gripped the armrests on his Alaskan Airline seat as the plane rocked violently from side to side and dropped periodically. He wasn't nervous; he didn't want to land in his seatmate's lap. The steep mountain called Barometer loomed dead ahead of the runway. No one else besides the pilots could see it, but they knew it was there, a wall of rock and stone. The aircraft pitched and dropped precariously closer to the runway that ended just short of the mountain ahead. Fellow passengers in his commercial Alaskan Airline screamed in fear, prayed, and laughed nervously.

"Oh. My. God!"

"We're going to die!"

"Wheeeee, do it again!"

"Padre nuestro, que estás en el cielo. Santificado sea tu nombre..."

(Our Father, who art in Heaven, Hallowed be thy name...)

"Please. Remain. Calm!" said a flight steward.

He remembered people had told him Alaska would be "closer to God." He smirked and remembered his cabin mates were not part of the Kodiak aircrews known for their turbulent aviation expeditions in some of the nation's worst weather. Nor were they hardened salty fishermen who were used to the pitch of the waves, which were part of their costly income on the high seas of the North Pacific. That's partly why the USCG was stationed in Alaska: to protect the inhabitants, fishery industry, and tourists in this remote, ruthless, and harsh land.

He had been airborne in these tumultuous skies many times in a previous temporary duty travel (TDY) and was returning for more. He seemed to have just hit his stride doing what he loved as a US Coast Guard Rescue Swimmer, and they even paid him for it. The temporary duty assignment to Air Station Kodiak on the island of Kodiak, Alaska, had been a fantastic and all too quick assignment of a few weeks almost a year ago. As of the previous month, he had his dream assignment for the next four years—another benefit of his CG career. The TDY had been handed to him by Captain Nissi the year before, and he was so grateful for the judgment call he had made.

Joshua loved what he saw in the few weeks of his TDY in Kodiak, even though it had been in the fall. Autumn in Alaska was like deep winter in coastal North Carolina, but he had enjoyed it immensely. That was why it wound up on his "dream sheet." That's what the CG called the assignments list everyone turned in when they were up for reassignment. He had primarily heard good stuff about Alaskan tours; "breathtaking" and "stunning." He anticipated more adventures like he had encountered on his TDY the year prior. Some of the previous experiences had taken his breath and absolutely stunned him.

Alaska isn't for wimps or first tours in aviation.

Joshua had proven gracious to sacrifice on someone else's behalf. He saved his aggressiveness for the rescues. Perhaps it was his childhood, his adopted worldview, or the determination to live under a higher purpose. The CG song had taught them, "High shall our purpose be." He enjoyed Rescue Checklist 1 when he and the crew were called out for a mission, but he lived for Checklist 2 when he got to relay what happened on the scene to the crew and perform the rescue. He had gotten into many sticky situations or, as he'd been teased and called, "icky" situations. His friends sometimes called him "Icky" after he got into more than one brave rescue that even most rescuers wouldn't have wanted to. He secretly hoped the name wasn't about his awful teeth. They were out of his control, but his uneasiness at his looks had dogged him his whole life. The reflection in the mirror every morning and night, while he tried to brush and floss, reminded him of his apparent weaknesses, which only solidified his dedication to do something about what he could control: be the answer to someone else's desperate need for help.

The most frustrated Joshua ever got was with those who did not acknowledge his authority and were unconvinced of him as their best advocate for their survival. Calm under pressure, he seldom let the stress show. As the old swimmer's adage went, the only thing that separated him from the survivor in those terrible circumstances was his attitude when he entered the water. At times, the work became personal somehow, and some days, he just had to take himself away from the position to deal with the stress and strain of what he could not control, what he didn't have authority over. The pressure from the missions added up for any man or woman. He hoped to learn how to manage the demands in Kodiak better. He knew severe stressors would be fierce elements, dangerous situations, and the world's most gigantic grizzly bears. Joshua laughed at the thought. That's why he came, after all.

He thought, *If I didn't come, fear may be my defeat, just like these scared people.*

The plane tipped severely to the starboard side, and everyone gasped around him. Joshua laughed, but under his breath, to refrain from further insult or humiliation to his seatmate. He glanced out the small window, two seats to his right, and saw the small town of Kodiak appear at the base of a different mountain with windmills on top.

He thought, *these people should be with the CG on some of our flights... or not.*

Commercial airlines would never fly in the hostile conditions Alaskan CG crews were known for. After almost a year, Joshua was still not as shaken by dangerous weather conditions as by the memories of the angry crowd that shouted at him and his crew while they left Air Station Elizabeth City. As a humble man, and yet perhaps one of the strongest mentally, Joshua had proven himself in rescues time and time again. That unwanted commentary about the tragic death of a teenager, Nic, on his watch may have been his first come apart. He hoped it was his last but knew better after being around many swimmers and their shared stories of burdens. He had plenty of people who screamed at boot camp and again at rescue swimmer school, but to build him up. Those civilians at the front gate of the Base at ECity who spat hateful words were different. They made it personal, and in hindsight, he realized what a gift Captain Nissi had given him to get away for a while. Indeed, the Captain had probably already been informed of the angry crowd when he issued the assignment an hour earlier. Somehow, Nissi had always seemed to know what went on everywhere.

I sure wish I could hone that ability...

The scenery was spectacular as his plane approached the narrow strip of land between the frigid North Pacific and the mountains of the island chain known as the Aleutians near Kodiak, Alaska. A shiver of excitement ran through him. Joshua had such a likable disposition and was of good humor. However, some other swimmers and old classmates sometimes deemed him too sober for his own good.

I like to have a good time, but never at anyone else's expense.

He was a brawny, 5'10" introvert of Hispanic descent. At least amongst his peers, he was introverted and liked to think everything through before he spoke. He had taught himself a new language as a child and later taught it to his whole family after he learned it in school. It made him a careful keeper of the words entrusted to him. Being bilingual didn't hurt, as he could also eavesdrop on conversations occasionally. Once, it was mentioned he might even get more pay if he tested and passed a language proficiency test, but then his secret would be out.

Joshua pondered, *It is way more fun to eavesdrop than collect extra pay.*

His fellow swimmers never knew, but he liked to help his survivors with good humor. Their crazed fear, interrupted by his jokes, usually immediately disarmed them, and they changed their outlook. Of course, he was always careful about what had happened, primarily as he assessed their dire situation. It often relaxed their features momentarily so he could earn their trust, which was important when they had just moments to spare.

The airline wheels screeched as they hit the landing strip. Everyone cheered.

"Hallelujah!"

"We made it, finally!"

"Gracias Dios!"

Strangers on the flight hugged one another. Others applauded the pilots' expert maneuvers after they'd just cussed them for their lack thereof.

That's all too familiar...

Other passengers tried to collect themselves while the nausea that plagued them on the descent receded. Flight in Alaska was not for the faint of heart. Almost everyone on board sighed with great relief as they began to collect their possessions after the plane stopped completely. Joshua turned to the mother and father seated next to him and assisted them with the several pieces of luggage in the overhead compartment. Their "near death" experience had rattled them. Joshua carefully regarded their child, about age 5, who shyly hid.

Joshua said, "That was the best ride, wasn't it?" with the goofiest grin he could muster.

The child giggled and hid. He was a bit bewildered and concerned about his parent's reactions to a stranger speaking to him. He looked back and forth between them all. Finally, he spoke up loudly despite his parent's hesitation.

He rested his gaze on Joshua and said, "The best day of my whole life!"

Joshua endeared himself to almost everyone he met. This family was no exception. The parents found their pride had dropped into their shoes.

They regarded Joshua and said, "Thank you" to him in a thick, foreign accent he couldn't place. Joshua had lost any accent from his youth unless he spoke with family members. He remembered that many cultures were represented in the rural town of Kodiak. Many participated in the vibrant fish, wildlife, and tourist industries. They realized he had turned what could have been a horrible experience into something to celebrate. Joshua again was in his element. He knew turbulence was just the appetizer for what was to come on the darkest night and in the worst storms. He nodded to them as if he understood, fist-bumped with the little guy, collected his bag, and strode toward the gangway. Except in Kodiak, he had learned you just deplaned right onto the tarmac on a steep airstair. An icy wind slapped him in the face.

Wow, this is cold and remote, even in good old summertime!

It was shockingly cold in June for most of the people who deplaned. Their spirits again plummeted as they trudged to the small terminal with open doors. The airline crew wore shorts and hoodies.

I suppose they have to make the most of summer while they, well... we can.

Joshua planned on it to be slightly warmer in June, but not with the wind chill. He certainly wasn't in Elizabeth City (ECity) anymore, but Kodiak was what he had asked for. He pulled his cell phone out of his pocket and began to look for the text about who was supposed to give him a lift.

"There he is!"

"My Man!"

"Mansoul."

"Icky!"

"Joshie, baby!"

Fellas called out to him as he made his way in the line through the terminal. Joshua turned around like he fully expected someone else famous behind him. They hollered greetings, and more welcomers continued to arrive as they made him feel like a rockstar in the tiny pick-up and drop-off area. It was crammed full of people who waited to board the very same aircraft he had just departed. The small terminal boasted just two flights out each day. His humility at their arrival en masse only made the hoots and hollers grow louder. The men and women confirmed he was indeed their long-expected guest. He had forgotten there was no walk to baggage.

I kinda wish I had a longer walk to spread out the "love."

The airport had two rooms; one was used to check in or pick up luggage, and the other was used for transition through security to board the same plane that had just arrived. A swarm of people with hot coffee razzed him with salutations and congratulations for making it to "the Rock."

Bless them for the hot coffee, he thought.

He wondered, *But how do they even remember me?*

The hot coffee was pressed into his hands, he got side hugs from strangers, and slaps on the back confirmed he was part of a close-knit company of rescue swimmers. These men and a few women were a select group on a mission many would never undertake. It bonded them; this was the camaraderie he was promised upon graduation from AST. He would learn to embrace it. The Air Station was also a large family, which included the ASTs. He almost felt like he had come home with such a warm, literal, and figurative welcome.

Wow, does that feel good? How is it possible to come home to an unfamiliar crowd?

A round of quick re-introductions and first-time introductions to far too many people with names he realized he wouldn't likely be able to recall five minutes later was made. They collectively recognized they had hogged the small terminal. Someone finally directed him to gather the duffle bag just unloaded from the plane a few feet away and delivered inside. He remembered this from the first visit, but only his sponsor had picked him up for his TDY. It had been dark and foggy that time, so he had missed entirely the excitement of the approach. He did remember how tiny the airport was. It felt smaller, full of larger-than-life people.

Wow, is this American soil? Did my pilot unload my bag, too?

The decision was made for Joshua to ride along to town for a good meal at the Aquamarine Restaurant. He was exhausted and would have preferred a nap after three airplane rides that covered some 4,800 miles. Of course, this crowd was not the group to beg off "tired."

Swimmers were never too tired for anything, anyone, anytime. *Semper Paratus.*

Joshua was escorted back into the wind that bit and blew sideways across the gravel parking lot. He began to understand why someone may not have loved their Kodiak tour if this was summertime in Alaska. Another muscular swimmer tossed his bag like a feather in the back of a rusty pickup truck. He jumped in the driver's seat, and Joshua climbed into the passenger's seat. They roared out of the lot and headed around some sharp turns into town.

The driver said, "You remember Deadman's Curve?"

Joshua smiled back, "Of course, why else would I return?"

He looked over the Pacific Ocean as it snarled against the shore a hundred yards below Deadman's curve and contemplated silently.

So, this was good enough weather to land in?

Excellent. I already have a family to welcome me with HOT coffee in July.

Things cannot get better, or can they?

At the table in the middle of the small restaurant, Joshua ordered a Fisherman's Pie because he had missed the fresh Alaskan fish.

I want something hot and savory.

He was excited that he would soon fish men and women out of their chaotic circumstances. He gulped down water as fast as the waitress brought it. Finally, she brought him a pitcher and set it heavily on the table as if it were his glass. He noticed his deep thirst, but not before she had.

Someone said, "Check out this handmade solid table and the engravements on each end."

Joshua pulled back from the table end and read, "Wherever two or three are gathered, I am with them."

Then the waitress added with a friendly wink and bragged, "This baby is from a local tree and was brought in here in ONE solid piece!"

Another swimmer said, "It's a 12-foot table of Sitka spruce felled not far from here. I'd like to have seen the guys that hauled it in."

The waitress said, "It came right through the window there," she pointed across the room.

The men grimaced at the thought of the dead weight of such an object. They all knew how hard it was to carry beastly loads. Conversation flowed freely with the group of swimmers and some of their spouses. Joshua was swept into their banter as if he had been part of their elite force since time began. One of them spoke from the other end of the table.

He said, "I heard that you did a bang-up job on that case out of Wilmington."

Joshua's heart skipped a beat at the introduction of that sentence, "I heard that," and hoped the news of *all* his rescues or failures hadn't made it to these Guardians. He took a deep breath to compose himself and spoke for maybe the first time that night. He knew they expected him to respond. Contented to be at the table to learn about Kodiak and their adventures, he wondered how to relay the adrenaline-pumping rescue from months back. He stepped with caution and answered the question with a question.

He settled on, "You know the quote from that old Olympic runner, Eric Liddell, from Chariots of Fire, the '80s British film? He believed that God made him for a purpose. But he said, 'He also made me fast, and when I run, I feel His pleasure.' When I'm on a rescue, I feel His pleasure when I swim. What can I say? He made me fast."

The surprised guffaws of laughter resounded through the place. Everyone was shocked at Joshua's statement since he had barely said a word since his arrival.

"Don't take me as arrogant. I hope you won't. I know I need all the help I can get."

Another swimmer answered, "I hear you, Mansoul."

Joshua replied, ".... and when I asked the survivors to follow me, everyone answered correctly *that day*."

The laughter grew quiet. Nods of mutual awareness were exchanged between swimmers, and their spouses or significant others looked at one another in respect. The rescuers' mission was physically intense. It was also emotionally stressful to be *Semper Paratus* with a mentality that would overcome the trials of the mind that sometimes seemed incomprehensible.

Joshua thought, *There it is.*

"It" was the freedom that swimmers found in the test of their wills and physical prowess. Freedom was the gift they found at the limits of what they were made for. Not to be free of limitations but to stretch their own on behalf of someone else.

I am home with these people. They get me, thought Joshua.

He sheepishly braved a toothy smile, and everyone smiled back.

Someone's cell phone rang, and the rest of the phones began to vibrate or ring all around the table. Money was thrown on the table while two men hustled out the door together. They ran out to ride back to base and on to the next rescue. Several guys groaned at yet another interrupted night out but, without question, decided it was time to call it a night. Joshua and those who remained off duty pulled out their wallets to pay their bills and those of the others. A rotund man approached the group and waved them off from payment of their dinner tabs. He smiled with a broad welcome smile and laid each of his hands on two of the men's shoulders. Joshua later learned it was Kodiak's Mayor Melchi and the establishment's owner.

Melchi said, "The CG's finest, I see, has come to grace my establishment. Your dinner is on my family. We are always in your debt. As are all the people," he waved his arms around the room, "Of the greatest state! The 49th!"

"Aw, thanks," said one swimmer.

He jumped up and gave the senior citizen a bear hug that lifted him off his feet. Everyone in the restaurant laughed at the sight of the much-beloved man's feet dangled in the big embrace the younger stout swimmer gave. They all clapped and appreciated the man's generosity and message. The endearment of the community was another warm welcome back to the whole community for Joshua.

Maybe these people were closer to God? I suppose I'll find out what that means as I go.

The fun had run out by the time they left, and the sun had just begun to set at 10 p.m. All Joshua could think of now was sleep. He was bone tired yet full of food and the kind of brotherhood that sustained a man for the next big unknown and breathless adventure.

Chapter 11

PROPERLY PREPARED

Elsewhere on the island of Kodiak that sunny night, Miriam tucked her daughter, Christina, into her cozy warm bed. She laid down next to her for a short snuggle and bedtime story. After one long story, Christina asked, “Another story, pretty please, Mom.”

Miriam replied, “Not tonight. We’ve got a big day ahead of us tomorrow. Did you remember we leave early to hike the Damascus trail?”

She got up and adjusted the blackout blinds to prevent the bright summer sun from its lateness and early creep into the morning for their complete night’s rest. Not that the brilliant summer sun, which hung out about 20 hours a day in July, could be blocked for long. As Miriam turned to switch off the little lamp and leave the room, little Christina, age 8, stopped her.

She said, “Mom?”

“Yes”, she replied.

She grew irritated by her three children’s continued questions at bedtime.

Christina added, “Mom, my friend Grace says prayers every night at bedtime.”

An empty silence fell over the room as Miriam stepped back toward the little girl. She realized that she had grown up and had questions she did not have answers to. She sat back down on the bed.

She whispered, "Okay, sure honey, why don't you do that, too, if you want."

There was a long silence in the slow summer twilight and semi-darkness.

Miriam interrupted the silence, "Do you want to start now, honey, tonight?"

Christina looked relieved, although she wasn't sure why. Her mom was agreeable when she asked nicely. Christina thought about what Grace had said about how Grace and her family folded their fingers and hands together, just like she laced her shoes and closed her eyes. She paused in thought for a minute. A "chat with God" was what Grace had told her it was.

She began, "Hey God, it's me, Christina, and my mom's here, too. Thanks for a great day and, um... for the salmonberries...and, um, for the wind to die down so we can hike...and um, for my favorite teacher, Mrs. Hill. Help our Dad to control his anger, please. Umm... I guess that's it for now. See you later. I mean, bye for now."

Miriam was choked up for a reason she could not explain. She could not contain her tears, so she just placed a kiss on top of Christina's forehead as a sort of approval. As she attempted to tiptoe from the room stealthily, she realized her unspoken prayers of late had been all too similar for her and her whole family's sake.

The next morning, the *Peanuts* cartoon that came to Christina's mind pictured Lucy saying, "There's no excuse for not being properly prepared" at a perfectly laid-out campsite. She ran around and piled all her favorite stuff she wanted to take on the kitchen table. Lucy was the only one in the cartoon who enjoyed her campsite, while the others were frustrated with lost or absent camp gear. Christina's parents packed lunches and filled water bottles for each of them. They had already begun an argument over the lateness of the hour for the day's hike. It was a lot of weight for three kids to haul water, especially since the twin boys, Silas and Jared, were just five. They, too, gathered things for the hike, like matchbox cars and Nerf darts, which the parents bemoaned due to their pointlessness and the extra weight.

Christina was humored that everyone's idea of being prepared was quite distinctive. The parents wanted bug spray, bear spray, and sunscreen.

Yuck, yuck, and yuck, thought Christina.

Every family member would pack differently for a trip, and it seemed like somebody forgot something each time they went out. It was imperative to bring bear spray in Kodiak, but the kids had never seen the world's most giant brown bear up close and wanted to see a 'Kodiak.'

They whined, "Why bother with spray to keep them away if we want to get close?"

Christina could tell everyone in the family wanted something very different on their hike.

She pondered, *How are we all going to have a good time at the same time?*

She thought, *Mom goes for the ripe salmonberries to make pies and jam. Dad has the outdoorsy, "let me show you how to make a trail in the wilderness, boys" attitude, which gets on my nerves every time. I can make one too. The twins only go for the promised cookies at the best bakery in town on the way home.*

They went to the bakery, Java Flats, every Saturday right before they closed to see 'Smily Jessie,' who would come around the counter and hand them cookies bigger than their hands...normally they broke the cookie in half to share. Every great once in a while, though, Jessie would say there were just too many left, and they each had to take one! Mom and Dad insisted the boys still share but took the other home to divide up later. It was the most routine thing they did together. The bakery was always busy, so it made sense to go at the end of the day. Plus, the bribe worked on the boys to keep their short, exhausted legs moving at the end of the long hikes. Her Dad, Sam, called the place his church. Only once did Christina ask why he called it that.

He laughed and said, "I never miss a weekend, see the people I want to see, skip the music, and still get the cookies."

His comment confused Christina because she liked all of that, especially music. Christina wanted to hike to get way out and away from everyone. There, she could hear herself think for a minute and talk to herself about whatever she wanted. Her parents encouraged her to talk on the trail, but they never had time to listen at home.

We had better hit the trail, or the bakery will close before we finish our hike.

She thought about mentioning it to her parents but decided not to. Her dad's anger was provoked quickly enough, and she heard the whine of the twins the whole trip about the missed cookie opportunity, which was not a pleasant thought.

She ran back to her room and quickly found her favorite stuffed animal, a sea otter named Otto, and snuck him into her neon yellow backpack while her parent's backs were turned. She had a flashlight, whistle, Otto, spare dry socks, and some more candy snuck inside. She was glad the sun shone so they probably wouldn't get wet. It rained more days in Kodiak than the sun would ever shine. It was a temperate rainforest. They were still sure to find mud somewhere to lose a shoe and get her socks nasty.

She appeared downstairs, back on her back, and said, “Ready for today’s long hike.”

She pasted a smile over her face to show her parents she was much more responsible than her little brothers. The twins still argued over who was carrying a Grave Digger toy truck or something stupid. Samson, her giant-sized dad, who some just called Sam, slammed his fist on the table.

“Shut up!” he roared.

The boys cowered and then slipped behind their mother. Christina winced at his already foul mood.

He declared, “We are already late. Get in the truck!”

The truck was almost packed, and everyone had yet to hit the bathroom one last time. There was no bathroom in the woods for a long hike, which the little boys loved for some odd reason. No matter how long she tried to hold it, Christina would eventually have to hide in the bushes. She had learned and was always ready with her stash of toilet paper prepared.

What else am I not ready for besides my mean dad?

Chapter 12

A SUNNY SUMMER NIGHT

Sam yelled over his shoulder sometime on Saturday, well after his kids' typical lunchtime.

"Stop drinking all your water. You must stretch it out over the whole hike up and back. You will finish the last drop in the truck or no cookies! We're almost to the top, and we'll break for lunch there."

They stopped early in the hike to pick the salmonberries from the thick bushes that towered over their heads. The beautiful red berries had ripened all over the island and were perfect to snack on along the way. They were known for the explosion in your mouth with a bitter taste if not quite ripe and sweet if ripened a deep red. The adults were more careful to pick certain berries, but the kids munched happily on anything they could snatch. Miriam filled several plastic containers full of berries for her baking at home. Hours later, the kids' stomachs groaned.

"Too far, too hungry, Mommy!"

"Too many berries, Jared."

Their legs burned from the enormous steps they had to take to climb over the boulders on the mountain. Mountain goats nearby looked pitifully at them while they stood and chewed the vegetation with contentment.

"Can we please stop and eat just anywhere like the goats get to?" asked Silas.

"NO! I told you we stop at the top. Quit your grumbling," snapped Sam.

Meanwhile, the goats peacefully munched on as if to say, "Find your own picnic." All the children looked on, filled with remorse for the peace the goats had with full bellies or fewer berries. On the mountainside grew the wild fields of Fireweed, a summer flower that bloomed upwards in stages from dark pink to white near the end of the season. That would already be the next month. The Fireweed practically grew on top of one another and covered the mountain in front of them in a gorgeous pink hue that bloomed as far as the eye could see. From below the steep mountainside, flowers reached to meet the sky.

Maybe that's why my family hikes every weekend all summer? considered Christina.

Due to the dramatic shifts in the harsh Kodiak weather, they and other Kodiak hikers had to hike while possible. It was only 50-odd degrees, but the hike went straight up to the top of Damascus Trail. It became roasting hot under the Alaskan sun. Miriam asked if they had put on sunscreen, which seemed pointless to them when they were already hot and sweaty.

The boys bantered, "Which kind of cookie are you gonna get today?

What did you pack for my lunch?

Can we trade our lunch stuff again?

Can I eat my WHOLE cookie?

I am so hungry."

They will never stop, Christina thought; *please don't get Dad even more mad.*

Christina interrupted them, "They brought what they brought. We'll find out soon enough."

She speculated on what her parents had packed for her lunch and hoped it was different than the boys. Sam, who always led the charge, went first through the thicker lower brush, unavoidable mud puddles, and poisonous plants that occasionally reached over their heads that they tried to avoid and set a hard pace. At long last, the top, or so she had hoped, came into view. More than once, they thought they had arrived only to find a false top or one that concealed the farther away top pinnacle from far below.

"AHHHHHH!" Sam yelled like Rocky, the prizefighter, when he summited the top with arms raised in victory over his head.

He helped pull Silas and Jared up and over the precipice. When Christina arrived, she was surprised at how narrow the trail had become and astonished at how little of an expanse there would be to share their picnic on "Top of the World." The view took their breaths away due to the realization their lungs burned after the hike exhausted them and in a scary way with a pinnacle top. They had to watch every move and simultaneously gawk at the 360-degree stunning views.

It's not a great place for the twins... or for me!

When Mariam arrived last, she exclaimed, "You've got to be kidding, honey! There's not enough room for all of us up here. I'll snap a quick photo, but why don't we head back down to a clearing."

Sam grumbled words under his breath and turned around several times to see the view, set his heavy pack down, and began to line up the kids for a photo.

He said, "I want a particular shot with the trail far below us, the ocean far off in the distance, and my three musketeers on top of the world."

He craved proof of his manliness. Miriam pulled out her camera and carefully balanced herself, cautious not to lean backward, while she followed his commands.

At that moment, a powerful, unpleasant odor settled over the whole family like a lightning strike to their noses.

The kids began to gag and said to one another, "Eww...what did YOU do?"

"It wasn't me, stupid."

"Please, just look at the camera for two seconds," remarked Miriam.

When Miriam regained their attention and got them to smile, she touched the screen for a focused shot of the family. She just as quickly saw something else in the camera frame.

Sam was always the biggest one in the picture, but..., she realized he wasn't. At. All.

"Whoa," Miriam said.

A gigantic, full-grown, teeth-bared Kodiak Brown Bear stood on its hind feet about 8 feet high and towered behind Sam and their children. Shocked and mute, she pulled down her camera phone.

She pointed and whispered, "It's...a ... bear."

"What?" boomed Sam as he spun around in total astonishment.

He gazed up, astonished, into the face of the colossal, putrid creature and stepped backward into thin air. As Sam fell backward hard, his gigantic frame crashed against the steep rocky mountainside. While on his back, he quickly slid and rolled head over heels down the dirt incline. There was nothing to break his plummet for hundreds of feet. The terrible moments were only trumped by the family's rapt attention on the bear. The massive Kodiak bear with long, shaggy brown fur had a horrible stench. Huge paws as big as dinner plates swiped the empty air and increased its enormous appearance. It swung its head back and forth as if to claim the top of the mountain and its rightful place at the top of the food chain. She snapped a photo once more.

She wanted proof of the cause of their demise. Stealthily, Miriam moved toward her children and gently tried to tug them backward inch by inch. Only a mama bear would take on a bear that size to protect her young. The kids stood with their eyes glued on the beast just feet from them, open-mouthed in awe.

Miriam calmly whispered, "Let's make ourselves look bigger together and raise your arms slowly."

The boys were slack-jawed and terrified. They stood amazed at such unmatched raw authority and power. No one had ever rivaled their forgotten father. They were not even sad, yet, that he had fallen to where they had no idea. They had wanted this bear encounter their whole lives, but it came at a steep cost. Oddly, they were enamored even as it had simultaneously become the best and the worst situation of their lives. The children were unmovable in their shock. Christina was so glad that no one else was startled, but she winced each time she heard her father's thuds as he continued to fall and yelp. She suddenly remembered the particular bear song taught at Salmon Camp in Kodiak.

Or was it at the Wildlife Visitor's Center?

She watched the gross drool drop from its massive jaws.

I didn't think the bear would be so nasty. Teddy bears aren't ferocious, either.

Christina felt her mother's tug backward. Softly at first, she did her best to mimic her mother's low tone.

She sang, "Hey bear, ho bear, whatcha gonna do...,"

The boys sang along, "I'm here, you're there, we're just passing through."

As they sang more and more robustly, they began to inch backward. The bear walloped back down on all fours and turned so they could see she was a mama with three cubs behind. The song faltered.

"So, we'll be on our way..." they all sang unanimously.

They were in awe of the mirrored image of a Mama with her own distinct three children that definitively outsized them. The situation had deteriorated. A strict rule of Kodiak was not to cross a mama and her cubs. Miriam courageously reacted like they were on the playground as one protective mother to another.

She said, "Oh yeah, you can have the whole mountain, Mama Bear; just let us go back the way we came!"

In keen observation, the bear regarded Miriam as if she pondered the thought. It shook its tremendous head, closed its jaws, and reared back onto both hind legs to make a point. She waved her massive paws towards them.

Jared said, "She's shooing us away, Mama."

This time, the kids all waved back and stopped their foot movements. Christina had sweat trickle down her back. She knew they'd have to turn around to climb down. She remembered she'd been taught at the wildlife center to stay calm and introduce themselves.

She responded, "Hi, I'm Christina, and this is Silas, Jared, and Mom. We gotta go find our Dad now, but thanks for making this the last summer hike!"

Silas said, "Mommy, I gotta wee, real bad."

Christina located her whistle on the backpack pull given to her by her American Heritage Girl troop leader. She turned to her mother as if to ask permission to blow it. When Miriam nodded, Christina blew it. The small bears turned and sauntered off the way they had come as if to say, "No more fun here." The mama bear walloped the ground as she crashed back onto all fours so hard the ground shook beneath them. She swung her huge, stinking hide away from them and followed her cubs in the opposite direction. Christina twisted, carefully swung her leg over the precipice, and jumped to the boulders below. When she looked up, she saw a long yellow stream arc from Silas's small frame. It seemed to chase after the bear's rump and splattered on the ground. Jared began to laugh, and Silas moaned in relief. Christina was thankful their backs were to her. Miriam went over the ledge and reached for the twins to assist them. They still laughed as they found their dad's backpack. That was fortunate since it had all the essential stuff. Christina called for each of her brothers to follow and rolled her eyes at their immaturity.

"C'mon guys, we'd better go back."

She heard Jared say, "Can we follow so I can pet them?"

"NO!" they all yelled simultaneously.

From far below, Sam wailed in pain, "Help me!"

Miriam exhaled and was relieved to hear his voice at all.

She said, "No kidding," to everyone and no one.

I'm glad he's alive, she thought.

The family, minus Sam, hiked back down to an open clearing while they unwound. They realized they were weak-kneed and set down for a much-needed rest. They looked around backward for the bears, so much their necks hurt as they stumbled forward.

"Keep up the talk and songs," called Miriam, "and don't go out of sight; just go behind us off the trail."

The kids wanted to eat, and Miriam needed to think through what to do next. She had checked the cell phone but knew it was out of range for service, which was no surprise in Kodiak. It was past two, and Christina knew they'd never make cookie time with Jessie, so she ate all her lunch ravenously. She kept that detail to herself since the boys didn't know how to tell time yet. Miriam decided not to find her husband with the kids for fear of what they would find, see, and remember. She spoke casually and hoped they wouldn't ask questions.

"I know you kiddos are famished; let's eat and then find out how much needs to be done this afternoon to get us out of here."

Miriam could not eat. She knew the adventure had gone dangerously awry. The burden that lay before her to get them all off the mountain was now heavier than she could imagine. She needed help. The kids dug into their lunches with fervor. Periodically, they would hear their father call up from somewhere below.

"Are you coming for me?" in a strained and pinched voice they'd never heard.

The boys yelled back, "Dad, where are you? Does it hurt much? We're gonna find you!"

"I'm coming," said Miriam in a strained voice.

She knew she had what could be a life-and-death decision to make.

She silently pondered her next step.

He needs me, but the kids don't need to see his condition or hear him roar. If he is bleeding, he may attract unwanted visitors on four paws, perhaps putting them in danger.

Miriam's quiet mood worried Christina, but she could tell she needed to think something important through. Miriam stowed her meager lunch and knew she would share it with her kids for dinner. After they devoured their lunches, the boys excused themselves behind some bushes and laughed again as they went. Miriam took the opportunity to speak to Christina, for once glad the boys were inseparable.

She said, "I must ask you to do something I've never wanted to do before. I must look for your father. Can you stay with the boys and protect them like you did so amazingly up there?"

She motioned to the top of the mountain, and Christina was immensely proud to have been rewarded with such responsibility. She nodded yes, not clear about all that would entail. She knew this was a tall order since there were no cartoons for miles. Her mother hugged Christina tightly and smoothed her hair back as she did at bedtime. Miriam forced a smile as she stood back up, already exhausted as the boys approached.

She regarded them thoroughly, "You know I must go find your father and send for help. You do EVERYTHING she tells you to do," she pointed at Christina, "and stay together to keep warm. Here's my jacket and my lunch. Save it for *much* later. Drink your water sparingly."

Miriam kissed them each on top of their foreheads. She slowly turned and walked further down the trail with her useless phone and the backpack with food and water bottles. When she came to a cliff and had to descend ladder style hand over hand, she knew she was glad she'd left the children in a clearing on the trail.

She thought, *What will I find below me? I'm not sure I can handle this on my own.*

She shuddered and exhaled deeply at the pain she would eventually face physically and emotionally.

Am I alone?

She paused momentarily and looked up, "If you're there, now's a good time to show yourself."

"Wait!" cried Silas into the emptiness that his mother had traversed. He realized he missed her immediately, "What about our cookies?"

Miriam had no words to answer him, but tears slipped down her cheeks.

Just because I don't answer doesn't mean I don't care, son.

That began a lengthy "partly sunny" experience in the midnight sun Alaskan wilderness.

A dense, wet fog rolled in while long sun rays waned in the evening. The separated family was in a desperate and dangerous situation as the temperature dropped with the sun before it rose again four hours later. They decided to stay where they were about half a mile apart. The light jacket mom left was barely big enough for the twins to fit in, nor warm enough. Christina unloaded her backpack and shared her clean hiking socks with the boys to put their hands and forearms inside like makeshift mittens. She was so glad she'd remembered to sneak Otto in for comfort. She used him like a puppet for her brothers' sake. She threw her voice into a high squeak.

She caricatured Otto, "Once upon a time, I drifted on the Pacific..."

She told the boys about Otto's incredible adventures on and under the ocean. She tried to distract them all from the harshness of the day and extended hours ahead without blackout curtains. The boys were thrilled that she shared her beloved friend and only slightly bemoaned they'd only brought darts and monster trucks. Those, too, were worked into the imaginative stories of rescue they hoped for without admittance. The children also made up stories from cartoons they had watched and told each other silly jokes. They huddled closer and closer until they were lying on top of each other and borrowed Christina's warmth as she tucked them beside her and Otto.

Otto's voice reassured them when the fog grew densest, "I'm used to this kind of weather. Out on the ocean, my mama always comes back. If we sleep, we hold hands so we don't drift apart."

The boys could not hold hands but hugged one another tighter. The only sounds so high on the mountain were the fog horns far out on the ocean and the steady schedule of the family's whistleblowing every hour. That was the signal sent to them that their mother was well, though she was far out of sight. They had given up the yells back and forth down the mountainside. The yells back and forth only made their nerves worse, their throats sore, and increased their thirst. The family could do nothing besides sit the night out together yet separate. They all knew it was better to sit and wait for help in Alaska than try to heroically rescue yourself and get far more lost. Their stomachs grumbled from the lack of dinner, and they began to wonder how long until help would arrive.

Jared finally asked the question the other kids had thought, "Is help even on the way?"

They had seen small airplanes fly nearby and waved, but to no avail. They'd even finished off all their mom's berries she'd collected. Although hungry, they decided collectively they didn't think they'd want another salmonberry, salmonberry pie, salmonberry jam, salmonberry anything, ever. Even the whining eventually stopped for missed cookies. The boys nodded off to sleep after what seemed to be hours of stories. Christina remembered her warm, snuggly bed and her first prayer the night before. She held her arms tightly around her brothers and dozed like a sea otter who clung to her siblings.

Christina awoke briefly and was stiff from having not moved. She still clutched her brothers. The dense fog had mostly rolled by, and she snuggled in again and imagined they were like sea otters on the surface of the deep Pacific. She looked up at the vast heavens above with the billions of stars that peeked around the thick Milky Way Galaxy that stretched from horizon to horizon. The clouds parted like curtains and revealed a dramatic show just for Christina. It seemed a comet streaked through the sky just for her.

She whispered, "Well, God, I see you. If you see me, rescue us."

And in the quiet, little Silas, whom she thought was sound asleep, added sincerely, "And bring cookies!"

Jared, not to be left out, said, "Warm milk, too, please."

They were cold and shivered but thankful for the warmth of one another before the sun began its slow creep up again. Eventually, they each drifted back to sleep after one more whistle blew at midnight. Their worries were paused for a few hours of much-needed slumber and close otter-like cuddles on the sea of forested mountains and valleys.

Down the mountain, Miriam and Sam took some consolation that Sam's wounds weren't somehow worse. Perhaps a fractured hip, lots of abrasions, and undoubtedly deep hunger. What consumed their minds were their exceptional, stranded children, lack of food, and rescue prospects. Their children were left to the elements of the harsh Alaskan wilderness overnight and alone. They realized they had failed to notify anyone of their plans or whereabouts, a cardinal rule of backcountry hiking. They tried unsuccessfully not to blame one another and knew they had to own their faults as time passed.

They wondered aloud how long until someone noticed they were gone. The terrible thought was never spoken, but their lack of genuine relationships may have been their death, especially for Sam, who couldn't stand, let alone walk on his feet. Their self-sufficiency was a burden their children had to bear, as well as themselves. Sam's enormous frame, too big for his little family to carry, would be left behind as they planned to hike out tomorrow for help. Sam knew better than to panic, but he did feel remorseful for his brave wife who suffered near him, cold and hungry.

"Wait," he said stiffly and pained, "I found this earlier in a bush."

He offered her a dirty old grey fleece hat he had found in some brush late in the morning. He just remembered he'd stuffed it in his back pocket. Maybe it had padded his fall and protected him somehow. She hesitatingly reached for it.

She asked, "Where did this come from?"

"What? No thanks?" he said condescendingly.

I'm giving it to her, after all...

He had painfully pulled it from his pocket. She turned over the man's fleece cap that hadn't been worn for several seasons. She inspected it and pulled it over her head without a care what she looked like. It covered her ears and eyes, too. It was not instant warmth but a welcome addition to her lack of preparation for overnight "camping" in Alaska. She smiled momentarily at the lack of light and, for a reason, not to look at Sam. She growled inwardly at her arrogant husband.

She pondered, *What happened to the man who lost the hat years ago? What happened to my man years ago?*

Miriam thought to herself, *Was he a more loving husband than mine? At least now I have an excuse not to look or listen. Ha, my overBEARing husband, indeed.*

She turned her back to him as she lay on the rocky ground. They both stared in silence at the dense fog around them, around their deteriorating marriage and their endangered children.

Miriam thought, *he finally met his match with that mama bear, or had he?*

CHAPTER 13

FORWARD FLIGHT

On Sunday morning that weekend, high overhead of the Kodiak range of mountains in an orange-tipped USCG C-130 (cargo) plane was Lt. Commander Elisha Joseph, or "Padre" as some guys called him. He was the aircraft commander and led their mission. He had the responsibility to help the CG keep a watch over the vast waters that surrounded the Kodiak area from Anchorage, several hours away by flight or twelve by ferry, to the frigid Bering Straits of Alaska. He flexed his arms over his head and stretched the dull ache in his back. He caught sight of his orange freckles that covered the back of his hands when he put them back on the yoke. He was glad to be out of the Florida sun and give his ruddy appearance a break from all that golden sunshine down south. However, the heat in the cockpit was surprisingly warm, and like a solarium in the Alaskan sun, it got toasty.

I'd better keep the sunscreen on here in Alaska, too. Bummer, he realized.

Padre was a bit older than most of his pilot peers and, therefore, took to being teased with the "Padre" in stride. His receding hairline gave him away. The wrinkles on his face formed by years of anxiety and disquiet were transferred into laugh lines. Too bad for him, the back strain continued with days and days in the cockpit.

I'd probably better mention that to Doc next visit...or not.

He had been relocated to Kodiak two months ago with his family. Being the quintessential family man suited him fine. He drove his family across the continent to arrive in Kodiak one miserable and rainy May day, unlike this day in every way he remembered. They had been stationed in Clearwater, Florida, and jumped at the opportunity to go North. All the way north. They had laughed and sang along to the old Johnny Horton song on that six-week trip, "Way up North (North to Alaska), we go North, the rush is on."

The "rush" in the song was a reference to the famous Alaskan Gold Rush. They rushed to get to Kodiak in time for his report date as a CG pilot before the arrival deadline. They, too, had been in a hurry for a new adventure. He was thrilled to be back in the air and do what he loved: rescue people and property instead of suppressing them as he once had. His life had shifted paradigms several times. The first time, he went from a farm boy to a US military member in an ugly war. The second shift was from single to married with children. He had found both shifts had led to bumpy rides he had never expected. He had a mess of a life that seemed senseless for a long while.

One day, Elisha met a guy who talked to him about his call to the CG mission. He was profoundly changed and decided to transfer himself. It didn't take much to convince his family, either. The shift to the CG was pivotal, and he gladly let go of his old life. He had found peace after he joined the mission to rescue others. In his desperation for help, he learned to request it from the correct source, which made all the difference. He had served in other units in the Department of Defense (DoD) and seen and done things he wished he could unsee and undo in his service time. When the time came for him to make a career move, he did it laterally into the Department of Homeland Security (DHS), where the CG welcomed him with open arms.

A weight was dropped when Elisha left the DoD to fly for the Coast Guard. Each decision had improved his life with his spouse, kids, and job. He was better at life and a much better person, which made him grateful indeed. He considered himself a warrior for the mission to rescue strangers instead of destroying them. That was a far cry from the warrior he pictured as a child, bludgeoning people. He eventually put those childish ways behind him when he became a man, thanks entirely to the mission.

Today's mission, Padre thought, *will be simple.*

"Ya'll wanna see anything particular today?" said Padre.

"Well, if you're asking," said Michael, his co-pilot, "I'd like to venture over to Adak and circle back to see some of the ring of fire."

They were on a fisheries patrol west of Unalaska to check out some fishermen who may have wandered too close to one another. Patrols were important cakework for the USCG, but a rescue would be the icing.

"Adak? That's a long way out to the end of the Aleutian chain. You tryin' to run away from someone?" said Padre and laughed.

"Nope, it's just so clear today. My great-uncle just told me he used to be stationed there when it was Naval Air Facility Adak, no joke. I'd like to see it and maybe get a few photos for him."

"Well, we're keeping the watch over Alaska, so I don't see any harm in going the extra distance. I can only imagine having been stationed up here during the Cold War. You know how scary it is when the forces of evil get too close."

Michael said with a smirk, "What was it like in the Cold War, Padre?"

Padre replied, "How old do you think I am? Geez, Louise, I'm only 45. This would be a much different flight back then. Do you know the

CG has been guarding these waters for over 100 years? I'm thankful we stood our ground then."

Michael said, "Let's hope we can always stand firm..."

There was a respectful silence that fell over the intercom.

Padre was glad he had come here to Kodiak and the CG in general when he did. Perspective played a mighty big part in the general optimism and gratitude that showed in his personality. He liked that "Padre" was now the theme that his life had taken on after many years of struggle. He was transformed and regarded for his gentleness, respect, and wisdom. The sun bounced brilliantly off the waters far below them as he helped fly their C-130 to head west along the chain of islands stretched out as far as they could see.

"It's good to be the old man and get paid to fly and protect you kids," he said.

His co-pilot, Michael, laughed, and added, "Padre, we all want to be like you when we grow up."

Chapter 14

WHEELIN' AND DEALIN'

Jessie's favorite family didn't show up at the bakery on Saturday for their weekly cookie date. She wondered what could have happened.

She admitted to herself, *of all my customers this year, I've come to love those three kids' visits the most.*

Jessie did more than bake for an income. She loved her guests, and the kids were the greatest customers. They enjoyed her food and unashamedly gave reviews on which ones were the best. With kids, the reviews were honest and accurate. She admired the weather while she locked up and went home for the day, thankful to have friends, even if she missed them. That was on top of gratitude for the hordes of tourists she knew she would never see again, who mostly gobbled up her goodies and, on a good day, stuffed the tip jar full of cash.

On Sunday morning, when Samson didn't show up for his job at the wrecker service in town, his boss was concerned because he had never missed a day yet. Samson didn't answer his phone either when they called him. The boss rode his wrecker past Sam's house to knock on the door, and when he couldn't raise anyone, he grew more alarmed. Their pickup truck was gone, so he surmised something was amiss and thought about who to call who might know the family's whereabouts. He later stopped in and saw Jessie at the bakery about lunchtime and mentioned the oddity.

Samson's boss said, "Frankly, Jessie, I'm growin' even more concerned by the minute. Sam never showed up for work, and it ain't like him, not even to call."

Jessie grew more alarmed when she shared that they had not appeared for their traditional cookie reward after their hike the day before. They came to the same conclusion. They agreed they probably should let the local authorities know they'd been missing overnight. Sooner than later, a community-wide search began for the family. That meant that the island trails network of people would alert hikers to begin a search at the typical trail heads where people would start and park their vehicles. That also would include law enforcement and any Coast Guard members already in the air. They would use their vast knowledge and resources to sweep the large and sparsely forested areas in Kodiak's immense wilderness. Kodiak Island is mostly a wildlife refuge and as big as the state of Connecticut. Not that a family hike could get too far in just a day, but with Kodiak's ridiculous weather, no one could afford to wait and see.

Meanwhile, Joshua Mansoul met his newly assigned CG Jayhawk crew Sunday afternoon and boarded the Jayhawk helicopter for a routine "fam" familiarization flight of the area. The crew consisted of the Pilot, Co-pilot, mech, a swimmer who had already passed the Kodiak syllabus, and himself. Kodiak had a distinct swimmer syllabus to complete to be proficient in its requirements. Kodiak tours were not for the faint of heart. The special agents who requested tours to Kodiak became cloud riders in a class by themselves.

The crew enjoyed the sunshine and, for locals, the balmy 50+degree weather, which was a reprieve from the previous week. They each wore their bright orange dry suit, watertight flight uniforms worn year around in Alaska. That meant that as the temperature climbed inside the cabin, they increasingly grew more uncomfortable with layers of sweat that formed underneath, unable to escape. They had to wear these due to their flights over the frigid North Pacific while on call. Joshua had worn the suit in the winters in North Carolina while stationed in Elizabeth City but never in July. In the lower 48, swimmers wore "shorties" or short wetsuits part or all year around. The temperature of the water was the factor that determined that.

They lifted off and crossed the same flight line he had raucously flown in on, crossed over the Buskin River, down the coastline of so-called Boy Scout Beach, and past the small town of Kodiak, a real one-stoplight town. It was so small and quaint.

Joshua thought, *I feel like I've stepped back in time. I guess it wouldn't take long to find everything.*

The crews talked freely over the intercom communication system that worked in the cabin through a headset he wore. The conversation was convivial due to the exquisite weather.

"My kids are at camp this week at Woody Island down there south of town," said the pilot, "Have you been to Abercrombie State Park yet?"

Joshua said, "I was told to go there to see whales in the spring, in the summer the old museum, and this winter eagles everywhere."

"You got it. If you see a cruise ship in town, wave off the museum and bunkers. It's a Kodiak madhouse," said the mech.

The mech laughed at the madhouse part since they all knew their sleepy town was rarely anyone's madhouse of activity.

"Do not forget the Wildlife Center for some hiking maps and grab a bite at Monk's Rock Café," said the pilot.

"Roger."

They soared towards Spruce Island and circled the island counter-clockwise to see some outlying villages, then through rugged mountain passes and searched the peaks for Kodiak grizzlies. The crew passed over the rocket launch facility and Surfer's Beach as they approached Womens Bay and the Air Station.

"This green is something to behold in July. It's so different than when I was here in the fall," said Joshua.

"You can leave your tour guides a nice tip at the end of your tour, thanks," said the co-pilot.

Joshua enjoyed the terrain of vibrant greens and purple wildflowers that covered hillsides and mountain slopes. He soaked in the marvelous views while his neck strained from peering out the airframe windows.

Joshua thought out loud to no one in particular, "We get paid to fly around and do this?"

Another crew member quipped, "No, he did not. You had to say it, Mansoul? Somebody knock-on-wood, quick."

Nervous laughter erupted from the rest of the experienced Alaskan crews.

The pilot replied, "No, we get compensated to do the stuff no one else does. This is just your bonus run. Since you said what you did, things will change for sure. Thanks for the reminder of how good we have it for the moment!"

Joshua's mind drifted to that old CG song he learned in basic training or 'boot' almost three years ago,

"We're always ready for the call,

We place our trust in Thee.
Through surf and storm and howling gale,
High shall our purpose be."

I'm ready. It seems like I am far from a "howling gale" duty today...

That song was almost 200 years old, but the lyrics could've been in the past decade. The CG had recently become prominently put into the news after more catastrophic hurricanes had made their rescues necessary from house to house, sometimes miles inland. He shivered slightly at the memory of the day he was stranded on a rooftop and needed the rescue warriors. He was glad he wouldn't be facing any hurricanes this far north.

He thought, *what other storms would we face instead?*

He was there for that, not for comfort and smooth seas, but for rescues. At that moment, the mic squawked, and "Padre," the Commander of the C-130 nearby, interrupted with a comment.

"Hey, ya'll, we just heard a report of a lost family that went out to hike yesterday. We should probably begin a joint search pattern over land."

The mech looked at Joshua grimly and made a gloved hand motion with two fingers waved between his own eyes and pointed towards Joshua to say silently, "I'm blaming you."

Whoops, thought Joshua, *guilty*. He threw his hands up in a surrender motion and grinned.

The pilots switched maneuvers from island orientation and sight-seeing to a Search and Rescue (SAR) pattern.

One announced, "Your tour, Mansoul, is over; please bring your tray table to a full and upright position and prepare for your first mission should you accept it. This fam flight may get noteworthy."

Semper Paratus.

Joshua immediately regarded his superior, the senior swimmer in the cabin with him. The more experienced swimmer pointed at Joshua with what he understood was the motion for "it's on you." He grinned widely because he knew the new swimmer, Joshua, was more than anxious to begin. Joshua leaned closer to the window to see the ground far below. They all switched from bear watch mode to missing person mode. He felt a thrill rise within him.

After all, I'm here to rescue. I may as well begin today.

Joshua peered with intensity out of his window through the azure sky. He licked his lips as though hungry for a morsel of hope. So many pairs of eyes between crews searched back and forth over the dense forests that stretched out for miles. The terrain sometimes dove into cavernous valleys or soared to rock pinnacles. They looked for anything odd, suspicious, brightly colored, and their pulses quickened unbeknownst to themselves.

Joshua questioned, *how in Creation will we find someone in this wilderness?*

Guardians lived on behalf of someone else they didn't know anything about except that they needed help immediately. They banked inland and set up the search pattern. The swimmers and the mech began to use the forward-looking infrared (FLIR) camera that would highlight the heat signal of any people or animals on the ground. They took solace in the fact help was already on the way.

Padre, not too far away, began to cross back and forth in a higher search pattern over the prescribed area where a truck had recently been located that matched the missing family's vehicle description. He zeroed in on this particularly densely forested range.

A missing family, he thought.

His teeth began to grind as he clenched his jaw. As a family man, he could not help but think what it would be like if he had lost one of his family members.

Is there any more significant loss?

They would commit to doing everything possible to get these people, these kiddos, home safely. He called out to alert and update the crew in the Jayhawk helicopter over the flight's radio channel they shared.

"Ya'll prepared to take this on with us?" asked Padre.

"Of course, we're still waiting on a description of any kind," said the pilot.

"It was chilly last night. They've been gone how long?" asked the mech.

On one side, the helicopter mech watched out his window, pilots out the front, and the swimmers on the opposite side scanned in every direction they could see. They also looked as far below as possible by the predetermined flight patterns. After about a quarter-hour of search patterns, Padre called out to them.

"Do you see that neon dot near the top of the mountain at three o'clock?"

The pilots recognized the directional input and banked their helo into a slow turn to reevaluate as they drew closer. It wasn't just one bright neon yellow dot they could see as they approached. There were three dots from that far away. They made good headway and closed the distance. The whole recognized three people waved their hands and wildly ran back and forth.

"We've spotted three survivors," added the mech.

"Nice, Padre. You may have found the target," said the co-pilot.

He added, "We're here for a closer inspection, but three people are excited to see us."

In the clearing, Joshua had the figures in sight and began to understand that maybe it was only part of the family.

Could it be the children alone after they've been out all night and all day?

He mused to himself, *Where are the parents? They must be frozen and half-starved.*

Joshua said, "This orientation flight just got way more involved."

The pilot and copilot agreed they wanted to try to land the helicopter in the closest place available. However, they needed to figure out how solid the ground was and whether they could take off without hitting anything nearby. The decision was made to lower a rescue swimmer down the line to visit with the children and assess the situation further. Joshua prepared to leave the aircraft with the mech's assistance and the other more proficient swimmer's vote of confidence. The crew was all smiles for having found lost treasure. Padre from miles up and away always provided cover to the crew below.

Padre spoke again, "So, the lost *is* found; give those kids a high five for me," with a smile in his voice and his heart.

When Joshua's boots hit the ground, he disconnected from the hoist cable. The helo had planned to fly away briefly. Far enough so that he could have a conversation without the thunderous sound of the helicopter. The children had run towards him too close for their comfort with the helicopter right overhead and its severe downdraft. When he turned to face them helmeted, they stopped abruptly about five paces away. Joshua appeared larger than life in his bright extra-terrestrial orange flight suit, a large blue bug-eyed rescue helmet, and the tremendous downdraft threatened to blow them over. He knew it was an unusual sight and, coupled with the horrific noise, had scared the young boys.

"Is he an angel or a demon?" yelled Silas to his siblings, though barely heard.

He tugged his sister back toward him as he clung to her and hid his face. Christina squared her shoulders and looked up at the orange-suited savior, put her hands on her brother's shoulders, and waited for him to speak. She had become the momma bear who faced an intruder on her mountain. Joshua removed his helmet and knelt on one knee to not appear so large and intimidating as the helo flew off. His size diminished when the bare head of shorter, trimmed dark hair appeared. He smiled shyly to comfort them and opened a gloved hand in a gesture of assistance.

Christina, a precocious and exhausted child, summoned her courage and marched up to Joshua. She spat out the words as her frustration and hunger overtook her sensibilities. She stuck her pointer finger in his face, shook it, and yelled at him.

"Are you with God? Did he send you? I knew help was on the way 'cause I asked you to come, but you're *really* late, and we are *really* hungry!"

Amusement erupted in Joshua's mind from the hilarity of his stern lecture from the child. He was amazed and pleased those deductions had come from such a diminutive figure with a larger-than-life personality. Calm and slow, he offered her a fist bump as a sign of peace. Next, he offered one to each of the boys. She continued to chat away as an acceptance of his appearance before he could answer.

She has endured a lot, and I need her help to get everyone home safely.

She said, "My friend, Grace, told me to ask God for whatever we needed, and my teacher, Mrs. Hill, once told me God would answer our prayers."

One boy broke in and asked, "Do you have cookies? We asked God for cookies!"

The other said, “I’m really hungry. Ya got any food?”

The first said, “Can you find our mommy and dad?”

Joshua thought, *Do I look like a take-out delivery driver?*

Joshua introduced himself and then asked their names individually. He did not have time for small chat like this, but he needed to gain their trust as part of his assessment of the situation. He also cautiously observed the rough terrain around them for a landing place. Joshua replied with a frown.

“Sorry, no cookies right now, but” he pointed upward at the helo, “I might give you a ride in a rescue helicopter.”

The boys broke into a dab dance and circled their newest hero while they pumped their arms hilariously around. He laughed to himself. He already had their trust, or the CG did.

Ah, childlike faith, he thought.

Joshua asked, “First, I’ve got to ask you a couple of questions.”

Cautiously, he continued, “Do you know where your parents are?”

Christina smugly replied, “Yes, but if you are God, don’t you already know where they are?”

Silas said quickly, “Dad slid down the mountain, and Mom’s probably still trying to find his big butt. She blew the whistle every hour last night and today all day. That way, we know she is still alive.”

Jared did not want to be outdone and added, “A Kodiak bear tried to eat us for lunch yesterday; she was HUGE,” as he flung his arms out as wide as he could, “and she had cubs, and I wanted to pet them, and Silas almost peed on them...”

At that point, Joshua cut them off and wondered what the truth from fiction was.

“Wow, quite the adventures, you’re all so brave ...so which way are your parents, if I might ask?” said Joshua.

They all pointed in one direction through the Fireweed and down the steep hill. He surmised a cliff was below them.

"The Damascus Trail goes that-a-way," pointed Christina in the opposite direction.

"How long ago was the last whistle?" Joshua asked.

Christina paused to look at her watch, "Oh, say about 30 minutes, but probably we can't hear the whistle anymore over your helicopter," she said with doubt and regarded the helo that grew closer.

Joshua knew the pilots would be impatient for good reason. They needed gas to get back.

Christina added, "She came up to find us and check on us a couple of hours ago."

She said, "Dad can't even stand, let alone walk, so they'd come up with another plan if, well..., but you're here, *finally*."

The girl pretended to pout about his tardiness to her rescue, but he saw the heavy burden lift with relief. Joshua presumed then there was no other plan. The adults stalled, like so many survivors. Little planning and no preparation made for 'what now?' It was an all-too-common scenario for people having the worst day of their lives.

Why don't people go prepared... primarily to protect others, mainly the children? thought Joshua.

"We will take you there," quipped Jared.

He confidently flexed his arm muscles and added, "She said it's really steep, but we're great climbers."

Am I willing to follow them?

Too many times, people were obstinate in his experience. They never thought they'd need help and then had too much arrogance to receive it.

Was it fear, doubt in their abilities or just pride?

He realized he needed their help as much as they needed him. Children lacked most of these frailties when they needed to be rescued. He liked that. He loved it, in fact. Joshua had lived it.

Let the children come to me.

Joshua radioed back to his crew to relay what he'd learned and that the ground was firm and clear enough for them to land. This was essential for the helo to conserve gas while Joshua and the other swimmer attempted to rescue the parents. He supposed he should let the little kids lead him to their parents and determine how to rescue them after that.

The rambunctious boys wouldn't stop their banter over Jessie and her prized cookies. He realized he vaguely remembered the café where her cookies were made, but it was a Sunday either way.

The café won't be open, and whoever Jessie is likely isn't making them cookies today. I'm not telling them that. This rescue is getting tiresome from their talkativeness, and we have barely started!

Joshua did not have the heart not to ask for the order with the kids who hung on his every word. He hoped there was a stash of something edible among the crew of his helo when it landed.

At least these kids were bright and strong. Do I have any food to offer them?

Joshua led them away from the rotator wash. The kids watched in awe at a safe distance while the Jayhawk landed precariously on the side of the mountain. Silas and Jared each took one of his hands as they knelt in the tall grasses nearby for added security. Christina covered her ears.

They are willing to follow me anywhere.

The sincere and unexpected act of trust stole Joshua's breath away.

He thought, *If you're misfortunate enough to need a rescue and staring at a rescuer, why wouldn't everyone act like these children, listen, and do what the nice rescuer told you to do?*

He radioed back to the crew, "We've got three cookie monsters that request cookies stat from some lady named Jessie. The monsters," he winked at the kids, "will take two of us to find mom and dad, who slid further down the mountain. Uncertain of location. The father is badly injured, and the mother is not. Any water and food would be appreciated, please."

He finished his radio call and nodded affirmatively at the children. They gave him huge smiles.

"We will conserve fuel and deliver the goods," was the callback.

After the helo landed, the other swimmer with more experience in these conditions than Joshua jumped out with the litter. The kids and Joshua waited at a distance. Joshua introduced him.

"This is Petty Officer 1st Class Joey Malakh. Malakh, these are our new buddies Christina, Jared, and Silas."

The children grinned and giggled. Malakh nodded while he quickly set down the litter, opened his gear bag, and offered three water bottles and glorious granola bars. The children ripped the wrappers off like they were the last candy bars on earth and inhaled them with wide grins as appreciation.

Joey asked, "What is so funny?"

Jared said, "You guys are twins, too!"

"Hey, were those mine?" Joshua teased his supervisor even while his stomach grumbled for his snack while they ate before him.

How did he know I stashed those in my overnight bag? I had only packed two, though...

"Way to be prepared, Mansoul," said the older swimmer.

He slapped his back and laughed at his expense. They grinned at one another.

They all headed through the fireweed. They acknowledged it would have been a pleasant excursion in other circumstances. Instead, the swimmers positioned the kids in between them. After about 100 yards, they found a sharp cliff face. Joshua was impressed at how the kids thought nothing of the scramble down the steep drop. He hesitated with the long orange litter for carrying an injured survivor in his hand.

"C'mon, Josh!" called Jared.

The climb down behind the kids in hiking boots was easier than he had expected. The litter he awkwardly toted one-handed was passed off to Malakh. The swimmers knew without a word between them; it would be nearly impossible to get someone who couldn't walk back up this rock face on the litter.

Why did I carry this down?

At the bottom of the cliff face, the ground became a knoll of grasses and tall brush. The kids hollered to the parents. They listened for the sound of the whistle and began in that direction. The children stopped briefly and enjoyed their new bottles of water. They continued their chatter about their overnight hunger and lack of entertainment besides a sea otter when a gruff male voice was heard in the woods below.

"It's about damn time!"

The two CG crew members immediately regarded one another with a wide-eyed look of disparagement.

Really?

"Dad, we brought rescuers," yelled Silas.

"Don't bother with me, just take them and go," was the angry reply.

At a charge, the children approached their parents through some dense underbrush.

The kids yelled over their shoulders to the crew members behind them, "Watch out for the Pushki!"

Malakh spoke only loud enough for Mansoul, "Pushki is also called Satan's celery."

Great, thought Joshua, *a tall poisonous plant and a poisoned soul on the same hike—a rescue to remember.*

Ignoring the comments, Joshua took in the scene of a huge, sullen man flat on his back with a tiny woman at about a 10-yard distance. She embraced her children in an emotional reunion for them each. She had stacked rocks like a cairn, an ancient trail marker device. They were still in use in backcountry places like this.

Marking the spot, artistic, or boredom? thought Joshua.

The quick assessment of the situation was his foremost job, and he noted the distance between the woman and the man, husband and wife lost "together." He was not surprised due to the disagreeable nature of the big guy.

Was it physical or emotional pain that caused him to shout out cruelly?

He had watched the children run to their mother for a collection of embraces but had little to no affection for their father.

Or maybe they fear him?

The mother appeared exhausted but relieved and smiled at her rescuers. She started towards them with the kids attached to her sides.

She said, "I'm Miriam. How can I thank you enough?"

The crew began to approach her first, but she joined them near her husband, and they all awkwardly circled the man. Sam rubbed his eyes as she introduced him.

Joshua replied, "I'm Joshua Mansoul, a CG rescue swimmer, and this is Joey Malakh..."

Sam spat, "I don't want your help; I'll make it off this mountain alone!"

His eyes narrowed toward the CG members as if he tried to threaten them from flat on his back. He was a pitiful sight as they looked down on a man who couldn't save himself if he tried, let alone threaten anyone else.

What had gotten ahold of him? Was he delirious with pain or always just a jerk? thought Joshua.

After his rudeness, even the children silently stepped back with their mother, and the crew followed them about 30 yards into the sunshine and out of earshot.

Miriam said, "I'm sorry you all had to hear that. I, for one, have done a lot of wheelin' and dealin' with the Master, I suppose, to get out of here. Thank you for coming for us. I can't imagine how you found us, but I'm grateful. You tell me exactly what to do."

Joshua smiled at the woman, full of compassion for this situation, but knew the helicopter couldn't wait forever. Once again, time was not on their side.

The crew got an abrupt message, "Fuel is low. Clouds are rolling in off the water again. Hurry this evacuation up. 15 to bingo."

Joshua and Joey, the other swimmer, knew they needed to move pronto. Bingo was the last moment they had to leave to return with the fuel that remained in the aircraft. Joshua had learned before he could be left behind.

I don't want to be left out here, especially since the kids ate my snack.

Joshua looked over the mountain towards the sea to verify what they had been too distracted to discern. He and the swimmer decided to split up. Malakh, the other swimmer, took the children and mother to consider where they could safely lower a litter carrier down to the patient and a rescue basket for the family. One thing was for sure: they could not possibly carry the huge man up and over the cliff they had just come down on a litter. They heard the helo as it transitioned to flight off in the distance. Joshua braced himself and strode to the man he'd learned was Sam.

Joshua sat down hard beside the man and began, "Hey buddy, I'm not telling you what to do, but if I were one of those great kids of yours and about to take the best ride of my life, I'd want my dad along for the memory."

After a long, silent pause, Sam turned his head away as if the conversation was over. Some survivors embraced their destruction. It was a condition of the soul as long as the history of the world. When what little they could control was threatened, their reason ceased.

Joshua said, "I wish I had more great memories with my dad. Why don't you take 30 seconds while we hoist your family and wrestle whatever demon... or angel you've been wrestling with for so long and leave the carnage on this mountain? Then, accept the grace of a free lift courtesy of your hard-earned tax dollars to go home with your family and have a good memory."

Sam snarled at him and said, "Do you not understand how humiliating it will be to be known as the big guy who had to be rescued off this little hike with his kids and wife? This is a small town, man, and you get to leave, but I'll never live this down the rest of my life... I don't need a miniature punk like you to tell me what to do."

Instead of the reaction Sam had wanted, Joshua calmly said, "So, your answer is no?"

He patted the man's arm like he would have a tiny child, stood, and walked away.

Brawn, hard-heartedness, fear, and ridicule. Oh, Samson...

Joshua mourned another lost man as he walked on to rescue the others. Miriam marched over to her husband after she agreed to whatever Joey had suggested. They passed each other with grim, deliberate nods like people share at a funeral. She had seen that Joshua had not convinced her husband of the error of his ways. She knew this might be her last conversation with her first great love and father of her treasured children. She was so torn, but she knew that her enablement of him hadn't worked.

She said, "You can crawl down this mountain on your arms face first and let the trail rescue team find you, but you'll be an even sorrier mess then. Or dead. Why are you so incensed to receive help?"

She knelt and kissed his forehead goodbye. She stood and turned away. She lifted her hand as if in a final wave of remorse as a tear slid down her cheek. She focused instead on the rescue of their children. She turned away from him for the sake of her sanity and her children. The little boys couldn't stand to see the rescuer and their mother turn their backs on their father. Children know no difference and relish the thought of their parent's heroism, even in their apparent weaknesses. They rushed headlong to him as they realized he may not join them. They jumped on him before he could yell out against them. Jared thrust his Nalgene water bottle toward him as he spoke.

"Dad, you said not to finish this water until we got home, and I haven't. I did what you said even though I was sooooo thirsty all day, and all night, and all day again. I will be just like you and as strong as you someday, see?"

He flexed his tiny arms.

Jared continued, "You can have my water 'cause the Guardian angels brought me more, so we can go home together, right?"

His eyes searched and implored him. They went to the bottle with just one or two swallows of water left inside. The water was back-washed with bits of orange Cheeze-its, and a few raisins floated on top. Sam looked at his son and back at the tepid water mixture. Something in him snapped. He closed his eyes.

Silas exclaimed, "Dad, are you dead?"

Samson realized, *it must have taken a lot of self-control not to finish that water off the night before... or all day in the hot sun. When will I learn that kind of control? Especially over my anger? I have so much to learn from my little boy for such a big man.*

Sam took the bottle and painfully unscrewed the top, raised it a bit to look at the raisins from beneath since he was flat on his back, and gave his son a questioning look.

Jared said sheepishly, “Silas put raisins inside and thought it would make grape juice.”

Sam nodded towards Silas, who knelt next to them both. Samson tilted it towards them as if he were about to toast the thoughts of hope and admiration they shared.

Sam raised it and said, “Cheers.”

Sam grimaced and poured the sacred water and bits over his mouth that gaped open. He took a second to swallow it and closed his eyes again briefly. Before the boys could react, he pulled Jared and Silas closer and put his hands on their shoulders in a painful squeeze for him, but gently on their small frames. The new development bewildered the swimmers, Christina and Miriam. Sam laid his head back, folded his hands over his broad stomach, and stared hard at the sky for several painfully awkward moments.

He said in a bold voice for all to hear, “You think you all can carry me out of here? It’s going to take more might than you think.”

At that comment, the CG swimmers suddenly jumped and retrieved the backboard to put Sam onto it. They were glad they’d carried it down with them after all. A 300-pound-plus man would take some heft to lift and carry between them. They looked at one another, grateful they were both there. It was rare to have two swimmers onboard, and this was still no easy task for them both. They raced the clock.

Wherever two or more are gathered... thought Joshua.

"On a count of three, lift. One, Two, THREE," said Joshua.

Sam was heaved, pulled, and finally put onto the litter. With his tiny wife and daughter on one side and twins who had their hands alongside, too, doing their best but only really slowed the process, they did it together. Joshua knew they would remember these events forever, so he did not preclude them from the rescue of their dad. Joshua and the other swimmer, Joey, needed every bit of superpower they could muster to get the enormous man over to the cleared spot for the hoist. They watched one another as if in a mirror and worked together. They cautiously strained every muscle in their bodies to heave the weight of the colossal man.

This is why we work out every day. This is why we train. This is Semper Paratus.

Sam was set down in a cleared spot to await a hoist into the helicopter. It hovered loud, far above them until Joshua signaled to approach them. Joshua raised one arm and extended it vertically with his palm open-faced forward. The other arm was raised so that it crossed his head and touched the extended arm at the elbow. It was the swimmer's signal for 'deploy rescue litter.'

While he signaled, Joshua thought, *There is strength in numbers.*

Joshua looked up. The USCG letters grew closer, and the thunderous ricocheted sound pounded in rhythm with his heart.

If I hadn't experienced what I had with my dad, I don't think I could have said what I did.

Grateful the mech was ready to begin the hoist, he and the other swimmer prepared to secure the man on the ground and prepare him for the hoist. It was another arduous task to get Sam into the rescue litter. The sun had dropped in the sky by then to cast a beautiful 10 p.m. sunset that glowed across the sky with clouds that encroached. Joshua went at a run to assemble everything lowered to him. He was glad to be under the watchful eye of his comrade, the more experienced swimmer. It was a comfort to Joshua to know he was guarded and for the second set of hands.

They and the rest of the family watched Sam disappear into the side of the CG helo that hovered above them. They all breathed a sigh of relief and exhaustion. The night air had cooled, and he could see the children shivered under the fierce winds of the helo. Next came the rescue basket. Joshua placed the boys next to each other on one end and Christina opposite them, backpacks clutched in the middle. Christina motioned wildly for them to wait. She unzipped her backpack to check for Otto and gave Joshua a big grin and a thumbs up. The thunder of the rotator noise precluded any spoken words. The boys' looks went from enthusiastic to apprehensive as they lifted off the ground. They had come to love and trust Joshua's big, toothy smile and good nature, so he wanted to wave as if they were on an amusement park ride. He knew better, as his hand signals were of utmost value to the coordination of their rescue efforts. They soared over the land and waved goodbye as they were pulled into the sky as cloud riders. Miriam followed by herself. Joshua quickly strapped himself onto the cable and enjoyed the ride up and off the mountain in the softened Kodiak light.

He thought, *You never know what the day will bring or, more accurately, who it will bring.*

Malakh came in last. Finally, inside the cramped cabin of the helo, Joshua assessed the situation of each of his new passengers. The mech had left the boys positioned together in a belt. They were wide-eyed, but they pumped their fists in the air in a non-verbal show of support for all the efforts on their behalf. They were excited to be on their way home in the powerful rescue vehicle. Miriam and Christina were practically sitting on each other but hugged tightly as if they'd have done so, no matter how much room was available. They were strapped in the swimmer's usual seat on a bench beside the mech. Still on the litter, Sam reached for Christina's tiny hand in a show of perhaps remorse for his previous actions, comfort for them both, and love without words. Joshua knew only those with headsets could hear him.

He spoke, "Anybody responsible for my granola bars? I need one after how much we had to pick up and carry down there. Maybe a record, you think, Malakh?"

Malakh, humble as always, shrugged and grinned back.

The co-pilot could not resist the jab and asked, "So, Mansoul, did you earn your wages today?"

The commander said, "Welcome to Kodiak," without expectation of an answer.

The co-pilot said, "What a turn of events from a familiarization flight to a family flight!"

Joshua sat curled up and felt his muscles involuntarily constrict.

He thought, *it's good to be home for as long as this is my home.*

The cabin grew very dark as they made their way across the island. The remarkable thundering of the engine and the gear that rattled were of comfort to the crew. However, Joshua noticed it had become tremendously frightening. He remembered those without headsets were unused to the tumultuous ride in a cradle of salvation. They were all jostled violently back and forth at moments.

What can I do to give them assurance in the dark?

Joshua sensed the fear that crept into the children. He reached over to the bag of unique seaworthy personnel marker lights (glow sticks) every crew carried.

"Crew, do you think it'd be alright to have a Jedi battle back here to entertain the young Padawans? We might save ourselves a good bit of clean-up later if I can distract them," said Joshua.

No one likes to end an extended mission and clean up someone else's vomit.

"Roger that," the pilots replied together.

He popped one neon green glow stick and handed it to Jared. The light lit up the whole cabin with a bright, eerie glow that was somewhat odd and a comfort. He popped a second open and handed it to Silas, who by then open-handedly grasped for one of his own to hold. He snapped a third and tried to give it to Christina, who rested her head under her mother's chin and waved it away to snuggle instead. He took the last one into both of his hands at the bottom of it. He began to swing it back and forth like Luke Skywalker in an epic *Star Wars* battle. The kid's spirits were revived, and their faces held smiles from ear to ear. The emotions were high due to exhaustion and dissolved into laughter and giggles as they fought back the darkness and fear. Though unheard above the din, their laughter was contagious amongst the whole crew. The sun had nearly been eclipsed by darkness by then, but light had won the day.

They touched down minutes later at the Air Station Kodiak. The door to the cabin was rolled back, and the crew climbed out first. The expectation was only for an awaiting ambulance as per the standard procedures. They were all surprised to see the hangar door stood wide open. A small crowd had gathered, which was enormously unusual for middle-of-the-night duty. The family crawled individually, dazed with exhaustion, to the cabin door. When they turned towards the hangar, they were deliriously mesmerized by the friends and CG members who cheered and waved them over. Miriam waited with her husband as the ambulance crew approached with a gurney to wheel him to a parked ambulance. She permitted the crew to take the children to the surprise party that awaited them.

Christina, dizzy with fatigue, said, "What is it?"

Malakh picked up her and her brothers and set them on the ground outside the helicopter. They all turned to see the bright lights that poured out from the large hangar doors. The people looked tiny in the shadow of the enormous hangar but waved wildly.

Malakh winked at Joshua and said, "Manna."

Christina recognized her friend, Grace, and her "bazillion" siblings who were there. She ran as fast as her little legs would carry her and broke away from her rescuers. Mrs. Hill, Jessie, her dad's boss, and many other CG people she had never met welcomed Christina and her family with open arms. Just as she leaned into a hug from her favorite teacher, Mrs. Hill, she smelled and saw the giant cookie in Grace's hand. She pulled back, shocked. Her stomach rumbled.

Christina said, "Where did you get that?"

Grace said, "Right over there, silly."

She gestured behind her where an eight-foot table had been set up with what looked like 100 giant café cookies and ice cream, too. Christina saw her brothers with one giant cookie in each hand, one in their mouths, and had eyes to try to pick up more. They nodded with mouths full that they also wanted ice cream to a CG member.

Relieved there was plenty for her, too, she said to Grace, "Thank you for helping me!"

She smacked her lips and started toward the desserts.

Grace quizzically said, "What did I do? I just found out like 30 minutes ago you were even missing."

Grace took another bite of her cookie while she shrugged like it was no big thing.

Christina giggled, "I meant you told me how to ask God for help before I needed him."

Grace said, "Cool," with a mouth full of gooey chocolate chip cookie and smiled.

It was so big she had chocolate smeared on either cheek. Then she turned their attention fully to the cookie table. Mrs. Hill and Jessie watched as she surveyed all the cookies and paused with wonder at which to take. It was like children before the presents under the Christmas tree.

Jessie caught her eyes and said, "Girlfriend, after we realized you were missing, I haven't stopped baking since. You can have as many as you want!"

Christina went around the table and gave her a big hug first.

Christina's energy returned, and she exclaimed, "Thanks, Jessie, I love church with you. Even in the middle of the night!"

Jessie received the hug and glanced at Mrs. Hill with a raised eyebrow. They both shrugged. Christina preferred ice cream. She looked at the far end of the table and motioned to a giant bowl of deliciousness with adoration in her eyes. Mrs. Hill noticed and was delighted. She remembered her student's love of the local Mission's specialty homemade ice cream. She was pleased she'd brought it, especially for her.

Mrs. Hill stroked Christina's head and had misty eyes that threatened to spill over.

She spoke, "I did not forget my favorite student liked ice cream best."

She gave Christina a big, squeezy hug. Then she gestured toward the ice cream toppings and offered sprinkles on top. Nodding voraciously, Christina accepted the delicious gift, and Mrs. Hill winked at her in that generous way she frequently did. When Christina had been in her class the previous year, she winked only when she mentioned the Lord. This time, it seemed different, like they had an unspoken secret coupled with gratitude. Christina liked being in on that expression almost as much as the delectable ice cream.

Wheeled closer for Sam and Miriam to see what was happening, they made a roundabout way to the ambulance. The kids were motioned over for a short goodbye before he was rolled away. Sam gestured for a cookie to inhale. Jessie laughed out loud and handed Miriam a takeaway box packed for the apparent trip to the local hospital. Sam motioned Joshua to his side as he was rolled to the vehicle for transport to the hospital. Without his helmet, Joshua could more clearly focus on the once distraught man who smiled despite his pain.

Samson spoke quietly enough for only Joshua to hear, "You were right."

"About what, sir?" responded Joshua.

He wiped his hand over his stubbled chin to clear it of crumbs. He leaned forward to hear the quiet words Sam was about to say with genuine interest.

"I did wrestle on that mountain. With the given name Samson, I've been expected my whole life to be bigger and stronger than everyone else. The older I got, the more afraid I got of my weakness. Even though I didn't know what it was going to be exactly. Eventually, I turned to anger, I think."

Joshua added, "You think?"

Sam paused to look at the sun that had begun to light the sky, a soft pink color on the horizon already in the wee hours of Monday morning.

Sam continued, "I found my weakness up there and realized it might be my greatest strength simultaneously."

Joshua just gazed down at the giant of a man and listened patiently to him as he tried carefully to find the words.

"My kid obeying me when he didn't have to.... He's gonna be just like me, I know it. That "juice" he gave me... it was bittersweet."

His voice was choked with tears. He offered his hand to Joshua in an awkward hand grab from a laying position.

Joshua returned the offer of a hand grasp and said, “So your answer to our offer of rescue went from no to yes because...?”

Sam paused and then responded hesitantly at first.

“From now on, I choose to be weak to be strong. I can still be big ol’ Samson ...who’s so big he can accept help when offered.”

Joshua spoke, “Like me, it’s a father’s love for his son that rescued you.”

A tear worked its way down Samson’s face unashamedly, and he smiled for the first time in memory. Joshua squeezed his hand once more and then let go with admiration. The gurney was pushed away and into the ambulance. Miriam squeezed his arm and mouthed the words thank you. She skipped with her box of cookies and their backpacks slung over her shoulder to keep up with her husband. Joshua watched and dropped his shoulders, relieved to hand over the man’s care to someone else. Approached from behind Joshua, a man’s arm went around his shoulder. Joshua turned to see a dim face that peered at him, clearly though a CG officer of senior rank.

“Nice work out there, son. Pretty good first mission for a rookie in Kodiak!”

He slapped his back with good nature. Joshua spun unexpectedly toward him to salute. Joshua read his name sign off his flight suit and recalled having met Padre during his TDY. He tilted his head, slightly embarrassed by the praise.

Joshua smiled and said, “Thank you, sir, for the opportunity of a lifetime. You find them, and we’ll redeem them.”

“I’ll look out for more men the size of Kodiaks and be sure you’re the one on duty. Samson may be one for the record books,” replied Padre with a laugh, “Carry on, you deserve a cookie.”

Joshua nodded in compliance and took a massive bite of the oatmeal raisin cookie he still held behind his back. He tasted it for the first time. The boys were right; he tasted it and knew it was good. The men walked over to the little crowd of all the CG members included at that time of night for a surprise celebration of cookies and ice cream. That kind of daybreak festivity was extraordinary, let alone the 1 a.m. sunrise for Joshua.

Well, there was evening... and then there was morning.

Chapter 15

SERENITY IN THE STORM

Joshua had climbed Kodiak's seven (road-accessible) highest mountain summits within a year. He had eaten far too many of Jessie's cookies, became an Alaskan fisherman, and made great, memorable lifetime moments over a few months. He participated in some frosty cold medical evacuations (medevacs), found lost hunters who were rescued just in time, and did other meaningful CG work. He had begun to volunteer at the local Mission in town in his downtime. The people there taught him, a city boy, many new things about how to live off the land, farm animals, and care for nature. He came into his own as a man on a mission while being part of the CG Mission. There was room for the convergence of his vocation and his avocation. He treasured it. He was a rescuer at heart and enjoyed life most with others on the same path of saving others, great and small. A few friends also visited or stopped in on their TDYs in Alaska.

Joshua said, "What a view... I think I can see mainland Alaska from here."

Ben said doubtfully, "No, you can't."

Ben plopped on the ground. He dumped his water bottle contents down his throat and emptied the bottle while sweat poured off his brow. Joshua neglected to tell his old friend, Ben, who had come to Kodiak on leave from another CG Station, that he'd hiked this trail more times than he could count already. Ben was *Semper Paratus* for an adventure, but not always quite *Semper Paratus* in shape for them.

Joshua added, "I thought you said you'd be ready for a marathon next time we met?"

Ben leaned back as if he were prepared to take a nap right there on the rocky ground. Joshua took a few photos with his cell phone but knew he'd have to wait to send them to anyone. Everyone was without cell service in this remoteness. There was a local competition for those who climbed and took photos for proof at the top. He wanted Ben to experience the thrill of the steep incline and spectacular views in every direction. He wasn't prepared that Ben would wish to nap at the top.

I should have known, surmised Joshua.

Swimmers sometimes challenged one another to run up and down these trails. One day every year, they tried to do all seven summits back-to-back. That wasn't necessarily fun for everyone, but it was a challenge.

"Do you want to eat lunch here atop Pillar or head back for a swim?" teased Joshua.

"Swim in the Pacific, here? You can do that?"

"Could and should are two different statements," Joshua answered.

"You're saying it's not unauthorized but highly discouraged," said Ben.

He added, "Ha. I'd love a swim now, but by the time we return, I want one or a dozen of those famous cookies after some fresh salmon for dinner. How many can we catch each day?"

Joshua said, "We can swim in the CG pool this weekend. They keep it pretty cool for training. The parents of the kids in swim lessons complain a lot, but it's not really for kids or the faint of heart. We train in that pool every weekday.

Did I tell you about the Christmas event when we swim the families around the pool in the Zodiac boats?"

"Wait, you swim them around how?" asked Ben.

"The families come to the pool to see the Christmas Decorations. They're all clothed regularly. Lights, music, people dressed in costumes, hot cocoa, and a movie plays while they wait their turn, the works. We swimmers power the boats and push them around the edge while in the water. The guests parade around the edge of the pool in the boats together. It's so great. Kids will remember that forever, I hope. I know I would've."

"You guys certainly make your fun up here. Now, tell me about the girls. Any around here? I asked what the limit was..."

Joshua rolled his eyes at Ben.

One track mind, thought Joshua.

He said, "Girls are limited. So are the salmon."

Joshua changed the subject, "I'll tell you about my runs. See that curvy road we drove up here to the foot of this mountain? We had a road race up and down from the Bear Valley Golf Course to the gravel lot where we parked the truck. It's called 'Run the Rock' and is a sweet 5K uphill and the opposite 5K right back down. Have you ever taken a jog in Bear Country, Ben? We should probably do that tomorrow. You'd love it, right?"

Not to be sidetracked, Ben said, "If you can bring some girls, you know I can outrun you from the bears...and probably the girls."

They started to share a good laugh when the rocks beneath them began to bounce. Birds rose away from the earth around them. At first, the earth began to rumble, but within two seconds, maybe three, the ground bobbed beneath them. Ben jumped to his feet wide-eyed in fear and threw his arms out to either side to steady himself. Joshua planted his feet in a wide stance to not fall off the high precipice they stood on. He had seen with his own eyes the damage that would have caused.

He spoke to Ben, "Earthquake."

Ben's face went white, and he said, "No joke, Dumbledore."

The rumbles and groans of the earth's movement snapped trees, and they crashed over to the earth. Some began to slide down the mountain face. In the remote place, it went eerily quiet as birds stopped their bird song. They listened intently to the rocks that ground against each other; all the while, Joshua silently counted how long it lasted.

...8, 9, 10. He turned his eyes out to sea to look for a wave.

"When will it stop?" asked Ben in shock.

As if the question commanded the cessation, all of nature seemed to stop. What had previously been a typical day felt like an exhilarating battle. The men stood at the highest point around them and contemplated the situation and their shared experience.

"That was one part thrill and one part terror. Will it happen again?" inquired Ben.

Ben had only arrived on the island days before and was unfamiliar with what the local earthquake experience could be. Since he was stationed on the other side of the Pacific, known as the Ring of Fire, on the west coast of the U.S., he, too, often felt small tremors caused by the shifts in tectonic plates. He had never felt this violently shaken, however.

"I'm not sure I want to feel a bigger one than that. Ever," said Ben.

"I wonder if a tsunami will form. That's more dangerous than the quake. We are safe up here from it, but not the Base. Perhaps we should head down. I know there will be a recall soon, and I need to be able to answer. Good thing I let my roommate know where we were headed," said Joshua.

"Yeah, I heard you tell him that, and I figured he was mothering you. Weirdo," said Ben.

"Nope, up here in Alaska, you always tell someone where you're headed for reasons like th..."

A wail, unlike Ben had ever heard, suddenly started to sound way off in the distance. It was an automated siren that began close to the Base and spread as if in surround sound through the valleys far below. They heard more sirens, which added to the wail. It came from the north and south, and soon, they blended in an ominous dissonance.

Ben spoke, "That must be way loud to hear it up here. Where does it come from?"

"Wow. That's the tsunami alarm, and it's so not a Wednesday," said Joshua.

"What does that mean?" asked Ben.

Joshua said, "We need to split from here. I'll tell you all about it on the way down. It's the warning system the whole island has for getting to higher ground because either a tsunami is on its way ashore or could be imminent. The tsunamis after the Good Friday earthquake in 1964 took out entire towns. They don't mess around with them in Alaska. That alarm normally sounds for one minute every Wed. at 2 p.m. as a test. Let me tell you how annoyed I've been to finally crash after a long duty and have that wake me up. Now, I'm grateful."

"Wait up, this part is like a vertical descent. I'm not gonna hurry if the rocks will cry out again like that," said Ben.

"Ben, can you eat while we descend?" asked Joshua.

"Mansoul, you know I can eat almost anytime, but not while I'm using my hands to climb down to get off this pyramid."

Joshua said, "I'll wait down here below you and take some time to watch the water. Those fishermen may get quite the ride if the wave is big. Better for boats to be in the open water than ashore."

"Hey, I want to eat my pickles while you go first. I've craved them since I packed them. This is a memorable day, Joshua. You sure know how to welcome me from out of town. You planned the whole Alaskan experience, eh?" quipped Ben.

"Sure. We'll be faster going down, and I am interested in seeing the CG response from up here. If you're extra fortunate, maybe we'll find a grizzly on our way back."

Ben went wide-eyed, "Ha. Ha. I remember what you told me that caused."

Only a few minutes later, the guys watched most of the CG aircraft get launched to survey any damage, recovery efforts if a tsunami were to hit, and for the practicality of getting the CG assets out of harm's way. It did not take the guys long to find the bottom of the trail. They slogged their way through the mud.

Joshua called, "Ben, you're jogging!"

"Very funny. Do I get a free t-shirt or just a cookie?"

About two and a half hours later, an all-clear was given. They realized the silence was deafening after they had to listen to the shrill sirens for the duration. When the threat of a tsunami threatened to spill over its banks, everyone lived on edge. *Semper Paratus*, Always Ready, never meant more than that day for the whole town and the base. Especially when the CG was not for strangers unawares, but for their very own friends and family who lived precariously at the edge of the Pacific Ocean, they were ready to answer their call.

After eighteen months, Joshua was invited to be part of the annual Christmas Live Nativity held at the Christian Mission each December. He was in the crowd the previous year while the story of Jesus' birth was reenacted. Townspeople of various ages had dressed in first-century garb, stood in the stable, and looked calm with the farm animals that surrounded them. When Mary, Joseph, and the baby Jesus finally appeared, the crowd collectively gazed at the baby in the scene's serenity. A choir of angels sang quietly from above them in the barn's loft. Stars shone down, and a special memory was made that Joshua cherished in his Alaskan collection of memories. He did not collect things but observations and a keen awareness of timeless significance.

Joshua presumed: *How hard can it be? I'll take a turn so someone else can enjoy that moment as much as I did.*

He answered, "Yes."

When he could, he always wanted to be of help.

It's who I am, after all. This will be the most straightforward request ever.

Within a few days, Joshua was confounded.

What is happening? he struggled to understand.

He and his friend Jakob, who had also been recruited as a shepherd, wrestled with a horned goat and a pesky sheep in a stable dressed as first-century shepherds. Joshua had worn plenty of fleece to stay warm outdoors on a cold Alaskan night. On top of that was a first-century costume robe and long, draped headpiece. He quickly became aware of his mistake when he began to sweat profusely. The sheep and goats became unruly and began to "baa" loudly while quiet, beautiful strains of "O Holy Night" wafted over the crowd of amused onlookers.

I don't remember if the shepherds held horned sheep last year...

He and some teenage boys, unaware of the danger ahead, had also been drafted into stable service. They, not as strong as Joshua, lost their restraint on the distressed stable animals. This was much to the hilarity of the onlookers. They almost controlled the idyllic scene until a harmless chicken began to squawk and awkwardly tried to fly away.

"Watch out, Mary!" said a tall, skinny shepherd that cast his staff aside to retrieve it.

The clatter of the staff on the stable wall made a sheep from a small shepherd's arms launch from safety, and it crashed loudly into the manger.

"Get back here," said the small shepherd boy to his scared sheep, who began to bleat obnoxiously.

The shepherd chased the sheep around the stable. Mother Mary leaped up to protect her newborn baby, and the manger fell over, as did the log she had been perched on. That got the choir's attention in the hay loft overhead, but they continued and missed only a beat or two while they wondered what had happened below. The goat Joshua had already restrained bucked back and set Joshua on his backside. His arms surrounded the goat's neck, which put his head precariously close to the goat's horns. The sprawled goat's legs took out the sheep's calm stance next to them, which sent it into the teen that grasped him. A cow began to moo as if it wanted to join the chorus of animal sounds. Like dominoes, the shepherds all started to struggle with the animals they were supposed to have silently kept watch over.

The crowd's laughter almost drowned out the choir at one point. Mary leaned onto Joseph's shoulder in a protective stance as his arms surrounded her and the babe. "O Holy Night" finished in the background, but next was "Silent Night." The disarray of chickens, goats, sheep, and a cow were all collected with grace by farmhands, some in costume and others not, by the end of the song. It was not lost on anyone that the crowd stayed longer than usual to see the mayhem brought under control.

Through it all, Joshua marveled that the Joseph figure remained calm and steadfast while he held his arms around Mary and the babe. His face was serene and, if anything, pleasantly good-humored about the madness that occurred all around them. Mary kept her eyes on the babe and only glanced at Joseph for reassurance. The first night of the Christ child's life was more like this than silent.

Joshua considered, *Joseph would have been a great rescue swimmer. He was calm under pressure, and he had undoubtedly helped to rescue humankind.*

One day, three years into his four-year tour, Joshua recognized it was spring. In Kodiak, a sign of spring was people had taken the chains off their tires to drive back and forth to town. The icy conditions for six months of the year encouraged big vehicles and fortified others to add traction to their tires. Joshua learned the hard way to wear shoes with shoe tracks for ice in parking lots that more closely resembled the local ice-skating rink. Joshua exhaled from his long third Alaskan winter. The weather still seemed to be winter to him due to his years in Eastern North Carolina and Texas of his youth. The sun was welcomed back from its respite of only being present a few hours a day. Through the winters, the sun had carved an arc in the sky just over the horizon. Most people had taken long lunch hours if they could, just for the benefit of daylight. Seasonal Affective Disorder was real at latitudes this far North, and Joshua could feel his spirit yearn for the light of day even more than the previous year. The snow had begun to melt, and the trails were technically accessible, but mud seemed to suck boots and gear into the earth. When it appeared, the sunshine lasted about ten minutes longer every day in spring. The whole earth and its inhabitants seemed excited to be turned back toward the glorious sun.

Joshua decided that after he had saved up, he'd take one of the "mail runs" to the outer villages and very remote places where the mail was delivered by seaplane. It was an authentic Alaskan adventure. It topped his list of Kodiak's exploits. He enjoyed his introduction to some folks who lived off the grid but was saddened at their choice to live outside the community. A bi-weekly mail run, which delivered mail, eggs, and produce, seemed unnatural. Something about the remoteness was formidable and yet sacred simultaneously. They broke their beneficiary's reveries and landed the float plane near rafts of sea otters on mirrored bays of the vast Pacific.

"See you again..." was each recipient's pronouncement as they accepted the blessings bestowed upon them.

No, I won't. Unless you decide you need the mission of the CG or other relationships, thought Joshua.

Kodiak had a couple of extraordinary places for their acclaimed bald eagles. The fish canneries collected their 'gold' from the sea, canned, and later dumped the waste. The vast number of eagles were sometimes called "trash birds" due to their prevalence around town and their preference for the canneries' easy pickings. The eagles were soon headed to other places, just like Joshua. They went north, but he had orders to head south.

Joshua had been given notice that he was being sent to the advanced helicopter rescue school (AHRS). AHRS was a week-long training in Astoria, Oregon, where he would have intensive training on crew coordination during the roughest ocean conditions. Air Station Astoria was there as well. AHRS was located along the Oregon coast because it consistently had the tremendously irregular seas that the school used for training in high surf, caves, and cliff rescues. Joshua already knew that crew coordination was essential for the mission's success. He was pleased when he learned that some of his previous Elizabeth City tour crewmembers would join him there.

He had a text from Jordan that read: Missed me yet? Let's get some more training behind us!

He replied: It's never as much fun to go it alone. I've got some crazy stories for you!

Jordan texted: I hear we're in for some wild water. Let's make history.

How well the CG worked together often determined the outcome and their resiliency afterward. Naturally, they all wanted a good outcome, and to succeed at the new training was crucial to their careers and character. However, success in the CG did not always mean smooth seas, but that's not what they were called into. A Coast Guard rescue crew was undoubtedly a team event, and no one made a rescue alone. The course was required after graduation from AST. Even if it wasn't needed, everyone wanted in on the fun that was known as AHRS. Because each class was just five days long, there were only certain days that the classes were given throughout the year.

Once aboard Alaska Airlines and headed south to the Oregon coast, Joshua wondered,

Will it be any milder there farther south, or is the cold Pacific churning?

The point was to head into tumultuous weather, and he shuddered slightly with excitement at what he would find.

That's the school's reputation: We should get there as often as possible for excellent cave work and whatever the sea can throw at us.

Chapter 16

HOPE IS A PERSON

Astoria, Oregon

"Class, class, class," announced Commander Ruth Kodesh. "During the next five days, you will encounter the roughest water the Coast Guard can train you in. We exist to prepare you for the most physically and mentally demanding trials you have yet to be part of. The water temperature is colder than cold. You will wear your dry suits this time of year, but it will make your swims, climbs, and rappels more strenuous. You will be tested to your limits and exhaust yourself entirely. Do not make big plans for the weekend: you have been advised."

Ruth Kodesh was one of the most experienced pilots in the United States Coast Guard and did not mince words with her new trainees. At 5'4" tall with a slight build, her presence did not command as much respect as her reputation. She was renowned for her calm under pressure, during which she and her crews had saved countless survivors after hurricanes, storms, and disciplined maneuvers. She, in turn, was asked to be their instructor and fly with them in the courses. She put her strong influence into words and actions.

Kodesh knew that some pilots and rescue swimmers were full of bravado and notoriously narcissistic. In her estimation, most may have put on that manner, but deep down, they were almost identical. They needed desperately to be needed. Their self-esteem waxed and waned on their essentialness to the missions at hand. Therefore, to make them *Semper Paratus*, Always Ready, she wanted them to feel the weight of the objective of the course. She wanted them to be the best they individually could and be trained under her tutelage to prepare them to work collectively. They swore to rescue men and women of the United States and others who found themselves in its territory on the worst day of their lives.

The desired outcome was that their worst day would become their best due to the training and counsel Kodesh and her school staff had given them that week. As an introvert, she gave critiques and reproofs with a few words when needed. Nevertheless, those who understood she was a coach and mentor appreciated her tenacity and toughness. Some found her insensitive and intolerant to the community in general for the expectation of strict obedience to the CG procedures that were time-tested and proven. If bossy was a practical term, she may have been just that because almost everyone wanted her as their boss. Kodesh got her pilot's nickname "Ghost" from many prominent rescues. It was as if her counsel helped them determine what to do every time and hadn't let anyone down. She wanted it to stay that way.

No hard lessons should go to waste on my watch. That would be the failure of the mission, she thought.

Joshua had anticipated being part of this advanced training for a long time, ever since he had learned about it in AST school at ECity.

He thought, *I can hardly believe I'm back in class with so little notice. I've dreamt of it for so long. I'm so stoked to be with friends from Air Station ECity again.*

Jordan Roi saw Joshua first and excitedly clapped him on the shoulder.

She began her usual rapid-fire conversational questions, "Where's the Alaskan bushy beard I see on *Deadliest Catch*?"

She prattled on, "I thought all you've done is fish? Did you bring me salmon, snow, sea glass?"

Joshua had missed her constant chatter sometimes. In Kodiak's soupy weather, he called her to listen to her share her stories. She was like sunshine in those weeks of overcast and gloomy weather. He regaled them with Alaskan stories, careful not to seem braggadocious. Not everyone had gotten their top choice of assignments. He understood Alaska was a coveted assignment for some and torture for others. At times, the assignments officer seemed to know more than they let on and made wise choices even if CG members were initially bewildered by their orders.

Joshua told them, "One time, some kids were rescued off a giant unicorn float."

"No way, a pool toy in the North Pacific?" said Jordan.

"Yep, I couldn't make this stuff up," said Joshua with a smirk and added, "They even had their dog on it with them. They crashed up on some rocks before they sailed to Russia."

"Did they have proper Coast Guard-approved life vests on and a paddle?" asked another Guardian and slapped Joshua's back in laughter.

"Nope, but I hope they will from now on," he said.

When the subject matter of rescue from a swimmer's perspective was brought up immediately at AHRS, Joshua couldn't help but remember the motto drilled into him throughout his previous training. Rescue Swimmers exist "so others may live." So far in his short career, the hot washes or debriefs seemed just as complex as the rescues.

Will my career be tanked over the responses of survivors unprepared to join me and prevent themselves from being rescued?

He knew that every rescue depended on the responses of the survivors. Whenever he was called upon, he didn't ask many questions. He responded in the best way he knew how, with preparation. Joshua understood that he would have men and women, young and old, be at his complete mercy to save them. He was stunned that some had refused the aid he and others offered, particularly at the cost of themselves and their country. He had not fully comprehended what it would be like to be rebuked and rebuffed for his willingness to be rejected. In discussion with other swimmers and CG members, he had learned that the survivor's answer had all too often eliminated the opportunity for them to save lives expediently. Instead of survivors, they were victims of the prison of their minds, which all too often led to their demise and the demise of those they were with. The question lingered in Joshua's mind like an annoying mosquito in a hot tent.

Will I get bitten again?

How do I persevere physically, mentally, and emotionally to be the only hope that these people may ever have?

Not far away from Joshua that same week sat Molek, an eighth-grade boy with an attitude of ingratitude. He was wedged between his younger siblings on a family trip to Cape Disappointment State Park in Washington State. The Cape was situated on the border between Washington and Oregon, where the Columbia River flowed into the Pacific. The giant river poured into the Pacific and, combined with the rough winds and cliff faces, created spectacular scenery and training opportunities for the CG. For Molek, the jaggedness was inside the vehicle with sibling rivalries over snacks, music choices, and who touched who.

"Really, Mom? The World Kite Museum and Hall of Fame? Can I sit in the car?" said Molek.

He thought, *The car is stifling, but better to sit in silence finally than be seen with my annoying half-siblings.*

"I thought there was going to be more adventure than the dumb kite museum," he said.

He loved trips to the beach, but his siblings were much younger. They weren't incredibly excited about the rugged Pacific coastline. Their idea of a good time was to build sandcastles and fly their firetruck red kite they had argued over at the last pitstop.

He promised himself, *I will not create another sandcastle, fly a stupid kite, or babysit them on my vacation.*

Finally, Molek's mom said, "Okay, okay...what do *you* want to do?"

Shocked at the thought of an opportunity for independence, Molek sat up straight in the car, and the kids quieted.

"Hmm...," he opened the map she handed him briefly, "I'll take the trailhead at Cape Disappointment State Park and rendezvous with you at the campground near the North Head Lighthouse by dusk."

The younger boy whined, "I wanna go with Mo...."

"Definitely no, buddy," Molek said, "Next time, maybe."

"Ouch, he touched me again!" hollered the younger girl, who held her arm like she'd been struck with an axe.

Again, Molek's mother was distracted by the other kids' behaviors. She nodded towards Molek. She slowed and left the car in park momentarily at the side of the road nearest the State Park. He popped open the car door before his mother could change her mind and squished the boy as he struggled to escape.

She seems glad to be rid of me for the day again.

"Please, Mo… I'll follow you, promise," the little boy begged, which only irritated the rest.

Molek rubbed the kid's head when he realized the boy admired his big brother and knew he wanted adventure, too. Everyone else called him Mo for short. Once his little siblings came along and all they could utter was Mo, it had stuck. Molek didn't mind the shortened form of his name. It only annoyed him when people wrote it down with an e at the end as if he were one of *The Three Stooges.*

"I just want to be alone," he said as he slipped from the car into the sunshine and wind.

Freedom.

His family drove off, and the kids waved out the windows that had been lowered. He didn't wave back.

The famous Long Beach lighthouse was located near the mouth of the Columbia River. The river met the ocean and formed tidal currents there. Plus, waves and surf pounded together to make some of Oregon and Washington's most spectacular and scenic wave action. Their vacation included both states if they could stand one another long enough. Mo pulled his beanie down over his long, dark hair and stretched his sore limbs from his time stuck in the back seat of his mom's tiny car. He was pale white from a long, dark winter in Washington, and the sun threatened to burn his skin where his t-shirt exposed his long, lanky arms.

Never mind, I am beyond ready for a sic time after I was stuck in the car with those snotty brats.

He hit the Beard's Hollow Trail in flops at a jog with just a water bottle, his favorite blue beanie cap, and the liberation he had longed for. It was just over a mile walk to the coast, but there was some significant elevation gain. At about 800 feet, he could see a long way away. It was a while until dusk, so he looked over the edge at several places to see how far down it was.

It occurred to Mo, *it would be super cool to climb over the front of the cliff, walk around Dead Man's Hollow, and rejoin my family and surprise them at their campsite in the loop at the State Park.*

Mo could see most of the way from up there, and the kites flown from the short stretch of beach flittered in the bright blue sky beckoned to him. He looked back and forth from north to south for an easier route to start his descent. The closer he got to the giant boulders, the more he was thrilled about his final look back up to the cliffs from the beach.

I will show off my sic skills to my brothers, who will look up to me even more.

He supposed they already did in a way no matter what he did, but this would also have been a sweet story to share with Lilah, his girlfriend.

The girl I want to be my girlfriend, he thought as he grinned.

Lilah wore her hair dyed jet black and lots of makeup, and she teased him mercilessly. She was somber and mysterious and yet always found a way to joke with him. He felt special when she paid attention to him, even at his expense. Occasionally, she showed him a softer side that intrigued him and made him want to know her more. She argued that there was no truth and no one could be trusted. For some reason, he tried to gain her trust. She claimed there was no god and there never could be. Just the thought touched a nerve within him. He remembered when he asked her, "No god, god. Does it matter?"

Nothingness? Why does that even bother me?

He sensed there must be some intelligence and design, but none had ever come to him. Since his dad had skipped out on them months ago, he'd given up hope in anyone. His mom tried, but she was too distracted to live.

Lilah's probably right.

He swore out loud to someone, maybe to no one, perhaps to himself, "Damn."

Why do I want to swear at someone if there is no one?

His dad's abandonment of them all hurt.

Maybe I'm swearing at him. Yeah, that's who.

Why, though, it didn't stop the pain; no one bothered to help Mo understand.

I need more risk and adventure to distract me from the pain.

Recalling the night his parents split, never to be seen "together" again, propelled him forward. He had heard his parents argue, but the question remained in his mind.

What did I not do to prevent my dad from walking away from all of them?

They argued over his mom, who spent their money, his dad's profanity in front of the children, and their unforgiveness toward one another in general. Their lists of wrongs seemed comparable, so it should've been a washout in his mind.

I feel like such a burden to both my parents. I don't think I'm the real problem, but it feels like it most days.

Mo's mom kept superstitious figurines around the house and constantly annoyed them with strong incense. Meanwhile, his dad used even worse language to combat the foul odors. Dad had kept it up to spite his mother's embarrassment and annoyance of the littles' schoolteachers when they repeated horrible words they didn't know the significance of in their classes at school and on the playground. She got blamed, and it was left to Mo to explain the words to the kids behind closed doors so they wouldn't do it again.

"Awkward," said Mo to no one and anyone at the same time.

He quickly passed by some danger signs. He looked over his shoulder again to see if someone had watched him.

"Nope, no one ever looks for me."

Mo found an open spot and scrambled down the wet cliff.

It occurred to him, *They are both, well, psycho... to name a god and curse it if they did not believe in it...or did they?*

His mom's awkward idea of forced fun was to make them all camp outside. It was her grand idea to compensate for the breakup of their family. They'd probably want Dad's help even more outside at night.

So what, he thought, *my friends all have family issues of their own. Mine don't beat me.*

When he spied an outcrop of tree roots, he investigated their ability to hold his weight as he tossed a leg over the ledge where he stood.

"Whoa, that is a long way down."

He resisted the urge to turn back since he wanted to tell everyone about his grand adventure down the cliff face. He knew he could do it in record time if he went quick, too.

If I tell Lilah about this right before I ask her out, she will have to say yes.

One foot by careful foot placement and hand under handhold, Mo descended towards the beach over the rockface.

The sun feels so good on my back, he contemplated as he found a foothold in the grass below him.

This is courage, he thought, *gotta demonstrate it to the world...or anybody who cares.*

Joshua was frigid, wet, and nearly exhausted after he had battled the heaviest surf he had ever swum in. These waves within caves were unlike anything else he had prepared for. He had taken turns between rescuer and pretend survivor. Jordan, his crew's mech, had watched the wave sets and anticipated how they would impact survivors in the water. The new dimension of wave action with rollers and waves that collided with a walled rocky shoreline nearby and exhaustion made Jordan, who was usually very chatty, a lot quieter and more hyper-focused to get her swimmer back safely. The crew was grateful for good visibility. A low cloud deck would have made the circumstances trickier if that was possible. The proper perspective and focus throughout the missions were paramount for the rescuers' success.

The pilots, too, had to fly, navigate, watch their instruments, and help time intervals between waves. The buffeted winds left them sweaty in their dry suits as they concentrated on the tasks in their hands and feet. The pilots used all their extremities in a dance of death over the abyss that threatened to pull them under. The next assignment was even more risky. They moved a swimmer from the water and took them vertically and horizontally along the cliff. The rescue swimmers were cautioned not to carry themselves across the rock face. Swimmers had been trained to keep positive contact with their feet on the surface, sit back in their harness, and use hand signals to the flight mechanic to tell the helicopter where they wanted to be moved. It was a dangerous dance between the swimmer, mech, and pilots. For Joshua, it was the most complicated dance he had ever done, a motion here and there, all for a life to spare.

He figured, *at this point, on the end of the hoist cable with the winds off the water and the down drafts, I've never been so much at the mercy of my crewmates.*

Within a split second, Joshua's body could have been slammed into the rock wall if they miscommunicated.

That would certainly leave a mark or worse.

Mo paused at what little was left of the grass and outcroppings. The grasses had become wetter, which made it harder to grasp onto. Then, it became apparent to Mo that he was only halfway down to the beach.

How far have I come from the lighthouse?

There was very little for Mo to hold on to.

He thought, *I'm used to this. It's exactly what it's like in my family right now. There's little to hold us together.*

Mo decided he'd try to find a ledge to stand and give his legs and arms a break. He climbed to the right. He groped as far as he could reach to search for handholds and another foothold to rest his weight on. He had not planned the climb to take so long.

"Wow, I need a break," he said as sweat dropped off his brow and neck underneath his beanie.

This was how he had felt in history class the previous week. They learned about the world's great religions. "Great" was the word he doubted. Judaism, Christianity, and Islam had many differences and began similarly. He had been confused and could not see the point. They all seemed like conspiracies to him. So much harm had been done to the world in the name of God. There were too many wars to count, and centuries of peace were barely interspersed when there was an occasional pause for the weary world. He had more questions than answers after those lessons. He left the class exhausted and more confused than ever. He remembered he needed a handle then, too.

Mo's water bottle dangled menacingly off his belt loop. He could not reach it while he clung to the rocks to drink, and it only bothered him and made him thirstier. His mouth went dry while his perspiration grew. He decided then that he could not go back up. It was too hazardous to continue down. He had to keep up the inch-by-inch push to his right and head toward the campground. He hoped for a sandcastle to build and for his safety. He scoffed and used that name he'd never comprehended.

"Jesus, my muscles are burning."

Mo realized there was some irony about his voice used to speak to no one who would listen.

Why did people around him use it? he thought, *Who was Jesus?*

Mo's neck ached from his tense body and his glances around him while he tried desperately to find handholds and footholds to hold his weight.

He knew, *Do. Not. Look. Down.*

Mo soon came to the point where it hit him hard; he was excruciatingly stuck in no man's land. A horrible fear rose in his stomach, and beads of sweat dropped off his forehead and made his palms even sweatier. He gritted his teeth.

"Damn it."

His beanie had always kept him warm, like a blankie. The same comfort threatened to betray him as it sunk on his forehead. It partly covered his eyes and vision as it filled with his sweat and the dampness from the air. He became desperate to live, he realized. A terrible fear burned deep within his soul and coursed through his extremities as water pressed and overflowed from his eyes.

Why am I crying? he thought, *I don't even have someone to cry to.*

No one can help me where I am.

No one will come to look for me when I fall.

Atop the far-off cliff, Mo's siblings ran back and forth along the Lighthouse Keeper's Loop Trail. Expectantly, the children played a version of the game of hide and seek. They fully expected their big, brave brother to have stood atop the lighthouse and waved at them.

The children looked and called out for him, "Mo!? Mo!"

They anticipated his yell back, "Got here first!"

At the top of the cliff, what they saw and heard instead took their breath away even more. A USCG helicopter's bold orange and white hovered nearby just off the cliff face and astonished them. It twirled and balanced like one of their new kites in the wind. The closer they moved toward it, the more they realized it bounced in the up and down drafts like an enormous kite further down the beach at the kite museum. They had begged their mother to stay at the State Park to see what Mo wanted. The Jayhawk helicopter's ferocious blades that chopped at the air to keep it aloft were not silent like a kite. It bit back at the waves and wind that threatened it and unknowingly them.

A helmeted person on their stomach looked down from the side of the helicopter cabin's door. The kids wondered what they looked for underneath. The Jayhawk helicopter continued its search north and south along the cliffs perilously close to the land. Mo's mother called the children backward, grabbed their hands, and pulled them away from the fierce down draft that sprayed them with bits of grasses, gravel from the path, wind, and seawater. They had never seen a CG helicopter so close. Although pelted, they were drawn to the excitement of action and the unusual vehicle. They twisted and turned in their mother's rough pull backward as they wanted to see what the helicopter crew saw. Annoyed at the inconvenience, she pulled them back down the trail toward their car. They would never forget their view of ferocious power combined with a graceful dance on the wind—the ever-prepared, hovered search for a survivors' sake.

Commander Kodesh's muscles strained as she held the collective of the Jayhawk helo in one hand to control the up and down motion. She carefully used the cyclic stick between her knees to control the aircraft's tilt. At the same time, she used her feet as well and brought the rudder into position. To put the swimmer into position was complicated on a good day.

This is a fantastic day to test my skills and proficiency, she thought, *focus*.

After a while, she offered the controls to the co-pilot while she glanced around at their surroundings once more, a bit more relaxed. She knew from experience she had eyes in the back of her head as a CG pilot. Those eyes were the mech or tweets. She also had eyes that roamed back and forth unceasingly. From her peripheral vision, Kodesh spotted a blue kite stuck on a rock about 100 yards away. Concerned about any debris in the air near them, she announced it over the intercom. She peered closer to see whether it had come loose with the enormous air disturbances they had created.

In shock, she realized, *Uh, oh. That's not a kite or a balloon; it's a beanie on a body.*

"Crew, I've spotted *someone* in distress. Bring the swimmer in now. Then we can edge forward for a closer rescue evaluation immediately."

Hung from underneath a CG Jayhawk and with the Pacific Ocean that pounded away underneath it, Joshua was exhilarated and exhausted. He was stunned when Joshua heard the chatter in his headset to come in for a rescue.

His first thought was, *WHAT?*

His second was, *Yes, Ma'am!*

He always obeyed orders and asked questions later if needed. The crew swiftly adjusted their mission to a SAR operation more rapidly than he had ever experienced. Once he was belted back in the cabin, they all gawked in disbelief as they cautiously flew closer by yards and eventually feet. Careful not to cause more harm, they each wanted to investigate what Kodesh had already announced.

A barefoot and slim young man clung for his life to a wet clump of grass and brush just feet above the waves of chaos that snarled and gaped at him when they hit the unforgiveness of jagged rocks below. Communication with him was impossible. As the co-pilot conversed with the Air Station, just a few miles away in Astoria, about the development, the crew pondered their next move. They swiftly moved from checklist number one to checklist number two.

Kodesh stated, "The man has moments to be rescued before he drops into the swells below."

Jordan, the mech, answered, "When he does so, he will be dashed against the rocks."

Kodesh stated again, "It would be best to deploy the swimmer immediately for a cliff rescue."

Fortunately for all involved, she had one at the door ready. She thought about the tenacity of Mansoul behind her. He was already prepared to head out the cabin's door and re-checked his gear. The crew understood the rapidity of checklist two was paramount. She knew that the swimmer would listen with intent to her every word. She spoke to her co-pilot.

"I like this, Mansoul. If this goes along with our training protocols, you'll have another wild but great story to tell."

"Aye, aye, Ma'am," answered Joshua.

Kodesh hoped it was the encouragement he needed in an already fatigued state. She took back the controls and had power management for the rest of the mission. She would not be able to see what happened immediately below her. That interaction was out of her control and view, although she bore the responsibility. They all feared how the downdraft would affect the man in his precarious state. Joshua took a deep breath and scooted to the edge of the helo.

Joshua thought, *All you gotta do is trust and answer me, man. I'm right here.*

"Swimmer is in the cabin door," he said.

"Deploy swimmer," Kodesh announced.

"Checking swimmer...Swimmer ready for deployment," Jordan responded.

Jordan thought, *Godspeed,* as she tapped him on the back per the CG protocol.

Joshua went back out the door, and the sea spray pelted him from the outrageous downdraft that thrashed the sea's surface below and ricocheted upwards off the wall.

This is a new feeling, a tornado within a cliff rescue, thought Joshua.

Joshua knew the intensity was bound to increase as he was lowered on the taunt hoist when it began to swing in the wind. His legs were heavy, and he was glad he no longer wore his flippers after all the water and cave work they had already done. His adrenaline had kicked in. The water began to needle his extremities, and he wondered how the survivor felt.

Joshua thought, *Semper Paratus, trained to rescue in the rescue. Saved by the water for the water.*

The engine noise screamed and precluded good vocal communication between Joshua and the survivor, who shook uncontrollably when he arrived next to him. As he appeared to Joshua, the teen was terrified and had his eyes shut tight against the water that pelted him. The beanie was very low on his head and almost entirely concealed his vision.

Joshua thought, *I'm surprised it hasn't flown off, and can he see me?*

Joshua did not want to alarm the teenager more, and he could almost reach him. He made the motions to Jordan above him to relay to the pilots what they had practiced. He needed to close in on the survivor with precaution and precision.

He thought, *don't let me make this worse; work with me, crew.*

With supernatural effort, Jordan had eased Joshua down through the forces that howled over the jaws of toothy rock and surf saliva alongside the teen.

She cheered into her mic, "You got this guy, Mansoul!"

If he's willing, thought Joshua.

Joshua cleared his throat, controlled his desperation, and hollered above the blade action over them as he extended his open-gloved hand to him. He lightly touched the man's shoulder to assure him of his presence.

"I'm Joshua, a CG Rescue Swimmer. Let me take your weight *before* you let go."

Mo had pressed his face against the rock so hard that his cheeks and lips bled. He only tasted the sticky blood on his tongue where he'd scraped it on the rocks. For a while, he had felt so alive. Then he clung to an unknown rock for his life well past exhaustion. Mo believed he had nothing but himself, the hard, cold earth, and weakness.

He had thought earlier, *I need no superstitions, no gods to help me; I'm invincible.*

He had roared with the foul language pent up within him. Within minutes, the adrenaline rush he had felt abated, and he could no longer see or hear but only taste his blood.

So, this was it? No first kiss. No one to see me. What have I done?

Moleck had felt more than heard a thunderous and concussive force that blew around and through him. His neck was too sore to look around for what it was. He willed himself not to look down, so he pinched his eyes closed. He couldn't even look up anymore. Mo hoarded the energy to see for his painful muscles. Too quickly, the sudden rush of aliveness had given way to despair when his muscles twitched in agony.

What is that force that pushes and pulls me against the rock?

Nothing left to do but let go...

Mo couldn't bring himself to finish the thought. It was then that he felt a touch lightly placed on his shoulder. His reflexes popped one eye open, and in his periphery vision, a man floated as if on a cloud closer than his father had ever been to him unless he was about to strike him. Mo clung to the rock-hard earth like a worm.

Mo's thoughts ran wild, *How is this happening? How can he be here?*

The "frog man" or "angel in orange," whatever they're called ... is here for me?

Am I already dead?

Mo blinked once with effort as the water pierced him all over. It made the already wet grass he clung to even more slippery. The blue helmet and orange armored man yelled something unrecognizable to him. His kind eyes and extended hand rested gently on Mo, and it captured him.

"Can't hold on," croaked Mo.

Mo slammed his eyes closed again and tasted the blood that ran from his lips. He wanted to pry them open once more to see a compassionate face. He was terrified to open them.

What would I see? My dad's look of condemnation, scorn, and judgment for my foolishness?

Joshua saw the complete exhaustion and brief vacant look in Mo's expression. Joshua squeezed his hand lightly on the teen's shoulder as if to confirm that he was real. He needed the man to acknowledge and cooperate to adjust the rescue strop and successfully hoist them both before he let go. Joshua's gaze never left the giant boy's face after Mo blinked once at him in what he hoped was acceptance. Joshua could use the quick strop with his own eyes closed, but he wouldn't dare.

Joshua's mind had leaped on the teen's eye movement. He hoped he had seen him there and would cooperate with his rescue. Joshua didn't have time to wonder, and it did not seem there would be any more discussion than what he'd yelled. Words were, at times, unnecessary.

Joshua surmised, *let your fear keep you frozen until I can get you secured to me, buddy.*

Joshua was desperate to quickly attach himself to the kid and then make the motion for them both to be carried up before he slipped away from him. He knew the entire crew held their breaths and prepared to take the load as Jordan relayed what she saw. Joshua pulled the strop that dangled beside him around the man.

He said, "Easy."

Mo turned his head away from what was in his mind, his father's gaze of condemnation. The only masculine face he truly knew in his thirteen years. He stiffened his back to Joshua, and a moment of eternity was split.

Mo cried out in his pain, "NO!"

Mo's eyes were open but hollow as if he had summoned his last ounce of strength. Regardless of what was to come, he pushed against the rock, the last place he had to cling to, of condemnation. He refused it, but in reality, he rejected rescue. He shook in fear like a dead man.

Joshua, completely taken aback, pleaded with him.

"Man, let me rescue you, please!"

For Mo, there was no fear of any god, no longer any fear of man. He only heard the shout. The need to be rescued and carried away was lost on Mo. He could not recall any man's trustworthiness. Mo only thought to end the drama and not bear more shame for his deep desire to be wanted.

Mo figured, *it's easier to let go and end the game. That was the only way I've ever learned to cope with my losses. 'Just go away,' they all told me. End the game.*

An unexpected, explosive, sudden jar of Mo's entire body weight fell back onto Joshua and pushed him off the rock face that only Joshua's feet braced against. Joshua's hands held the strop not yet clasped around the teen. Joshua grasped desperately to grab the wet teen while his hoist cable swung him away simultaneously with the push backward. In the quick succession of motions, the teen, Joshua realized, had thrust himself away from the rock on purpose. Joshua looked down in horror at the upturned face that looked up. The teen not only lacked trust, but he also intentionally pushed Joshua away.

"No!" Joshua bellowed.

Mo looked disoriented as he fell through the air and grasped upwards with empty hands at Joshua, who shouted fearfully down. Joshua's arms were outstretched toward Mo while he swung wildly away above him in a pendulum motion. Mo's body hit the icy water below, while Joshua's body simultaneously slammed into the cliff face from the unanticipated swing from Mo's push. Joshua's eyes had been trained below him on his survivor. Joshua had desperately watched the lost teen fall away and took the tremendous blow as it punished him further. His helmet of protection saved his head. Figuratively, his mind and heart were crushed instantaneously.

Joshua urgently used his hand, with his finger pointed down, and rotated his arm in a horizontal circle. It made the motion to his mech for lower down without a second thought.

Please, give him back to me!

Mansoul's intense physical pain didn't compare to his hurt when he was so close to the young man and lost him. Jordan sprang into action and requested the pilot to maneuver away from the rocks. She waited cautiously to lower Joshua down into the swells. They threatened to dash him against the rock walls beside and under him. The already palatable tension in the cockpit was only raised at their realization that this was now a water and rock rescue their swimmer had yet to be thoroughly trained on this week. They all recognized that tests, too often, come before the lessons.

Jordan called out, "He's been hurt! He wants to be put back in. Are there more nasty caves here, too?"

Her voice was strained with fear for her swimmer friend and survivor. The exhaustion and anxiety were evident in Jordan's quick line of rapid questions. Commander Kodesh was always calm under pressure and moved her crew into a higher hover out of Joshua's harm's way to reassess the sudden change to the situation and SAR rescue. Joshua began to spin on the hoist below them. Jordan kept the crew up to date.

Over the intercom, Kodesh said, "We all need to take a deep breath. Let's collect ourselves about a water rescue."

Her co-pilot relayed, "We're near bingo."

This meant they would soon be required to leave the scene due to the remaining fuel requirements to return themselves to the air station.

Joshua said, "I request to be lowered. I have a visual."

He knew it would take one minute tops to be lowered into the swell, swim to the survivor, use the strop, and be hoisted to freedom for them both. The agony in his voice was apparent to all who heard him. They knew he could barely see anything in a spin, let alone anyone.

"We could leave a life raft," added Jordan, always full of hope.

It was clear to Joshua that the teen was too weak to pull himself into an inflated raft.

Joshua added, "One more time, please, lower me, 'Ghost.'"

The co-pilot perfunctorily said, "You've got one minute, and we leave."

They all knew that time was against every rescue situation. Eventually, their resources, strength, or will would break, and the whole crew depended on the clock. That wall of time as they knew it could never be traversed.

Kodesh had the final call, "Deploy swimmer."

Jordan called the wave action and put him inside the jaws. The icy chill of the water doused Joshua's entire system as it threatened repeatedly to drown him. He swam with the sting of salt water in his wounds that bled where he had last seen the man and his bright blue cap as it bobbed beneath the surface. Wave after wave came at Joshua as he slid down the front of a wave only to be smashed under the surface as another hit him from behind in the chaos of waves that churned off the rocks.

Another 30 seconds.

He remained calm in the mayhem. He looked right and left, took a huge breath, dove under the surface, and saw something.

Last chance.

Joshua's lungs burned, but he swam bravely toward the beanie. He grabbed the knit blue cap and pulled himself towards the water's surface. Bingo.

Kodesh ached and involuntarily repositioned herself in the cockpit. She looked around and adeptly guided the Jayhawk back and away from the cliff face. She brought the helicopter up and arced over the nearby lighthouse, called North Head, as it flew away. She noticed several children who jumped up and down and waved like they were thankful for their rescue "demonstration" that day. A mother pulled them backward away from the tremendous power of their helicopter, understandably. Her heart dropped further when she saw their happiness in the moment. She and her crew briefly flew along the coastline and were immensely disappointed.

All the power needed was readily available and miraculously on the scene. However, there was no salvation for the CG missionaries. She searched to find joy buried deep in the attempted SAR. Off they sped through the bright blue sky towards the Air Station and a medic for the battered and bruised Mansoul. Another helicopter was en route and entrusted with the continued search for the teenager along the broken, rocky shoreline of destruction at Cape Disappointment.

Kodesh snuck a look in her cabin view mirror. The Jayhawk she flew pressed through the dusky haze that had come ashore in the afternoon. Behind her, she saw the tight grip of Joshua's one hand around the soggy blue cap as the other held his helmeted face full of regret. Joshua's chest heaved with what she supposed was remorse and exhaustion. His eyes were uncommonly pinched closed. He grieved in silence.

Kodesh longed to say, "Another save for Mansoul," but instead summoned a brief, "Return to base."

Jordan couldn't let the heavy silence hang over them for a full minute as they rode the clouds in the air. She looked directly at Joshua and remarked instead to the pilots through her mic.

"'Ghost,' you're good to have spotted him... we did all *we* could to rescue him."

Kodesh remarked, "He wasn't prepared to answer his rescuer."

Chapter 17

JUST COFFEE

The next day, classroom instruction continued at the AHRS Aviation Training Center. The crew was somber, and gloom and sorrow shadowed the schoolhouse. Jordan continued her admonition to anyone who would listen that they had done more than anyone could have expected. The stumble upon a SAR was unusual.

"We were there and ready," Jordan said, "no one should have perished."

Other crews had been sent to look for any signs of life late into the night and again at first light. About noon, there was a notification that the young man's body had washed ashore further down the beach. Kodesh announced an extended break at that time. She knew that Joshua and Jordan would appreciate the time to collect themselves. Joshua, worn out emotionally and physically, lowered his head down on the desk in front of him. Classmates filed quietly out of the room to give him space. Some paused to touch his shoulder to remind him they wanted to help shoulder his obvious pain. Kodesh proceeded toward him and laid a hand softly next to his head on the desk.

She nearly whispered, "Why don't you head over and see Chaps for a hotwash of your very own before we have ours this afternoon?"

Out of respect for the officer, Joshua sat up and nodded his obedience to her request. He looked up at her full in the face. She had wisdom he did not in the moment of defeat.

He consented, "Yes, Ma'am."

Joshua moved stiffly and somewhat hesitantly towards the door. His wounds from the previous day were bandaged carefully under his flight suit. His invisible wounds still seeped and were raw inside. Too often, a trip to see the chaplain was misunderstood as a collaborative procedural and disciplinary process. In this case, everyone completely understood it to be restorative. Most Guardians liked their chaplains for different reasons. What they discussed was confidential, and it was a relief to unburden oneself. Joshua realized he walked taller and taller down the hall toward the chaplain's office. An unburdened soul was what 'Ghost' ordered, and he realized he wanted it as he stepped through the door frame.

Chaps had been aware of the tragedy the previous day and expected one or more crew members to swing by. He understood the importance of what he called a time for J.C., "just coffee." For some in the mission, it had been a time to vent, confess, or for others to listen about rescue. Some wanted to receive, follow, and answer with humility and respect the hope Chaps found in his commission. Therefore, he always kept an open-door policy and the coffee hot.

When Joshua's muscular frame filled his door, Chaplain Johnson smiled and beckoned him inside further. He raised the coffee pot in a gesture of hospitality.

"Yes, Sir," said Joshua.

Chaps read the name tape on the flight uniform that said Mansoul. Chaplain Johnson put two-and-two together that he was likely the swimmer on duty for the SAR the previous day. Chaps loved assignment to the 13th District of the CG from the US Navy. The slower-paced land-based unit was a welcome tour to be home with his large family after he served on a carrier in the open ocean for months at a stretch. The close-knit CG community also made it easier to develop longer and closer relationships. Joshua accepted the coffee and tried to glance around for something sweet to put in it covertly. He had developed a sweet tooth and could barely drink plain bitter coffee anymore.

Chaps noticed and apologized, "Sorry, I'm a JC freak, 'just coffee' guy."

Chaps laughed at his joke and opened the glass dish of jellybeans sitting on his desk for Joshua. Joshua laughed out loud for the first time in over a day, and it felt strange as it came out of him. They both knew that a family was likely in deep emotional pain elsewhere, and they quieted in compassion and reverence for their pain.

The sorrow followed me here, thought Joshua.

Chaps kept those jellybeans on his desk for several reasons. They were a massive expectation for his kids whenever they dropped in to see him. They were a cheery reminder of his favorite holiday, Easter, year-round. They were offered at odd times when conversation was awkward for people in a "holy person's" office for the first time. He'd ask the Guardian about their first name if the Guardian didn't want to talk to him immediately. Names told him a lot about a person. While they ate jellybeans, they had to chew slowly; the time passed less uncomfortably. Chaps did not know where Joshua was emotionally or spiritually, but he waited patiently as he regarded the beans.

Joshua carefully pulled out a white jellybean, popped it into his mouth, and smiled again despite himself. He carefully fished out two more, pink and purple, which he knew to be sweet-flavored. To Chap's surprise, he plopped them in the cup. They shared another laugh. He leaned back in his chair and lifted the mug in a "cheer" toward the Chaplain across his desk, who watched him amused.

"I've never seen that done," said Chaps.

"Desperation sugar," said Joshua.

"Resourceful," followed Chaps.

"Semper Paratus," answered Joshua.

Their conversation flowed easily, as did the coffee. Chaps reminded Joshua that "we are rescued to be rescuers." Joshua's physical rescue as a child and his vocational experiences shaped his outlook on every person he encountered. He knew everyone on this planet needed rescue at some point. Death was not the primary enemy, but to be unprepared for it was. They spoke about the unseen enemy's obligation to seek, kill, and destroy. It was usually with fear and pride. Joshua, as a Guardian, was to do the opposite. He lived to bring life, abundant gratitude, and joy through the redemption of those who suffered. Chaps put his mug aside and leaned forward, elbows on his desk, as if he had to share some secret.

He lowered his voice and said, "I've found only three kinds of rescues in the CG."

Joshua cocked his head to the side, surprised that the chaplain was about to share rescue advice with a swimmer. Chaps opened his hands to demonstrate he referred to a physical and supernatural rescue scenario.

Chaps said, "We come alongside in three distinct ways:

1) To enforce the crisis of decision that authority has in every person's life. Does one answer with acceptance or rejection of the authority of rescue?
2) To reveal the realms we inhabit on Earth. We don't make judgment calls on peoples' circumstances; we're here to rescue them from dominions they cannot see, no matter what one has or has not done.

3) The upside-down value system and Guardian's ethic. Every life is valuable, EVERY single one. No matter how large or small, young or old, no matter how good or bad."

Joshua slowly nodded his agreement. He sat back with his coffee and let the words soak in. He meditated on them for a few minutes. He had never heard the CG ethics explained so concisely. He asked for a minute to type them into his note app on his phone.

"That's deep. May I use this to share later?" said Joshua.

He knew he'd want to share it with Jordan later that day. She would like it written down for sure. She wrote everything down.

Joshua reflected momentarily and listened intently to his new confidant and friend. He finished his coffee with one last gulp and saw the remnant of the jellybeans stuck to the bottom of the cup. He looked at the Chaplain directly and smiled with his big toothy grin.

"Thank you, Sir."

Joshua sobered as he rolled up his flight suit's sleeve to reveal his bandaged flesh, torn and bruised. He wanted to entrust himself more fully to the chaplain. Chaps grimaced. He had not realized the extent of Joshua's woundedness inside and out.

Joshua said, "These wounds that mark my flesh are just the second part of the checklist... my soul is overwhelmed with sorrow for the lost, but they only strengthen my determination to continue. Some guys intentionally add tattoos to demonstrate what; I'm not sure. It seems the wounds I bear validate my love of strangers. If only they would readily answer my call to rescue them."

Since it had been about an hour, Joshua glanced at his watch as he rolled his sleeve back down and knew he had to report to his class. Chaplain Johnson acknowledged the wane of their time together. He stood and regarded his newest friend with respect and admiration.

Chaps spoke carefully, "Just like coffee, life is full of bitterness and can often be made sweet. You are to drink deeply and enjoy all the flavors. Allow both to form who you are. Your mission is to allow this human experience to be redeemed. The culmination of your life's work will be the most rewarding part of your life and your legacy."

Joshua stood and handed the empty cup back to Chaps. Chaps stood with him and placed the mug on his desk.

Joshua said, "Thanks for the fill-up in my cup," and added, "May yours always run over with just coffee."

He placed a firm hand on the Chaplain's shoulder as they shook hands goodbye. Joshua departed through the door with his shoulders straighter than when he'd entered. Goose bumps raised on Chaps' arms. His encounter with Petty Officer 2nd Class Mansoul was different than usual.

He thought, *hmm.... maybe, just maybe, I've entertained a warrior angel unaware?*

The AHRS instructors usually critiqued the previous day's flights every morning of the class. Kodesh had made the executive decision to reverse the order of the day's events. Joshua walked in from his visit with Chaps before the video began to cue up from their previous day's training evolution. As the room darkened, he sat and watched as wide-eyed as every other student did. He struggled to detach himself from the personal and tragic experience he viewed on the screen. Sweat again formed on his brow when he saw the teen he now knew as Moleck as he clung to the cliff face. Jordan put her hand on his forearm to signal he was not alone. Not prone to sickness in the aircraft, a wave of nausea caught him off guard. He purposely opened and closed his fists, thought of something to smell, tasted the jellybeans in his imagination, and breathed deeply.

Breathe Mansoul, breathe the breath of life...

Joshua found he could stomach the hotwash with supernatural strength, probably thanks to his new friend, Chaps, who gave him a unique mission perspective. Each helicopter had a video camera on the hoist that looked down. It also audio-recorded conversations between the crew. Instructors used these recordings to debrief nearly every single mission as a hotwash. They critiqued and reminded the students how and if they had progressed day to day. When the video concluded, the lights were snapped back on. After such a dark episode, the intrusion of white LED lights seemed cruel as the trainees straightened in their chairs and cleared their throats. Commander Kodesh strode to the front of the room.

'Ghost' gazed out over the class and began, "I'll start with a familiar quote from Mario Vittone, retired CG AST,

'Becoming a helicopter rescue swimmer is usually much more difficult than actually being one, but for those who make it through the training, *the job becomes one of delivering hope.* All rescue crews are teams, but when swimmers leave the helicopter in an attempt to save someone, the outcome is in their court, and they know it. That burden is the real price they pay for the job: There's praise if they save you, or a lifetime of guilt if they don't.'"

The room went silent as the trainees felt the weightiness of the extreme physical and emotional shared burden. They knew that Mansoul bore the brunt of the affliction. They couldn't help themselves but glanced his way. Joshua felt the eyes of everyone upon him in the silence of the room.

Was this mission a success or a failure?

Joshua responded to their heartfelt eyes and knew they wanted him to respond. Time awkwardly stood still like for those who attend funerals and don't know what to say. Often, those in misery are the ones who respond first to open the floodgates of shared grief. Joshua knew they waited on him. He tangled his heart-wrenched words with his native youthful language of Spanish.

Joshua said, "We were ready for the call, los amigos. We offered hope. We place our trust in Dios."

The men and women in the AHRS course that week always remembered the grace and honor of Mansoul and his crew. The mission was successful, even though the loss was unforgettable.

Joshua was relieved at the wisdom of Kodesh to have already given him the gift of a personal hotwash, or he'd have probably been a terrible mess in class. He was free of guilt, thanks to his relationships with his friends, commanders, and father. He knew he had to look up, especially in the worst circumstances. He had already determined that he would faithfully follow wherever his Papa led. Answering the call had never let him down. He remembered he feared the hotwashes from earlier trials.

They are not getting easier, yet I look forward to them now. To show others, it's okay to do hard things, unforgettable things in obedience to the mission. Like my physical training, I will discipline my mind and soul for the greater good.

Joshua smiled to himself and thought, *Jedi-like, you will be.*

Joshua was moved to make hotwashes an essential part of his overall mission and incorporate them into his relationships, friendships, and conversations with family. He decided that he'd make it a priority to offer a hotwash to anyone who'd take him up on his offer for "just coffee" but also to have a spoon full of sugar *always ready.*

CHAPTER 18

NO MORE KRYPTONITE TONIGHT

One of the best parts of Joshua's Kodiak tour was the community he had embraced. Joshua learned summertime in Alaska only meant lots of uncertain weather. If, however, the party planners were fortunate, a warm-ish sunny day they called "summer" fell on the 4th of July. Holidays and ordinary days were best had with others. He enjoyed life off base as well as his CG duty. He relished the invitations for open-mic nights in town, volunteer opportunities at the Mission, and meals people frequently shared in their homes, particularly in the long, cold, dark winters.

Joshua anticipated his return to the chapel community when he returned from AHRS. He decided to throw out the invitation to more of his peers. Joshua introduced himself and some new friends for "just coffee" after worship. They found the chaplain to be a terrific person. He was more recent to the island than most and liked cold coffee. Joshua learned Chaps had just had a tour with the Navy in Hawaii.

That is weird, thought Joshua; *what's the point of that in Alaska?*

Joshua told him, "Surely Kodiak will turn you to the light and drink hot, sweetened coffee if you prefer or 'Just Coffee'..."

Chaps replied, "I've been out to sea too long to drink hot coffee and not expect a parade of critters from the sugar bowl. It became cold fast anyhow, so I just started it out that way."

There were other looks of affirmation after Chaps' words from the CG surface guys. They, too, recognized food on board ships and smaller vessels had to be monitored more closely than in an aircraft. Each unit had its peculiarities and nuances for life as a Guardian. A few aviators lived aboard a vessel, sailed on cutters for months at a time, and experienced both. The other airframe, the MH-65 Dolphin, was the helicopter that flew off the deck of the Kodiak-based vessel Alex Haley, called the "Bulldog of the Bering." Those airmen truly embraced the entirety of the mission to be *Semper Paratus* on land, sea, and in the air wherever called upon. To land an aircraft on any ocean-going vessel was no small feat, but doing so on the deck of a CG Cutter pitching up and down on the Bering Sea was borderline ridiculous.

The amiable chaplain told the new friends gathered, "I was taught always to be ready to preach, pray, or die at a moment's notice. Those roaches, the Navy had almost sent me overboard once or twice."

One of Joshua's favorite pilot friends, Lt. Commander Joseph, or 'Padre' as everyone called him for short, was present and also attended chapel services.

Padre replied, "Well, you should join these crews soon on their missions in the Bering, and I promise you'll be prayed up, Chaps!"

Padre then invited them all to a potluck. It was planned in front of his base home on a cul-de-sac for the Fourth of July.

They all laughed when Joshua asked, "Do you know whether or not summer will make an appearance for the party?"

"Hey, Chaps, can you arrange that for us?" Padre added.

Chaps groaned and replied, "That's not exactly how it works."

On the morning of July 4th, Joshua and some buddies did the 10K run to town from base. Then, they watched the local downtown parade in the one-stoplight town. He got a lift back to the gym for a much-needed shower. He realized after two years he had finally acclimated to the temperatures because it was a balmy 72 degrees, and he was truly hot. Summertime had arrived, and with no time to spare. He cleaned up, rushed through the commissary on base, and picked up some chips and a dessert on the way to the potluck just a mile away. He had to stop to cross the active flight line, which had remained unusually inactive because of the holiday. He knew that duty-standers would miss the holiday to keep the mission on point.

I'm hungry.

When he arrived, he was shocked at the masses of people: children on their bikes, roller skates, playing ball, using makeshift water slides, water gun wars, and genuine fun in whatever ways they could imagine. The adults mingled amiably and savored the warm temperature and brilliant sunshine. Several tables were full of food, and he could smell the meats on the grill. His newest favorite was the salmon. It was as plentiful as hot dogs and hamburgers in the lower 48.

I miss seeing carefree kids and the senior citizens who must be here on vacation.

Base life, in general, was limited to a very healthy population from ages 18-50. When Joshua was around the Red Cross as he grew up, people of every age loitered. On base, there were very few older people. These were parents who came for a visit in the long summer days. He wished for his mama, but the finances weren't there for that expensive trip.

I'm happy to send home some of my paychecks so my brothers can eat well and even head to college soon. Their lives will likely be more carefree than mine.

Living amongst a mostly healthy 20-something population day in and day out had its advantages and disadvantages. He put down his contribution to the meal with the rest of the spread on a long portable table. He savored the smells of grilled halibut, salmon, burgers, and hot dogs wafting off the grills and waved to several people he recognized. Kids ran through a sprinkler and splayed themselves out on a homemade slip-and-slide made from blue tarps and a hose. Kodiak's fun was often combined with duct tape and a can-do attitude. He knew there would be no fireworks in the sky over Kodiak that night, not for lack of patriotism; it was just the practicality of it being far too sunny.

"Gracias Padre," Joshua said.

"Happy Fourth!" said Padre.

The two men shook hands when Padre welcomed Joshua to the party. At about that moment, two kiddos ran up to them and begged Joshua to return a ball that had been lost over the nearest fence, which separated the housing units from the flight line. They knew they were forbidden to cross the chasm. Joshua assessed whether it was wise to demonstrate how to climb the fence while they watched. He knew when he had been their age; he would love to have seen how a strong man could rescue their toy in a single leap. However, he knew they would try and repeat whatever he demonstrated.

He said, "Sorry guys can't now- I'm soon on grill duty."

One boy replied, "Oh, c'mon, Superman, we thought you could just jump over it quick!"

Another was frustrated with Joshua's refusal. He looked up at Joshua with a warning gaze and murmured inaudibly. Joshua bent over to listen to him repeat it in his ear.

"What was that, buddy?" Joshua said.

The boy replied in a whisper, "There's kryptonite in the salmon; you've been warned."

They dejectedly turned away and continued to scheme about what they could do next. Padre had witnessed the interaction and slapped Joshua's back with laughter.

He said, "Parents have a similar job to the CG. We're always on call to rescue our kids. Funny they asked you, though."

Joshua looked back over the fence and decided he may have been able to vault over it quickly but thought better of it. Soon after, he stealthily slipped around the units and behind the woods to retrieve the soccer ball. He vaulted over the fence easily as he had hoped. Joshua relished the thought of their joyful faces when he returned with it.

The hero of the hour, he hoped, *mission accomplished.*

When Joshua rounded the corner of the woods out of sight to get to the ball, he not only found a massive stash of Nerf guns and darts but a plastic enclosed container also full of old hard candy, a walkie-talkie, and all of that was inside a pieced together broken pallet fort. He laughed out loud.

Well, well, what have we here? What a great childhood to have.

Those kids are outlaws and living their best lives.

He rummaged through the candy and took a small package of licorice, of which there was plenty. Careful to leave the rest of their secret hideout concealed where it would remain.

Well, it's somewhat of a secret.

"Now, we know why you didn't want Padre to find the ball, you boys, ha."

After he had retrieved the soccer ball, he returned, and with a short piece of licorice hanging between his teeth, he walked over to the boys with the ball held high over his head. They jumped towards him, desperate with joy.

He spoke to them with a wink and a fake outlaw's long Texas draw.

"Lookie here what I found, fellas."

They saw the licorice and stood shocked and open-mouthed in front of him.

The littlest child piped up, "You can be part of our secret hideout club, Superman, but only if you bring more candy… and make it the good stuff. Chocolate does NOT melt around here. But ya gotta secure the lid tight, or BEARS," and his eyes grew large and round with fear.

Then, with a serious look and scrupulous eyes, another boy asked Joshua, "Do you even eat candy?"

The third child punched the second in the arm and said, "Sure he does, look at those nasty teeth."

He pointed at him and continued his accusation against Joshua, "My mom said that's what happens if you eat too much candy."

Joshua grimaced at their candidness, shook his head, and thought, *so much for a good deed.*

He knelt in front of them all, placed the ball in front of them, and then slowly looked over his shoulder and back. He leaned forward and waved them closer empty-handed.

He spoke softly and painfully said, "I do eat too much candy. This," he held up the last bit of licorice, "might be the kryptonite you thought was in the salmon, but so that you know… no more kryptonite tonight for me. You, amigos, should eat your fish and veggies, just like your mamas tell you."

They nodded warily, took the ball, and scampered away to play. The last one looked over his shoulder as if he had to ensure the visit was real.

Joshua thought, *It sure feels good to make a rescue of any kind, even if I am reminded of my awful teeth.*

He couldn't seem to make everyone happy all the time. The boys scampered away with no thanks at all. Joshua stood and headed toward the grill for his turn to make something tasty and fulfill his appetite. He remembered there wasn't much extra food while he grew up, let alone candy. Now, though, he ate like a king. Maybe one day, he could afford dental work and have a smile he wanted to share. Until then, he'd work to remember to keep his mouth closed figuratively and literally.

He suddenly felt a small hand in his. The tiniest grip squeezed his big, strong hand three times in quick succession. He looked down in surprise.

"You know what that means, Superman?" said the smallest of the boys who'd received back their ball.

Arrested by the fact that one of the boys had come back and touched him, he just shook his head back and forth, *no*.

"It's our secret handshake. It means you're in the group without saying anything. Thanks for the protection of our fort's secret and the rescue of our favorite soccer ball. My mom was upset I had lost it again. She'll be so happy it's found."

He tugged Joshua down to his eye level, looked over both shoulders quickly, and spoke secretively.

He said earnestly, "You can come after school to our meetins'... if you bring Snickers. Unless that's kryptonite, too?"

Joshua tussled the boy's hair as he stood. He stepped back and saluted the boy.

Joshua said, "Aye, Aye Chief!"

The six-year-old stood up as straight as he could. He appreciated the salute, which he had seen plenty around the base.

The child returned the salute, said, "As you were!" and scampered off.

Joshua couldn't help but grin as he watched the child retreat and was amazed at the child's gratitude and invitation. Then he turned and followed the scent of fresh grilled salmon and could not help but grin widely.

The responsibilities of the four-year tour had flown by in Kodiak for Joshua. The rescues each had more exhilaration than the previous, it seemed. The crews continued to gain proficiency and rank as their careers developed. Some new people cycled in each summer to begin their three to four-year tours. This reminded them all that their four-year tours would come to an end. It made most CG members relish their opportunities in the 49th and most spectacular state in the US. It certainly had the most coastline, for sure, and that kept the CG quite busy.

Besides his CG duties, Joshua had learned to fish for salmon and halibut. He fished the ocean and bays, as well as coastal rivers. Therefore, he also saw plenty of bears since they were there to fish. Once, Joshua had come closer than he wanted to a colossal Kodiak bear when a lovely stringer of salmon nearby became its prey. His buddies teased him and remembered he had walked over the rushing water to snatch up the stringer of salmon and make his escape.

Joshua took his turn and kayaked the many bays in awe of the sight of sea lions and sea otters in their natural habitat. He laughed over the memory of his day dressed as Sammy the Sea Otter in the hot Florida sun. The kayak's stillness allowed him to slide up next to the animated creatures and listen to their huffs while they cracked open the shellfish upon their stomachs. Creation never ceased to amaze him every day in Kodiak. The gorgeous weather more than made up for the stormy and tempestuous days.

He loved to use snowshoes in winter and ice cleats around town. He purchased big, heavy, industrial boots called *Xtratuf* to wear year-round. Mud was an Alaskan way of life if one went outdoors, and since he couldn't get enough of the adventure of a lifetime, it clung to him often. His new friends came and went with their CG orders, temporary duty (TDY), and some were in and out of port aboard CG vessels that patrolled the North Pacific.

Joshua had one more escapade on his list of desires that he'd heard about and jumped at the opportunity. He particularly looked forward to doing the 'milk run' on a couple of days of leave before he left. The 'milk run' was a series of quick stops by airplane in rural villages for supplies that could only be reached by plane. Alaska Airlines had commuters that would join the 'milk run' frequently. Though not cheap, it was the locals' only option at times. His only destination was to quickly see the remote places and pass over much of coastal Alaska by an airliner, which included famous glaciers and fjords.

To fly from Kodiak to anywhere, one had to go by way of an hour or two flight to Anchorage. Joshua learned Anchorage was not the capital of Juneau but the biggest city in the state. It also boasted the best reindeer pizza. He flew on to Ketchikan for an overnight in the tiny tourist and fishing village. He was stunned by the number of tourists that poured off colossal cruise ships and vanished immediately before the same ships sailed up the inside passage of Alaska. Ketchikan was unique in that it was unreachable by car, so anyone who traveled to the remote place had to come by air, boat, or ferry. It was Alaska's southeasternmost settlement. The Air Station in Sitka covered much of this region in Alaska. Still, he had heard tales of their heroic stories and enjoyed their similarities and differences, such as the totem poles and historic preservation.

From there, he rejoined Alaska Airlines for the scenic tour otherwise commonly known as the 'milk run' to locals. He flew to Sitka, Juneau, Yakutat, and Cordova and never left the commercial aircraft! When he returned to Anchorage, he joined a C-130 "hop" back to Kodiak with a returning CG crew from the Air Force/Army Joint Base Elmendorf-Richardson (JBER).

What a memorable trip!

After he dropped his overnight bag in his room, he immediately phoned his mama.

Joshua said, "I don't know if I'm more thrilled to stretch out or tell you about the incredible experiences I've just had to share with you!"

She said, "Do both! Tell me everything, niño ..."

After the shimmering lights of the Christmas holidays had been packed away mid-January, the end of January was gloomy at best. There had been lights all over the boats in St. Paul's harbor that reflected off the water to illuminate the town. The Eastern Orthodox Church still influenced the community; everyone welcomed their delayed holy-day traditions. The Eastern Christians celebrated the birth of the world's Savior thirteen days after Western Christians' traditions of celebration on 25 December. The four possible hours of sunlight rarely appeared just days after the winter solstice. It was one dreadful week of weather after another when it seemed like all was lost in the fierce winds, the dense fog, and little to no sunlight visible. Alaska, especially in the winter, gave people plenty of time to wrestle with their thoughts. Some people even agreed vampires would need to be counseled if the weather didn't lift.

In a time of deep thoughtfulness one night, Joshua remembered Christian's statement, "I want what you have." Joshua had been through a lot in his short career and meditated on how far he'd come with his soul from losses. He thought it was time to reconnect and have a 'just coffee' debrief with Christian.

If he still wants to have a relationship with me.

There was no chance of an immediate interruption, so Joshua picked up his phone and dialed Christian's number to check in on him since it'd been a couple of years. The phone rang several times and eventually went to voice mail.

Ugh, the time difference!

Joshua remembered it was four hours earlier in Alaska than on the East Coast, and by then, it was after 11 p.m. He decided to leave a very brief message.

I've probably already awoken him anyway. By now, I should've known better.

"Hi, um, it's Joshua Mansoul, CG Rescue Swimmer. I hope you're well. Just checking in with you. It's been a while..."

Maybe he's forgotten me...I'll never forget my rescuer.

He decided to give it more time if he didn't hear back. He would never press the teen and presume he wanted to follow him into the CG mission, but he still hoped. The next day, he slowly woke up to his nightstand lamp as it increased its glow like a sunrise.

My sunshine for the day... he already knew the forecast was for more gloomy skies for a week or more.

Joshua sighed and pressed favorites on his phone, found his mama's name, and called to surprise her. He always called on Sundays before chapel to catch her off work on the East Coast Sunday afternoon.

She answered, "Joshua? You okay, son?"

"Hi, Mama, yes, I'm fine. Just a slow day here on the Rock, and I wanted to surprise you," he said.

"Oh, very good; my heart always flutters when you call unexpectedly. It's always good to hear your voice and know you're thinking of me!"

"Do you have a minute, Mama?"

"For you, always, although Jude has to be at swim practice soon."

"Sure, well, I'll make it quick. I've been thoughtful about my next tour of duty, and I need to put in my dream sheet soon. What would you say if I listed Florida or Michigan? I've loved the adventure up here, but hear great things about aviation in those places, too. Plus, I'd be closer to you all and be able to get home for graduations and stuff like that."

"Oh, you know I want you closer, but you have to do what's best for the mission and your career," she said.

"That's the issue, Mama, what is best? How do I get those answers?"

"Well, that's the million-dollar question. Just look up and talk to as many wise people as possible. And one more thing niño, remember there are NO hurricanes in Michigan, at least that I'm aware of..."

As his mom's voice trailed off, he smiled and knew she gave reasons that were not just in jest. Ever since the chaos after a hurricane had taken his dad away from them, her son's safety was still her most genuine concern.

"Gotcha, Mama. I love you, you know that, right?"

"Oh, niño. I do. I do. Hurry this way when you can. Michigan people have funny words for things, but that's still better than hurricanes and tsunamis."

"Si, they may, but you do, too!" they laughed together knowingly, "Every place has something... or they wouldn't need the Coast Guard, Mama. It's who I am."

"Si, and you make us proud. Your brother has been toying with the mission, too, but you didn't hear that from me. You should call him more."

"Si, si. I will. Love you, Mama."

"Thank you for calling my love. Adiós."

Oddly enough, Joshua realized as he hung up that his mother had never wavered in her support of him. He risked himself repeatedly in terrible conditions and situations on behalf of others to support the CG Rescue Swimmer motto, So Others May Live. Her faith in him and the mission was paramount. He realized she gave from her heart for others to live. He had regaled her with epic stories of powerful waves in the Bering Sea, terrible on-scene rescues due to the rigging in giant fish trawlers, and SAR events that he couldn't have made up. She had never wavered in her encouragement, but the hurricanes still gave her great pause a decade and more later. It was the invisible enemy of her soul to have stolen what could not be replaced in this lifetime.

Well, he thought, *that is it then. Michigan. There are no hurricanes in Michigan, ever.*

Where is Michigan?

It couldn't be any colder than Alaska, right?

I wonder if they have a milk run, salmon run, or a sunshine run, for that matter?

He smiled and typed 'Traverse City, Michigan' in his phone's search bar.

Chapter 19

AT YOUR MERCY

Sometime in March, after submitting his final dream sheet listing his hoped-for follow-on tour, he awoke with an awful toothache. After reporting to work, he mentioned his problem to his Chief, who sent him to the Base Clinic to wait for an emergent appointment. It was unique to him that on this base, they had not only shopping, gas pumps, and recreational opportunities like a bowling alley, theater, and gymnasium for fun but also excellent medical care.

I've heard enough from my other struggling high school buddies to know how great I have it, even if I don't feel great now.

Joshua realized help was on the way as he sat for several hours in the clinic's waiting room for the on-call dentist. When a petite middle-aged Hispanic woman in a white coat over her uniform appeared and called his name, he gasped. It was like he looked at his abuela from long ago.

I'd only recognize her from my mother's photo albums now, he realized sadly.

This woman's contagious smile was on the face of a USCG Captain. She repeated his name, this time slower, and laughed with him in his apparent disbelief. He stood sheepishly and nodded mutely, unsure of what to say.

He thought, *Can I tell a woman she looks just like my grandmother?*

Is that a compliment?

No, do not say that to a Captain!

Especially one about to work on your teeth.

Captain Eva Paz had a warm smile and, with a twinkle in her eye, introduced herself.

She said, "I am Dr. Paz. I apologize that we are short-staffed at this late hour. I do want to eliminate any pain you have pronto."

Joshua followed her to the exam room and did not remember seeing her. He was uncomfortable in the chair as he opened his mouth for her to look closer.

Why is she so familiar, disarming, and high in rank?

She was masked by then, and he closed his eyes as he leaned back for an inspection. There was nothing as awkward for Joshua as the display of his terrible teeth to someone up close. One time in boot camp, a hygienist gasped at the sight of his crooked and misplaced teeth upon inspection. He had little to no orthodontic care his whole life. There was no money for such extravagances. He still remembered his classmates' complaints about excellent dental care. They waltzed through life with perfect teeth and so little gratitude. He did not want the pitied look from this woman who looked like his grandmother, but he was literally in her hands and, even worse, in pain. Joshua gripped the armrests with white knuckles, which was a rarity.

Rescue me, please.

"Hmmm.... very nice. I think I have found the culprit to your woes, Mansoul," said Captain Paz. She patted his arm as she raised the back of his chair. "Today, I will ask to remove a tooth from you, and soon, you will discuss a serious matter with me, si?"

Joshua felt small and weak in front of this tiny force of nature with her hopeful smile. He would have followed her anywhere, even an expeditious tooth loss.

He faltered when he replied, "I'm at your mercy," as he rubbed his sore jawline.

"Yes, you are in the good graces of the USCG. You clean your teeth well; you were just given a bad start with your first set, which has not helped your second set. I recommend that once you are back in the lower 48, you get help for a much-improved set with a rescue from the CG! When will that be for you?"

"I PCS this summer," he said shocked.

An improved set?

She added with a sly grin, "Now we'll take the one in the worst situation out to make room for the rest to breathe a little, si?!"

In that tense moment, without thought, Joshua could not answer in English or his native Spanish language. She immediately prepared for the extraction and lowered the chair again near her lap. He was still lost in his "bad set" comment and sunk further in the shame of his youthful experiences due to his terrible teeth. He remembered the other kids had teased him about his awful teeth from before adolescence. It was as if a dam had burst. A lone tear of grief mingled with relief worked its way down his neck unchecked as he regarded his newest and closest friend in the world through blurry eyes. He was grateful to close his eyes while she worked. He let the pain of the extracted tooth and all the excruciating tooth memories roll away.

While the Captain eased him back up in the chair from the extraction, just a few minutes later, she handed him one tissue with a wink. She smiled like his mother, and without words, she seemed to have understood the years of agony of teasing, discomfort, and shame over his teeth being malformed and growing up in poverty. She tenderly patted his shoulder.

"All gone," she said.

"This is the best pain relief I've ever had," he tried to joke with her.

They both knew he had failed to cover his unchecked emotions. He blew his nose and wiped his eyes like a child as he sheepishly regarded her. She waited patiently for him to collect himself. She saw past his youthful banter and squeezed his arm.

"Dios has seen and will deliver you; you must trust him, Niño. He wants you to live abundantly, too, no?"

Joshua wanted to either lift her off her feet or kiss her feet for physical and emotional relief but knew neither was appropriate.

"Aye, Aye, Ma'am."

He lowered his voice, spoke to her in his most heartfelt Spanish, and shook her hand with his, "Muchas gracias."

She replied with a wink and a smile while she peeled off her gloves and mask. She asked to have him schedule a follow-up visit soon and waved him away until the next visit. Joshua could not remember a visit to the clinic ever feeling so light and peaceful.

All from tooth pain!

Did she offer that the CG might help me get orthodontic work?

I might have enough money saved to do it... Why haven't I thought of it before?

Joshua looked forward to his next PCS if for the relief alone of the crookedness in the mirror that awaited him every day as he shaved. Astounded, he returned to work, but not before a quick call to his mom.

"Mama, I was rescued by a little 'Angel de Dios' who wore the rank of a USCG Captain."

Weeks later, another SAR alarm screamed overhead as Joshua threw back a wool blanket from his tired frame in the dark. The lights were snapped on and glared overhead. Joshua's body pumped with adrenaline as he quickly dressed. The men who shared the ready room groaned as they tugged on their dry suits and boots, which were always required in Alaska. The crew shuffled out the door of that room and wondered collectively,

who in the North Pacific needed them and why?

The polar vortex included hurricane-force winds on any given day that no one in the lower 48 would dream about going into. Nevertheless, on any day, it was nearly a typical situation in parts of Alaska.

"Just another Tuesday," they joked among themselves.

Except it wasn't for those who attempted to fly directly into those glacial winds that threatened their survival. Many discussions had to be held, but in the end, every crew member needed to be heard. The entire crew voted whether they felt the risk was worthwhile to fly into the madness that awaited them.

"Aye."

"Aye."

"Aye."

"Aye."

This time, they faced a mission to a vessel that had stalled and taken on water near Resurrection Bay close to Seward. Not only was it a vessel, but it was a tourist vessel out to regard the gray whales that so frequently gorged themselves on amphipods before their migration south to warmer seas near Hawaii.

"Why is a sight-seeing tour boat out at this hour, and in this situation, no one yet understands," remarked the Officer of the Day (OOD).

The real question remained: how many souls were on board? That would determine how many crews would need to be awakened and launched. The crew had already unanimously agreed the mission was worthwhile, and they prepared their Jayhawk for departure as they waited for more information from Sector Anchorage.

Joshua fastened himself into the seat in the Jayhawk and rubbed his gloved hands together as he reviewed his checklist before the flight.

Ah, rescue checklist part one...preparation.

He and his buddy, Jakob Day, were glad to be in one another's company in the back of the helo in the darkness. Although they didn't say much, Joshua understood it was great to be with an Aviation Electronics Technician (tweet) he knew and wanted to work on their mutual trust in every situation.

Tourists flocked to Alaska for wildlife tours, and people were already out to look for whales in April. The crew had learned before they departed that the vessel's engines had quit the day before; therefore, they gradually took on water, and at this late hour, they were precariously close to being hung up on some rocky shoreline. The best estimation was that more than fifty souls were on board (SOB).

Joshua said, "The tour guests have gotten more than they paid for with the outrageous winds from the vortex bearing down on the six-hour-long cruise that is probably more like a nightmare for them."

Jakob sang back, "A three-hour tour..."

The pilot joined in, "Without the courage of the fearless crew..."

Jakob Day had flown often with Joshua and become a friend over the past several years. Their tours overlapped, and they enjoyed the camaraderie that guys of the same rank and life situation: unmarried, adventurous young men who suddenly lived in a one-stoplight town.

Jakob was the sociable one. He was the life of the party, loved rock music, but kept his hair entirely buzzed. Jakob admitted one day that he thought the ladies would prefer him if he kept the military crew cut even shorter. Most everyone saw through his "cut" to be advanced hair recession and that he wanted his head not to look like he was bald prematurely. In his early twenties, it was understandable. Joshua never mentioned it or teased him about it, and for that reason and more, Jakob was his faithful friend.

The best option the crew decided was to lower some dewatering pumps and allow them to wait for a tug from Seward that was on its way. Joshua's Jayhawk helicopter would only comfortably hold three survivors plus the crew. Records had been shattered in Hurricane Katrina and other heroic days, but no one wanted to repeat that misery unnecessarily.

The crew watched the snow that fiercely blew around the tarmac. They pulled away from the hangar and their safety "so others may live" and lifted off into the whiteout conditions. If Joshua could have rolled up his sleeves, he would have, but in his mind, he went over and over the procedures he'd been trained for years to be prepared for whatever he faced, *Semper Paratus.*

After some significant turbulence in the long ride, the helo eventually hovered over the coordinates of the vessel's location. These were immensely valuable since the visibility was down to mere yards. The pilots turned on the highly powered light underneath the helicopter called the midnight sun (Nightsun), and Jakob showed it around the deck of the small cruise vessel at their request. No crew or passengers were visible, but inside, the crew imagined they were cramped and very uncomfortable.

Joshua thought, *most are nauseous in the crashing waves and terrified in what would feel like a sinking cage.*

Jakob said, "I sure hope they don't trample you to get off, Mansoul."

They all remembered the stories told to him of other rescues gone awry. Survivors had made irrational responses in situations that threatened their lives and those they loved. That was as old as time. A vision of the Titanic flashed through Joshua's mind.

Focus on rescue checklist two...

Joshua requested to be put down as the boat lifted precariously high in the water and dropped down again with each large wave that passed underneath or crashed over its foredeck. Without power, the vessel was like a toy that floundered in a toddler's bathtub. The passenger vessel was precariously close to the extensive outcrops of boulders from endless wilderness peninsulas in these remote Alaskan areas. Because of the distance from Kodiak, the crew operated on a slim fuel margin. They immediately lowered Joshua, followed by the dewatering pumps, to the tour vessel for Joshua to use.

Joshua spoke to the crew inside the boat's cabin and shook off the snow and ice that collected on his suit.

"Evening, gentlemen, a fine night to go sightseeing, isn't it?"

They smirked at one another just like Joshua had hoped to relieve some of the tension. Joshua extended his hand to what he hoped was the Captain. They were all red-faced, but that man was almost purple. Joshua didn't know if it was anger or shame.

He spoke loudly, "My name's Joshua Mansoul, CG Rescue Swimmer, and you are?"

Most Alaskan fishermen were crusty old guys who knew how to handle large vessels and the tumultuous seas. Sightseeing guides tended to be younger and less adept at handling large vessels in a polar vortex, let alone in the black of night. This was different from their standard cruise. Though they were trained to use equipment, doing so when their lives and dozens of others depended on it was worrisome.

Their noticeable relief that the Coast Guard had made their way to them gave them a triumphant spirit in the middle of the controlled terror. The staff's redness abated as they continued to speak with urgency.

"Aye, I'm Captain Shamus, pleased to have you aboard."

By the look on your face, thought Joshua, *I don't think you are. I won't stop to ask about your blood pressure.*

Joshua recognized that he had only minutes, so he jumped into action.

He asked the crew, "Do you know how to use this dewatering pump?"

They nodded yes uneasily, but no one moved. Joshua was not convinced. Joshua assumed this could only mean they had been taught but had probably never used one personally.

He thought, *and the truth is probably that you don't know how.*

Joshua said, "I'll show you the way and the truth if you show me below deck."

The three men nearest and most afraid jumped at the opportunity to show him below the passenger deck to the engine room, where the water had collected rapidly. Joshua grimaced and stopped only to report quickly to the helo crew and all the Guardians on alert what he had found and that he would have to demonstrate the process.

His CG crew circled overhead, and the C-130 was out of sight but constantly overhead to watch them. So much pressure was unburdened for Joshua when he realized earlier that it was Padre who once again looked down on all of them. Padre's voice comforted him in his headset earlier and had brought a balm to his raw soul. In the sky, powerful forces worked on their behalf and kept track of them, advocated for them, and could send in more resources like life rafts for all involved in the dangerous, extensive rescues. It was reassurance and standard practice that the Coast Guard would fly far overhead for their protection as they rescued others. It may have appeared to the vessel that Joshua was alone, but no one was truly alone in the mission. Because Joshua had practiced and practiced *Semper Paratus* to set up pumps, he adeptly began to pump water back into the sea where it belonged. The crew cheered and laughed in relief as the water level slowly receded.

One tour crew member hollered, "We did it!"

The others stopped and stared at him in disbelief. The youngest crew member spoke up quickly and chastised the first while he pointed to Joshua.

"The Coast Guard did it, you dummy!"

Joshua chose that moment to remind them what they already knew.

He said, "Sector Anchorage said a tow vessel was coming from Seward. Within the hour, you will be pulled opposite from the shoreline and back through Resurrection Bay towards home *if* you keep these pumps going non-stop. Don't make me come back here for fifty souls. Keep them on!"

He thought, *they could be home before daybreak.*

Joshua climbed carefully atop the vessel to the main cabin as it pitched from side to side into the passenger compartment. He was met by Captain Shamus, who stopped him from his exit. Joshua expected him to offer a word of thanks but instead informed him that there was an elderly individual, Jonas, who, without medication for his uncontrolled health condition, would not survive the long night in the terrible sea conditions. The family was bereft, never thinking that joining a six-hour scenic cruise would have become a life-threatening excursion. When Joshua looked at the older man, he was ashen and as humble as Captain Shamus was arrogant. He passed his eyes over the huddled and frightened passengers.

He thought, *They should've taken the 'milk run.'*

"Please, help us. Help him!" the family rushed to Joshua and began to beg him for assistance.

Joshua regarded Shamus' expression as one of contempt for the added aggravation and inconvenience.

Once again, Joshua radioed his crew to converse and rapidly requested they prepare a basket for the survivor. Sector Anchorage overheard the conversation and was concerned there would be enough fuel for the helicopter to return to Kodiak. They all knew the distance they could cover grew shorter by the second. The flight was then diverted to a closer helo-pad and hospital in Homer. Joshua tried to be of encouragement to Jonas and his family.

Joshua asked Jonas, "How about I meet you in the aircraft before you can count to 100?"

Jonas said, "Throw me overboard and be done with it..."

Then, the older man patted Joshua's helmet like a football coach would have.

The crew and all the souls who remained on board cheered them as they each prepared for departure. Joshua could barely hear their voices of appreciation when Joshua and three crew members opened the hatch and disappeared into the storm to carry the frail man to the hoist cable. The forces of nature rocked the boat heavily, and they strained not to drop him. The door had slammed shut behind them, and the howl of the chaos of wind, ice, and waves threatened them all to be thrown overboard imminently.

Jakob Day, the tweet lowered the basket, and the elderly individual, Jonas, was expedited inside the frozen wet metal basket. The fierce winds howled outside the protected passenger area where his bereft family stood and watched wide-eyed with fear. Joshua dreaded that the man could be blown out and again instructed him firmly to hang on for the ride of his life. He clamped his hands around the man's and pressed them down on the sides of the basket to urge him to hang on tight.

Probably, he can't hear me...

"Don't go overboard on me, Jonas..." he spoke again.

Joshua did not want to go into the water tonight to retrieve him. Jonas did not comprehend what was said, but he nodded appreciatively, then drew a shaky hand to his forehead in salute.

"Roger that!" said Joshua with a big grin as he returned the salute.

Finally, somebody understands good order and discipline! He answered me!

While the basket was hoisted, Joshua held onto a trail line attached to it to prevent its spiral motion in the furious wind and downforce. Joshua knew there was nothing Jakob could do to stop it, nor could he once it began. It was dangerous and messy for Jakob, especially since it was cold and wet, but he was confident in his abilities. Jakob felt the wet snow and ice prohibit his traction inside the cabin and feared for his life. For all their lives if he did not get the survivor and the swimmer back.

Though Joshua tried, the rescue basket spun out of control until it reached the helicopter's side. In astonishment to the crew, the older man was caught in the full gale force winds and spun at a rate that no human would want to have experienced. Joshua was glad Jonas' family could not have seen what happened to their beloved family member from inside. He knew that a matter of life and death was of more excellent value, and he could only hope that the man would hang on and not suffer further from the rescue operation and nausea he must have felt. The basket was brought inside the cabin, and Joshua exhaled a sigh of relief he didn't realize he had held.

Next up ... oh, man.

One crew member pulled Joshua to him in a quick embrace with a sudden force that Joshua had not anticipated. He took the trail line from Joshua's hands and slapped him on the back. Without a word, the stranger communicated his respect and awe for what Joshua had to endure on their behalf.

Joshua's heart continued to race as the quick strop was lowered, and Joshua snapped into it. He made the hand signal, thumb up, for Jakob to retrieve him. As expected, he sailed into the sky and spun uncontrollably. The spin crushed him, yet he spoke not a word. He closed his eyes, gritted his teeth, and focused on each breath he took, not to black out.

Sector Anchorage had rerouted the Coast Guard crew to Homer instead of back to Kodiak. It was a shorter distance, and they could treat the patient with a similar level of care in the closest town. The Jayhawk could also refuel there to return to Kodiak when the weather cooperated and after the crew rested. Joshua was as nauseous as the elderly survivor who could barely lift his head. Joshua attended to his survivor and made Jonas as comfortable as possible. Meanwhile, he fought back his own body's reactions. In minutes, they collapsed in misery, grateful to be inside the helicopter as they went into forward flight.

The crew was on approach to Homer, and the pilots gasped suddenly into their microphones.

They asked one another, "Did you just see that?"

"What was that?" snapped Jakob Day.

Joshua rolled his head to the side and opened an eye in response to their surprise.

It's a memorable moment to shock a CG pilot in a polar vortex while in flight...

"A flare!"

They immediately notified Sector Anchorage that they would pass by the same area due to a flare the pilots had seen. The pilots spoke to one another in controlled tones and decided they had but a small amount of fuel to make another pass toward the flare that had been shot off. They could only presume it was an attention-getting maneuver for the US Coast Guard to begin a SAR. The storm raged around them, but with permission granted, they flew as close as possible to shore. Once again, the light of another flare appeared near them—that time, too close for comfort.

"Not AT us!" shouted the aircraft commander.

Due to the progression of events, Joshua had composed himself enough to watch out the small crew window at the helicopter's side. A dark sky against white snowflakes reflected the lights on the helo for a *Star Wars* appearance around them.

He thought, *If I go back out there, I may as well go through a galaxy far, far away.*

"There, at 3 o'clock!" shouted Jakob.

This time, it looked like a gas fire on a beach where the flames shot up twenty feet quickly, and then it was gone again. Joshua sat up further as he peered out the window. He had only caught just the tail end of the flash in his peripheral view. The flash in his night vision was extraordinarily bright and was gone again. He prepared himself to be deployed again even though his eyes felt blinded momentarily. The pilots coordinated the mission with Sector Anchorage and decided to leave the previous route to the small hospital in Homer to try to assess this situation further. An agreement was made that it was a SAR case. They had fuel for just about seven minutes on scene.

After they made a third pass, one brighter, orange fan of flames shot into the air along a strip of land. Day used the Nightsun that swept the beach, and they saw a fire had been made on a vast beach. As they lowered the aircraft, they were close enough to see a small whaleboat beached at high tide alongside the small fire. There must have been at least one survivor to have set the homemade blaze and the flares off.

"Maybe there are more survivors since someone threw something like gasoline on a flame to get a flash that big to get our attention," said Day.

After making a tight figure eight in the air, the Coast Guard crew hovered over the beach, and Joshua, nauseous, prepared himself to be lowered again to the open beach. They closed in 50, 40, then 30 feet. Jonas reached over and tapped Joshua. Joshua turned with a concerned look on his face towards his survivor. Once again, Jonas saluted, but with more strength this time and a glint in his eye.

Joshua knew, *ah, he knows help is on its way, and he's recovering.*

This bolstered Joshua for his second deployment that night.

This is going to be some hotwash...

"Mansoul, you've got five minutes until bingo," said the co-pilot.

"Swimmer deployed," said Jakob Day.

He lowered Joshua on a long cable line to the beach as his NightSun revealed that Joshua descended again in a spin. The motion ensued as Joshua felt the nausea rise within him.

Joshua's feet hit the sand and rocky beach; he stood and quickly unhooked himself from the hoist cable. He still felt unwell and did his best to find his equilibrium. He was focused solely on the mission, unpredictably as it had become, and took a few steps to right himself.

Find the survivor or at least the cause of the flare, he determined as he strode forward.

He tried to tamp down the disbelief to make a rescue on the way to rescue someone else.

"I am thankful for that Nightsun that Day gave me up and down the beach. It showed me the boat and the small fire in front of me. Here's to being my eyes, Jakob."

Joshua began to trot the distance of the boat about fifty yards away. It was then that something else occurred to Joshua.

I am walking on a beach in the middle of an Alaskan snowstorm, looking for a survivor, but what else may be waiting for me?

I could be found by a hungry grizzly instead...

You're tired, Mansoul. There are no grizzlies out here setting off flares and having s'mores, he reconsidered.

He smacked his helmet with the palm of his hand as if to remind himself that he was under a time crunch and picked up his pace. He began to jog toward the red embers of the fire before him.

Maybe ten yards to...

WHAM!

On top of Joshua was a body that appeared from the periphery of his vision without notice. He hurled sideways, out of his mind with fear, with a reflex he hadn't known he had. Joshua staggered to regain his stability and turned to face the creature on him and expected a grizzly.

Day yelled simultaneously, "Human!"

A small figure clamped her arms around him in an unexpectedly tight grip for such a diminutive size. Joshua only hoped that it was a human and not a wild animal. He caught himself as he stumbled sideways with the additional force. The tiny frame of a middle-aged woman who clung to him nearly knocked them into the sand and rocks.

They grabbed one another and righted themselves to a full-standing position. She put both hands around his helmeted face, surprisingly brought it down to her, and kissed him on the only exposed skin of his face, his chin. He pulled back in astonishment, put his hands on both her shoulders, and stood her back on her feet at arm's length. His exposed skin was so cold that he hardly felt it after just seconds outside.

What in the world is happening?

"THANK YOU," her lips formed.

Joshua could not hear the words but knew what she said. The moment was so unexpected that he laughed out loud despite himself. Joshua only knew it was a woman because of the long, dark, curly hair that had escaped her parka and bright red lips. The fur trim on the parka was wet and frozen and revealed only her thin mouth. She was dressed for the storm but was wet and icy with the sleet and frigid temperature. She trembled with uncontrollable shivers, he realized. He tore into action. Usually, he identified himself first before he made any physical contact, but she evidently knew who he was and expected him. In fact, she had called upon them and nearly shot them down with her flare.

He shouted and mouthed the words slowly so she could see them, "Are there any other survivors?"

She shook her head, "No, thank you for saving me, thank you, thank you, thank you, now, please take me."

She collapsed into his arms again. He realized now she cried with tears of gratitude that froze on her puffy, hypothermic, and swollen cheeks. He picked her up in a cradle hold and returned to the clearer part of the beach, away from the hot embers.

He heard her yell, "Oh, how I have prayed, and you are my deliverer."

She threw her free arm and pointed upward towards the Nightsun that shone down on them from above in a white light. She closed her eyes and hugged Joshua's neck with her arms wrapped tightly around him. He set her down on her feet at about the place he had been lowered, and she swayed as if in a worshipful reverie. She then began to wave her arms over her head in jubilation. It looked to the crew like she danced and sang, though they could not hear her.

A two-armed overhead wave was symbolic to the crew as a distress symbol.

Jakob Day told the pilots, "She's either crazy, high, or exuberant with joy."

Joshua signaled them for a quick hoist and laughed at her memorable rescue.

I sure wish everyone was this cooperative and glad to see me.

Joshua radioed to the crew, "Ready for recovery, one survivor is a happy soul, once lost but found."

Jakob had already helped the older man out of the basket and put him into Joshua's typically assigned seat. They all anxiously waited to see who Joshua would appear with inside the cabin. It seemed to get fuller than they anticipated, and they weren't sure how many survivors were on the beach until his radio call.

Joshua held onto the trail line dropped briefly to keep it from spinning again in the torrential snow. He stood with some effort and realized he was worn out while he waited for what he presumed was their last hoist.

We need to go together; there is no time for her in a less painful trip in a basket.

Joshua tucked her frozen limbs against his chest. He yelled in her ear but didn't know if she could hear him. He patted her shoulder for reassurance. She turned her head away from him and pursed her lips to blow a goodbye kiss towards her boat.

He thought, *that must've been painful with the frostbite forming on her face.*

Joshua snapped them into quick strops for each of them and prepared her as best he could. He made hand gestures for her to hold on tight as he pointed to convey that she needed to hold on to him. She laughed and happily clung to him. He gave the thumbs-up hand signal for the hoist. Under the intense Nightsun in the middle of the bleakest night, he realized he was on a stage like no other. Day's Nightsun spotlight was on him, and together, they conducted the rescue of a lifetime for this woman. She was frozen and yet jubilant. Her pained smile reflected the evidence of the hope within her soul. He brushed the tears that began to spill over her cheeks, but instead, they were soon frozen on her face while she smiled. She gazed up at him then, and in a motherly gesture, she patted his helmet with her mitted hand that he realized was frozen solid as if to say, "My son, well done." He thought of his mama, who had also been rescued before they were raised into the heavens long before. He clung to this woman, someone else's mom perhaps, as they spun together into the vortex.

He marveled; *This petite person's salvation miraculously came on the darkest night.*

Because she was prepared to ask for help in whatever way she could.

The rescue had come just in time.

He, too, felt the joy that arose in his soul. Only then did he look around the barren beach, and he saw miles of open beach strewn with driftwood, the battered old boat, and the empty gas can turned on its side that blew away in the wind. Then he thought of the brilliance of the woman who used the gasoline in the extra tank to throw on a fire as a bright flash of hope to get their attention in a sea of darkness and a whiteout.

She didn't just wait with hope. She expected it. Inexplicably, she knew help was on the way and answered the rotor call before we knew she needed us. Semper Paratus.

The unexpected mission was nearly accomplished, they all hoped. Above the roar of the wind and the storm and the loud noise of the helicopter engine, Joshua celebrated that what had once been lost had been found twice that night. The mission had been successful before anyone else knew otherwise that she had been lost. She expected them to be out searching for her.

Rescue checklist three... Wait until she hears why we were out here...and she was already dancing.

Upon arrival in Homer, the red-lipped woman explained she was headed home to her nearby remote Alaskan island when both the boat motors quit. She had tried to row when the polar vortex had slammed into her adrift in the channel. She was swiftly stranded on the beach with a boatload of supplies but no communication.

Still, in the wee hours of the morning, the crew sought to tend to their own needs at the small Homer airport terminal. They shared a hot meal and had their brief hotwash from the middle of the night alarm onward. The turn of events that escalated with the second rescue case was extraordinary. Eventually, one of the pilots started to laugh uncontrollably. It became apparent to Joshua that the crew's contagious laughter had something to do with Joshua. Exhaustion made fools of everyone, but for his life, he didn't understand why they chuckled at him. The hilarity continued at his expense until finally,

Jakob pointed toward Joshua's face as his tears of laughter streamed from his eyes.

"You. Your face. Look at it," Jakob snickered.

Joshua said, "You guys have lost it."

Jakob motioned him to look toward the wall behind him. Joshua tentatively turned toward a long mirror behind him on the wall and fell silent. He was stunned at his reflection. One of the pilots could no longer contain himself.

He nudged Joshua, "So Joshua.... Do you want to explain all the lipstick on your face or not? We won't tell anyone how young or old she was..."

"Very funny," Joshua replied.

Joshua stood from the table and wandered to a condiments counter to find something to wipe away the red evidence.

Flatly, Joshua responded to the whistles and guffaws.

"Wow, some real thanks are due to you guys. How long were you fellas going to leave me like this?" he continued in disbelief.

The crew wiped their faces with their hands as they cried hilariously. Someone snorted, and that sent them into more riotous laughter. They teased him relentlessly about his "beach rendezvous." Exhaustion had indeed made fools of them all.

"We must be deliriously tired. This isn't that funny. Or is it?" asked Jakob.

The pilot said, "Only because it's innocent, Joshua."

They roared even louder and attracted the attention of the people at the bar across the room, who glanced with annoyance at them all.

Jakob said, "I had planned not to mention it until we returned to base for the hotwash. I at least told you now."

The pilots' laughter grew as Joshua glared at them and then softened with a shake of his head. Joshua excused himself to the men's room to wash it off. Quick. He just shook his head back and forth and laughed to himself.

Who needs enemies with friends like these? Jakob, the deceiver, and my friend.

The pilots stretched out their limbs with a brief walk around the tiny terminal area. After Joshua washed his face clear of the red lipstick stain, he was more awake than the rest of his crew. He watched the sun continue to slowly rise in the early morning hours over the famous Homer Spit. They procured a ride to their motel to sleep until they could safely return to Kodiak the following day.

Full of gratitude, Joshua added two more saves to his catalog of saves versus losses. The reminder of saves versus losses was inevitable in a swimmer's psyche.

It is hard to let go of what could have been even after all this time on duty.

He found it essential to reorient his mind when the darkness of losses crept into his attention, all too frequently, when he was exhausted.

It is never helpful to go down that road of should haves.

Joshua began to make another list. He had things he knew he needed to do to prepare for his permanent change of station (PCS). He anticipated the next move to Traverse City, Michigan, and had been given orders for his PCS midsummer. On his list in his flight suit pocket, he added Snickers bars. He looked forward to one more visit to the pallet fort soon. Perhaps, before some of the boys left for their change of station to follow their parents' careers,

I should leave a stash of the good stuff and a note.

I would like to have seen each of them find a pack of Snickers as a goodwill gesture towards friendship, camaraderie, and childhood. Or those cookies from the café?

He surmised to himself, *I'd prefer to leave coffee and donuts and have a little hotwash on their tours to Kodiak. Nevertheless, the kiddo had requested Snickers. That'll do.*

One day, he would pay it forward with coffee and doughnuts if these kids grew up and wanted to join the mission. He noticed that he had missed a text at four in the morning. Several calls had come in from East Coast time in the wee hours of his days that tour, and he did his best not to be annoyed at anyone who forgot the time change.

At least this time, I'm already awake!

He was pleased it was a familiar number and name, Christian.

It'll be relaxing to unwind with some conversation tomorrow.

Except it is tomorrow...

First, I need some good sleep, and then I will answer after I get back to Kodiak.

He realized he had daydreamed about sleep. The crew piled out of a transport van after he nudged them awake.

"I should've let you guys stay asleep on the van..."

The storm was over. He stumbled into the Land's End Resort and wished he could appreciate the resort part of his stay. Likely, he'd never return to Homer to enjoy the "end of the road" as they called it.

I am grateful for the end of a long day, whatever time it is this morning, and it was a good one.

He tightened the blackout curtains shut on a beautiful pink and yellow Alaskan sunrise that spread across a violet sky. He fell into bed and noticed that just a fraction of light showed around the wall of windows. He enjoyed the thought that it was impossible to hold back the light.

Chapter 20

ANSWERS

Midafternoon Joshua awoke from a deep sleep and flew back to Kodiak in the refueled Jayhawk over crystal calm waters.

"What a difference a few hours make," said Jakob over the mic.

Joshua realized, *I'm famished.*

"Jakob, you got anything to eat?"

"Nothing to share."

Jakob proceeded to open a bag of nachos he'd swiped from a vending machine before they left. Then he opened a Coca-Cola bottle, and Joshua waited for its contents to spew everywhere.

Joshua threw his hands up in the air with indignance.

What? Are you kidding me?

"Nacho, problem, right Day?" laughed a pilot who caught the interaction in his rearview mirror of the amiable crew.

Joshua just shook his head, laughed, and closed his eyes for more shut-eye on the smooth ride.

Joshua said, "I'm not going to clean that mess up."

The guys on the crew teased him for his attempt to sleep most of the way home.

"Mansoul, you think you can sleep through anything?" said the pilot.

"Only because you're so good at what you do!" he quipped back, "and there's no in-flight snack service."

Once they landed back on the tarmac at Kodiak, Jakob said, "If I'd had some lipstick, I'd have redrawn those lip prints!"

Joshua returned home after a cheerful hotwash and, still famished, fixed himself some salmon. He'd saved the king salmon from a fishing expedition offshore the previous fall. Afterward, he remembered to check his phone. He dug into the food, still amazed he'd eaten so well off the land and out of the sea for years.

How I love being "closer to the earth" in Alaska.

He had surprisingly missed several texts. One was from his brother Jimmy, or James as he had recently renamed himself, and another was from his old buddy, Caleb, from ECity. It seemed like he'd been gone for days, but only a few hours before they had left, not even a whole day. The first text was from none other than Christian, the young man he'd rescued in North Carolina.

It read:

Hi, You'll be glad to know I've joined the Coast Guard since you last called me!

I hope to finish boot camp by the end of summer and rendezvous with you in Alaska or at your next duty station.

Let me know where UR headed.

Excited to follow in your wake.

Ah, excellent wordplay. He's following me. Wow. I'm honored.

Somewhat stunned, Joshua sat for some time at his table. He remembered his first real conversation with Christian outside the kite shop and again in two subsequent coffee and donut chats before he left for Alaska.

I miss those Duck Donuts.

He had hoped the teen would continue to recover from the loss of his buddy, Nic, whose life was sadly shortened by the refusal of rescue.

On my watch duty.

Joshua paused and wondered, *have I recovered from his tragic loss and Mo's?*

He looked way off in the distance over St. Paul's Harbor, and the sunlight that bounced off the shimmering water made him squint. He wanted to leave their burdensome tragedies in Alaska before he left. He looked at the other random messages and decided his answer to them should wait. He re-dressed quickly for an adventure, stuffed a bag with gear, and headed off for some alone time on a mountain top not far away. He glanced at his watch and went faster, unsure why.

First, just coffee.

When Joshua pulled up in his rickety truck next to Island Coffee, a well-established drive-through coffee stand. He smiled at his preferred barista, Sara. She knew he only splurged for specialty coffee after a save, as did some Guardians. Others preferred to celebrate in a host of various ways. He also knew she was flirtatious. Or at least she worked hard for tips. She leaned out the window close enough to almost hug him.

She said, "What will you have today, Coastie?"

He gave her a polite nod, self-conscious of his smile in front of the cute woman.

It's just hot coffee, but it seems a waste not to pick a flavor with all these options, but I'm not in the mood to decide.

He answered, "Hot tall coffee with a flavor, but please surprise me."

She smiled widely, "Hmmm.... Surprise me, that's adventuresome... awesome sauce."

He pulled a $10 bill from his wallet and offered it to her, "Keep the change or pay it forward."

Who am I to tell her what to do? That was a dumb thing to say.

I want to palm my forehead after that comment, but that'd only worsen this.

She smiled broadly, began to giggle, and turned away. A minute later, she returned to the window and handed him the hot coffee wrapped in a coffee sleeve that had writing on it and had steam that wafted off the top.

She leaned out too far again and hesitated, "Thanks, sweetie pie; I wrote my number on your cup."

She watched him roll up his window and drive away. His face reddened from the collar on his shirt up. Somehow, her words and accent took him back to North Carolina.

He wondered, *what had brought her so far north from her roots?*

I'm not headed back to Carolina any day soon; sorry, Sara.

He pulled away from the drive-through to leave Near Island, where the stand was located. He saw what she had written. The cup had a different message: "The most difficult trails lead to beautiful destinations."

A difficult trail it is, then, he thought, *whew. Everyone wants to see me blush.*

He pointed his truck towards Barometer Mountain for a short, very steep hike up the side of a mountain that overlooked the CG Base. Everyone saw the same mountain when they flew into Kodiak each time on an airliner if the weather cooperated. He came to Kodiak with questions and still had more questions that needed answers.

Answers are important. I need to be ready with answers for the hope that I have.

As he drove south from town, he hadn't anticipated the recent sleet, and slippery conditions quickly turned to an icy glaze as the sun dropped in the late afternoon. He wasn't prepared to climb on ice, and as a good Guardian, he knew better than to start unprepared.

He contemplated, *where to head instead for a "mountain top experience" close to sea level?*

He guided his truck to a stop in front of the Boy Scout Beach parking lot. He walked the short-mile path through the mushy leftover snowpack. He was glad it was familiar enough to go over the covered, worn trail between green mosses and beneath the Sitka Spruce trees that towered overhead and lifted his eyes heavenward. He was oceanside before his coffee had cooled entirely, and he took a slurp where the path met the empty beach. It wasn't a difficult trail, but it was a gorgeous destination when the view of the Pacific Ocean opened to him at his feet. Cliffsides sat back from the tide's pull as demarcation lines of how far the open ocean could reach.

I got to my beautiful destination with little difficulty today.

He looked at the empty cup again and reread her message. He laughed at his humiliation just prior.

I hope I don't cross paths again with Sara. I should have known better than to think she'd have left her number.

He plopped down on the vast coastline with the beach all to himself.

I will miss the dark sandy beaches and lull of this rocking ocean.

He redirected his attention and heart and looked up. He always wanted to get away and spend time with his Father in seclusion like this. The busier his activities made him, the more he knew he needed to avoid endless activities to keep his perspective on what was most important. Today, he wanted answers. His gratitude soared as the last warm swig of coffee smoothly went down.

With a hint of raspberry, he thought while he smiled to himself, *or was it salmonberry?*

Berries would be on their way, but he would not see nor taste them this year in Kodiak.

What kind of berries are grown in Northern Michigan? he wondered.

He knew he would find out soon enough.

Papa, are you glad I'm following you? Have I done what you've asked? Are you proud of me? The saves were such glory, but I have trouble with the losses.

Joshua fell back on the wet sand in defeat and felt the cold earth beneath him, but his view of the vast sky was unencumbered. He still missed his papa ever since his youth when he was suddenly gone.

But you have never left me.

He wished for a conversation to share what had happened in the last few hours. Instead of a phone call, like most Guardians got to make, he took the time to get away and share out loud, if possible, what was on his heart and mind to whoever listened. Some people he knew emptied their minds to meditate. He preferred to fill it with purpose. His papa had promised him rescue, and it had come. It would come again.

Joshua focused on a cloud that passed and an arc higher in the atmosphere. It was a contrail that swept from horizon to horizon in Alaska for those long-haul flights that skipped across continents.

Look how far I have come, Papa.

Rescue Checklist One I have done. I am Semper Paratus.

Help me, please, be freed from the burdens that I have hoisted and tried to hoist, like Mo; take them from me, Rescue Checklist Two.

I'm excited about Christian joining us in the CG. I suppose the loss of Nic has played an immense part in the life choices of Christian. Only you know the truth if they both could've been saved. I'm going to trust that you will redeem both situations.

Survivors had two options when presented with the Coast Guard Mission to rescue them. Communication was notoriously tricky, but discernment was vital, even across language barriers, time constraints, and dangerous circumstances. The CG made it clear to survivors you could engage or negotiate at your peril. Joshua and his crews wrestled with the unseen forces that cloaked people's minds and discernment.

Why do people try to negotiate and risk everything? I want to save them. It's who we are.

Joshua sat up and looked for a big rock to heave into the sea. He wanted to throw it into the waves that crashed nearby and, therefore, leave the weighty losses at the bottom of the abyss. He got up, dusted the sand from him, and ventured down the beach by the shoreline. He found nothing worthy to be an escape rock close by. He walked a short way down the line of the tide that came in. Joshua remembered how he felt when he walked through the HS cafeteria long ago and looked for someone to rescue during Hurricane Ike. The same worldview came back to him like a blanket of comfort.

I am a survivor of storms, not a victim of them.

Thanks, Papa... I will not fear what they fear.

Joshua saw something tumble around in the surf's foam, which he supposed was driftwood. Upon closer examination, he saw a large chunk of sea glass. He danced with the tide as it rolled in and out and then just walked into the water since he had on his trusty Xtratuf boots. He picked it up carefully and inspected it in his hand. The once broken and jagged edges of what he supposed was an antique blue bottle were now rubbed smooth. He lifted it before the sun, its last rays of sunlight, and the blue shone brilliantly as if it were a sapphire.

It is beautiful in its time.

He had heard from a friend that blue sea glass was some of the most valuable to be found. He'd only previously seen tiny fragments of blue, and this piece was the size of a half-dollar coin. Kodiak was known for its sea glass. Anywhere in the world, "blues" were prized by glass collectors.

This is undoubtedly cherished, but only in the eye of the beholder.

Broken, old, and discarded junk had become valuable over time, and years of rolling around on the sea bottom had worn it soft to the touch. It had to be rescued from the beach and found by someone who could see and feel its value. A timeless treasure of great worth was valued simply because of the progression it had been through and in a collector's eye.

He smiled despite himself and felt like a kid with a candy bar.

Should I keep it or give it away?

The response reverberated in his heart. It was a poignant answer to his previous question with his papa moments before.

The brokenness in loss, with its jagged edges of hurt and remorse, could one day be made whole when worn smooth among the sands of time, hope, and the anticipation of cherished treasure in a new creation. What was considered wasted could be made valuable, even beautiful, with time and perspective.

Thanks, Papa.

Joshua pondered whether to take a quick picture of the piece of glass for a souvenir but decided it was too sacred to try to relay in any conversation except through his memory. The purity of the moment hardly deserved words, let alone explanation. He held the big blue in his palm, closed his grip around it, kissed his fingers, and pitched it as far out as he could, past the surf that broke yards away. The blue was simultaneously lost and rescued. This time, it was given up willingly and with gladness. Joshua's burdens had slipped from his hands and rested at the bottom of an Alaskan coastline, safe for time and eternity. If the blue surfaced again, perhaps it would rescue another time-worn and burdened soul for redemption.

Snickers bars in hand, Joshua pulled away from the commissary in the hurricane-force winds several weeks later. Grocery carts sailed in various directions through the parking lot like children let loose at recess, frolicking on a playground in every direction at once. A sign nearby read *PARK AT YOUR OWN RISK*. Now he knew why.

He said, *I won't miss these ferocious winds, and I'm glad I've got a beater truck.*

He wasn't concerned about cart damage. He planned to give away his truck and everything else he could manage. Easy come, easy go was his motto, except when it came to the rescue of souls on board.

Geez, imagine explaining that to my insurance man...

"Why were you shopping in a hurricane?"

No, sir, just another Tuesday in May on Kodiak Island, he began to chuckle aloud.

In the lower 48, they had weather advisories about storms this strength. He felt poorly for the local festivities planned for the Crab Festival downtown that day. The rides, events, and booths would fare badly in these extreme conditions.

Joshua realized, *things will likely be very different in Traverse City.*

Do they have a festival like the Crab Festival?

He'd enjoyed the excitement of the annual Crab Festival that had happened the previous year. He particularly enjoyed a swimmer demonstration for the crowds at the harbor and the flyover later in the morning.

Joshua parked and looked around for his little candy stash buddies as he retraced his steps to the pallet fort for his stealthy candy replenishment. The 60 mph winds covered his covert stash of candy. He had also prepared a note to leave them.

It read,

> *Kryptonite Kids, here's to building on a firm foundation. May you each have a long life of looking up and following closely in your Guardian's footsteps.*
>
> *Your Rescuer and friend,*
> *Joshua*

After he left the base, Joshua remembered his latest discussion with Christian and their plans to rendezvous at his graduation from boot camp or shortly after that.

Christian had said, "I'd be honored if you could come, Joshua, I mean Petty Officer Mansoul. I wouldn't have done this without your inspiration... Well, the truth is, and you know it, I wouldn't be here without you."

"I'd be honored to represent the ASTs, but any of us would have gladly rescued you. It's who we are. I'm thankful you decided to join us in the mission."

Joshua had been so gratified since they had spoken. He remembered that Christian had also decided to try to join him as an AST. He would do his best to encourage him.

He explained, "There's no way to prepare you for that training adequately."

Christian replied, "I've got to try."

Imagine that? Christian has suffered so much, but it could be used to build perseverance. If he had perseverance, he would have the character of a Guardian. As a Guardian, he had to develop hope. With hope, the mission would never disappoint him.

Semper Paratus was Christian's new call. It seemed lots of people were joining up these days. The news had prompted Joshua to call Jones, who had recruited him back in High School to join up.

What a riotous conversation that was, Joshua remembered, *and meaningful.*

The retired swimmer made him laugh until his sides hurt about recent events and old CG stories. He had been delighted Joshua reached out to him, especially from Kodiak. Before he ended the call, Mr. Jones surprised him. Jones admitted that each day before he "fell out of bed," he began it with consideration of Joshua and the importance of his mission to the world that day.

Jones added, "Makes getting up every morning as a broken old Coastie easier, knowing I played a small role in today's continued mission. I'm a happy man you answered the call, Mansoul. I don't know where I'd be without it. You saved me in my old age."

Joshua kept silent. Jones got a little choked up and lowered his voice to a whisper.

He added haltingly, "Son, ...you make me proud."

"Thank you, Sir, as do you."

"Until next time then, Petty Officer 2nd Class Joshua Mansoul."

Joshua was stunned to feel how much the words, "Son, you make me proud," spoken through the tiny device in his hand from thousands of miles away, had wrapped around his heart and squeezed it hard. He wasn't sure who had saved who when he hung up.

I suppose that's the natural gift of being a rescuer.

Joshua glanced inside the back of his friend Jakob's pickup in June when he arrived to pick him up for their departure from Kodiak.

"Sorry, I got all this stuff, Day. Hard to part with everything, but I tried," said Joshua. Joshua had a duffel bag and two large plastic totes that held all his worldly goods. Most of those were uniforms, to be sure, a computer, some cards his family and friends had sent that he couldn't part with, some random magnets, clothing, seashells, and sea glass from North Carolina and Kodiak. He had a small red kite tucked into a long tube with some maps and photos he'd collected from his adventures. He wore his Xtratuf boots, Carhart coat, and a favorite flannel shirt and planned to most of their trip. They were headed south to Canada, which was fun to tell people.

Joshua's travel buddy, Jakob, was shocked and said, "That's it, Mansoul?"

Later, Joshua stood astounded as he watched Jakob strap his fat bike, snowshoes, hiking poles, and surfboard into the truck bed with another ton of stuff. Joshua pitched in to load the bags, totes, and other gear his friend expected to haul. The truck towered over a small camper they planned to use along the Alaska-Canada Highway (ALCAN) on their way to their follow-on permanent stations much further south. Jakob had so much stuff, and Joshua just looked on, amused at how many treasures the man had collected and wanted to take with him.

"That's it, Day?" Joshua added with a tease.

"Ha, ha, very funny. If you want to give it all away, Mansoul, fine with me. I like my stuff. I can see a future with all of this in Detroit."

Joshua sighed, *leaving anything here to help someone else feels great. It's worth more to the people here.*

"What good is it unless you can give it away?" said Joshua.

No need to be burdened by stuff on our journey.

"I wouldn't have had any room to bring anything else anyhow," Joshua added with a hearty laugh.

Jakob shrugged in agreement. They were off to meet the Alaska State Ferry in town that would take them to Alaska's inside passage. Then, they would jump on the Alaska Canada Highway (ALCAN) to the lower 48. It was a gorgeous day to sail, and they had to be there promptly to queue up for the scheduled boarding hours ahead of time. The state ferry system was persnickety.

Joshua thought, *I've been waiting to travel "home" this way for most of my tour.*

"I can't believe the day has finally arrived, Day..."

He had missed the opportunity on the front end to travel across the continent. There would be daily stops on the ferry, much like his milk run the year before. In Haines, they planned to depart the West Coast of the continental US and have the most fantastic cross-continent truck-camping adventure of a lifetime.

They arrived at the ferry terminal dock, and the MV Tustumena, or "Rusty Tusty," had already been tied up. After parking their truck in the appropriate queue for embarkation, they noticed a party in full swing. An Air Station gathering was already near the exit from where the ferry was unloading. The traditions of new island residents being heartily welcomed like he had been at the airport years ago were still in full force.

Jakob sighed contentedly, "Ah, it ends as it begins for someone else."

The coffee was hot and flowed into cups with the Fly-By logo. One of the favorite coffee shops had set up a temporary stand. That was frequently when the ferry arrived for those who came ashore and unloaded. It was a bitter or sweet last souvenir for those like Joshua and Jakob who wanted a cup to depart with much later after having parked the truck and camper on the ferry.

He and Jakob were in for a surprise when they made their way to the stand after they marked their truck with the appropriate tag. They recognized a small crowd that chanted Joshua's name and waved him over. He turned red as he felt the blood rush to his face when he discovered a diverse and wonderful group of friends had gathered to see him off. Sam, Miriam, Christina, Silas, Jared, and Jessie were present, with plenty of cookies to share. Little Christina stood next to Mrs. Hill as they held a cardboard sign that said, "King of the Rock... We will miss you."

"Joshua," they hollered, "over here for hugs!"

Joshua was stunned and speechless. The kids had grown so much in four years.

And they remembered me?!

Another woman, who looked vaguely familiar, huddled with a box of donuts next to some of the local Mission employees. She broke free from the group as he neared, and her bright lips again found his cheek. His face turned purple from embarrassment. Everyone laughed at his expense. It only underscored how everyone knew he was a favorite amongst the ladies for all the right reasons. This cheery woman was clueless until it was pointed out that she'd left her mark. She hurried and tried to wipe it off, but she made a big red smear instead. She apologized repeatedly, and Joshua finally embraced the woman for one last hug to stop her chatter. She eventually just threw back her head in inexplicable joy. She pulled back at arm's reach for Joshua and spoke for everyone to hear.

"Everyone's coffee is on me! Thanks be to God for my rescuer and hero, Joshua!"

"Hoorrah!" exclaimed Jakob.

Jakob cocked his head and made a motion with two fingers that pointed at himself, like, 'Where is my attention?'

Jared pipped up as they all turned to go and line up at the coffee stand, "But I want milk with my cookies!"

The lipstick lady promptly handed the box of donuts intended for Joshua to Silas and Jared. They looked at one another and shrugged. They tore open the box without regard to their parents and dug in joyfully. Jakob helped himself, and the boys laughed at his rival greediness.

Padre stood with his wife, two small boys, and Chaps nearby to greet and farewell Joshua.

Padre spoke while he hugged him, "Hey man, you're going to be missed."

"You're on your way soon, too, aren't you?" said Joshua.

"Soon. That word doesn't mean much in the CG mission world. You know that," said Padre.

Padre's wife rolled her eyes and then elbowed him in the side. The boys at their feet swayed back and forth, pointed at the ferry, and looked partly nervous and restless.

Joshua asked the boys, "You guys want donuts, too?"

They nodded hopefully towards Joshua.

"Let's see if they can feed the multitudes," Joshua said.

He appreciated them waiting patiently for their portion.

They've got great parents.

Joshua ushered them to his buddies, who munched happily and asked them to share their gifts. They warily obliged and handed the box over. They continued to chew and smear sugar with their sleeves across their smiling faces. They had gladly shared, and Joshua acknowledged that with fist bumps of praise. Padre nodded his appreciation for the shared gifts and added another comment upon Joshua's return.

"We're on the same ferry out of here with you. The boys saw the party, and we saw the coffee line. Chaps here spotted us. It's a great reunion day for sure."

"Chaps, it looks like you've come to terms with hot coffee on a June day," Joshua said.

He tipped his cup towards the chaplain in the manner of a toast.

"Yes, well, looks can be deceiving," Chaps replied.

Chaps waved his Yeti for all to hear the ice cubes clinking inside, "No one has converted me yet!"

Padre, his wife Starr, Joshua, and Jakob groaned at his joke.

A pretty blonde stepped beside Joshua, and he gulped when he realized who it was. His barista friend, Sara, had come way out of her way to say farewell. Her influence on Joshua was pronounced.

He thought, *I've never seen her outside of the coffee shack!*

She drawled, "Honey, I couldn't let you get away without a hug goodbye. All I had to do was ask around, and everyone knew this was your last day. I guess I've been hoping you would take me with ya'll."

Sara winked at the unmarried men, Jakob and Joshua.

Joshua looked in shock at Jakob, "Ummm...."

Jakob looked back over his shoulder at his truck; it already overflowed, and he suddenly seriously considered the option.

Full of sudden regret, Jakob said, "Well, we're kinda loaded."

Joshua was extremely relieved that Sara's attention was focused on Jakob, he hoped.

Sara crept between them, smacked their backs, and laughed at the heat that arose in their faces. Joshua was humbled by all the attention and made introductions as best he could. Self-conscious of the fact that he had red lipstick on his cheek already and a pretty woman next to him, he changed the subject and stammered,

"Are you just here for an undercover Fly-By coffee taste test, Sara?"

"No, Sugar, I've never seen you outside the ratty old truck you've been driving, and I wanted to shake your hand."

She batted her eyelids only at him and offered her slim hand.

Joshua took it and awkwardly shook it three times in quick succession.

"Plus, no one on this whole island tips as great as you do, and I am finally paying it forward as you say," she added.

Joshua felt the heat rise again in his cheeks and locked eyes with Padre. He sent him a silent, wide-eyed gaze he hoped he recognized.

Help.

Padre's wife, Starr, stuck out her hand to shake Sara's hand. Starr had caught the look.

She replied, "I'm Starr. I could use a coffee, thank you very much."

Sara said dejectedly, "Oh, well, I meant Joshie-baby, but okay, I suppose."

Padre and his wife steered Sara toward the coffee truck, and Joshua took a deep breath.

Starr replied loudly, "Let me introduce you to my friend, Eva."

"Oh, Okay..." said Sara while she waved her hand towards the guys in farewell.

Chaps promptly burst out in laughter. Joshua realized he'd held his breath for a minute. He grimaced and exhaled.

Chaps said, "You forgot to breathe, Mansoul."

"Glad you can laugh, Chaps," said Joshua.

Chaplain grinned and said, "We're all out here to help others in any way we can, remember?"

Jakob said, "I'm not laughing," and followed Sara and Starr dejectedly toward the coffee.

"Keep looking up, my man, keep looking up. Things could be a lot worse. Let's get that lipstick off you before you board the ferry."

"Como estas?" said a bright female voice.

Joshua stopped in his tracks and turned towards the voice that had spoken. He faced a miniature Captain that belonged to the accent he had just heard. Wide-eyed, he took in the petite Hispanic woman who drowned inside a short parka in June. Her face appeared inside the muff of fur that framed her head, but recognition hit him.

Joshua said, "Captain Paz! I'm honored that you're here, too. No, you must be here for someone else?"

Joshua looked around him humbly and searched for someone else she might have spoken to.

She said, "I've heard about these Air Station welcomes and farewells. It's my honor to say farewell, Joshua Mansoul. However, I hope to hear from you and your progress."

She motioned toward her teeth and winked. She shivered and then laughed at herself for her cold condition in June.

She spoke again, "I know it's June, but I'll never get used to these temperatures. Enjoy your friends, but we will talk again, I hope when you arrive at your next station. I'll do my best to help you set up your appointments through your new provider in Traverse City. I've made some recommendations in your medical records."

"Muchas gracias! I will never forget your kindness."

Captain Paz opened her tiny hand, spoke graciously, and gestured towards the people who celebrated near Joshua.

"Just as your community will not forget you, who answered them in their time of need. May Dios make his face shine upon you and be gracious unto you, young man."

He has indeed, he is, and he will.

Joshua looked around at all those who had answered him agreeably in the past few years and smiled sheepishly. Those with lipstick, sugar, and coffee smiles returned the grin. Rescuers were made to rescue. The rescued, he learned, could also make the most faithful of friends and, in return, liberate their rescuers if needed. He nodded appreciatively at Padre.

"This is a great way to spend our lives," Joshua said to no one and everyone.

Jakob returned with two coffees in hand and a donut in his mouth. The steam rolled out of the tiny holes in the top. He offered one to Joshua and then took the donut from his mouth.

Jakob said, "You talking to yourself, Mansoul?"

Joshua smirked at him.

Jakob said, "We've got 5,000 miles to go, and you need to explain why everyone wants to *talk* to you, yet you talk to yourself."

They believed in the mission and its principles and followed their leaders well. *Semper Paratus* meant to show up for people when called upon in their hour of need or of abundant celebration and was most worthwhile in both circumstances. This was the best life could offer for Joshua and others he hoped would follow and answer him.

PART 3

REMEMBER ME OR HOPE DESTROYED

Chapter 21

I SCREAM, YOU SCREAM

Traverse City, Michigan

"We're gonna remember this forever," said Joshua.

"I'm trying to forget," said Jakob.

Jakob Day was his friend and travel companion for the past month. They both scratched at another bug bite collected on their North American cross-continent trip.

"Seriously, this was the most incredible trip. I can't thank you enough for going the extra distance to drop me in Traverse City," said Joshua.

Joshua was thrilled to have made the 3,000-mile trip and have finally landed at his new home. His buddy, Jakob Day, had been a Tweet at the same Air Station they had come from in Kodiak, Alaska.

Jakob said, "I need a Coke. No, I need a shower, a hamburger, *and* a Coke."

"Let me find a public beach first to get clean, and then the celebration meal is on me," Joshua replied.

"Why a beach?" said Jakob.

"Free showers. Nobody wants us in a place that serves food," he replied and added a smirk when they regarded one another.

Jakob nodded in consent. The friends were filthy and regarded the state of one another like they were looking in a dimly lit mirror.

I want to look better than our current status when we enter my new hometown and, more precisely, an actual food establishment, thought Joshua.

Jakob thought, *Mansoul looks rough. Rougher than a Guardian should look.*

Joshua and his friend Jakob rolled into Traverse City, Michigan, late on an unseasonably hot July day. Jakob's truck and camper were even filthier than the men. The Alaska plates on the front and back were *almost* unreadable. Someone had drawn "Wash Me" on the backside in the brown caked mud.

Jakob joked, "Funny how cleanliness hasn't mattered for the past 22 days, but it does now."

It was an ambitious drive over horrendous roads and wilderness across four time zones.

"I'm grateful. We camped all along the way just as we planned," answered Joshua.

Jakob quipped, "And we have the memories and mosquito bites to prove it."

"We also gotta get the flat tire fixed and back on your truck instead of the spare," said Joshua.

The stinky men peeled themselves out of the truck for an anticipated "end of the journey" photo opportunity near the shore of Lake Michigan at Traverse City State Park. They decided on the way to the shoreline from the truck; they couldn't waste time for a photo. The beautiful crystal water beckoned to them. They were sore, tired, and itched unmercifully. They saw the pure water, and it beckoned to them like thirsty men in a hot desert.

"Is it real or just a mirage?" asked Jakob.

Joshua picked up his pace and hollered, "The last one in is the loser," as he passed Jakob in a dead sprint.

Delirious with joy, they sprinted across the beach and tossed shoes, phones, and wallets in a pile on the sand. They plunged fully dressed headlong under the water's surface, and it did not irritate their skin like saltwater did. The marvelous obliteration of grime freed them. They jumped up and splashed one another and laughed at their state. Fully clothed and waist-deep in fresh water, they gawked at one another like mischievous kids. They submerged themselves repeatedly with the glee of children who discovered the joy of unrestrained splashing in the water. Jakob fell backward with a flop and tried to float while he scrubbed his scalp vigorously to scour away a month of camp grime. Joshua swam like a showy dolphin and sliced through the water in wide circles around the nearly empty swim area. The cool temperatures of the Bay off Lake Michigan did not bother the men. It was the warmest water they had been in outside in years. Alaskan water was just above freezing. This shallow Bay off Lake Michigan was luxurious in comparison. Joshua remembered some billboards they had seen earlier in the day.

He repeated the signage, "Welcome to Michigan, Great Lakes, Great Times."

"Yup, great times indeed," said Jakob.

Jakob fell backward again into the water, then did a summersault and attempted a handstand on the sandy bottom of the lakeshore. He came up and sputtered the freshwater out of his mouth.

Joshua admitted, "We could use a bar of soap right about now, too."

"Nope, I'm gonna hit the free shower for that and then trash these clothes later. We're like a couple of ugly civilians after three weeks without a shave and shower!" said Jakob.

Joshua told his friend, “We’re unrecognizable from the guys who left Kodiak and our Air Station duties a month ago.”

“It’s nice to be incognito,” replied Jakob.

After a few more minutes of leisure in the freshwater, their stomachs grumbled and demanded to be fed. The guys waded out of Grand Traverse Bay for food, but first, cleanliness.

After “luxurious” hot showers courtesy of the State Park, the guys agreed they were thankful for the good taxpayers of Michigan. They headed towards their truck and carried the soggy clothes from the beach. They wore the freshest clothes they had found in the bottom of a tote packed a month ago and felt like new men. They dumped the old wet stuff in a trash can.

“Why am I surprised they, too, have bear-proof cans in Michigan?” murmured Jakob.

“There’s more to Michigan than Detroit,” teased Joshua.

Jakob said, “Yeah, where are we on the mitt again?”

Joshua remembered his old friend Ben from his time in boot camp, who was a Michigan native and from Traverse City. He looked forward to a rendezvous with him at some point while he was stationed in his hometown. Joshua lifted his right hand and demonstrated the mitt as the state of Michigan. Ben had done “the mitt” frequently and pointed to the tip of his ring finger.

Jakob grimaced and said, “And where is Detroit?”

Joshua then pointed to the base of his thumb near his wrist.

Jakob replied, “That’s a long way unless you’ve come from Alaska.”

Joshua was so refreshed that he took a deep breath and looked around the park for the first time since his eyes had met the open water. He raked a hand through his shaggy, long hair and over his bearded face. He enjoyed the anonymity of a grunge look he had never had before. They were due to begin their newest assignments this week. Jakob was headed to the United States Coast Guard (USCG) Air Station Detroit, four hours farther away on the opposite side of Michigan on Lake St. Claire. That large lake was nestled between the Great Lakes of Lake Huron north and Lake Erie south and east. Traverse City was Joshua's new hometown while he served at Air Station Traverse City along the Grand Traverse Bay of Lake Michigan.

"Ope..., s'pose you're new here. From Alaska, eh?" a voice behind them said.

The guys whipped around and saw a family of five who stared at them and not so subtly tried to control their laughter.

"Welcome to Traverse City," said the father of the family.

He smiled knowingly and said, "Bo's the name. Jeet? (Did you eat?) You fellas will find the best ice cream at Moomers, the best burgers at ...."

A small child who held his hand interrupted, "Chic-fil-a's THE best. And they sometimes have a cow, no, really, a cow."

Bo's wife said, "C'mon, crew," as she waved them away and smiled over her shoulder.

Bo called over his shoulder before they got into their vehicle, "I'm sure we'll get to know one another soon. Enjoy your freedom."

Jakob and Joshua looked at one another and then at the license plate as the car backed up and around them. It read *Alaska* and had a vanity CG frame around it. Jakob was disconcerted but still oblivious.

He said, "Did you get the name of the burger place?"

Joshua chuckled as he subconsciously raked his fingers over his head and tried to comb through his wavy dark hair, which felt so unfamiliar.

So much for anonymity, he thought, *Ope.*

Later that same week, Joshua officially reported to the Air Station unit. A wielded coffee crew of Guardians again mobbed him. Bo, short for Boaz, was his new Chief and had anticipated the renowned swimmer from Kodiak. The CG was small enough that reputations got around, and Bo was pleased to put a clean-shaven face with the name he'd expected at last.

"I put it together when we briefly met at the beach," Chief said.

He offered a firm handshake and then a wide grin when Joshua's look of alarm crossed his face as he remembered his run-in at the State Park with the Chief and his family.

The Chief added, "Some say those meet-ups are a coincidence, but not for me. I call that an 11-letter word for God. I trust you're all settled in at the Victorian?"

Another crew member said, "Glad you're over that nasty camp odor! No 3,000-mile camping trips for me!"

Joshua wondered, *How does Chief know about my lodging situation?*

The men laughed, and then the Chief introduced Joshua Mansoul as their newest experienced Kodiak swimmer. It seemed like a much smaller operation than Kodiak or Elizabeth City. He observed the clinic when they passed but almost missed it.

Joshua hoped, *Will Captain Paz's claim that some orthodontic work was ahead for me happen*?

"Is there a dentist at the Air Station, Chief?" he inquired.

"Nope, ya gotta go into town for that. You need one today, Mansoul?" he regarded him concerned.

"No, no. Not today. Soon."

He waved off the Chief's look of suspicion. Bo briefly touched Joshua's shoulder as a sign of concern.

Bo said, "We're like family here. We are a small unit, as you've observed. You gotta take good care of yourself. 'Cause when we're a man down, we all feel it. You understand me?"

Joshua nodded.

One after the other, the duty crew regaled him with facts, observations, and information.

"The area we cover is vast: to keep the ships and recreational adventures safe, the pace is difficult on our Traverse City Crews."

The Air Station was a close-knit group that offered to take him to the quaint downtown area for pizza and drinks after hours. The small town seemed to jump with Chicago, Detroit, and Canadian tourists. The Guardians told their favorite stories.

One said, "We just enjoyed the Cherry Festival, complete with musical entertainment, carnival rides, an air show, and a cherry pit spitting contest."

Joshua began to comprehend that cherries were the new salmonberries. The fellas looked forward to coming to work on cross-country skis and fat bikes again to work.

"Skiing to work?" Joshua said.

Zephyr replied, "Yes, the lake effect snow dumps on us. The snow falls on the prepared and the not prepared. You have to keep a good perspective to live in the mitt."

Joshua immediately thought of his buddy, 'The Mitt,' and smiled.

Incredible, he thought, *Skiing to work was not an option in Kodiak or ECity.*

His next thought was, *That's going to mean there's more snow to shovel than I imagined.*

Joshua's attention snapped back to the conversation as their voices grew serious. He tried to cover his concern about the amount of snow removal he had agreed to for his new home.

"Make no mistake," Bo told him with emphasis, "If you think being a swimmer here is easy, you've missed it. The lakes are as tough as any ocean you will ever see and merciless."

It was an ominous warning.

The initiation to the freshwater I felt recently didn't seem to be terrifying in the least.

A mech who sat opposite him said, "The CG wouldn't have made a station in Traverse City if it weren't necessary."

He added, "Do you like to fish, Mansoul?"

Joshua sat back in his chair with an appreciation for the subject change.

"Of course, you know of a great salmon river?" Joshua asked.

Bo said, "Yep, we'll also be fishing for walleye, trout, northern pike..."

He leveled his gaze at all the crew around the table, "But we fish the lake after first things first..."

Joshua wondered, *Why the dramatic pause?*

There was an uncomfortable silence around the table, and Joshua concluded this was an important lesson. All eyes focused on Joshua.

Oh man, they're waiting on me to answer, he thought.

Joshua's mind reeled with possible answers.

"What must we remember *most* as Guardians of the North?"

Bo asked the question in a different way for Joshua to answer. Joshua looked up and realized the ceiling had a mirror effect, and the crowd of diners that surrounded them was diverse in age and ethnicity.

Semper Paratus went through his mind.

Joshua admired his new Chief immensely when he reminded them of their duty and honor.

"Mansoul?"

Joshua answered, "We fish for souls."

'Unsalted' was the billboard that welcomed Joshua's mama at the tiny regional airport when he picked her up in early August. The same airport had the USCG Air Station Traverse City adjacent to it. Joshua had swept his mother, Maria, off her feet and into a huge hug. They had a joyous reunion after four years of separation. Tears of joy were still in her eyes as they left the Cherry Capitol Airport and headed to Moomers for ice cream. Joshua had deliberately waited on his first trip there as a special treat for the anticipated rendezvous.

"I hope it'll be worth it after all the hype about this place," Joshua said.

"I could eat cardboard and be happy as long as I'm with you, Niño!" she said.

While they stood in the long line, they kept talking over one another as they tried to catch each other up on all the escapades of his cross-continent trip and his brothers' antics. His mother embarrassed him because she continued to reach out and hug him as if she couldn't believe he was in person in front of her. He decidedly wrapped his arm around her at last.

He said, "Here, just stand and hug me, Mama; I know you want to..."

When they had almost reached the front of the line, a family of five covertly cut in front of them from the opposite door. They entered the "out" and handed over a golden ticket. Joshua pointed out the absurdity to his mother. She raised her eyebrows at Joshua and wondered what had just happened.

He thought, *I thought people around these rural rolling green hills were more respectful...*

They waited and observed. While they tried to watch and listen inconspicuously, the youngest ordered a "Moomer the Mouse," and the rest placed their orders indifferent to the ever-increasing line. The staff seemed to invite the rude behavior. He felt his mother's spine stiffen at the indignity of them cutting lines, especially one so long and at the exit. Her eyes cut to Joshua's.

He sensed her thoughts, *Who did these people think they were?*

Joshua looked toward the softening sky and smelled the sweet aromas that wafted around him. He looked up to the ever-present calm of the USCG in his imagination, and he often focused on it when he needed calm and clarity. This was the mechanism he'd learned to use to cope as a young teen after his rescue by the CG.

He refocused, *Remember the mission to save the lost. These people are lost.*

Maria smiled at her niño as she gazed up at him. She admired his brute strength contained.

He speculated on her thoughts, *His father would be and is so proud...*

She leaned in close and said, "I scream, you scream...."

They shared a laugh.

Perhaps there was more to the story, Joshua thought.

The family looked innocent as they turned to go and wore guilt-free smiles before they began to lick the ice cream that dripped on the waffle cones in their hands.

"Next, please," said the girl behind the counter.

She smiled broadly and noticed the exasperation on Maria's face still on the family that exited as they stepped forward. The counter girl had followed their gazes.

She said, "Sorry about that. We give special golden tickets for 'fast passes' to regulars who live here year-round. It may seem rude, but it's supposed to be a reward for loyalty."

Joshua replied, "Well, how long do you have to live here to become a local?"

The young woman, with a long ponytail dyed purple and whose name tag read Lydia, sized him up.

She said, "Come back often in the middle of winter. Ya know, when it's dark and the snow's all piled up, then you're considered a local. Ya got me?"

She winked at Joshua with obvious flirtation and then snorted at her joke.

Why do these girls flirt with me?

He turned pink unconsciously.

Joshua's mother said, "Cherries Moobilee, one scoop, waffle cone. Thank you."

"You betcha, and you?" The teenage girl smacked her gum, frustrated he didn't flirt back.

Joshua replied, "Double scoop of mint chip, waffle cone, please.

The counter girl winked at them again and spun around to fulfill their orders.

His mother turned at once to Joshua, "Aha! I knew it!"

"The last shall be first... what a marvelous concept, Mama, don't you agree?" said Joshua with a sly grin.

"That's not what I was thinking, my boy, you have admirers everywhere," she said.

He laughed at her, tried to look shocked, and quickly changed the subject to the room's décor.

Let's not go there...

When the cashier exchanged money for Moomer's famous ice cream, she added, "If you come on your birthday, then you'll get your birthday number as a percentage off your order. I hope to see you again."

She batted her eyelashes unashamedly toward Joshua only.

They accepted their cones and wandered outside. They tried vainly to lick the drips before they splattered on the sidewalk. Together, they found a picnic table under the shade of a bright red table umbrella next to one another. Maria couldn't help herself and nudged her niño in the ribs.

"I suppose this will soon become a favorite indulgence..." she said.

Joshua replied, "It's better than average ice cream. I gotta admit it."

Joshua and his mother vacationed for the next few days until she was exhausted. They hiked the dunes and swam in the crystal-clear fresh-water around them. Joshua's appetite to return to the rescue "business" was stoked. At the top of one of the Sleeping Bear Dunes, a sign read, 'Warning: Avoid getting stuck at the bottom!' and 'The only way out is up. Rescues cost $3,000.' Joshua was reminded that the CG rescues were paid for in advance.

He said, "Taxpayers collectively sought the common good, and rescues should be taken for granted."

Maria and Joshua had stopped by the Visitor's Center and were overwhelmed with tourism prospects and recreation. One pamphlet had data about the origins of the local US Life-Saving Service.

Maria read aloud, "As far back as the 1870s, surfmen, and keepers began to rescue over 178,000 people from shipwrecks. Later, they became formed the USCG."

Maria tried to tousle Joshua's cropped hair; by then, he had it cut back to its regulation length.

"I'm so proud of the long lineage you've come from, a chosen one!" she said.

Joshua nodded in agreement. Humble to a fault, he wanted to change the subject as they later strolled along W. Front Street in downtown Traverse City.

He explained, "I found the older couple's advertisement for a room in exchange for assistance in their enormous old Victorian home not far from here."

In exchange for his services to mow, do general maintenance, and later shovel the drive and walkways, he had a terrific room to stay in with access to the kitchen and a private entrance.

Maria asked, "Niño, have you ever shoveled snow in Michigan?"

"You think I'll have a difficult time with it after my tour in Alaska, Mama?" he laughed.

He had gratefully accepted the hospitality and befriended the couple immediately. They described themselves as followers of the way, which considerably warmed his heart. They, too, had been part of a mission much of their lives and were glad to host another CG member. They had a long line of Guardians who had found welcome and mutual assistance in their home.

They had told him, "We hope your tour here lasts longer than we do."

Joshua did not know how to reply.

They grinned, and the frail woman spoke, "Ah, the valley of the shadow of death is a long trek for us. The good Lord must have His reasons, though."

She tapped her cane on the floor and added with a coy grin, "But you know, young man, God is with us. Our cup overflows, and soon we will dwell with Him, forever."

She winked at him, and then her husband told Joshua about the requirements for the upkeep of the large home. No restrictions were mentioned. Joshua had debated whether to mention his mother's imminent arrival.

The gracious old man said, "Out with it. You have a question in your eyes."

"My Mama, she will be visiting for just a few days soon."

The elderly couple, Bryan and Naomy, reacted to him joyfully.

Naomy said, "Your mother is coming? She must stay with us. A great reason for you to help me clean another room."

They all shared a hearty laugh, and Joshua breathed easier. He had relayed all of that to his Mama and more.

He added that they had told him, "We are thrilled to have a young CG member in our home. We feel safer already and will treat you as our family."

"I was thrilled, because when I moved here, I had nowhere to lay my head," Joshua said.

He added, "This way, I plan to send the money I receive for my housing to you all."

Maria reached over to hold his hand in deep appreciation and affection. He knew that his mother had experienced that situation herself as a young woman and would appreciate that they would all be cared for financially as a family. They appeared in front of the gorgeous mansion, now his home, and stood momentarily to take in the property and stately but comfortable house. It had more rooms than Joshua could fill, but he was one of many who had graced its halls.

"What a place for you to stay and to serve. It's big. I'm most grateful, too," she said.

Maria added, "I know the CG Mission will guide and protect you. I put my trust completely in them to do so. It has been so hard to let you go. Soon, I will face the same with James..."

“Hey, Mama, maybe one day everyone can stay with me in my big house.”

Maria buried her face into Joshua’s chest and sobbed yet again. All too quickly, the long weekend rendezvous was over. Joshua’s mother hugged his waist like he had done to her as a child in his early school days. They could hardly speak as the goodbyes lodged in their throats. All too soon, Maria’s bag was packed, and they drove back across town in the weighty silence of an unhappy departure. Joshua glanced at his mother again and again to reassure her. A sword pierced her soul at the thought of the ride up into the clouds and away from her firstborn and precious boy. Even when he towered over her, she still wanted to wipe his tears and cradle him as she once had when he was entirely dependent upon her. The Cherry Regional Airport bustled with tourists who came and went.

This life of absenteeism from my family seems to get harder instead of easier, he thought.

“Let it not be four more years until we’re together, my niño...”

“Mama, I’ll come to you next time.”

She spoke through her tears, “It doesn’t matter where we meet, just so long as you know your Papa and I are with you.”

She poked his chest and pointed at his heart.

He finished the conversation with a tight hug and spoke into her ear, “I am with you always and forever.”

Joshua had been up for promotion and leaned into his work tirelessly when he was back at Air Station Kodiak. They were shorthanded as it was a tumultuous Permanent Change of Station (PCS) season. Single Guardians were in high demand to cover various jobs around the base. In contrast, newly acquired people and those who left the base with families and their school schedules shuffled their lives around the country and sometimes beyond U.S. borders. He offered to welcome and mentor younger Guardians and kept the coffee hot as promised.

Joshua thought, *I remember being young and far away for the first time. It took work, discernment, and discipline to fit in well.*

Joshua was calm among his crews, in his unit, and to those he knew around the base. He had learned his time in Kodiak would end too soon. He had quickly volunteered for this coveted duty when it opened way up north in Michigan. How pleased he had gotten the station of his choice. Even though it was technically south of Alaska, it was north for almost everyone else in the CG besides those in the Seattle area, Lake Superior, and northernmost Maine. He had heard great things about the crystal blue waters and laid-back schedule of Traverse City. After all, it was a Great Lake with no mighty ocean breakers and no hurricanes.

They said it would be like a 'vacation station,' he thought.

The turnover of events and constant readiness to remain *Semper Paratus* with the smaller amount of people made Joshua appear early to work and late to get off duty. He realized the extra hours in Kodiak were the new expectation in Traverse City to complete the tasks on time every time. He was motivated and finished his syllabus to stand full operational duty in record time.

"Glad I had leave saved and took a vacation on my way here. I don't see any in sight," said Joshua to his Chief, Bo, one day after some exasperation on a maintenance issue.

"Be glad you live in paradise and your off-duty days are somewhat flexible, Mansoul!"

Joshua said, "These crowds make paradise a little hard to enjoy. I suppose I got too used to my one-light town."

Bo said, "Oh, be glad paradise is crowded for now. The next season will be upon us like a thief in the night. You do have your winter weight training circuit down, right?"

Chapter 22

FREEDOM

The Trail Life Group of teenage boys rendezvoused at Sleeping Bear Dunes National Lakeshore for a highly anticipated paddle-board trip. The guys jumped from their vehicles at Esch Beach, excited to get out on Lake Michigan after another warm summer in Traverse City.

"Perfect weather... sunny, no wind and waves for a September day," called their leader, Matthew.

The Trail Life (TL) organization stood upon the shoulders of a man named Baden-Powell. He had formulated a plan to instill skills, initiative, citizenship, and character in Britain's youth more than 100 years ago. No matter their backgrounds, he realized boys would likely not volunteer to learn about values and citizenship until they were presented with the critical component of *adventure*. Baden-Powell created the worldwide scout movement, which was the predecessor to the Trail Life organization.

The teens in this TL unit had run towards their great water adventure, only to be very surprised. When lean and lanky Andrew hit the lake at a full run, he splashed up to his waist. He was shocked by the temperature of the water and abruptly retreated with a wail like a hurt animal.

“What in the world?” yelled Andrew.

Since he had been the first teenager to get soaked, the group was behind him at the shoreline and laughed at him. They recognized it was too unpleasant for a quick swim near shore. The recent cooler weather brought a westerly wind across the lake and dropped the lake’s temperature to about 50 degrees. That was a far cry from a pleasant swim.

Matthew stroked his gray beard and spoke up with a lesson.

“You should know about the natural process of the lake as it turns over. When surface water becomes as dense as deeper water, it sinks. The downward movement of surface water forces deeper and colder water upward. The water begins to circulate, and that is called fall turnover.”

“Blah, blah, blah.... Are we going or not?” said Andrew, still impatient.

The rest of the group decided to stay dry and on top of their boards. They were prepared with a float plan, wet suits, life vests, a cell phone, and a backup to their backup plans.

“Geeze, these leaders are over the top on safety,” Andrew muttered to his friend Bart.

Thad asked no one specifically, “Do we *really* need to wear the vests? Can’t we have them on the boards?”

Matthew, the leader, answered him, “If the Coast Guard comes around, it’s not going to do us any favors if your board is the one with the jacket on it.”

Christopher double-checked his gear, which included a new paddle that floated. He had gotten it for his birthday and had yet to use it.

“What good is a gift if you can’t use it?” said Christopher, demonstrating the features to Matthew, “Today is my day.”

The group took their preparations seriously. It made them slower to get onto the water than anyone wanted. Nevertheless, parents were included in the day's float plan, and an estimated arrival time was given to all. They rechecked the weather to be sure it had cooperated. Eventually, they attacked the surface of the vast body of water like Vikings from another era.

"Mid-September is our last chance to get out before next year," Matthew said.

"This is so going to be worth it," said Christopher, admiring his new prized paddle.

Christopher thought, *and maybe I'll share it around.*

Matthew and the five guys pulled hard against the small swells near shore, happy to be afloat and on an epic adventure. Christopher was in the lead and thankful for such a great bunch of friends to do cool stuff with every season. He raised his arms with his paddle held over his head.

He shouted, "Freedom!"

"FREEDOM," they all shouted together in reply, and the sound carried across the lake.

About 200 yards from shore and a mile down the shoreline, the guys enjoyed their magnificent perspective as they looked back toward the high windswept dunes along the shoreline for miles. After the hordes of tourists had gone, the beachline was empty at that time of year. Surprised at how vacant it was, they felt they had the whole lake to themselves. As far as their eyes could see, they had a calm lake to voyage upon. Adventure was what they were mainly after, but the constant paddle motions had grown slower after an hour.

Matthew knew he had the guy's attention because they closely followed his cadence.

I've waited for the pace to settle and for silence. Now is as good a time as any to ask, he thought.

He wanted to start a long overdue conversation. In his opinion, many guys were more into "trash talk than truth talk." Trail Life was a mentor and discipleship journey, and his challenge to himself that day was to discuss different world views. He did not know all the teens' backgrounds. However, he knew they were exposed to other world views at school and online. Just because they grew up a certain way did not mean they would claim their parents' views or those of TL.

If they're like me, they're probably already testing their parent's views.

He knew from his history that he had searched and floundered as a young adult as he "tried everything."

It can't be easy to make your way in a diverse world that's getting more crooked every minute, he supposed.

He was a TL leader because he wanted to spare these guys the same painful choices he'd made around their ages. He decided the direct approach was best.

Matthew looked to the clouds and whispered, "Help me with the truth."

Matthew cleared his throat, "Ahem," and said, "Uh, guys, I wanted to ask you something... What are your worldviews?"

Andrew, Christopher, Bart, Thad, and Phil turned their heads at him simultaneously dumbfounded. They kept silent, paddled along, and thought to themselves for several minutes.

Andrew, always the first to speak, said, "Um, I guess American. Isn't that what we all are?"

Matthew smiled.

He replied, "Good start, not the answer I expected. Yes, we are. I mean, yes, we're Americans. Then we're what? I meant, how do you make decisions? What's your code of ethics? What informs your attitude, values, how you treat others...expectations from life?"

Phil said, "Geez, Louise, can't we talk more about football?"

Bart said, "I dunno. I think I'm in between stuff. My dad's parents were Jewish, and my mom's Catholic. It's totally chaotic at home because of that. They're asking me what I want to be, and I don't have a clue. I don't want to have to pick a side."

Christopher spoke next, "Sorry, dude. That's rough."

Quiet paddle sounds through the water were cut off when Christopher answered a minute later, "You guys aren't gonna believe this, but I've got a Christian worldview."

They moaned at his joke about himself.

Bart said, "No, you? Always quick to pray at *every* meal; even worse is how you always want to burst into a song. You're a walking musical. What is up with that anyway?"

Matthew was encouraged by their banter and prodded them further.

He said, "So why do you have a Christian worldview, Christopher? Is that just 'cause your parents named you that?"

Christopher retorted, "No way, man. Have you been in world civ class lately?"

All the guys guffawed since Matthew at age 45 was, well, *ancient*, in their eyes.

Christopher said, "We studied these world religions in history class. It's wild. I went home and asked about it all, and my folks and I had some great discussions. For days actually.... My parents were just as interested in what I was learning, no *more* interested than I was. It totally helped me sort some stuff out."

Thad said, "You're lucky 'cause I got questions, too, and my parental units said I'm not old enough to understand and won't talk to me.

No, they said, 'You can decide when you're older.' Well, I got news, I am older. Still no idea."

Matthew asserted, "That's why I'm here, I mean Trail Life is, to help you get good answers to your questions. Give me one, but be gentle."

Phil said, "I got one."

Matthew said, "Shoot."

Phil paused and replied, "Who's gonna win the Super Bowl?"

They all groaned. Thad tried to splash him with the end of his paddle and nearly fell off his board.

"Whoa there, big guy," said Andrew, "Okay, I got one. What's up with all the religions? Isn't there just one God? Why are they fighting? Isn't our religion our worldview if that's how we decide our values? Some people are whacked out on that stuff."

"So, that's like five questions, buddy," said Matthew.

"Okay, fine. What do all the religions say, and then we'll decide," said Thad.

Matthew let out a long breath, uncertain of where to begin. That was the question he had the least knowledge about.

He thought, *I should've gotten more training before I asked about this...*, he looked up, *Help me.*

After a few minutes of quiet paddle strokes, Thad spoke again, "See what I mean? Nobody has answers."

"Wait, Thad, let me try, will ya?" said Christopher.

Christopher paused because he knew how important this discussion would be. He looked up and remembered the conversations that had flowed naturally with his parents. He was thankful for those long discussions. He continued to paddle with his buddies on the serene, magnificent lake. He remembered his dad's encouragement to be audacious with his faith. His dad had said, “If you mean to follow Jesus, then you especially need to when it gets uncomfortable.”

Christopher thought, *I can’t repeat all those discussions in just a few minutes.*

I don’t want to sound like this is judgmental, but I’m glad my Dad prepared me for this.

I know these guys are pressured with different belief systems and sometimes poor examples of Christianity.

Christopher took a deep breath and dove into the conversation, “Okay, this is how I understand them. You have to consider them all carefully ‘cause it determines the direction of your life and maybe an afterlife you want to be part of.”

Phil said, “I want to go to the Super Bowl, and it’s always on Sunday, so what does that make me?”

Christopher smiled at his friends’ comic relief and began again.

“Eastern religions like Buddhism, Hinduism, and Shintoism collect gods and expect morality, wisdom, and enlightenment... you receive Karma. That’s the idea that you get what you give, cause and effect. Then there’s Islam, which is complete and total submission according to the Prophet Muhammed and his principles. There’s Judaism, which is to follow commands and traditions, then try to create justice and mercy to appease God ‘cause you can’t always follow the commands. They’re still waiting on a rescue.”

Christopher took a deep breath. No one else said anything, but he could tell they had listened carefully.

He began again, “Of course, there are those who are ‘not religious,’ they live mostly without hope in anything, person, or cause. Justice for them is awkward to say ‘cause it’s hard to define without a guiding principle for making decisions. Christianity is good news for me ‘cause it means Jesus came to rescue us and taught us how to live so we can bring others to him to rescue. We rescue each other because he first rescued us from how messed up we are."

"Nice," said Matthew.

Could not have said it better myself, Matthew thought with thankfulness.

"Wait a minute," said Bart, "you never mentioned the most populated country; China's got Confucianism...it's confusing, ha, ha!" he laughed at his terrible joke.

Thad remarked, "No, I heard India just passed up China. And they believe what?"

The paddlers slowed as they all waited for answers to the tough questions that flew back and forth. Christopher thought hard for a response when Phil answered the question with a question.

"What if it's all a game, and some people just watch, and others participate?"

Matthew said, "The Roman Empire did that. They worshipped many gods and used humans for sport. When the gladiators got injured, they just pulled them off dead or alive and threw them in a heap or fed them to the lions. Have you guys ever seen *Gladiator*? No thanks."

Phil asked again, "So it's about who has the power, eh?"

Thad spoke solemnly again, "I learned in World Civ that the Chinese value stability and blood family. Not me..."

To change the subject, Matthew said, "What about the people from India?"

Bart looked up and remembered, "It's been a couple of days, but they've got the universal law of cause and effect...Karma, like what Christopher mentioned. But not all Indians are Hindus, by the way. My sister's friend, Susanna, isn't Hindu and is from India."

Thad asked, "So more of, you get what you dish out?"

Matthew decided to brave an answer.

He said, "Hmmm, do you think that's how you want to live? Have you ever accidentally done something?"

Phil said, "I guess that's why we've never seen anybody from Rome, China, or India play in the Super Bowl."

The guys snickered despite his awful and singular focus on football. They hoped he had made the joke with sarcasm.

Matthew braced himself and added, "Religion complicates, Jesus clarifies: love God, love people."

The guys had paddled strong for the duration of that conversation. Their leader, Matthew, cautioned them to slow up for a long paddle back if the wind picked up. It had been an hour out, and they discovered they'd gotten further than planned when they turned around.

Christopher spoke quietly to the group, "Jesus' point was a rescue mission. We should follow him and serve God with everything we've got to rescue others as much as we grasp his having rescued us."

"Whoa, deep thoughts," Andrew admitted, "I'm tired and need a break."

The guys slowed, stopped, and found that standing on a paddle board proved more difficult than forward motion on one. They stood awkwardly in silence while the deep thoughts undulated around in their minds and souls.

"Dude, this is like a track stand on a bike. It's easier to paddle forward than stand," said Thad.

While they stood there, Bart bent over to try and sit on his board. The guys were either lost in thought or distracted. Two watched Bart humorously attempt to sit on the tippy board. A swell had built up from far across the vast lake that they had not anticipated. The silent yet swift sneaker wave was on them before they saw it. They all bobbled with the jolt that lifted and rocked under them as it passed. Their arms flailed to keep themselves upright as they quaked on their boards. With a sudden splash, they realized together Bart had gone overboard. The whole group gasped as not any one of them had anticipated a plunge into the frigid water. Bart surfaced and held onto his paddleboard for a few seconds before he tried to haul himself onto his board. Some roared with laughter; others held their breaths.

The leader, Matthew, said, "I am so relieved we all have wet suits and lifejackets on."

Bart shivered, and his arms were worn out from the previous hours' paddle. His inexperience had rendered him weaker than he wanted to admit. The more he tried, the less able he was to haul himself out onto the board at neck height. He vigorously kicked the water in vain.

Matthew carefully paddled to him and thought, *I don't want to get too close and end up in the water myself.*

Lord, thought Christopher, *this isn't good. I've got to do something.*

Christopher maneuvered closer and got down on his hands and knees to offer Bart a hand. Bart cursed at his heavy vest that repeatedly caught on the side of his board.

Matthew hollered, "Wait!"

When Christopher reached for Bart, he saw Bart's panicked eyes. He realized too late as Bart pulled him into the water in his distress. As Christopher hit the frigid water, he rethought the wisdom of his hand too quickly offered.

"Whew, it's cold!" Christopher said after he sputtered out the cold lake water.

If it had been a different scenario, Christopher would have laughed, too, as he swam up to his board. After he surfaced, he made eye contact, and the looks on everyone's faces were not funny. Unease had muted them all, and their silence was louder than their laughter had been earlier. Christopher hauled himself out of the water easily enough onto his board. He was sorry for his friend, Bart, who thrashed in the water near him. He hand-paddled on his belly over to a few feet from Bart's side. The others tried to calm him down without a touch.

"Bart, dude, you got this."

"Man, just take a couple of deep breaths and relax."

"Bart, buddy, chill... oh, my bad."

After a struggle with the cold water for what seemed like minutes, but what was probably seconds, Bart was so spent that he relaxed like an exhausted bull in the ring, barely able to stand. Matthew grew increasingly concerned and remembered how he had been trained and the protocols for TL.

Matthew spoke with authority, "I'll call for help before we have a bigger emergency."

His call went first to another leader on shore. Immediately, the land-based troop leader made a direct call to emergency services with their exact location given. That call activated a search by local authorities, the launch of a CG small boat, and a CG helicopter. Matthew knew they were in trouble but relied on the guidance and trusted the checklist in his head and on his phone.

Christopher was trained as a lifeguard at a pool previously. He spoke calmly to Bart. By that point, Bart could barely tread in the icy water. Christopher assured him they'd get him out of the water, but he needed to lay back and trust the life preserver to float him.

Thad spoke, "You got this, man. You relax, and we can help you on your board."

When he finally consented, Christopher slipped back into the water to boost Bart onto the board. The weight in the water was nearly impossible to clear the flotation on the board and the life preserver. The others paddled their precarious boards against the opposite side of Bart's board.

Matthew thought, *I can see they're afraid they, too, could go in.*

Christopher went under repeatedly to boost Bart up each time. Christopher had begun to shiver himself.

I wish I were wearing more than a wetsuit... he thought.

He said, “Dry suits? Is that what they’re called? Next Christmas, I know what I’m asking for...”

Matthew had pocketed his cell phone in a waterproof case around his neck. He was grateful that someone was prepared to answer his call for help since their circumstances had deteriorated fast. He spoke calmly with the other guys in the troop, Thad and Phil, about his plans. He lowered himself on his knees, then to his stomach, and braced his entire body perpendicularly across their three parallel boards. Andrew and Thad did the same with theirs and then reached their hands onto the shoulder straps of Bart’s life jacket. They pulled while Christopher pushed. Finally, they hoisted the motionless Bart onto the board. He breathed hard, but the strain of the event rendered him immobile.

The young men looked around then to assess how far they were from shore. They realized one of the six boards had floated a long way away. They all knew the fun was over.

Matthew said, “Likely from the struggle in the water and the wave action,” he waved it away, “it is too far to retrieve. We need to focus all of our energy to get home.”

They were down to only four paddles. One floated away in the opposite direction, and another they discovered had sunk. They all rested on their boards for a long minute, collected themselves, and tried to control their breathing from their stress and exertion.

Christopher said, “Why do they even make paddles that don’t float?”

Flight Surgeon Esther Rapha, or Doc as everyone referred to her, ran toward the spun-up CG Jayhawk helicopter and mumbled under her breath. She was slightly frustrated, again, at the interruption to her busy schedule of patients by yet another Medical Evacuation/Search and Rescue (MEDEVAC/SAR). She did not normally accompany the CG crews on their rescues, but when her medical expertise was requested, she knew she had to go. It wasn't that she did not want to fly. It was an excellent diversion from her day-to-day requirements, but it was time-intensive and typically unpredictable, which meant patients had to be rescheduled.

Lately, with all the people who love to come to Traverse City, there seem to be more cases than usual, she thought.

She was only one woman, but the crews relied heavily on her since she was trained to do the advanced kind of emergency work the CG was called upon to offer. The CG constantly trained swimmers for basic lifesaving skills, and she oversaw that, too.

What don't I participate in around here, for goodness' sake, she thought.

After she declared she was buckled in, the cramped Jayhawk helicopter lifted off the ground and headed west toward the National Lakeshore. She had learned minutes before they were to rescue boys offshore that would most certainly be hypothermic.

"It's cozy in here already. These boys had better be small, or I'll have to swim back," she said to the crew over the intercom.

I'm glad my boy is safe in the trombone section at band rehearsal.

She did not relish the thought of attempting CPR on children, but it was her job and the rescue swimmers. The swimmer would assist her, but she hesitated to ask. She knew it was brutal to do it, especially after a difficult rescue in icy conditions. She paused to reassess their individual roles spelled out in the CG protocols. Swimmers performed CPR until someone else determined the survivor deceased. It was not for them to decide such a fate. That had meant some awful circumstances on which to fly in a cramped space for an extended period to no avail.

"Has the local hospital been informed we may be on our way soon?" she asked the pilot.

"Yes, Ma'am," said the co-pilot.

The pilot in command replied, "The kids have a cell phone, so we have a definitive location. This should be quick. 5 min. out."

How comforting to recognize both pilot's voices, she admitted to herself.

Rapha remembered a conversation she'd had with her son's friend the previous weekend. The friend misunderstood her occupation and asked how she enjoyed surgery.

"Surgery?" she replied.

"Yea, you're a surgeon, right?" he implored her.

"Oh, I'm a flight surgeon, which means I'm a doctor that flies in an aircraft. No surgeries in flight for me, I hope," she admitted to the teen with a smile and a heartfelt expectation.

Esther had known both pilots as patients on her Traverse City tour over the previous two years. She involuntary nodded and smiled to encourage the tweet and swimmer. The tweet had a familiar face, Monica Goodspeed, who returned her look and flashed a bright smile. Monica had the most beautiful countenance, even inside her flight helmet. It was a mysterious comfort to Esther to have a tweet that did her job well and that she could identify with on several accounts: a shared faith, love of family, and being an active-duty mom.

I can't remember her kid's ages...

Lucky me, she fished around in her flight suit pocket. Esther was relieved to have found she had stowed something to eat earlier. Doc turned to look out the window from the back bench she sat on and pushed a piece of candy into her mouth.

I don't even have time to eat lunch anymore, she thought as her stomach growled in acknowledgment.

Before she bit off another hunk of the candy bar, she offered a piece to an unfamiliar face who stared across from her. He smiled after she caught him, shocked to see her about to chow down a candy bar in flight. She laughed and shrugged her shoulders and ate hungrily. Monica gazed out the window, distracted. Doc looked back at the swimmer to read his uniform and read Mansoul.

She thought to herself, *Hmm... I've seen that name come across my files recently. Why?*

"Now, you know me as the candy-eating doctor," she spoke to the crew after she had swallowed.

The co-pilot said, "Wait, did you bring me some, too?"

The aircraft commander said, "You must be hungry to eat while in flight. This is no taco truck."

"No worries, guys, I *nacho* make you clean it up later," she retorted.

"Doc, that was bad," said the co-pilot.

"Made you laugh, which is the best medicine," she said.

She planned to attend her son's marching band performance that night.

This may be quick, and I could make the halftime show, she contemplated.

She was sorry again for her husband and kids that her work had eclipsed their lives. They seemed to understand more than she did that her service to her country was just as important as their dependence on her presence for every event in their lives. She remembered, *It's teenagers who required rescue. Perspective was what I needed. All jokes aside now.*

Esther Rapha leaned her heavy helmeted head back on the seat webbing behind her and briefly closed her eyes. She decided to rest and meditate briefly while she could amidst the jarring of the aircraft.

If only my body did not feel like I was in the back of a dump truck rattling down a pot-holed Michigan road. God only knows how long we'll be searching until we find these half-frozen kids and in what condition.

"Let's hope this a quick one, friends," she spoke and then exhaled.

"Aye, aye, Ma'am."

Esther Rapha sat up straighter after she heard "Ma'am." She remembered an email from several weeks ago that regarded a Mansoul. With her eyes closed on purpose, she tried to recall the rest of the message. She did not remember what it was about, except it had come from a different command.

Hawaii? No, Alaska.

She mused, *Probably his previous command regarded his up-chit or fitness for flight approval.*

She dared to look at him again and opened one eye in an odd wink face. Joshua caught her gaze, and he smiled widely then. She smiled back and closed her eye again.

She thought, *He laughed at my attempt for a siesta in the back of a wild bucking ride, or he knew I was trying to identify him.*

She spied what she needed to at his kind gesture, his teeth.

That was it; the gaining command requested orthodontic assistance from OCONUS (Outside Continental US).

Yep, she thought, *those teeth could use a rescue, poor guy. I'm on it.*

Esther smiled as she thought about her kids and their orthodontia. Then she remembered her braces long ago.

Look at old "braces face" now, world.

She quickly began to count her blessings instead of sheep.

NEVER LATE

Matthew said, "I think it would be better to keep warm by paddling than to sit and wait."

The Trail Life group was relieved that help was on its way. The leader pulled the board strap off his ankle and attached it to Bart's ankle to pull him behind him. Andrew also put his strap onto a still inactive Bart, who shivered while he lay on the third board now towed behind them. Christopher feared he would upend another paddleboarder in any attempt to climb onto yet another board already occupied.

"Let me swim alongside for as long as possible," he said.

Christopher realized as he swam, *In my desperation to swim to shore, I've never felt so comforted.*

He knew his friend suffered from hypothermia and exhaustion. Christopher carried on in the same conditions in a different manner.

Why the difference? he thought.

Surprisingly, they had both gone into the water. Due to Christopher's lifeguard training, he had been prepared for the elements. He looked up at his leader silhouetted by a bright blue sky.

I am grateful for his calm amidst the storm, Christopher thought.

He noticed the long brown dunes that grew taller by the moment. They spanned the horizon and beckoned him home.

He recalled, *"I lift my eyes to the hills; where does my help come from?"*

Christopher thought again, *The tan sand had roasted my feet in the summertime. That warmth will come again. This is my faith. Stroke by stroke, I'm living in faith.*

Bart coughed and cried to no one in particular, "I'm sorry!"

His chest heaved, and his shudders wracked his frame. His friends called out to him and reassured him that help was on the way.

Matthew spoke, "You're being rescued now; you just have to believe with us."

The determined paddle caravan lasted about two minutes. Until the silence was broken again. Christopher's strokes had begun to falter, and he ceased his feat of heroics.

Christopher admitted, "Guys, wait... I'm too cold to continue in here."

Thad piped up, "Well, I think you broke some kind of record, you frozen weirdo."

The boards were pulled against one another again to brace them.

Christopher said, "Pull me up!"

Andrew's board tipped precariously, but they braced as if their lives depended upon his efforts to pull while Matthew and Thad held him on the board.

"Argh!" they said in unison.

"Freedom," chattered Christopher with a big smile of appreciation as he was deposited on the top of Andrew's board, stiff and spent physically.

Christopher pulled himself into a ball to sit on the front with his arms around his knees for warmth. The paddlers who remained began to draw again with all their might for those who didn't have them. They all felt a breeze that had started from offshore.

"Is that pushing us backward?" asked Phil.

It brought discouragement and added a cooling effect for the wet passengers.

Christopher asked Matthew, their fearless leader, "Hey, you know that Toby Mac song you're always humming?"

He thought, *I gotta encourage us.*

Christopher spoke again, "It's my dad's favorite, too, ya know? Could you sing it now for us?"

Matthew was typically a reserved guy who didn't sing out loud. However, he had hummed that exact song in his head for the past few minutes.

I'll take that as my sign, he reasoned.

"Be forewarned, it won't be pretty, but here goes," he began to imitate his favorite singer-songwriter but blurted offkey instead, "'Help Is On the Way.'"

After a few bars, Matthew dared to swagger his head to the beat. The boys laughed and shrieked like fans. He stopped the paddle motion and swept his long paddle into an imaginary microphone. His voice grew stronger as he felt all their tension roll away like the wake behind them.

Matthew thought, *At the same time, this is a terrible and hilarious idea, but I know they needed to settle themselves with a moment of levity.*

In their various strengths, all the boys began to join in and sing about the help on the way. Together, like in the YouTube music video, several had watched repeatedly, they were also part of the rescue mission. Christopher, Matthew, Thad, Phil, Andrew, and even Bart, who only murmured, joined in the refrain, "He's never early, He's never late!"

Christopher focused then on his parents and their faces that smiled at him in his head.

He thought, *Mom won't want me back out here for a bit.*

Dad's gonna be so proud of me for keeping it together and doing what he told me to do.

I can't wait to share this one with my sister, Kira. However, she'd have seen this whole thing coming. He laughed to himself.

Grateful for their "endured" preparation in Trail Life, Christopher turned his face toward the sun for every little ray of warmth he could absorb.

Christopher shivered and thought, *I love the responsibility of being prepared. God, make the end of this story one we all want to tell someday, especially for Bart.*

The song lyrics continued around them all like a sea shanty song. It reminded them to hold on a little longer for help to show up in a mighty way. The song grew louder, and they drew strength from one another. The paddlers became synchronized. Their bond was tightened with each stroke.

Exhausted and nearly unconscious by then, Bart no longer mumbled at all. When the chorus came around, his friends did their best to encourage him. The sea shanty had synchronized their brave caravan like seafarers of old. By then, instead of Vikings on a power trip, they were crusaders for a rescue mission with spirited adventure over the chaotic abyss they were surrounded by.

"There it is," said Matthew, "See that, fellas?"

Out of the clear blue sky, just over the horizon appeared a tiny black dot over the dunes. The guys held their breaths momentarily until their eyes and ears were opened. On its way toward them was a revered orange CG Jayhawk. The helicopter's engine that rumbled in the distance and grew louder and larger by the second.

The Jayhawk's drop over the dunes and toward the isolated paddlers on the lake was a calm loop. Right where the crew had been directed, they found the tiny caravan that bobbed on the lake's smooth surface. The tweet, Goodspeed, prepared the basket for retrieval as soon as Joshua was dropped into the lake for the first time. When Joshua hit the water, he was still surprised at the lack of the sting of salt in his face.

When will this become normal? he thought, *Where is the saltiness?*

He swam in the unusually calm water for a rescue and remembered the local sign, Michigan: Unsalted. He swam adeptly to the caravan of guys who cautiously celebrated his arrival in unique ways. One teen was on his knees, head on his board...

Joshua thought, *I'm not sure if he is exhausted or bowing down to me.*

Another guy pumped his arms up and down like the prizefighter Rocky who had just won the fight of his life. His actions threatened to throw him and his wet passenger in front of him on the board back in the water. The passenger also had a big goofy grin as if to say, "What took you so long?"

Here we go, thought Joshua, Rescue Checklist two.

The teen who was in desperate need of rescue shook uncontrollably from hypothermia and was on his side curled up. The last man was evidently the leader and sat down on his board with his feet on the hypothermic teen's board to stabilize it and a hand on his ankle to remove a strap. The helicopter flew off briefly for Joshua to evaluate the situation and speak to his survivors.

Joshua yelled to them all, "You guys order a ride share?"

Most of them laughed and whooped.

Joshua continued, "I am Joshua, your CG Rescue Swimmer. Who will follow me?" as he pointed skyward.

To Joshua's surprise, they all exchanged looks and, in a chorus, began to sing to him in one accord, "He's never early, he's never late, he will stand by what he claims. I've lived enough life to say Help is on the Way."

It was a song they all knew by heart and apparently had just practiced. The lyrics and syncopation were perfect.

This is a first. A sung response, Joshua thought dumbfounded.

It was a familiar song to him, "*...help is on the way.*"

Except for the hypothermic friend, they broke into guffaws of laughter, thrill, and relief. Joshua conversed with them about the next few minutes of procedures. He wanted those with hypothermia off the lake as soon as possible.

"I'm going to take both of you wet guys with me for sure," he concluded as he assessed them individually.

Joshua smiled and made the overhead motion for the tweet, Monica Goodspeed, to send him down a basket that looked more like a robust cage for the teen who was obviously in most need.

He instructed, "The rest of you need to paddle 50 yards away so you all aren't blown in."

Christopher yelled for Andrew to stop and, with teeth that chattered, called out into Bart's ear, "Remember you told me you once were baptized, buddy? You're all wet again and getting rescued! You're saved through the water and can have a clear conscience before God. My pastor told me, 'Remember your baptism and be grateful.'"

Bart smirked then for the first time in an hour. In pain, Christopher splashed a little water over Bart's hope-filled eyes. They shared a sly grin. Andrew untied their caravan and paddled away as quickly as he could to catch the others.

They all called out behind them to their buddy in dire need, "You got this, Bart!"

"See you soon, and enjoy the ride for us."

"Good luck and Godspeed."

The basket was lowered, and Joshua reassured Bart about what he needed to do for him.

Joshua said, "Just let me have you, and soon you'll be with me in the sky."

Bart could only blink his appreciation. His long, wet eyelashes looked to Joshua like those of a fawn desperate for rescue from a trap.

Thankful that this kid should quickly go in and out of the basket, thought Joshua, *I've got you.*

They neared the orange floats that floated at the water's surface and identified the submerged basket beneath. Joshua pushed the mercy board away from them when Bart was rolled into the basket of grace. Bart's eyes widened when he was suddenly hoisted into the air and freed from the watery grave.

In standard procedure, Joshua held onto the basket until a few seconds after it was in the air. The guys watched their rescuer and friend suspended above them in awe. He had indeed appeared in front of them right on time. Joshua was strong enough to hold onto the basket as it left the water and splashed back into the lake. Joshua had let the basket go and fell back a few feet into the water to keep it from spinning as it was hoisted.

The survivors all gave an unplanned cheer, "Hallelujah!"

"Yeah!"

"Whoo Hoo!!!"

Christopher still sat on the board with Andrew. They were quickly joined by Joshua, who had swum over to them, and Christopher shivered without control by that point due to the downdraft of the helo on his wetsuit. Christopher acknowledged his chauffeur and patted Andrew's foot with a *thank you for the ride.*

Joshua instructed Christopher, "Roll back into the water carefully. I've got you!"

Andrew steadied himself while Christopher happily surrendered his body back to the wet oblivion that threatened them all in complete trust. He did not fear the chaotic waters as some did. He dreaded the creator of the waters and knew the order of the man who would draw him up was trustworthy. Christopher was dragged away from the caravan of paddleboards by Joshua. Christopher did his best to twist in Joshua's grip and came within an inch of Joshua's ear.

Joshua was surprised when Christopher yelled at him, "No, not yet."

Joshua was incredulous and couldn't hold back the shock on his face as he thought, *What? Rejection? Not again...*

Christopher yelled, "I'm sorry we had to bring you here. Will you forgive us?"

Christopher's eyes searched Joshua's shocked face. A long second passed as they stared at one another.

Is he mad at us for getting him into this? Christopher wondered.

Mansoul released his grip just enough to turn him face-to-face and show him his kind eyes. They were the sincerest Christopher had ever encountered. It truly amazed Joshua, and he could not contain himself. He awkwardly bear-hugged the teen, which sent them both under the water and inadvertently kicked one another.

"Are you kidding? You called for me and were singing to me!" Joshua said, "This is what I live for!"

They laughed like the best of friends in the most awkward situation possible.

"I don't fear what they fear!" shouted Christopher.

Goodspeed lowered the hoist cable and strop line as the pilots held the helo in a hover. The rotors, in the shape of a cross, spun so wildly in a hover that Christopher and his friends could only see them as a blur of fierce power contained for their benefit. Joshua's strong right arm went around Christopher again as he swam to meet the perfectly timed cable of conviction that met the water's surface. Joshua hooked onto it and then joined them together and, with his thumb raised above his head, motioned, "Ready." Christopher left the water that tugged at them both, embraced by Joshua, and looked up at his sweet ride into the heavens. He saw the USCG emblazoned on the bottom of the helicopter and raised his numb hand over his head, "Ready!"

He yelled, "Freedom!" for the third time that day and truly meant it.

Much to the caravan's surprise and relief, while they held onto their boards so as not to be blown into the lake while the Jayhawk hovered nearby, a small boat that belonged to the nearby USCG Station Frankfort appeared. They had hoped for a small boat and dropped to their knees in appreciation and for lower centers of gravity when the boat's waves reached them. The small boat crew idled up first to the leader, Matthew, who had more gray hair than he had begun the day. Thad vaulted in on the other side of the boat before the crew could even offer to help.

He said, "We knew you'd get here."

The small boat helmsman was surprised by Thad but shouted, "Welcome aboard!" to the others.

Andrew said, "Ya know, hope does float. Dudes, you brought the glory boat."

They were exultant when they had all climbed aboard the vessel dry with the experienced crew. It was a great day when the CG worked together tangentially to rescue people and even their gear if there was room. Andrew gestured to the boards, and they all began to collect the gear nearby and tie it down in the vessel. Lastly, they searched further away and gathered the lost gear still afloat before they made for shore.

Thad admitted he didn't care if he got his paddle board back or not.

"It'll be a *very* long time before I'm back out here!" he said.

With great relief, the dry survivors serenaded their amused heroes lustily and slightly off-key with the CG marching song, "Semper Paratus is our GUIDE..."

The small boat crew was all smiles despite the complexity of the group and gear that needed assistance to get home. Matthew stood by the helmsman and shouted over the waves while they headed towards shore.

He said, "You're out here daily to rescue knuckleheads like us, thank you."

The helmsman grinned back and said, "That's the kicker... this is what we prepare for every single day. Rescues on the water are our jam. 'Cause life happens, ya know. Folks go home with a good conscience when they remember to ask for help before it's too late. We're always ready either way. Thanks for your request earlier instead of later. It does make our mission easier."

Joshua and Christopher clutched one another while they dangled beneath the Jayhawk in their strop hoist.

Joshua thought, *This is simultaneously the most physically unpleasant and incredible gift of any rescue.*

Christopher prayed, *Thank you, thank you, thank you.*

They dropped backward inside and were tangled together on the cabin floor when the tweet, Goodspeed, hauled them in. For a few seconds, they both just lay there hilariously while they slapped each other like father and son who congratulated each other after a hard-won game. Goodspeed interrupted their celebration with a friendly swat to them both and helped buckle Christopher in next to Bart for forward flight. Christopher shivered but gave Bart the biggest smile he could. He raised a fist as if he wanted to bump fists but knew Bart was in no condition yet. Goodspeed closed the cabin door. Their assurance of their rescue was confirmed.

Joshua said, "Rescue checklist part two complete."

It was then that Doc's face appeared and hovered over the teens who trembled with hypothermia. Her face beamed, and she mouthed to them through the deafening roar of the engine, "Do. Not. Be. Afraid." Rapha helped them place their frozen arms, which did not want to cooperate with their minds, along their sides for better blood flow. She forced each to lie back, which was difficult with a small, crowded cabin full of men and women. She began to assess the heart rate of the teens and placed a dry blanket around them.

"That was quick, nice work," said the co-pilot, who glanced in the mirror.

Joshua caught his breath and looked at Doc. He was genuinely relieved to have a suitable helper for these teenagers to render advanced first aid.

Joshua said, "Begin rescue checklist part three."

Wow, thought Joshua, *this kind of rescue is incredible. When people are ready and more than willing to be rescued, it goes exactly as it's meant to. They asked for forgiveness, serenaded me, and followed me exactly as I told them! They even remembered to plan to call for help.*

Joshua spoke to the crew, "These guys were prepared. Maybe more guys for our mission one day?"

Monica added, "Aye, aye," and smiled broadly.

She sat back in their chariot of liberation, which they all understood was a masterfully maintained instrument of goodwill. The passageway into the cabin had become the declaration of their salvation. The cabin door was closed in flight to the relief of the survivors, but Joshua was hot after all the exertion. The respite was palatable for all. The cabin became a way forward into a renewed awareness of humility and gratitude for life. The crew members still in the helo were hospitable in every sense of the word. They welcomed the survivors expectantly in the grim condition they were in. They were comforted, aided, and treated as the valuable souls they were. The teenagers' eyes were their only form of communication, and the crew in the back of the cabin could see they were surprised at all they observed inside the cabin of controlled chaos for their rescue: equipment and gear, brash noise, more uniformed personnel, and pure joy.

Joshua and Monica glanced at one another as the helicopter sped for shore and the closest hospital landing pad. Each admired the smoothly coordinated crew members' contribution to the successful rescue. They nodded towards Doc, who was in her element and hovered herself over the teens. Despite never meeting formally, the crew's coordination was precisely how the CG mission was meant to operate. The genuine spirit of gratitude and confidence in one another's role was such that it solidified the mission mindset and left rescuers hungry for more experiences like this one again and again.

Joshua recalled, *My up-chit to fly was signed by the Flight Surgeon who covered Rapha from Detroit. I'm looking forward to an introduction to Doc after our first flight together. These cases sometimes kind of bond us. Maybe, just maybe, she'll help me out, too.*

Joshua licked his lips and teeth subconsciously.

Christopher gazed up at his rescuers' faces one by one as tears of thankfulness streamed from his eyes, not that he felt them on his frozen cheeks.

He realized then, *I'm too tired and relieved to care if anyone saw me. Besides, I'm so wet no one would notice. Please, don't let me forget this.*

He pulled his numb arm that tingled from under the blanket tucked around him. He motioned for Joshua's hand with his exposed frozen stubs of fingers and tried to fist bump him but could barely lift his arm. Joshua carefully wrapped his gloved hand around the tender extremities to strengthen the courageous young man even more. He gave him a crooked smile. Christopher knew he witnessed a great gift that warmed his heart and the rest of him. Joshua had gripped Christopher's hand, mind, heart, and soul.

When Christopher and Bart fought the uncontrollable shivers, exhaustion, and abrupt desire to sleep, Doc shook them gently on the arms. She leaned over Bart, then Christopher to check their pulses and treated them each as if they were her son. She made a funny face and sang hilariously to the crew and, most importantly, to Christopher and Bart, who were already delirious. They could not hear her, but they could see her antics.

"Wake me up before you go, go. I don't want to ride back here solo...."

Christopher suddenly recognized her as a band parent from his sister's band. He could hardly believe a band parent would have a job as unique as hers. Soon, he would tell her about his rescue and the rescuers. He would tell anyone who would listen about them.

"Home, James," Doc quipped to the pilots in general.

She had shortened the old quote.

The aircraft commander replied with the rest of the quote, "And don't spare the horses."

The pilots happily obliged as they whisked over the lake shore and the Sleeping Bear Dunes below.

The aircraft commander asked, "Mansoul, you know the legend of Sleeping Bear?"

"No, Sir," said Joshua.

The co-pilot relayed, "A mama bear's cubs drowned, and her heart was broken. She waded ashore, lay on the bluff, and looked over the water. They surfaced as the two little islands. She still lays there looking after them."

Doc replied, "Well, I am certainly glad these mama bears back here can deliver these cubs home safely!"

The Guardian crew acknowledged with a "yep, yep" while the aircraft dipped forward and gained speed over land. They were all exhilarated for another quick and successful rescue. This one had been made in record time.

Christopher regarded the blue-helmeted, orange-suited rescuers with his last ounce of energy. He could only cling to the earlier song, *"Help is on the way, Comin' for ya,"* when his eyes dropped closed with exhaustion and gratitude for the assurance of his salvation and Bart's.

Chapter 24

TENACITY

Joshua's breath was taken away. He watched it waft away and escape in little puffs of vapor into the crisp autumn air.

"Spectacular," he whispered.

Orange, red, brown, and yellow erupted from the created order in a marvelous showcase of splendor. Fall in the Midwest was unlike anything Joshua had ever experienced. His youth in Texas was bereft of hardwood trees for hundreds of miles. The loblolly pines of coastal North Carolina had been gracious in their height but not in foliage. Between the farms and the beaches of the intercoastal waterway, he had enjoyed the scrub brushes and wetlands that held water cypress and oaks. Kodiak had boasted mainly one species of tree. Almost entirely, the Sitka Spruce had been transplanted there from a volcanic eruption a hundred years before that blew the seeds from hundreds of miles away.

The volumes of Michigan's deciduous trees that gave up their mighty canopies of leaves blew his mind. He had driven around the peninsulas of northern Michigan and gawked at their glorious autumn colorations.

"You gonna help us tap some maple trees this spring, tree hugger?" voiced his coworker and newest friend, Eli.

"I have no idea what you're talking about, but if it involves these trees, I'm interested," replied Joshua.

They were out to scout the countryside not far from their CG Air Station in Traverse City. They each sipped a Cow Tracks Malt from Moomers as they sped down the highway.

"It's a big deal around here. Maybe you know about Canada being the Maple Capital of the World, but we're farther north than most of Canada's entire population."

"You're kidding me, right?" said Joshua.

"Would I kid you about that? Nope. What I will kid you about is Lydia..."

Eli teased and waggled his eyebrows when he said, "Lydia."

"Eli, I'm getting braces next week as a 28-year-old man. You're not going to try to fix me up now."

Joshua smiled widely then to remind Eli why he needed braces for his crooked, messed up teeth and to remember for himself.

I am probably the most excited person ever for orthodontic work.

He had saved and shared his pay for his mother and brother's needs and only recently discussed orthodontics with his mother. The new orthodontist Doc had sent him to, Dr. T, assured him he'd be happy for him to get the needed work accomplished.

Maria encouraged him, "Who are your mother and brothers unless they encourage you to do what is good and right? Your Papa would want it for you, too."

Would it be a splurge on something for himself or for them all to be less self-conscious? he pondered.

Ah, to smile without reservation. That's something to smile about already, he thought, still tight-lipped.

Joshua's mother's reminder of his papa's goodness finally tipped the scale to get it done.

They rode along in companionable silence while Joshua's mind returned to the recent conversation with his mama. She mentioned that his younger brother Jimmy was about to graduate college in the spring. After that, he wanted to be called James instead of Jimmy. There was also some discussion about James' plans after school. James might be interested in following in his big brother's wake and joining the CG mission. Joshua grinned despite himself at that thought.

My little bro coming on board would make me proud.

Jimmy, er, James.... He must decide on his own, though. I can't coax or pressure him. It's his leap of faith.

They would likely be stationed separately. Instead, their delivery of hope to those lost in the world would be magnified as brothers physically and vocationally.

Mansouls on a mission has a nice ring to it, he thought.

He was thrilled that his brother even considered the mission. More importantly, it would be further redemption for their papa's loss while he tried to help their neighbors, some strangers, get rescued. He had cared more for them than his self-preservation.

Joshua looked out the window and thought, *I still want you close, Papa.*

Each mile they drove, he thought more about his papa and the few memories he could recollect of their carefree time together. Somedays, it was still a struggle to comprehend the power of nature that caused so much damage in the world. The natural world broke hearts and bones. The solace for the mission of the CG was being part of the effort to mend and heal what could be, to redeem the pain with purpose.

Eli said, "Are you okay? You're like a thousand miles away, Mansoul."

Joshua quoted Henry David Thoreau, "Many men go fishing all of their lives without knowing that it is not fish they are after."

Joshua took another sip of his malt.

Eli didn't understand him and said, "You want to go fishing?"

"I know who I am fishing for, men and women desperate for rescue," Joshua said.

He was sure it was their souls, not just their bodies, he searched for in the rescue effort. He had recovered both, but too often, sadly, it was only the latter he feared was found. He preferred the victory of lost souls and not just their earthly shell found.

How, he contemplated, *can we convince them all that we are the way for life abundantly apart from their fears?*

He reminded himself, *I left the losses on the beach in Kodiak and moved on.*

"We could've gone fishin' if that's what you wanted. Not sure what's in season today," commented Eli.

When the next storm came, whether the survivors answered affirmatively to Joshua's offer of hope, he would be prepared with gentleness and respect as the CG had trained him.

I should call Jimm...er James to talk this over with him. He needs to know he's signing up for a pro-limb and pro-life organization. We rescue everybody, no questions. But he's gotta know the truth about the suffering involved, and he can't go alone.

Almost no financial cost is considered when lives or limbs are hung in the balance. The CG had six primary operational missions: defense, security, transportation, safety, response, and enforcement. So long as collectively, the rescuers' lives are not conflictingly lost, extraordinary efforts were made for rescues. Joshua's mind rewound to the memorials he had seen. There was a long list of courageous men and women whose lives were listed on several CG Memorials. They willingly volunteered for the mission and gave their lives for others to live. It wasn't just the swimmer's ethos "so that others may live." The collective CG missions agreed there was a justifiably high value for human life "so others may live." To always be prepared to answer the call literally and figuratively was the only way to exist, *Semper Paratus*. The storied history of the Life Saving Service and the legacy of laying one's life down for another was understood.

"You still thinking about Lydia?" Eli broke the long silence.

"No."

"Good, can I ask her out then?"

Joshua just leaned over and offered his buddy a fist bump.

"Do it. I've got a date with an orthodontist instead."

"You're sure you're good with it, man?" Eli inquired.

"Just don't forget to introduce me to this maple tree project."

Eli laughed, "Aw Mansoul, we need all hands on deck for that. The unit makes syrup in the spring to sell for a summer fundraiser. It's to benefit the spouses club."

Joshua twisted in his seat and asked, "Well if we don't have a spouse...what's the benefit?"

A big grin spread across Eli's face.

He never missed a beat and replied, "To find one."

Traverse City's gorgeous fall colors finally waned, and the leaves dropped within a month. That only seemed to make way for spectacular winter snows. The snowflakes fell and stayed for weeks at a time. In Michigan, temperatures stayed continuously below freezing, and the whiteness was sometimes blinding. The Great Lakes began to freeze up. Although they seemed like vast oceans, they were smaller and, without salt, would ice over on top. The little lakes inland froze during December.

One day at work, Joshua proclaimed, "This place is like a snow globe that gets turned over for a fresh covering of white every week."

A crew member asked, "You gonna buy a snow blower, ya know it's only the first part of December? You can't hold out forever."

This was unlike Joshua's previous experience in Kodiak when the snow fell and the rain turned it to mush days later. The mush mess froze and thawed until it drained away with another rain. Piles of dirty, sooted, and gravelly snow were pushed around for months on base before it melted completely.

His housemate and friend, Naomy, asked him after work one night under the kitchen's fluorescent light, "Son, you ever going to shave that crazy mustache you have had on your face the past month?"

Joshua replied, "Soon," after he pulled the knit cap she made off his head. It was pretty warm inside while he took a quick break from the fresh powdered snow removal workout he got most days.

"Well, not soon enough for me!" she exclaimed.

"Why don't you like it, may I ask?" asked Joshua.

"You look like a movie charlatan. Where's my nice Coastie under there?" Naomy laughed.

"Okay, okay... It'll be gone next snow. I grew it out for 'Movember.'"

"What in the world is that?" she inquired.

"It's a friendly wager at the Station to see who grows the thickest and longest mustache, and the winner gets bragging rights. I'm not interested in hearing anyone boast, so I'm keepin' until you say no more Movember. All the money made supports testicular cancer awareness. With my dark hair, who do you think won?"

"Ah, my boy. Leave it a little longer then," she added with a smile, patted his face proudly, and turned away with her cane further into her warm home.

Her son had suffered and lost the battle to the very same cancer. She shed unabashed tears as she toted her mail to a back bedroom and shared the mustache victory with her beloved husband, Bryan. Joshua retreated again to the driveway with his cap pulled down while he unknowingly redeemed another sad night with gracious benevolence.

"How kind of our boy to live it forward," Byran said.

His eyes shimmered as he watched the snow fly up and off the drive, thanks to Joshua's strong arms and the mission that brought him into their home.

"Do you think he knew about our boy?" Naomy replied.

Subconsciously, she wrapped her arms around herself to hug her man-child, who was gone but never forgotten.

Joshua only knew, *As soon as the roads are cleared and I finish my homeowner's long driveway, I can expect them to be full again tomorrow, just like shaving around this mustache daily.*

He could only laugh when the globe of lake-effect snow turned over repeatedly. Another beautiful layer of fresh snow would appear, and he would shovel the drive again. It began to be a routine, and he considered it refreshment and a way to start each day with an excellent warm-up workout. He enjoyed coffee before and after the first month to warm himself. In the second month, he just needed the first cup. By the third month, he acclimated, and it was as expected as his workout routine. It had become as routine as brushing teeth, and he nearly replaced the coffee with tea in the company of Bryan and Naomy.

Joshua wondered, *What will I do with the extra hours of my day all the rest of the year?*

There were plenty of extraordinary things to do that he'd never done in his life before Michigan. He was introduced to sledding down the enormous sand dunes covered in snow. He visited Moomers as a local and got his golden ticket, too. Hockey was what most of the fellas at work wanted to do, and he was intrigued.

Eli convinced him, “You have yet to experience the best of what Michigan offers.”

The arrangement was revealed one bitterly cold late January day. The escapade of ice skating on a natural lake was the oddest sensation for a boy raised in Texas. Joshua found himself walking over the water. He tried to act nonchalant, but in his mind, he screamed inside.

This is not normal.

Joshua said, “When you said hockey, I thought we were headed to the inside rink.”

“Looks can be deceptive, eh?” Eli said.

“Uh, yeah...This is hard to stay upright.”

“A dose of humility for grown-ups who wait too late to learn a new skill,” said Eli and laughed at him.

“Oh, you of little faith...,” said Joshua.

He was more determined to learn to skate when Eli laid down the challenge.

Keeping my feet together is tougher than it looks, let alone backward and in quick turns with a stick and puck.

Eli skated circles around Joshua and turned backward and forward with little effort.

“Finally, I found something to beat you at. But...I’m going to teach you how, Mansoul, ‘cause I’m cool like that,” teased Eli, “Lean side to side, increase your speed as needed.”

Eli gestured to the children learning around them and added, “Want me to skate backward holding your hands?”

“I’ll let the children lead. Thanks anyhow, amigo,” Joshua said.

Lots of people swirled on the lake around them. They admired the way the ice had formed. It was crystal clear, and they could see the bottom, which included the slow-moving fish and other natural parts of the lake that only seemed frozen beneath. Joshua tried to skate like he'd seen others, but it seemed unreasonable. The push and pull of his feet together were effortless on the slick surface, yet his body seemed unable to coordinate the efforts on the blades. His buddies, at last, skated away in a flurry to play hockey.

Eli called over his shoulder, "You learn hockey; you get the girl. And, hey, you may lose some of those teeth!"

He was left wondering: *How do they make it look so easy?*

Joshua supposed, *I don't think hockey is how I want to lose my teeth*, and he grimaced.

Joshua decided to become a trainee again and study the kids around him. He could stand on the skates when he relaxed his upper body and bent his knees. Then, with a brush outward with one foot, he could glide a few inches on the other. He stopped and started again with the opposite leg. Some parents skated backward and held their toddlers' hands for support. He did not have that luxury, so he stumbled forward and mimicked the motions he saw while his arms flew out from his sides at awkward angles. Eventually, he could glide along and finally made a wide turn.

The guys all pulled their skates off and gave Joshua a hard time about his skate school.

"You lasted longer than the last guy we brought out here, Mansoul," said a Michigan native called a Michigander.

He added, "He said he preferred being in the water than on top of it."

Joshua said, "I think I might be able to play hockey with you, fellas, about when I PCS."

Joshua wondered, *When will I use these skate skills unless I stay here for a lifetime?*

"You betcha, but not a bad way to spend a marvelous Michigan day, eh?" said his Michigander friend.

February gave way to March, and the snow and ice began to thaw. That was a gloomy time for ice fishermen, sledders, skaters, and skiers, downhill and cross country. Joshua had made a good snow removal routine, but the snowflakes came in less frequent bursts by the week. Joshua's duty load had been noteworthy since the cold weather environment he thought Alaska had prepared him for was different still in Northern Michigan. Rescues of people, ice breakers that needed aid to keep shipping lanes open, ice fishermen stuck on ice floes, and distressed mariners were among some hazardous SAR cases in sometimes whiteout operations.

Joshua went to work in the dark and came home in the dark. He enjoyed the toasty fireplace with his frail but companionable housemates some nights. They loved to hear his stories as he regaled them with his adventures of rescue. They always seemed to soak up his words as if their lives depended upon him to bring the good news. He also learned a lot from them; they were always to bed early. At times, he went out afterward to meet friends from work and explore the starlit skies that shone so clearly in the far north. He had time on his own to read, study, and reflect. Joshua especially loved ancient texts about the unity of a worldwide mission.

One Saturday, Joshua was standing duty when the SAR alarm sounded. It reverberated throughout the ready room and interrupted a Midwest game of cards called Euchre. The guys played it during the long hours between calls or when there wasn't something else pressing to prepare for on their weekend duties. They dashed over to the call center for further instruction from the command. The 9th District Command Center was far away in Cleveland, Ohio, on another Great Lake, but they directed local sector responses in the Sault Ste. Marie and Sector Lake Michigan vicinity.

The Operations Officer said, "Two youngsters are stranded on an ice floe in the middle of Green Lake."

The men gawked in unbelief at one another.

"A rescue on a nearby lake?" said a Petty Officer.

After they unanimously decided to go, the responders ran for their Jayhawk helicopter while the details continued to come in.

An hour earlier, Sophia and Beth had strapped their skates on while they sat on some rocks near the edge of Green Lake. They enjoyed the warm sun that beat down on them. A golden lab sauntered over to them, which surprised the girls.

"Awe, she's beautiful. Where do you think she came from? said Sophia.

Beth tossed her long dark hair over her shoulder and opened her hand to pet the good-natured dog. The dog immediately trotted next to her and sat at her feet as she rubbed its head behind its ears.

"Aren't you cold, girl?" asked Beth.

"Is there a tag with her name? I don't see an owner anywhere," said Sophia as she looked around.

She cupped her hand over her forehead and roamed her eyes around the ice to see another human in sight. She saw none and bent over to put on her favorite old skates.

Beth answered with her thick Brooklyn accent, "Oh, here ya go, the tag says, 'Luna.' And there's a phone number. Should I *cawl* it?"

Luna took the close opportunity and licked her face repeatedly. Little skin was revealed under the heavy jackets, jeans, hats, scarves, and fingerless gloves the girls wore.

"She sure is friendly. Maybe the owner is close by. We can take her back in with us and call when we're done if she hasn't already gone home," said Sophia.

"My bums getting wet," said Beth, who had just finished all the laces on her pearl white skates.

Beth chatted on, "I don't remember feeling wet before when we *was* out here last month."

Sophia replied, "Yeah, you're right. It does seem warmer today than on other days. Maybe we should head in?"

Sophia was a very petite 17-year-old ballet dancer with waist-length strawberry-blonde hair tied in a loose ponytail.

Beth said, "Aw, but we've just got our skates *awn*. Let's stay a little while and enjoy the ice while we can. Who knows, it may be the end of the season soon."

Luna ran circles around the girls and slid sideways on the icy, wet surface. She repeatedly tried to jump on the girls.

"She must be happy to be outside," said Beth.

The girls stepped off the shore and regained their skate legs. They each made more prominent and comfortable strides as they went.

"Lookie, I can see the bottom of the lake," said Beth, "It's not like that in Central Park!"

"I prefer not to look down, thank you," said Sophia.

Beth said, “It feels so awesome to be back on these.”

The fifteen-year-old friends skated from the shoreline and away from the Interlochen Center for the Arts, where they attended school. They lived on campus during high school while immersed in the dance program and the arts community in general. The boarding school was internationally renowned for its art programs and holistic education. The girls came from different backgrounds, and neither was from Michigan, but they had become great friends in their first year of the very selective high school. They had watched the ice fishermen and skaters enjoy the glassy surface most of the winter. Adjacent to the school was Green Lake. The lake was 2,000 acres and over 100 feet deep. While it was not a Great Lake, it wasn’t a pond either. They planned that the day was theirs and to make it an adventure.

Beth said, “This is the perfect Interlochen experience for emphasizing our...”

“Mindfulness, wellness, and resilience,” they said in unison.

Their laughter rang out over the ice while they continued to skate toward the middle of the lake. The yellow lab jumped and slid around them as they went along. The sunshine reflected off the lake’s surface as if it shimmered like diamonds. The brilliant reflection blinded them at points and made it hard to see ahead. The girls compared stories about their childhood memories when they skated in NYC’s Rockefeller Center Rink or at Central Park.

Beth said, “This is so great. It’s like we have the entire lake to ourselves. So much liberty. I love this place. Remember, there used to be shacks all over the ice, *whack* people. Did they live out here? Who would want to live on ice? I wonder where they’ve moved?”

Sophia shrugged and then changed the subject, “It is good to be away. Sometimes school feels like it’s boxed me inside. The schedule is so tough. Too much pressure isn’t good for our “wellness.”

They giggled, and Beth said, "No joke."

Sophia pointed to the shore opposite them, "Wanna go across and back?"

Beth replied, "Sure. I always love being here. The pressure keeps me focused. There's somebody awake at all hours, things to do, shows to watch, concerts to attend, and all the coolest people who will one day be famous, like us!"

Sophia said, "I'm glad we have each other, but I guess I prefer the library. This is great, too."

I haven't been on my skates since I was home in Brooklyn last Christmas a year ago. Glad our legs are strong from our dance," said Beth.

The girls chatted amiably as they continued to glide across the surface. They gained speed and had loads of fun. Beth looked over her shoulder to see if anyone was behind them. She was used to the stage and preferred the thought of people who would watch and admire her. Several hundred yards from shore, she could still not see anyone. The buildings from her campus were barely recognizable. The campus looked miniature from that angle—the aloneness she felt suddenly hit her as an odd sensation.

"Professor Winters said, 'Tenacity and adaptability are the keys to our future.' What do you think he meant? I'm supposed to write a paper on it today," said Sophia.

"Umm, well, when life hands yous lemons, yous make lemonade. Tenacity is like 'hang on for the ride of your life.' Kind of like I feel after our endlessly long dance practices on dress rehearsal week," said Beth.

Sophia said, "I'd say that's just perseverance... He made it seem like it was as if your life *totally* depended upon it."

"What was the other word?" said Beth.

"Adaptability."

"Umm... geez, it's like skating. I might plan to do a 'triple salchow' jump but do a double instead. Yous gotta land it either way."

"Nice," said Sophia, "You're good. I think I'll study with you more often for research."

Beth answered, "Don't yous think dancers are described as tenacious and adaptable?"

The girls continued to glide across the surface that shimmered as they practiced their twirls. The sun seemed to get brighter and hotter. The ice became wetter. Beth looked over her shoulder to see if someone was behind them again.

She spoke, "Did ya hear that?"

Several hundred yards from shore, she could not see a soul. She gazed in every direction around her in the middle of the lake. All the places began to look the same from so far away.

"I wish I had brought my sunglasses. It's way brighter out here," said Beth.

Luna scampered around them then yapped and lunged at them several times.

"Why's she doing that?" said Sophia.

"No idea," said Beth with frustration.

She found avoidance of the dog on her skates increasingly tricky. Luna began to growl then and snarled at them suddenly, giving the girls pause. They stopped and looked at the dog with shock and uncertainty.

"What in creation?" said Sophia.

They looked at one another. Then, they heard several short pops, snaps, and bursts. A long white bubble whooshed under their feet beneath the surface of the ice away from them. A slow groan began deep around the thin ice around them. A crack eight inches deep started from about six feet in front of them and cut underneath them another twelve feet behind them. They flung themselves together and caught each other and hugged barely upright. The sounds and cracks continued as they clung to one another.

"Oh, My God!" Sophia screamed.

They waited for the ice to crumble beneath them flung together. Luna began to whine, and her tail thumped the ice loudly behind her. The reverberations of her tail pounded across the glossy, wet lake. The girls started to look around with wide eyes over one another's shoulders. They pulled apart and still gripped one another at shoulder length. They weren't wet yet.

"Stand still, would ya," commanded Beth.

The horrible cracks, bursts, and tail thumps continued. A large pop sounded to their side. Another ice crack slowly opened, and they tilted towards it.

Sophia began to scream.

Beth slapped her with a gloved hand to stop so she would stay calm as long as possible.

"Shut. Up. Sophia!"

Luna began to bark but strangely sat still except for her ferocious tail that thumped and wagged as fast as their hearts beat.

"Oh, my God, we're gonna die," whimpered Sophia.

The giant ice sheet they stood on rocked back and forth and stopped altogether. They stood and held onto one another's shoulders on their skates for what seemed like minutes. They collected their composures. They scanned around them to see if the ice continued to crack and crackle underneath them. There were huge cracks, but only one that opened within a few feet of them. Behind Beth, open water now lapped where they had come from. The ice sheet they precariously stood on with their slick skates lilted back and forth as their weight shifted.

"We must stay calm and stand up straight," whispered Beth.

She continued, "What do you see behind me, Sophia?"

"Umm... well, there's still ice, but it looks all broken...cracks...," she sniffled, "everywhere."

"Did you bring your phone?" Beth asked Sophia.

"This is no time for a selfie!" she spat back.

"I meant to call for help, thank you," Beth said.

"This is like a continual balance board," said Sophia with a whine, "on skates."

Luna barked once more as if she wanted to second that thought. Her tail thumped on the ice and was the only sound for half a mile as it reverberated oddly. The ice continued to pop erratically, which made Sophia cry. Snot ran down her face, but she refused to let go of Beth.

"Sophia, you have to hand me your phone, but real slow," Beth demanded.

Sophia carefully took her mittened hand off Beth's shoulders and bit her glove to remove it one-handed. She fished her cell phone out of her pocket and sighed when she saw one little bar of service. She handed it to Beth and dropped the glove from her mouth. She was very hot from the adrenaline that pulsed through her.

"Sweet Jesus, pick up," said Beth.

Sophia met Beth's eyes with tears in them.

Sophia said, "We're gonna need all that tenacity *and* adaptability."

Beth stammered, "Oh, we've got it. But can we get help?"

A lump formed in her throat as she dialed 911. She realized she held her breath and braced her sore legs as the phone rang.

"911, what's your emergency?"

Joshua and the rest of his CG crew were on the scene and hovered high over Green Lake after only two minutes once they were airborne. The helicopter had already been prepared from a previous flight, and the crew had been dressed, which was fortunate for all. The day was spectacularly clear, so they easily spotted the two figures on the lake.

"Looks like there's a dog, too," said the aircraft commander with the best view.

Joshua considered the new information, *a pooch in the helicopter.*

"How big, I wonder? Can somebody get permission to bring it in, too, if we can?" Joshua said.

"Roger that," said the pilot, "Prepare the swimmer for deployment."

The mech said, "This ice looks crazy thin to be skating on."

He added, "Don't forget those skates have blades, Mansoul. Don't cut yourself, your suit, or them."

The Jayhawk circled the girls to evaluate their situation once and plan for the hoists as part of rescue checklist one. The crew was relieved they weren't already in the water. They did not want to submerge them underwater due to the helicopter's downdraft.

"We don't want them under the ice sheet," said the mech.

"The basket will work, but I don't want to set it on the ice. Can you hold it real steady, Commander?" said Joshua.

"You put them inside, and we hoist. No worries, calm air today," said the aircraft commander.

They're still standing on a small ice floe, but where will I fit? Joshua thought.

He slapped his orange dry suit with his heavy neoprene gloves and knew he'd be fine in the water for a minute.

The pilot said, "You're a go for the pup after the survivors are in."

Joshua replied, "Aye, aye," with relief.

"Mansoul, you are a softy. You do like every-*body*."

"It's probably best for me to go in the lake and not put the girls in the water. I'll try to steady the basket so they can climb in dry," announced Joshua.

The mech said, "I'll put the basket right at their knees, Mansoul. Don't let them push it away and have it swing back into them."

"Begin rescue checklist two," said Joshua.

Joshua was lowered carefully to an enormous ice sheet within ten yards. Joshua didn't want to be the one who upended the ice and inadvertently dumped them into the frozen water or, worse, bury them underneath an ice sheet. When it hit the ice, he feared his weight would send the whole ice sheet toward the girls unexpectedly, which could be deadly. The crew wouldn't know until he got there. Joshua kept his arm moving in a circle beside him. That was the 'lower' motion to the mech who controlled his descent. A small Sherriff's boat had been launched nearby, but they had encountered enough ice it was slow going for them. The rotor wash hit the girls, and their hats flew off their heads in different directions. They fought the vicious winds to remain upright with every ounce of their strength, even as it waned.

"HOLD ON!" yelled Sophia.

"It's never-ending pirouette pain!" said Beth, who wore a tight grimace.

The girls were terrified they would be blown over and land in the water. They clung to each other tighter and tighter until they fully embraced each other as one body with four legs and arms encircled. Their legs burned and shook in the fierce gusts. They could no longer communicate except to squeeze harder as though their lives depended on the embrace. The ice beneath them began to sway. They tilted and slanted. Tenaciously, they dug deep to hold on to one another and to life that seemed to worsen with help as it had come with such force.

"Jesus, help us!" one screamed.

"Tenacious and adaptability... tenacious and adaptability... tenacious and adaptable," Sophia said repeatedly.

She said them for herself and Beth.

My paper is already written, if I live to write it, she thought.

They each peered up to see the USCG on the bottom of the orange and white helicopter. Their hair whipped hard in the mighty wind. The sun peaked around the animated vessel of rescue, and the fluffy clouds high in the heavens made a perfect backdrop to the outline of the Jayhawk that hovered high above them and out of reach. It threatened to blow them into the lake and simultaneously offered hope. Then, an angel in orange descended slowly from the sky as if he were casually on a ladder to the earth.

Joshua descended towards them on the hoist cable as cautiously as the mech could lower him. They planned for him to be set down where there was still ice that might hold his weight.

The question on everyone's mind was, *would it hold him?*

When his feet hit the ice, there were pops and groans, but no one heard them over the roar of the engines. He planted his feet and stood up in a wide stance, prepared to hit the icy water.

Well, I'm thankful for those skating lessons now. Semper Paratus! Joshua thought.

Joshua unclamped himself from the hoist cable for it to be drawn back into the aircraft and the basket to be lowered. It was hoisted while the aircraft flew off slowly in a large circle for the rotor wash to cease over the survivors. Joshua needed to act fast and communicate with the girls. Joshua shuffled forward as he had before at his first skate lesson.

Let's make this a redemptive story for Eli's hockey lesson, he thought.

Easy, big guy. Don't hurry, or everyone will be wet. I don't remember this training day at AST.

Despite the seriousness of the dire situation, Joshua addressed them from a few yards away. Their red-hot faces pressed cheek to cheek, and their big dark eyes implored him for rescue.

"Hey, ladies," he said.

He noticed they weren't children.

Why did I think these were little girls and not young women?

He did his best to diffuse the situation that had them terrified. He saw how tightly they clung to one another.

He wondered, *How to get them into a basket together or individually?*

"Did you call for an Uber? I'm a CG Rescue Swimmer, and we'll get you out of here."

He could see the face of one young woman who looked paralyzed with fear, and the other gave him a desperate grin. He eased toward them in inches and began to hear the ice pop.

No es bueno, he thought.

He knew his time was limited to how long they could hear him, so he began to yell directions. He expected the ice wouldn't last long, either.

"When the helo comes back, they'll drop a big basket down, and I want one of you to climb in first while the other holds it steady."

"It will go up and back down for the other one. If I can't get to you, can you do this?"

There was no response, except for the dog's tail that thumped. Then, it barked as an acknowledgment of the conclusive plan. Miraculously, it hadn't moved and sat as a good guardian.

“I need to know you heard me and if you can help one another,” said Joshua.

“YES!” they both exclaimed.

“What are your names?” Joshua asked.

He tried to distract them from their fears as he continued to inch closer. The helo was already en route in return, and he couldn’t quite catch what the teens said in reply. As the basket lowered between them, he moved closer in an awkward dance. Joshua decided when he began to see the cracks under his feet to hold still and see if the girls could get into the basket themselves. The rotor wash was intense. It bounced upward off the ice and nearly sent the girls flying since they were on skates. The struggle to remain upright exhausted them all.

How long have these girls been out here? he thought.

The basket was right to their side, and the dark-haired girl let go of her friend to grab it before it threatened to topple them over. She held it with one hand, but her friend was frozen with fear. He could see that she shouted to her, and she let go of her to climb inside. Relieved that they had not fought to go first, Joshua exhaled. Five seconds passed, and he realized they weren’t strong enough to hold the basket, let go of one another, and maneuver themselves inside. As one moved, their ice block tipped, and they abruptly stopped. The aircraft hovered perfectly, but it couldn’t forever.

I must move forward to make this happen, whatever the cost.

He slid one foot in front of the other at a low crouch to test the ice’s strength and focused on the basket. He glanced at the girl who had closed her eyes and buried her head in her friend’s shoulder, probably panicking.

Will I have to pry them apart or toss them in the basket together?

The dog, too?

The dog wandered around on the ice and sniffed at the basket.

You know that's your ticket outta here, too, eh girl?

The dog laid down obediently when Joshua neared the ice sheet, but its tail still wagged. The ice was wet from the direct sun that had melted its surface and from his additional weight. He noticed his feet sloshed when he moved.

Both girls in the basket together, he decided. *They're small, and it'll be a quick ride.*

Joshua felt the ice drop beneath him, and his heart thudded. It was a ride he'd never ridden before. When the ice gave away under him, he sank slowly as he wobbled back and forth. His arms flew out as if to catch himself in thin air. The ice floe dislodged from the rest of the ice just a few feet from the girls in a large sheet. Joshua knew he could not let them slip beneath the water's surface, or they may become trapped under the ice once it shifted. They sank gradually towards the open water behind them. They were forced to let go of one another, and in fear, the girls grabbed the basket when it swayed towards them. One held it courageously as she screamed for the other to get inside.

Joshua was almost next to them when the ice sheet he was on again tilted up behind him. He began to drop and slide into the water in what felt like slow motion, but he knew it happened in a split second. He grabbed the basket and held it steady from the bottom like a weightlifter over his head. Half of his body was submerged. He held himself up by his grip on the bottom of the basket and appeared in his crew's sight underneath the basket.

Please hold this hover steady, he sent his thought heavenward.

His weight underneath stabilized it for the girls to clamber inside wet halfway up their torsos. The girls twisted their bottoms into the basket as he held it steady. Both girls unintentionally sat on his fingers, and he groaned in pain. He feared how he would get his fingers in his thick neoprene gloves wedged out before the basket was raised. The mech could not see him below them, caught by his fingers.

Leave me here in the water, but don't take my fingers!

The girls were sitting twisted on one another with legs that dangled outside the basket and skates that hung splayed awkwardly in various directions. They had grabbed the outside of the basket with one hand and clung to one another with their inside arms. The basket dropped when their weight collapsed inside and conked Joshua on top of his head.

He thought, *Should have seen that coming.*

The hoist isn't supposed to be like this, but they're mostly inside.

Joshua kicked the water vigorously to keep himself upright; his fingers were wedged underneath their backsides around the basket's bottom.

How am I going to free my hands?

Crew, he thought, *don't hoist me up and drop me back on the ice...*

He didn't want to for propriety, but he quickly jabbed his thumbs into the girl's backsides, which sent their bottoms up just momentarily for him to yank his fingers free. His body dropped immediately under the surface of the water.

COLD! Ugh... my gloves?!

He gasped after he bobbed to the surface of the lake in the icy water. He carefully waved his arms around his head to protect any ice from flowing over him. He did his best to keep his hands out of the water. The basket bounced up when Joshua's weight dropped off, and the mech expertly began a quick but controlled hoist of the teenagers into the aircraft that hovered above.

It's gonna be a frosty minute while my mech untangles those girls from the basket with skates on. My hands will freeze out here quickly!

Joshua looked up and saw his gloves that dangled from the bottom of the basket. He focused on the magnificent big black letters, USCG, on the underside of the Jayhawk. He held his hands out of the water and kicked vigorously. He looked like a man who had surrendered to the water with his hands over his head. He was everything but forfeiting his efforts. He continued to tread with determination when his booted feet seemed to pull him down into the depths. He was somewhat more buoyant in the dry suit, but it was heavier by the second. He assessed his environment again. The sun streamed down on him, and the USCG held his focus.

Breathe Mansoul. Life is good. I must hold on for one more minute...

Some people choose to take ice baths. Things are going great—two more survivors are almost in the cabin.

His face was not the only exposed part of his skin that had begun to turn red from exposure. He knew he needed to get out of the ice bath soon for his nose and fingers' sake. *Two more rescues in the middle of a card game on a beautiful afternoon. Nice.*

"Whoof, whoof!"

The dog!

Joshua spun his feet around as quickly as he could while his dry suit restrained his motions like a swimmer in concrete. There in the water, not six feet away, was the wet and pitiful dog that struggled to keep her head above the water. There was no way to hear the whine, but Joshua could see the pathetic look and knew she whimpered. About six feet of ice was between him and the pup. He scanned the area and looked up to see the basket disappear inside the helo. He knew he had but a few seconds to get to the dog and try to save it, too. The dog seemed to attempt to swim towards Joshua, but the ice between them made it problematic. Joshua tried to grab the ice sheet. It was over two inches thick and too slippery to grasp, especially without gloves.

Don't push it over the pup... careful, Mansoul.

The dog tried to get a paw on the ice, but it was too weak and the ice too slick to get on top of it.

What do I do?

Joshua looked up for help. He closed his eyes for an instant and spoke out loud while he kicked repeatedly and still held his hands above his head.

"Please, Papa."

When he reopened his eyes, he saw the basket was lowered again in a quicker hoist maneuver. Joshua pumped his hand to the mech to move it so the basket went first to the dog.

Let's see how smart you are, Buddy. Swim on in there.

The mech recognized the motion, and the Jayhawk's pilots expertly maneuvered to the new target six feet to where the pup paddled. The basket had orange floats on either end, so it floated beneath the surface when lowered into the water. The dog swam away from it for several seconds while the crew collectively held their breaths. Then, phenomenally, the pup turned slowly and swam back. It sniffed the bars and licked them once or twice. The rotor wash splattered the water away from them and prevented Joshua from yelling anything the dog could have heard. Joshua flung his arm and exposed frigid hand through the water with exasperation. It sent a massive splash of water over the dog. The spray over the dog's head propelled the pup to paddle into the basket. The cold water was like knives on Joshua's already frozen extremities. The mech raised the hoist slightly to be sure the dog was in. Joshua made the hand signal, a raised thumb up, for the hoist, and the mech quickly retrieved the dog. The basket soared upwards, and the dog shook the water from its back as its tail wagged in relief.

"That's a girl!" Joshua hollered out loud.

One more save for the crew. Not sure my thumb will rise next time...

Joshua shivered and continued to tread water with his feet only among the ice chunks. His thigh muscles burned, and his fingers for very different reasons. The sun reflected off the surfaces around him as it began to lower in the late afternoon denim blue sky. He watched overhead as the basket was brought inside the cabin. The water stung his unprotected hands continuously while the downdrafts kicked up an immense amount of water that slapped him. He blinked uncontrollably, and the water that ran down his face felt hot on his exposed, frozen face. The other part of him that was exposed, he remembered, was his big goofy smile. He ran his teeth over his new braces with appreciation as his teeth chattered.

I'm sitting pretty, and those girls should be happy to have their wet dog back.

His teeth hammered involuntarily inside his head, but he beamed with anticipation of a smile that was being made new.

I'm glad to have my "smile help" on board, too, but these hands... This rescue may leave a mark...

He regarded his raw hands over his head that had begun to turn an awful shade of purple-red with frostnip. Within seconds, a hoist strop was lowered to him, and he connected with sheer determination and a well-practiced motion. He was grateful he could still use his palms for that last connection to his lifeline.

Maybe the basket would've been better to roll into...

He raised his orange dry suit's yellow-banded arm with his hand held high for the sign to be raised. He could no longer feel his fingers from the icy condition, and giving a thumbs-up was impossible. He waved his arm back and forth vigorously. That was the first time Joshua understood he was in trouble without an immediate end to the evolution. Joshua had never felt more exhilaration as his ascension skyward for his rescue of body, mind, and soul.

I want to keep my digits! For you, Papa, three more saves!

Chapter 25

PIT SPITTERS

"I just cannot thank you, gentlemen, enough," said a distinguished man with salt and pepper hair in a cherry red polo shirt.

The General Manager (GM) of the Traverse City Pit Spitters Minor League Baseball Team was welcomed in the Air Station hangar. The warm summer day was made tolerable in the shade of the giant home of the aircraft assigned to the Station. The hanger had been set up expressly for a distinguished guest. A gentle breeze blew through between the doors that stood wide open. Gigantic CG and American flags unfurled overhead and made for a spectacular welcome. The VIP visitor approached the gathered unit and greeted them informally before a special presentation was made.

"Please, call me Paul."

He shook hands warmly with Joshua's Chief, Bo, and the rest of the crew that had saved his dog, Luna, who was leashed at his side and attempted circles at their feet. Luna proudly wore a CG orange bandana tied around her neck. Luna wandered among her new friends as her tail thumped back and forth between human hugs and ear scratches. She enjoyed all the attention and sought out a host of new smells and smiles. She finally sat on the station deck and listened intently as her master spoke to the assembled CGAS Traverse City crews and other guests.

"You know our city is grateful always for what you do, but my girl, Luna, here is part of my family," the GM said.

The respected gentleman was nearly beside himself while he gushed his gratitude.

"I've heard about the CG and honestly been annoyed at the sound you've made sometimes over my house!"

The gathered crowd suppressed laughter.

"When you brought her home to me, well..., my family and I cannot thank you enough. Now, I'm a believer and proponent of the mission, and I'm here to show my deep appreciation. I want to spread the word everywhere about you all."

Joshua remembered how grateful he had been that he had been on duty some months ago at the right time. He was part of the crew that rescued the teenage skaters and what the crew assumed was their dog. When they arrived back at the base, it turned out that it was not theirs. The girls babbled their gratefulness for the dog who had accompanied them and warned them at the last minute about the thin ice in front of them. Base personnel had called the number on the dog's tag and immediately connected with the rescue dog's anxious owners. They arrived almost as soon as the girls' schoolmaster. All the souls were collected for safe returns home after promises to meet again. Joshua's attention returned to the VIP who addressed them.

"Guardians of the Great Lakes and especially of Green Lake...," the GM began with a smirk, "We want to honor you all with..."

Joshua and his buddies Eli and Ben passed through the gates into the new home of the Pit Spitters baseball team. It was a perfect summer night under the big lights around the field. The sun was bright late into the evening in Northern Michigan, but they were already on as fans began to assemble early in the stands. The GM gave the CG unit free tickets to that night's game as a gift of gratitude. Moreover, the same crew who rescued the girls and Luna had been asked to throw out the first pitch. They all tossed coins to see who would throw the ball across home plate. Joshua had held his breath until he eventually lost the toss to the flight mech.

That is an honor I don't want, he thought as he exhaled in relief.

When they found their seats, they were astounded that they had been given terrific seats on the right field behind first base and over the dugout.

"Sweet!" said Eli.

"I figured we'd be in the outfield with free seats," said Ben.

"No, gentleman, I want the best for our honorees," said the GM, who stood behind them.

Embarrassed they'd been overheard, the Guardians blushed.

"Follow me, please, as we make our way to the field. I want to introduce you to some people along the way," Paul, the GM, said.

The crew made jokes to each other as they trekked behind him about how they'd given up their illustrious baseball careers to turn wrenches, fuel helicopters, and were forced to watch ball games from the stands. Some shared that their families would also be in attendance. The kids were incredibly excited for free additional bottomless popcorn buckets, Monty the mascot hugs, cherry hamburgers, cherry pop, and cherry floats. Fireworks had been promised, and the crew wasn't supposed to be called away suddenly that night. The men recollected going to games with their dads decades before. They compared home teams from all over the country.

Joshua listened in until he realized he was more distracted by how much he truly missed his papa than any ballgame opportunities. When he and his brothers were small, he had been to a ball game with his papa, but the memory was fuzzy. He didn't know much about baseball at all. He played it cool and learned as he watched and listened. It was just another reminder of how much he had to learn about the world around him that others seemed to understand already.

Joshua's passion early on had been time in the pool. When he stroked through the clear pool, he had time to himself to think and no rules to remember. He disciplined himself to get in the pool and swam faster than the guy ahead of him. His coach kept it simple: pull ahead of the competition on the last lap to win.

But it never built fun memories with my Papa, Joshua contemplated.

Focus on being glad I'm not the one trying to throw the ball tonight, Mansoul, he thought to himself.

Joshua was never one to aim to be the center of attention. He looked up. The brilliant lights glared down and around the field and grandstands. He noticed they resembled the Nightsun that the CG often used in darkness to light up the area they needed to see. The similarly powerful lights were meant to light up the fun game.

Joshua mused, *The same powerful light is used in good and bad situations, but always to make it better.*

The crew eventually assembled on the back of the pitcher's mound near center field. Joshua beamed as the crowd cheered the CG and applauded all the Guardians and their families in the stands. He didn't care about people seeing him with braces tonight. It was not often that the CG was so spectacularly recognized. He was glad for the community and his peers' admiration. His pseudo-parents and landlords had joined the special event, although they planned to leave early to beat the crowd.

I bet they don't last until the halftime. Wait? Does baseball even have a halftime?

The press box announcer said, "Let us stand for our National Anthem brought to us by the Interlochen School for the Arts chorus."

"Hey, isn't that the same school those girls were from?" said one of the crew members.

He elbowed Joshua playfully in the arm. Joshua shrugged with nonchalance.

The first pitch went well, and the crew returned to their seats and enjoyed a great game against another Michigan team. There was entertainment between innings, and the CG kids were often invited to participate.

This is more party than play, thought Joshua.

Eli said, "Mansoul, you do a mean chicken dance."

"Where's Ben? He's been gone a long time," said Joshua.

During the seventh inning stretch, entertainment was planned on the field that Joshua had never imagined could happen. The crew was in on the "entertainment" beforehand, and the GM had coordinated it earlier with Bo, their Chief. Poor Joshua was unaware of the surprise that awaited him.

The crew was invited back on the field for a supposed "game" between innings. Joshua was blindfolded, spun around a ball bat five times, and told to run to first base with voiced directions. The crowd watched animatedly when Sophia and Beth replaced Joshua's crew. The crowd cheered louder as the petite teenage girls tried to coax their gentle savior forward and then right and left. The jumbotron showed a photo of the damsels with him on the afternoon of their rescue. They had been wet and freezing, but their smiles were enormous. Joshua looked to the crowd like a warrior on the screen in his orange and yellow dry suit, helmet under his arm, flanked by the young women who hugged him tightly and Luna, too, mid-bark. Their tiny arms were thrown around him like their lives depended on him. His last name was prominently displayed underneath in flashing lights: MANSOUL Rescues Three.

"Mansoul Rescues Three, Mansoul Rescues Three, Mansoul Rescues Three!" chanted the crowd, louder and louder.

The teenagers did not touch him on the field as he staggered in every direction. He kept himself poised and simultaneously tried to keep his feet under him while he stammered forward. Joshua's reaction was hilarious since he realized two unknown girls replaced his crew. He could not hear their directions over the crowd and stood motionless to gain composure.

Wait, those voices aren't my crew.... but they do sound familiar. Who is it?

... focus Mansoul, he chided himself.

Then, just to his right, Joshua heard a dog bark.

Whose dog is allowed on this field?

Joshua felt his face as it began to flame under the blindfold.

What is happening?

The "Mansoul!" refrain grew louder until his feet finally found first base. Beth and Sophia bear-hugged him and stripped his mask off. All around the stadium, the fans were on their feet and chanted, "Mansoul!" They all waved orange neckerchiefs like the one Luna wore while she ran exuberant laps around them. The lights were so bright Joshua had trouble seeing anyone else in the crowded stadium. He immediately looked for the crew that was supposed to have vectored him, and they were all gathered near home plate doubled over in laughter. They knew the meek Mansoul was next to undone in front of the exuberant Traverse City crowd.

The GM leashed Luna and approached Joshua and the girls as they headed toward him near the dugout. The GM used the microphone and briefly explained the relationships to an enamored crowd. He quickly retold how the crew, who also joined them near the dugout then, had heroically saved the three souls the previous March. He also extended his appreciation to all the service members, past and present, in the stands. He mentioned that under his leadership, one game would be CG appreciation night every season henceforth. The crowd began to chant again, this time, "Coast Guard. Coast Guard!"

The crew and ladies left the field with glad hearts. The ladies spoke up before Joshua returned to the stands.

"Mr. Mansoul, sir?"

"Yes," said Joshua.

He slowed up, then stopped, and turned fully around to them.

"Thank yous again for saving us that day. As God is my witness, I was begging Him for maybe the first time in my life, and yous was the response," said Beth.

She shook his hand vigorously as she smacked her gum with vigor and a wide smile.

"My parents said, 'If yous ever in Bucktown or NYC, we's gotchu. We'd a been lost withoutcha."

Sophia added, "I wrote a paper on being tenacious and adaptable for one of my classes this spring. At first, I thought that's what we had to have been to survive. The more I considered it, the more I realized that's exactly what you are to help people like us live. It's probably silly, but I brought you a copy. And look here," she said, pointing to her signature, "I hope to be a famous ballerina someday, but I wouldn't be here without you."

Sophia beamed at him, courageously reached up on her tiptoes, and kissed his cheek briefly. Joshua flushed at her youthful dreams and for her sincere appreciation. He stepped back and cleared his throat, unsure of how to reply.

Ben appeared with nachos and a face that read, "What did I just miss?"

Eli stood with them and sensed the awkward silence.

Eli said, "You going to introduce us to your friends, Joshie?" while he winked at him.

With some reluctance, Joshua introduced Eli and Ben to Sophia and Beth. Only then did Joshua realize the ladies wore CG t-shirts with their cutoff shorts, orange bandanas in their hair, and orange Chucks shoes.

Eli added, "If the ballet doesn't work out, the CG is always looking for *more* tenacious and adaptable people."

Joshua added an warning, "Once you've turned 18," directed toward Eli.

He nudged Eli in the side, but Eli ignored his friend's cautionary tone and invited the girls to sit with them for what remained of the game. For Eli, it seemed a suitable end to an exciting segment in Joshua's career of saves and an opportunity for himself.

Joshua wondered, *Can Eli be saved from himself?*

Ben regaled the girls with lively CG tales of heroism, and his beautiful sisters also joined them before the end of the game. That spread out the conversation enough so that Joshua didn't feel obliged to entertain them. He had already been tongue-tied with all the attention. Joshua enjoyed nightfall as the lights lit up the dark sky and the crowds wandered away. Eli seemed to be pumped up by all the attention and acclaim. Joshua solemnly considered the turn of events as the CG's mission was twisted somehow to make him the point man. It did not suit him to be the focus but to share the glory with his extended CG family.

What a thanks I get! My crew knew I'd rather not be in the limelight...

He shook his head, still in disbelief at all the unwanted attention. He knew he was not solely the rescuer of those girls. The mech had put the basket near them with expertise and single-handedly fished the dog out. The pilots' near-perfect skills at hover and precision had gotten the mech in place. The mission had been misunderstood when the crowd chanted his name alone. When the crowds chanted his name, he realized he had become uncomfortable in a way he'd never known.

I think I'd rather be an undercover AST, Joshua thought.

I'm a far cry from that night in ECity when the crowd chanted hateful words.

Eli slapped Joshua's back as they neared his car in the almost vacant car lot.

"What a night, eh? Should we go back and play some Euchre now or go out?"

Joshua said, "Not tonight, Eli. I'm toast."

He said farewell to his buddy and knew Eli didn't understand him and the importance of his time alone to think and meditate.

Joshua drove home to a dark house with a tiny porch light left on that illuminated the front and back steps.

A light in the darkness.

He was lost in the thoughts of his parents and wanted to share the comedic events and incredible appreciation everyone had participated in. He'd call his mama the next day. As for his papa, he missed him even more than he had words.

So long as you are the one who cheers me, Papa, I'm a contented man.

That is what I do know. Baseball, girls, and friends, I'm still trying to understand...

Chapter 26

FACE THE STORM

Summer gave way to the expectation of glorious fall foliage. Joshua looked forward to the harvest season and the winter snows that would follow. There were a few more rescues, but life was at a joyful slow pace. Joshua's orthodontics work progressed nicely. He developed a good relationship with his off-base dentist and orthodontist, though neither comforted him as Dr. Paz had in Kodiak. He was hopeful within two years, he would smile like a new man. He had planned that all the ortho work would be finished before he PCS'd again to his next duty station. He was working hard to promote and take the Servicewide Exam required of all the Coast Guard enlisted corps.

One late September day, Joshua hiked alongside the still waters near the Beitner Trail. Joshua received an urgent bulletin. A massive hurricane had formed in the Caribbean. The hurricane's trajectory had not yet been confirmed, but additional crews had been called to Elizabeth City, North Carolina. They would meet there and then forward deploy for post-hurricane assistance operations. The question was, would Joshua be available and willing? Joshua's forehead rippled with concern. This is what he trained for, *Semper Paratus*, always ready. He lived for this to help others in their direst time of need. However, he knew his mother and his family would be terrified at the thought of Joshua heading into a named hurricane. A similar disaster brought back so many days and nights of turmoil and sleeplessness. Mainly for his beloved mother, it was still raw and painful.

Who are my mother and my brothers? Many more families need the mission to succeed.

After he had thought on it for just a few minutes, Joshua knew in his heart that he could not say no to the opportunity and the privilege to do what was asked of him as part of the Coast Guard mission.

Joshua was packed and forward deployed from the Air Station near the Cherry Regional Airport within hours. He was headed first toward the Norfolk, Virginia, airport to be picked up and bused to his old Elizabeth City, NC, home. He had spent years of his life in and around coastal North Carolina. Questions swirled in his mind as he made his way there and cautiously informed his family and friends of the scenario as it unfolded.

Joshua gazed out his airplane's window and thought, *What and whom would he find in the days ahead*?

He used the travel time en route to catch up with friends, his brothers, and even Christian, whom he had rescued and heard graduated from CG boot. As a seaman, the Coast Guard had sent Christian to a small boat station at Fort Macon, NC, in his first tour of duty. As the crow flies, it is just a short distance from Elizabeth City, but the duties required of Joshua on this temporary duty (TDY) would preclude him from any attempt to see Christian.

"So close, and yet so far," they had laughed together.

How a crow and a Jayhawk could fly was quite different.

When Joshua arrived in ECity, he was assigned a room in the barracks and relaxed briefly. In an oddly familiar environment, he walked to the chapel a few hundred yards away. He was reminiscent of his first visit to the chapel years ago as a nervous Airman. He longed for a sense of peace that the chapel represented then, and what he yearned for was peace of mind and soul before he was sent into a storm. He was encouraged when he tugged the door, which swung open and invited him in. The base chapel was silent when he slipped inside. Joshua regarded the same illuminated stained-glass windows that glowed from the sunlight that filtered through them and colored the floors in hues of oranges. These windows were unique to any he'd seen anywhere else. The CG symbol of the double anchors within the circle of orange was set in them, and they seemed to wash over him.

Will my life be like this, with the mission filtered through me to shine as a comfort, a calm reassurance, and an invitation? he wondered.

It was as if time had stood still here in this place. The chairs were still in the exact rows. *No,* he noticed, *the carpet was more worn, and there were more speakers and musical equipment. This place has had some good use.*

The organ was gone, but he did not want music. He searched for solace. It was a serene moment, and he knew he needed to wrestle with the emotions that stirred within him as he prepared to face the storm within and externally.

His papa had used his axe to break through their roof with them after Katrina.

Papa, you knew help was on the way and directed us into the hovering USCG helicopter for a hoist to our salvation.

Joshua's papa had said he'd meet up with them later. He never did. Neighbors later told his mother he'd been seen with his axe as he swam from rooftop to rooftop. Strangers had desperately called out to him, and he never gave up.

He swam with an axe!

The neighbors were amazed and grateful for his courageous rescues, hard work, and wisdom, which allowed them to climb on the top of their roofs for the CG to come. He wore the biggest smile and reassured older people and children alike that help was already on the way. They admitted to Maria that he had demonstrated supernatural strength.

"We hadn't been forgotten," they said, "and were loved."

I can hardly wait to meet up with you again, Papa, he hoped.

Hours earlier, Joshua had met up with friends and fellow CG members across the service on the bus from the airport. His phone blew up with more acquaintances on their way. They already knew Hurricane Ian had increased in power and strength as it churned its way through the Atlantic and headed directly toward Florida. Souls had already been saved and lost.

Whom else can I save? Where else can I go?

When Joshua left the small chapel, he glanced at the Memorial Wall of Aviation to those crews who had so courageously given their lives on behalf of strangers. It drew him to reevaluate, and he turned and walked the granite wall's length. His eyes canvased the names that listed far too many brave men and women who had given their all. He thought then of their families who, like his, had suffered immeasurably, missed ball games, birthdays, and all the holidays.

Where were they now? Have they moved on? Had their loved one's lives been redeemed in some way?

These lives all mattered to him. In some great irony, it stirred courage within him to bravely face what was before him. Perhaps to fly into the jaws of death to fight a battle not with flesh and blood but with unseen forces that threatened to tear apart things. More importantly, the unknown forces would de-create people of immeasurable value. Joshua's fists, he realized, were clenched and sweat dripped from his brow. He was already ready to combat the unseen battle of wills.

These lives given have not been in vain. Mine won't be either.

Joshua dared to reach out and lean on the cold granite wall. His forehead pressed against the stone, and he sweat profusely. He tasted the bitter saltiness of his tears before he recognized he shed them. He did not draw strength from the memories but from the hope of humble sacrifice given in love.

Your will be done, Papa. The mission must be accomplished.

"High shall our purpose be."

The next day, Joshua reported to duty early and entered the familiar hangar to join up with the other guardians who had already stood duty. Crews were formed from those flown in from across the country to help with the additional duties and preparation for the category five hurricane. By then, Hurricane Ian had not exhibited that it would directly hit the Coastal Carolinas. Florida was its target. The location at Air Station Elizabeth City had become the forward operations base for the entire East Coast. Other air stations evacuated farther south, including Miami, Jacksonville, Clearwater, and Savannah. Those crews arrived hourly.

It is terrific to have run into old classmates and previous acquaintances. Sorry for the occasion, though, thought Joshua.

This mission, more than most, solidified why the USCG was unique. Due to its strict procedures and policies, every crew member could work with any other crew. Mechanics could fix any aircraft they were trained to, no matter where it hailed from. Their work included staff preparedness, vehicle readiness, and mission appointments.

"Mansoul, well, if I didn't know better...They let just anyone in this hangar, I guess!"

Joshua bear-hugged Caleb, "Nice to see you in person again, too, amigo!"

Suddenly, the SAR alarm screeched overhead and reverberated through the hangar that overflowed with equipment and personnel. The men and women who stood duty jumped and ran for their stations. The data was collected, and they began to make their way through the hangar into an aircraft that the OPS boss directed as the duty aircraft for the day. Joshua was off duty and awaited orders for the hurricane mission efforts elsewhere. The Coast Guard resembled an ant hill that spilled over with resources and feet that scurried in every direction. Joshua wished he had more of a part to play and volunteered wherever possible.

Mariners preferred to get their vessels out to sea instead of being beaten inside marinas and docks where they were typically moored further inland. When hurricane forces or tropical storms came near, boats were the first to be damaged or lost. However, those same boat owners were only sometimes proficient at how to sail or motor in torrential rain, strong winds, and frightful weather. They had often put themselves and others in grave danger in the past. There was a real reason why the Outer Banks of Coastal North Carolina was called the Graveyard of the Atlantic.

Joshua shuddered and recalled the surfers who had once, they thought, bravely surfed the giant swells, and that added strain to the lifesaving services along the coast. Although only sometimes unauthorized, it was highly unadvised. Joshua's heart was with all the duty standers and first responders up and down the coastal United States as this gigantic storm began to batter South and Central Florida. He remembered the families like his who hid in the attic through the long, dark, terrifying night. He trembled as the warm temperatures began to rise inside the shade of the hangar.

I should call my mama again, but what do I say?

Joshua's reverie was interrupted when Caleb plopped down next to him at chow.

"Hey, have you seen Jordan yet?" Caleb said, "She's supposed to be here already."

"Not yet," replied Joshua, "We'd know if she was in the vicinity."

"I heard 'dat!" said a jubilant Jordan from behind them.

The guys leaped to their feet, and their hugs went all around. A joyous reunion was held between old friends right back where they had begun in ECity. The Air Station and all of Coast Guard Base Elizabeth City worked frantically. The meals were their time of refreshment, and guardians savored the camaraderie they found in coming together again. Crews and reinforcements were called all over the central Atlantic Coast to stand up for the emergency evacuations and SAR cases that would surely come farther South in Florida and the Carolinas.

Preparations were made, and Joshua was frustrated to be put on a standby hold one more day. His standby duty only lasted 24 hours until the Air Station Elizabeth City crews had exhausted themselves. They'd received hourly cases of stranded boaters and missing vessels and persons. Fisherman worked at a frenzied pace to retrieve nets and get in what could be their last catch of the season.

Joshua volunteered cheerfully for the local duty since he knew the area well after his tour of duty there. He loitered near the ready room and snacked out of the vending machine on what was left of grape juice and crackers. He, his friends, and new acquaintances enjoyed their swapped stories as they tried to distract themselves from the zone of the Weather Channel and continuous desperate news feed.

The destruction at least overwhelmed them and at most exhausted them as tired crews began to trickle back in from long, difficult flights. Joshua texted Christian, Jones, and his family to check in.

It was only a short time before an urgent call came in for a SAR due to an overturned and empty tandem kayak in the Chesapeake Bay.

One guardian said, "Are you kidding me? Who goes out in *this* on *that*?"

Joshua said, "They don't know what they've done."

Jordan said, "We do what is good. We will go out and never let fears alarm us."

Caleb looked between them both and shrugged.

He spoke, "I'm in if you are."

A favorite sight for many in the Chesapeake Bay area was the beautiful Chesapeake Bay Bridge Tunnel. One may travel by automobile over 17.6 miles of engineering innovation and see vibrant wildlife and ocean views without a single stop sign, traffic light, or intersection in sight. It was a toll road and a pricey drive, but a great way to sweep around the busy interstate area of Hampton Roads or have an excursion to the beach. It was also an excellent demarcation for the CG. The Bay was inside the bridge-tunnel, and the open Atlantic Ocean was on the other. The greater Hampton Roads area was home to the Portsmouth Naval Air Station and many other Department of Defense units and contractors. The giant ships of the Naval Base and the container ships could traverse the bay's tunnel system, and smaller boats could float under the miles of bridges. Truly a construction marvel of the 20th century. Joshua had enjoyed the view over it each time they routinely swept up the Atlantic coastline in flight.

Watchstanders at Coast Guard Sector Hampton Roads in Portsmouth, Virginia, received a radio call at about 6:20 p.m. that a kayak had been seen overturned in the water in the vicinity of the Chesapeake Bay Bridge-Tunnel. Sector Hampton Roads issued an urgent marine information broadcast. Coast Guard 29-foot Response Boat-Small crews from Station Little Creek in Virginia Beach launched to assist in the Search and Rescue efforts. By 7 p.m., aircrews launched from Air Station Elizabeth City included a H-60 Jayhawk and a C-130 Hercules.

Once on scene, Station Little Creek crew members pulled the vessel aboard to search for any owner or contact information description. They noted the location of the red tandem kayak as just west or inside the bridge and technically inside the Bay. Finding no personal distinction, they radioed back and began a patrol that swept the Bay in the rough seas.

The Jayhawk crew lifted off on an overcast day with gusty winds that rocked the crew around inside the aircraft. The crew began to discuss why kayakers would paddle so far out into the Chesapeake Bay just before the threat of a major hurricane. In the back, Jonah, a mech that Joshua had taken an immediate fondness for because he had volunteered to stand the duty with him, spoke over the intercom. Joshua was taken aback when Jonah complained about their duty and the SAR case.

Jonah said with indignance, "Why do we have to go out and search for one or two persons who should know better?"

He continued, "Don't you guys agree? The demands of the Coast Guard have rarely been higher due to Ian. Why did the Air Station commander send us to find these punks?"

Joshua spoke, "Remember the mission. Rescue checklist part one."

"Why are so many resources spent on someone who lacks better judgment? This dude has put so many of us in danger in such a great time of stress already," said Jonah.

"Word will get out and create similar stunts and behaviors for others to do the same, I think..." he continued.

The aircraft commander, Lexi, interrupted with a remarkable reply.

"Honor, respect, and devotion to duty, my husband says, is another way of saying, "Being kind is not an endorsement."

"You all remember what they said in the movie *The Guardian*?" said the other pilot, Gabe.

He continued, "I take the first one I come to or the weakest one in the group, and then I swim as fast and as hard as I can for as long as I can. And the sea takes the rest."

Joshua added, "The old timers in the Life Saving Service had a rule that read, "You have no choice but to go out. I think this storm will teach them. But will they remember?"

The rest of the ride was quieter as the mood turned somber. Joshua had watched the movie *The Guardian*, loads of YouTube videos, and even 'Coast Guard Alaska' on the weather channel. Some of the portrayals and information were realistic, but others were not so much. It was part of the ethos like Chaps had told him once. The responsibility was to rescue, no matter the insult or injury. "So Others May Live" was about souls saved, not condemnation in the process. Those who had never requested the mission nor embraced it were condemned. The mission's offer to help had been made since 1790. The Life Saving Service was conceived on the shoulders of rescue missions like it since ancient days, loving your neighbor like yourself.

Information was continually fed to the crew from the District 5 headquarters base nearby in Norfolk. Joshua could see Norfolk on the horizon from the helicopter's windows as they approached the Chesapeake Bay.

Joshua thought, *How ironic that the watchstander was just a few short miles from this person or persons if there were any.*

"Maybe somebody's kayak got away from the dock, and we're on a fool's errand," replied Jonah.

Suddenly, new information filled their headsets. A missing person's report had been placed to the Coast Guard via the 911 call center. This was an appropriate use of emergency services, but the services were strained with the many people who struggled with their own homes, businesses, evacuations, and shelters that were formed. Many other responders were prepared to head into the storm that may barrel up their coastline within hours. It was still unknown if the category five storm would reach the low-lying Chesapeake Bay area. A man's name, Nabal, was given as being the first kayaker unaccounted for. He was described as a Caucasian 50-year-old male with an athletic build, and his son, named Mayim, was age 17. They were three hours overdue off the coast of Virginia Beach.

Joshua knew the surface water this time of year was warmer in the Atlantic than in Lake Michigan. At about 70 degrees, Joshua knew he was fortunate it was September. The warm currents kept the water at a higher temperature than the Great Lakes, further north. No one knew how prepared the men were for a long duration overboard. Some kayakers took a risk and did not carry an EPIRB (Emergency Position Indicating Radio Beacon) or wet suit. The USCG required only a personal flotation device every day for situations like this. The EPRIB was strongly encouraged, particularly in the open ocean.

"What do you want to bet they're *not* wearing their *Coast Guard-approved* life flotation vests?" said Jonah.

Joshua thought, *I'm beginning to wonder about my friend Jonah's sincerity to the mission.*

Joshua responded, "Back to the checklist. Remember me, crew, if they're prepared."

Or not..., Joshua thought.

Joshua began to search the vast open Bay behind his open visor and hoped to spot a colorful life vest. He understood he would go to the ocean's unpredictable surface whether the survivors were prepared or unprepared. The outcome difference would be obvious, but his role was the same.

He requested, "Permission to open the cabin door?"

The crew knew in salt water, someone could float for a long time but become dehydrated quickly if they exerted much effort. Whether it was fear or exhaustion, they could succumb to the elements long before a rescue could be made. The crew had been informed a CG small boat crew had been on the scene and recovered the kayak. Small boats rarely could see far with a lot of wave action. There were plenty of waves that day, and they increased in size further from land. The helicopter and a C-130 for cover began a search pattern that sometimes took days. Days were not what the Coast Guard had to give.

The Coast Guard Jayhawk pilot spoke again from the cockpit as they made their way north along the beaches of Virginia. He knew the men in the cabin had all been previously stationed at ECity.

"Does this view make you guys homesick?"

Joshua looked down and saw the beach he had stretched out idly on with his family that day years before. That day, the surf pounded the shoreline, and the long stretches of beach were vacant. It was the great memories of the relaxation and the bright future ahead of him that brought joy to him in that moment. They began the search pattern, and Joshua made himself as comfortable as he could on his knees while he peered out his designated watch window at the waves that continued to build below. The sky had turned a deep blue as the blanketed sun began to set over the far westerly horizon. They knew they couldn't run the search pattern long after sunset.

Joshua listened carefully in his headset as the pilot, the aircraft commander, began to share a story she had heard told the previous weekend.

The commander, Lexi, relayed, "Hey guys, I just remembered a story about a man named Nabal. I haven't heard that name for a long time until this week, and now twice! Crazy story, his name meant *fool* ...anyone else heard that story?"

A voice from the C-130 overhead relayed, "I know that ageless story all too well. Let's hope it's not replayed again today."

Elijah "Padre" Joseph, aircraft commander of the Hercules, flew high overhead for surveillance and support of the CG mission below him. "Padre" had also been sent TDY from his new Clearwater, Florida station to assist in hurricane efforts out of ECity. He knew his job that day was a comeback tour. He had flown out of the Norfolk area when he had been assigned to the Marine Corps and Department of Defense a decade before. He knew the territory and longed for good news.

Padre spoke again, "Chance favors a prepared sailor."

He paraphrased Louis Pasteur's famous line, "Chance favors the prepared mind."

"I think Pasteur was a rescuer in his own right... Let's keep looking vigilantly," said Joshua.

"You're well-read, Mansoul," replied Padre.

"I'm glad you're with us, Padre," said Joshua.

The Coast Guard swept the area in a grid determined by policy and coordinated efforts for over an hour. They flew back and forth over the water around the bridge. Since the small boat crew had located the red kayak, the CG plotted how far in three hours or so the men could have floated. To find a 50-year-old man with or without a life preserver in the vastness of the outflow of the Chesapeake Bay into the Atlantic Ocean was akin to the search for a teardrop in the tide. They all knew the inevitable was that they likely would never be found, not before sundown. All had committed their lives to search tirelessly for the lost, so they persevered. Therefore, the search continued until the pre-coordinated metrics were exhausted. It was someone else's decision at headquarters to call off a SAR.

The lack of visibility and wave action made the small boat turn back to shore. The Jayhawk still had better visibility and continued the search long after the big orange sun had hit the westerly horizon. In the twilight, an oddity far below caught the eye of Joshua.

He jumped and shouted, "There, 2 O'clock!"

Joshua couldn't contain himself. He pointed, but no one could have seen what he pointed towards in the back of the aircraft. Immediately, in the direction he mentioned, the Jayhawk began to bank.

The pilot said, "We have little time left with light or fuel. We can mark the spot and send another crew."

"No!" said Joshua, "Please, fly closer."

The mech replied, "We could drop a life raft, too... see any movement?"

They flew in closer to see the neon orange life vest around the neck of a man's head. They flew in a tight circle around the life vest that floated on the water's surface a couple of miles from the bridge in the Atlantic. The coordinates were recorded and relayed to headquarters. A hand barely lifted from underwater and slightly waved with exhaustion.

"There, he's waving, he waved! Please put me in!" Joshua announced.

The pilots and crew disagreed and were disgruntled at the lack of fuel in their tank.

Lexi said in accordance, “Mansoul, we’re at bingo in two minutes.”

Joshua told Jonah and the pilots, “You must understand he won’t last for the next crew. Drop the life raft and put me in it with him. Return for both of us. I’ll administer aid, and you can find us fast with my EPIRB.”

There was a long, weighty silence as the crew evaluated his thoughts and their own.

Joshua began to prepare himself for a deployment and attempted to persuade them by his off-key rendition of their CG song.

He began, “To fight to save or fight and die, Aye! Coast Guard, we are for you!”

They all burst out with laughter in disbelief at his determination.

“Geez, Mansoul. Lay it on thick, why don’t you?” said Jonah.

The pilots consulted with one another and headquarters as the precious seconds of time and fuel ran out.

“It’s why I came. Put me in.,” said Joshua.

“There’s no need for you to become a martyr, Mansoul. You sure?” said the aircraft commander.

“Nevermore, Ma’am! It’s who I am. You’ve got me, right, Padre?” Joshua declared.

“Roger,” replied Padre.

Without a second to spare, the agreement was made. Joshua was at the cabin door, which had conveniently already been opened. Jonah shook his head in disbelief at what he prepared Joshua for and glared contemptuously at Joshua. Joshua nodded to his crew mate in appreciation as though he could never fully understand his passion for the call to rescue. Joshua heaved himself from the safety of the cabin and into the watery chasm ‘so others may live.’

“Swimmer is outside the cabin,” said Jonah.

Joshua’s head popped above the surface after his free fall into the water close to the first man. It was the older survivor, Nabal; they could tell from his full head of gray hair.

“Swimmer is in the water. Mark, mark, mark!” said Jonah.

The crew marked the exact location Joshua was left and anticipated the C-130 overhead would stay in continuous contact with him. They would never leave him until he was swiftly retrieved by the helo already spun up in ECity to rescue their own. Joshua felt the cool water and gasped in wonder at the size of the waves that crashed over them. He made the sign of the cross to deploy the life raft. He held both arms extended vertically and crossed them over his head with his fist clenched. Then, he expeditiously swam up a wave and down another to his first survivor.

Salty! I’ve been in Traverse City maybe too long, he thought.

Chapter 27
EMPTY

Chesapeake Bay, Virginia

Joshua was alongside the survivor immediately. Joshua's crew and Jayhawk backed away. The rotor blades' tremendous sound wafted into the cacophony of water and wind that broke over their heads. Joshua spoke to the man once the noise had slacked.

"I'm a U.S. Coast Guard rescue swimmer. My name is Joshua Mansoul. What's yours?"

Because he already knew the man's name, it helped Joshua; the man could only grunt. The man's eyes could barely open in two blinks of acknowledgment that he was no longer alone in the chaos and madness. He could not speak. The life raft dropped immediately as the Jayhawk passed over them. It plunged within yards of them. The helo made one more circle overhead as if the crew waved farewell and Godspeed. Joshua's heart sank when he knew he was nearly alone with his survivor in the mayhem. The blink of the lights of the Jayhawk faded, as did the engine's roar. His heart was not downcast for himself. He knew that he could withstand the one or more hours at sea. The precious life raft dropped to them both would easily hold them. The raft was made for six men.

Joshua wondered, *If this man is already so frigid, would he hang on for just another hour?*

Where is the boy? I have got to find the other guy!

"I heard your name is Nabal. Is that true?" asked Joshua.

Joshua, with precision, swam around the man and assessed him in the wave-tossed ocean. The man grunted once more, and his eyes fluttered open and closed. He knew these moments were a matter of life and death, and to get the barely conscious survivor alive and into the life raft on his own was going to be difficult at best. He was prepared.

Joshua replied, "You've got to hang on, and we will get you out of here. I will inflate this life raft and then get you inside. A crew will return shortly, and help is already on its way. Then, after we get home, we will fight a hurricane. You got all that, Nabal?"

The survivor went completely limp. Joshua knew many survivors did this in the last moments when they sensed that help had been found. They gave up entirely their own will to survive. Joshua slapped him carefully on the cheeks several times to revive him as they slid up and down the waves.

"You've got to stay with me, Nabal. You got any kids? Where's your son? When did you last see him? You got a pretty wife at home? You need to start thinking about them. Live for me. Live for them. Live for us," he pleaded.

Joshua swam over and opened the life raft. It ballooned in size. Joshua's eyes widened when he remembered how big and tall it was and how quickly it inflated. The wind tore the raft from his grasp and threatened to blow it away from them and across the billowed surface of the ocean that raged against them.

"Whoa, boy," said Joshua.

He dove for the raft that skipped away like a kite on the wind. He swam it down, and then, with one arm, he tugged the giant raft towards Nabal. He swam ferociously with his other arm and his mighty fins that churned beneath the surface. Joshua fully committed himself and clamped his jaw down tight around the mouthpiece of his snorkel. He tasted blood.

My braces aren't any help with this rescue, he thought.

With heroic strength, Joshua reclaimed the distance and put a seat belt grip around Nabal. The waves seemed to continue to build around them. Joshua knew he had precious seconds to hoist the man inside. Joshua hoisted Nabal's head and life vest into the entry point on the raft to keep him steady. Joshua pulled himself into the raft entrance, climbed inside, and lost his fins in the process. He leaned on his stomach precariously over the edge and grabbed under both of Nabal's arms. He pulled Nabal's deadweight up the front of the life raft's slippery entry point. He wrenched the large motionless man into the open side of the raft when a sudden gust of fierce wind picked up the opposite side of the raft, and it slanted out of the water. The blustery wind blew the raft over, and before Joshua knew it, it capsized. He was forced underwater and trapped under the raft. The raft had a cover, and the men came up under the heavy cover, which sent Nabal into a sudden frenzy. Joshua took what breath he could and pulled Nabal underwater away from the 150-pound rubber raft. The huge, buoyant man still in his life vest was a tremendous load.

Joshua thought, *I'm pulling an elephant underwater.*

Joshua swam away and clear of the raft. They both came up and gasped for air. Nabal was conscious after his plummet under water. He coughed up ocean water and cried out in rage. Joshua searched around them to grasp the upside-down raft.

"That was not part of the plan!" said Joshua.

Nabal came at Joshua and swung his arms in an angry fury. He caught Joshua by surprise and bloodied his nose with a right hook.

Joshua's eyes stung with pain, and blood squirted across the water and hit the life raft inches away. Salt water stung in his nostrils as the blood continued to pour. Joshua grabbed his nose to pinch it and shoved it back in place when he realized it was broken. Joshua swam backward, and when he did, he let go of the life raft. He swam away from the gruesome scene and then watched as his survivor pulled himself toward the life raft. Joshua rode up one wave and down another in awe of the quick turn of events. Seconds felt like minutes as Joshua reassessed his situation and their circumstances.

Nabal flailed in his attempts to keep hold of the raft he regarded for the first time as his salvation alone. Nabal captured and hung onto it by an exterior line. He laughed in agony or arrogant pride. Joshua needed to learn which. Nabal claimed the raft like a child's game of King of the Hill.

Nabal called out, "It's all mine."

How had this become a matter of wills so fast? thought Joshua.

Joshua momentarily allowed the man to pirate their life raft, intended for Joshua to save the men and himself. With Nabal as a stand-in for the part of the dragon creature from the ocean's depth that mariners had feared for ages. Joshua considered his words and plan quite cautiously.

The question remained, *Did Nabal speak to the abyss that nearly ended his life or to us, his rescuers?*

Joshua knew at that moment he would give the raft away. He would give it all freely; even the darkness and the man's eyes could not overshadow the light in Joshua. He was the arm of the Coast Guard. Survivors did not get interrogated nor condemned to the end. He would not destroy a stranger he had come to save. He knew he would not push his will on the survivor. With regret and remorse, though, Joshua acknowledged his survivor had made it all too apparent that he alone wanted to survive the night in the life raft he had provided him. Nabal, in his state, wanted to fight to the death for it.

What irony? thought Joshua.

Where's his son?

Joshua rode the waves up and down and kept a few yards from the raft. He knew Nabal would not leave it but could not hang on to it for much longer.

He's not even asking about his niño?

Joshua looked in every direction. He turned and dove away to give clearance for himself and assessed his new injury and situation.

Broken nose, no fins, still need to find the second survivor while Nabal screams.

He figured when Nabal hit the water, he was suddenly and viciously awoken from his near comatose situation. His terror had enacted his fight-and-flight subconscious.

Or maybe he was always a dragon...

How much fight did Nabal have left?

What to do with an overturned life raft?

Joshua calmed himself and regarded the circumstances in the near total darkness. Joshua broke the green chem light and placed it on his forehead for added light. It would be needed for the inbound crew to find him anyhow. Nabal desperately searched for a better handhold on the raft's side. Together, they could have assisted one another. Joshua heard him swear and curse the darkness. Joshua was embarrassed for him.

How pitiful a creature that rages against the darkness he has brought upon himself.

He used the time to call the C-130 Hercules that circled overhead to relay what had happened. They were none too pleased to relay he'd overturned in the first raft but assured him they would drop a second within minutes.

Padre said, "You okay, Mansoul?"

Joshua replied in short spurts between waves, "Cloud rider, I've been bloodied and bruised. Combative survivor."

Padre said, "We won't let go of you. We have your chem light in our view. Engine problems on the second Jayhawk. Turning the crew and passing gas to the earlier 'Big Iron.'"

"Mansoul, we see the other survivor about 25 yards from you due west, but he looks face down. Godspeed."

"Thanks, amigos, and sorry for all the trouble. Remember me, will ya?" asked Joshua.

The C-130's aircraft commander, Padre, said, "Dragon slayer, what you are doing will never be forgotten."

Joshua swam back and calmly treaded water beside the raft. He resigned himself not to use combative force to wound the survivor. When Nabal's movements slowed, Joshua reengaged the man within seconds. This time, he approached with procedures he had trained per policy with combative survivors. When he attempted to put on a C-clamp grip, Nabal reached out with surprising strength and grabbed Joshua's head. He tore at his mask, snorkel, vest, strobe, and anything that he could catch on it. The fight with the madman was about to turn deadly. Joshua's personal locator beacon was ripped from his chest, and in the struggle, Nabal let it go. It blew out of sight in the blink of an eye. Joshua controlled his anger and knew that the C-130 that droned overhead still had eyes on him from high above in the near darkness for a bit longer.

At least until they realize I am no longer with my beacon, strobe, or with them at all.

Joshua only allowed himself to mutter these words,

"I am grateful for the sky ruler's coverage, but my beacon would have been helpful, to say the least."

He did not know if he had spoken to them, himself, or his foe. He looked up and willed himself to see the black USCG he'd always admired and laid back momentarily. Instead, he saw a crescent moon on the opposite horizon from where the sun had set.

I need more light and more time, he mused.

Re-engage, Mansoul. Find the other survivor and the new raft.

Joshua followed the last order and looked to his right at 25 yards. Joshua saw a life jacket wash up and over a wave with a head in it. He swam immediately to the survivor and, to his surprise, found the young adult wide-eyed in fear, not death.

"Please, take me ...with you..." the man-child choked out, exhausted.

"You're all mine, Mayim."

The teen's eyes flickered with emotion at the mention of his name. Joshua confidently placed a cross-chest carry around him and began to swim him to the life raft that bobbed away in the wind with Nabal, who desperately clung to the side.

And there was evening and then the morning..., Joshua thought.

They were all in the deep abyss, a chaos of mystery, and headed toward what Joshua did not know. Nabal saw Joshua approach as if for the first time and turned his anger towards him sadistically. He fought at the side of the raft still.

Nabal screamed at him, "Why have you done this to me?"

Joshua contended for all their lives using a cobra grip and other tactics to keep Mayim afloat. The rough water and westerly winds continued to push them further out to sea. Joshua had watched the second life raft get dropped from the C-130, but with the wind and wave action, he believed it would be harder to attempt to get to the new one than the one within reach. It was almost out of sight, and he desperately wanted to keep the survivors together.

"So, you've made this personal. Mayim, *your son*, is alive, and I won't leave you," said Joshua.

"It's all mine," Nabal hissed.

Joshua kept clear of the man who had fought him vigorously. He placed Mayim, Nabal's son, between them to prove his goodness by his return of the man's son. He hoped the son's deliverance would be atonement for whatever Nabal had against him. He never doubted that he could outswim the man. Joshua knew it was Nabal's manner that would be their demise or their delivery from death. Joshua's resolve thickened when he realized Nabal wanted to fight over the raft to save himself.

I have come to save them all.

I will not leave them or forsake either of them.

How ridiculous to have found a hurricane of a fight in the middle of a rescue outside the hurricane, Joshua thought.

Where else can I go? Where else will my help come from?

Joshua knew they needed to be inside the life raft. He swam for it with Mayim in tow and caught it, which was no easy task. He strained, pulled with all his might, and tried to regain the raft. Mayim was barely alive and coherent. Nabal yelled obscenities between his plummets under the surface when waves crashed over their heads. Joshua knew he needed to make life-and-death decisions. He had to get Mayim in or on the life raft himself. He timed the waves and wind, released Mayim quickly, and scrambled atop the raft. In the next tremendous gust of wind, Joshua yanked the righting strap of the upside-down raft into the next wave that towered over them, and it flipped again.

Nabal had been pushed under the same crest of waves and cursed Joshua, his birth, his family, his ancestry, and his legacy. Joshua plunged beneath the surface into the chaos again, but the taunts rang in his ears. Joshua resurfaced and then reclaimed Mayim briefly.

The young man begged, “Please don’t leave me.”

They dove under the next wave together. Joshua’s lungs screamed for oxygen. Joshua resurfaced and, again with a cross-chest carry, dragged the teen to the entrance side of the raft. Nabal had also seen his opportunity to climb aboard and met them at the entrance.

Joshua yelled, “You will climb into the life raft after Mayim is in.”

He no longer trusted Nabal in any manner.

How will I keep him from destroying this rescue without harming him?

Nabal spat between waves, “I’ll pull him in once I’m in. He’s mine.”

A salty mouthful of water made Nabal choke on his last words. Joshua hoped that would be the case and consented at last. He had little choice but to allow him to get them all inside. Joshua had nearly exhausted himself to get the raft upright. His nose and braces still dripped blood from the hits earlier and later. Blood in the ocean attracted sea monsters from miles away. Not only did he have a monster on the surface, but there were those underneath on their way to contend with later if he could not prevent blood flow and get out of the water.

“So others may live.”

He knew it was more than his job to help the survivors inside. That was why he was there in the first place. It had never been just a job. In the dark, without communication, the raft was his salvation, too.

“Let the sharks eat us, damn you,” Nabal railed.

Nabal struggled repeatedly to enter the raft as the waves pushed them around. He wanted to eliminate Joshua with a vengeance. The hopelessness he had drew him to the conclusion that nothingness awaited him. It made him fiercely contend for an approach to death devoid of consequences and eliminate hope for others. He continued to fight Joshua even while Joshua held Mayim's head above the surface. Joshua timed the waves and pushed the raft's entrance toward Nabal repeatedly. The man was out of his mind, with fear and wickedness displayed in rage and condemnation. The irony was Joshua's silence with one arm around Mayim, another arm for his attempt to hold the raft, to kick for his own life, while buffeted in different directions was a slow, painful crucifixion.

Nabal spewed hatred, "I'm dying of thirst. I'll burn in hell, and you will, too!"

Joshua murmured, "I thirst for innocence."

With newfound resolve, Joshua suffered while he held the raft to allow Nabal to get inside. The other outstretched arm went numb as he held up Mayim's head. With one last hoist, Nabal pulled himself half onto the life raft's entry point and clawed his way in. He connected his life vest's belt to a hand grasp line.

Joshua yelled, "You should NOT attach yourself to the raft, Nabal."

Nabal roared back, "I'll do what I damn well want."

He howled over their heads and the darkness of the chaos that shrouded them and briefly blocked the entryway. Nabal sat back at last on his throne of inhumanity.

He screamed, "I am KING."

Joshua thought, *You have nothing that hasn't been given to you.*

Nabal cackled a menaced laugh at Joshua's attempts to lift Mayim up and inside. He spat on Joshua and stomped on his hands at his attempts. Joshua retreated momentarily and held fast to Mayim, who was about to lose consciousness.

He said, "You saved others; can you save yourself now?"

At the entrance to the raft, Joshua maintained his resolve to rescue one soul at a time. He knew his attitude must remain singularly focused on his mission. Joshua began to sing over the chaos of wind, waves, and monsters of the deep.

He called out, "We're always ready for the call, We place our trust in Thee. Through surf and storm and howling gale, High shall our purpose be."

Nabal cackled, "What the hell?"

Joshua gave up the expectation that the dragon of a man would assist his son, Mayim, inside the raft. Joshua waited and supported Mayim as his own child. Nabal eventually flopped backward onto his back at the entrance to the raft since he was strapped to it. He was in apparent physical relief but still cursed the darkness for the circumstances in which he had found himself and called for death.

Joshua regarded Mayim and wondered, *Are you any relation at all? Your father has chosen not to love you, but I already know I do.*

Joshua looked up to the vast heavens, *Thanks, Papa, for loving and rescuing me.*

He re-focused on his mission and continued to sing over Mayim, "*Semper Paratus* is our guide, Our fame, our glory too. To fight to save or fight and die, Aye! Coast Guard, we are for you!"

Mayim struggled to breathe and had enough strength to white knuckle Joshua's bicep in terror. Nabal continued to swear and curse God in vain from inside the raft as it tipped precariously back and forth with the increased swells. The hurricane is upon us. Joshua sensed Mayim about to give up in exhaustion and pushed the same thoughts from his mind.

For Mayim, he thought, *and for all who are a part of the mission.*

Joshua hoisted Mayim's head and arm up onto the entry passageway. He transferred his grip onto the raft and scrambled himself inside first. From there, Joshua strained as he knelt on the rubber raft's slippery entryway. He hauled the deadweight of Mayim inside while the fierce waves threatened to topple them over again and again. Nabal roared from his place where he crouched at the door so close to them, but he did not touch them. They were somewhat out of the ocean at last.

Joshua focused his eyes on Mayim's as he leaned over him and vowed, "Today, you will be rescued with me."

Mayim's eyes slid closed. Joshua knew Mayim had given up and surrendered his life into Joshua's hands. Joshua sat back on his heels and breathed heavily. He continued to pull themselves further inside their cocoon of safety by the collar strap on the back of his vest. Joshua worked themselves around the sprawled-out Nabal that shook in cold water shock. Joshua noticed ironically that their life vests were not CG approved.

Gotta remember to tell Jonah about those vests, too, Joshua thought.

The precious moments that ticked by would result in their submission to death or death while they confronted the monster at their side. Joshua's blood tricked down his face and dropped onto Mayim as he pulled him away from Nabal. Joshua pulled Mayim into a half-upright position against the far wall of the raft so he wouldn't drown in the water that sloshed back and forth with the waves inside and more violently outside the raft. Joshua, too, was tossed side to side, front to back, with the increased waves.

Glorious rest, thought Joshua.

He took several deep breaths on his knees and relaxed his arms with relief. He wanted to stretch out his worn muscles, but his mission was still far from over.

This night won't be over for the unimagined future.

Joshua attended to Mayim. He checked Mayim's pulse and realized his own arms shook from exhaustion and exertion. He gently attempted to wipe his blood off the man as if to bring dignity to his innocent survivor. He swiped in surprise at the increased blood stains on the raft. He made two swipes, one left to right, another from top to bottom, closest to his reach. He knew he was about to face Nabal and a long night in the raft with an angry man. Joshua pinched his nose and once again tried to stop the blood flow. He looked up and tasted his blood trickle in the back of his throat.

I am grateful to be out of the water and to have found respite.

Joshua closed his eyes, and in his imagination, the USCG letters swam before him as he made himself remember their ever-watchful presence. He thought he heard the far-off drone of a Jayhawk that circled or the Hercules and ever-watchful Padre. Joshua knew that gratitude was the greatest of all virtues and the parent of all others. He knelt with a hand on an unconscious Mayim, the other on his broken nose that throbbed.

"So thankful, Papa," Joshua muttered.

Never stop your search for us. Remember me, he thought.

"I have won this battle," Nabal sneered from behind him in the enclosed life raft. The green neon glow of Joshua's chem light cast eerie shadows about them.

You are too proud, thought Joshua.

Nabal cackled with a blood-curdling laugh. In his madness, he leaped on Joshua from behind. Nabal threw his immense weight forward and brought his hands together and down like a hammer squarely on top of Joshua's head. Joshua crumpled on top of Mayim, who moaned as Joshua's bulk crushed him. Joshua was blinded with pain and half-stood quickly and slipped to defend himself from another attack. The life raft tipped perilously when their weight shifted, and a wall of water pushed them up. The raft was tossed vertically like a toy. Both men were tossed off their feet and slid towards the entrance of the raft. Joshua instinctively reached out his hands per his blindfolded swim and dunker training he had routinely had. Instead of the raft's handles, he caught Nabal's life vest. They both slid through the entrance that had become an exit. They flailed simultaneously backward into the Atlantic Ocean before they knew if it was man's will or the dreadful wave action.

Joshua had a severe concussion that left him unable to see. He only felt the cold and consuming, watery grave that enveloped them. Joshua felt the top of his helmet for the last light that remained and realized the chem light was gone. No one would see him in the darkened abyss, and he saw blackness. He began to retread water, though only for himself.

Nabal cursed Joshua between waves that flung him into the air, plunged him underwater, and said, "You...did this ...to me..."

Nabal's vest was still clipped securely inside the life raft. It had caught him and hung him upside down from it, face first in the Atlantic Ocean. Nabal sputtered and cursed briefly until the chaos drowned his voice. The sea had claimed its dragon king of oblivion.

Joshua knew, *Nabal was silenced by his own choices.*

The three souls washed away from each other as the whitecaps continued to increase. Joshua knew it would be a long night on the ocean with no EPIRB, no way for the C130 overhead to contact him, and no sight. The crews desperately searched and circled some distance away. Joshua was alone on the water's surface but knew the CG mission's cloud riders carried on.

He recited, *They will never leave me or abandon me.*

He fought the doubts, *If only they could find me, that is. Will they remember?*

Who knew the drone of a C-130 would bring such peace? he marveled.

Joshua's breaths, body, and soul calmed as the wind and the waves picked up. Joshua had a strong will to survive and listened to the engines that hovered and flew around him. He had reassurance in the sound of the multitudes in the heavens who surrounded him in larger and larger circles. Utter darkness had fallen across the Atlantic Ocean, and the storm clouds prevented even a sliver of moonlight for the crews who searched from the sky. Joshua's concussion made everything dark to Joshua. Torrential rain began to beat down on him. He supposed the life raft drifted further and further from him.

Where will my life drift?

On that tragic night, there was nothing for the C-130 to do but not give up on the mission or their champion, Joshua. No light shone to glisten on top of the chaotic waters below. No EPIRB or radio transmissions were received. It seemed all hope was gone.

Padre spoke to reassure the crews that always kept their duty to circle overhead.

He said, "He's out there and can hear us."

Orders from up the chain of command kept them on the scene throughout the night. The waves continued to grow. Joshua understood that Hurricane Ian was nearby and the sea conditions would not improve for a long time. Joshua felt terrible that his rescue would incur a more robust search by the Coast Guard than for Nabal and Mayim. The CG would never leave their own. They would search long past anyone else's life expectancy. Or so he hoped.

Nabal was a strong man with a stubborn will to die on his terms, he decided.

My will is to do my papa's will and live. He is not far from me.

Joshua looked up in his blindness at what he knew was the night sky. He dreamed of the stars he had once watched with his father. He gasped with increased ragged breaths between the waves that towered over him. He fought back the taste of blood and swallowed it not to attract more aggressive monsters of the deep. He knew his extremities had started to swell after hours in the water. He kept his eyes closed and focused his imagination on the USCG on the underside of the aircraft that he could hear but could not see him. He did his best to fight off exhaustion and delirium. He listened intently to the C-130 circle overhead. Finally, he spoke to them as if they used a radio. He imagined their conversations. He treaded the mountains of water while in the shadows of the valley of death.

Will the mission forsake me?

Joshua listened intently when the second Jayhawk went far away from him. In what direction, Joshua could not know. He could not begin to swim for his life to shore until he could see something: a star, the moon, his watch, and a compass. Their search pattern was miles away, and he figured he had drifted far and fast offshore. The survivors were but tiny bobbers on a ferocious ocean. His victory at the lost being found was shortly drowned out by darkness and chaotic water. He continued to tread with his feet and then alternated arms back and forth. One rested while the other burned like he was on fire. He shivered when his heart rate had slowed.

I've never known fire and ice simultaneously.

Joshua had one last nearly invisible tool and pulled the cord in his final act. An Osprey Low Profile Flotation Collar (LPFC) inflated around him, and he relaxed his muscles and succumbed to the effortless flotation on his back for the first time as a rescue swimmer. The monstrous large waves dumped him repeatedly in their powerful exchange of motion and energy. The waves battered his body, and without sight, he was tossed like a buoy between them. The CG searched for hours but could not locate him. All his tools were lost or destroyed. He had exhausted every resource. Joshua was at the complete mercy of a mission bigger than himself.

He thought, *So, so thirsty. I'm surrounded on every side by 'water, water everywhere, nor a drop to drink.' Now, I'm quoting from the Rime of the Ancient Mariner... High school English wasn't a waste, after all.*

Joshua struggled to speak over the rain-filled gusts and whitecaps, "I know you will blow me wherever you will. Please, just not out of your will, Papa."

At first light the following day, two Jayhawk helicopters were seen over the horizon that searched a renewed SAR flight pattern. A C-130, a Coast Guard cutter, two CG small boats from nearby Chesapeake Bay Virginia Beach, and other first responders braved the turbulent waters. Hurricane Ian churned farther inland but made the coastal regions unsuitable for boaters. Coast Guard Auxiliarists and civilians on a mercy mission were inbound and went to where 2nd Class Petty Officer Joshua Mansoul of the USCG had last been seen. The Department of Defense also sent some assets not tied up in hurricane evacuations and relief to search. Hundreds of people searched, some prayed, and his inner circle hoped for the best.

At about an hour of flight time, the first life raft was found blown listlessly across the Atlantic Ocean. A CG swimmer was lowered to the raft on calmer seas than the previous night, but not for the faint of heart. When the CG life raft was spotted, everyone's primary expectation was to discover Mansoul alive.

The rescue swimmer, Pete, made the cruel discovery of Nabal's bloated and lifeless body. His life vest's harness attached to the raft's side had oddly twisted and submerged his face in the open water. The rescue swimmer entered the life raft after he verified the first survivor was deceased. He gasped and immediately radioed to the crew what and who he found. When he saw the scarcely alive Mayim alone, he was unprepared for the blow of loss he felt. His disgust and powerlessness in the situation made him wretch into the raft beside him.

There's no evidence of him at all; where is Mansoul?

Pete paused far too long when the crew summoned a response, "Where's Mansoul?"

"He is not here," he said.

Pete's head hung low in disbelief, and the finality choked in his voice. He prepared the unconscious survivor for an urgent hoist. He also noticed that what was unusual was wiped blood inside the raft, though Mayim had no evidence of blood loss or a struggle.

It seemed, *there was a fight of some sort...*

Just as the rescue swimmer tugged unconscious Mayim through the raft's exit, a swimmer's green light stick rolled toward him.

"Mansoul's light!"

He was here..., thought Pete.

Recovery of the deceased also required the aid of the hoist cable and the mech's assistance with a different liter. Pete carefully but quickly searched again for details while the soulless individual was hoisted. With great despair, he checked and rechecked that the life raft contained no survivors nor evidence of Joshua, except the light stick, which was almost spent entirely. It was as if he could not believe his eyes that there was no other evidence. He made the motion to deploy the rescue sling with both arms extended over his head with his fingers interlocked. Afterward, he clutched the chem light in his hand before he was hoisted again to leave the scene. He stabbed the raft so that it would not be a nuisance as they continued to search for Mansoul. When he knifed the heavy plastic, it immediately deflated. His hopes and those of the crew were deflated, too.

After Pete reentered the Jayhawk cabin at long last, he relayed his discoveries to the CG world. The crew became very quiet. They all assumed the worst but carried on and continued to look desperately for any sign of their comrade as they flew the survivor and the deceased back to a trauma center. The most frustration was centered, of course, around why the EPIRB had been lost. Pete wracked his brain.

Where is he?

All contact with Joshua Mansoul was gone. The CG collectively knew he would never have let that happen on his own accord. The second unopened life raft was located within the hour. There were too many unanswered questions. They all grew more concerned when the evidence of blood was reported as wiped on the wall, purposefully in the shape of a t or a cross. This loss, they realized, unnerved them. It was not just tragic but deeply disturbed them all because the survivors had been located, but not the swimmer.

What on earth had happened?

Twenty-four hours after his concussion, Joshua opened his eyes again with relief since his eyesight was finally restored. Joshua, still enveloped in his floatation collar, was numb and stretched out on the surface of the Atlantic. He embraced the Milky Way Galaxy that appeared over him as a glorious friend who had come to visit him in his time of need. The heavenly visions were brief between cloud sets and ocean swells that he slid up and down. The water rocked him like a child in his mother's arms.

Are the stars a sign of welcome or a sign of warning?

Some of those stars had fallen from their intended purpose. They had added to the monstrous chaos of the ordered cosmos. Chaos that he had been and was consumed by at that moment. He appreciated he had a mostly good existence, but he was despondent for his mother's continued grief.

I want the mission to continue, but will others take courage or flee in fear?

Maria's fears of another hurricane that snatched her son would pierce her soul. Joshua settled himself to grasp that her fears very well may be realized.

Who will care for my Mama now?

He closed his eyes again, then in sincere grief. He had no more hydration to even form a tear.

How long have the raft, Mayim, and Nabal been gone?

He couldn't say. His tongue was swollen and stuck to the roof of his mouth. He knew by his watch he'd been afloat for 28 hours. He was trained to be in heavy seas for 30 minutes.

Joshua thought, *Perhaps no one will ever know the real story. It may be better that way.*

I will have died and given my life for someone else, doing what I loved. Hopefully, I'll be remembered as loving them as myself "So others may live."

Joshua's face was salty and burnt from sun exposure, and his shriveled skin had become white. The drone sounds of a C-130 had stopped in his ears, and he had never felt more alone. The vast expanse of the universe soared over him and waited to collect his last breath. It was not a hurricane precisely that would take him out. The insanity that pursued Nabal was the deadly force.

Papa, I followed you as you told me to.

He struggled to speak, "Where are you, Papa?"

He had dozed off in the waves as they crashed over him. His breath came in ragged fits as he tried not to ingest the saltwater and coughed it painfully back into the sea. He lifted his gaze and looked towards the farthest galaxies.

I never knew it could hurt to open my eyes. It's so beautiful, though, I don't want to close them. Forever.

Joshua's sight had returned more clearly, and with it, his head pounded from the concussion and severe dehydration. He had never seen the sky so clear before. Hours rolled on, and behind the dark storm clouds that rolled in again, the stars of light taunted him. He yearned for their company in his solitude and suffered much when the blanket of darkness covered the vast expanse again.

Has the storm passed over, or was I in the eye of it?

Joshua tried vainly to lick his cracked, bloated lips and only caught the rough edge of his braces. The harshness of more agony caused him to whimper and clinch his eyes. While his floatation device held him up... he could no longer hold on.

Papa, it's over, rescue me.

With an uncharacteristic loud cry, Joshua exhaled again and gave up his spirit. Joshua's head rolled back on the flotation device, and his body surrendered entirely to the waves that encompassed him. His last thoughts were of his papa. He had, at long last, joined his beloved papa.

The evening became morning, and hours turned into days. The second day became a third. The Coast Guard assets were stretched as thin as they had ever been before. They valiantly searched for Mansoul and made heroic efforts to rescue life and limb in the aftermath of Hurricane Ian elsewhere. The hurricane had torn up the coastline from the southern tip of Florida and caused billions of dollars in damages: lives lost, property damage, and historic floods.

For the Mansoul family and the CG, the cost was invaluable. The Mansouls had been notified and rushed to ECity. Joshua's friends and family were in various stages of grief: disbelief, despair, despondence. The Mansoul family accepted that Joshua was lost at sea when his green glow stick was pressed into their hands. The crew that had recovered it, the last item touched by Joshua, were undone with their own emotions and speechless. His family sat in reverence while they watched the last of its lit filament die in their tearful hands. James and June rocked Maria back and forth in her personal storm-tossed sea of grief.

Flags across the United States were planned to be put to half-mast on Coast Guard Stations and Bases. Funeral arrangements were made ready to include the Commandant of the Coast Guard as well as Joshua's crews at his Traverse City Station. It was to have members of the Coast Guard who knew him from Kodiak and Elizabeth City as well. His family was assigned a chaplain and an officer who accompanied them. Maria, James, and Jude were also escorted to the various planning events by Mr. Jones, whom they would not allow to be left behind. Friends of Joshua's, Eli and Jakob, took immediate leave and made plans to rendezvous with Caleb in ECity. Everyone agreed it seemed that only the good die young.

"Joshua wasn't good. He was faultless," Jordan said to Maria.

The Coast Guard had lost a member. It was clear that it was not only the members, community, and world individually whose lives were diminished by his loss. Joshua, who had shared the utmost courtesy and respect for life, had made their lives better and them each better at life. Jordan Roi, Ben, Caleb, and more of Joshua's friends were already in ECity on Temporary Duty for Hurricane Ian. They were more resolutely tasked with search and rescue efforts they wanted to continue with on his behalf.

Maria Mansoul, of course, took it the hardest. She had first lost her husband in a hurricane and now her firstborn son. She moved as if in a trance. Her sons, James and Jude, stood with her and hardly left her side. Every moment, they provided for her needs in rote action with raw emotions of disbelief, grief, and waves of hope. What they could not provide was an escape from the blessings and the bruises of the life of a son and brother who was so selfless. For Maria, it was as if a sword had ripped through her heart and torn apart the wounds that had begun to heal from the loss of her beloved husband.

She wondered, *What will each day bring without my precious first-born, Joshua, my rescuer?*

It was in the quiet moments and the dark hours that were void of his mother's direct presence that James Mansoul wrestled internally. He wanted to join the Coast Guard's mission. He deliberated over two things.

Is it out of admiration for what my brother has done so selflessly or as a tribute to my father? Is it the rest of the mission being conducted so firmly for the saving of every willing soul?

The CG's tight-knit community gathered around them, active and retired, and supported their every physical, emotional, and spiritual need. James determined this was what he wanted to do for the rest of his days. James knew if he were to be called upon to give his life as a ransom for someone else's, he would want to do it as courageously as his brother had. James had come of age and was willing to serve and give his all so others may live. He wanted to be *Semper Paratus*. He needed a reason to hope. That he did not yet have. The second part was the worst.

James thought, *How and when do I tell my grieving mother this?*

James pondered, prayed, and waited as the stars set their courses above, and the sun made its next approach on the horizon.

Word about the missing swimmer spread like a tsunami throughout the Coast Guard. Every unit on the East Coast was on alert. Joshua's young protégé, Christian, whom he had rescued off North Carolina's shores years before, was distraught. He was grief-stricken when he heard the news about Joshua's SAR, but in a way, he couldn't imagine it. For many, they reconciled, it was the only way for Joshua to "go." Christian had never met someone so courageous, steadfast, kind, and humble. He knew Joshua would have gladly given everything he had to let one person have their soul for another day. Christian determined he would not grieve yet.

He thought, *But am I in denial?*

Distracted by all the work around him to be done, Christian moved forward with renewed determination. He and his new unit in Morehead City at the small boat station were focused on recovery and patrols post-hurricane. He longed to join his peers in Elizabeth City, who could gather and mourn the loss of Joshua Mansoul. He could not get there without time off at the onset of his career. Plus, there was emergent work to be done after Ian battered the coastline and inland of the Carolinas. He pined for his friend in private as he continued his mission, albeit distractedly, to serve the last, the least, and most certainly the lost.

Is my future lost with my rescuer, Joshua? he contemplated; *what would be the point without him?*

CHAPTER 28

REMEMBER ME

MOREHEAD CITY, NORTH CAROLINA

On the same beautiful Sunday morning of Hurricane Ian's retreat farther inland, Levi and Kristen's friend, Michael, called 911 and reported their vessel was well overdue. He had hesitated for hours but could not focus on anything, so he finally gave up and did what he could. He knew their circumstances vexed him but did not want the operator to hear it in his voice.

"911, Please state your emergency."

Michael said, "Hello, my friends told me they were going fishing, but we haven't heard from them since yesterday. Their truck is at the marina, but we can't get ahold of them. Can you help us find them straightaway, please?"

"We'll connect you with the CG immediately," said the dispatcher.

A few tense minutes passed, and Michael began to sweat profusely in the hot North Carolina sun. He leaned on Kristen's truck over the hot pavement. It seemed pointless to call there, but it was his only connection with his friends. As he lamented, his irritation had become fear that crept up Michael's spine.

Where are they?

Suddenly, a CG operator and watchstander said abruptly, "Coast Guard, how may I assist you?"

"Yes, my friend Kristen and her family are overdue a day, and we can't get ahold of them on her cell phone... she should've been off the water by now, but I'm by their old truck at the marina, and this is unlike them not to answer."

Michael knew he rambled, but he had never called 911 before.

The CG operator asked the question, "Where was she going?"

Michael gulped and replied, "Fishing..."

The CG Operator spoke again more slowly the second time.

"No, sir, that's an action. Where did she go..., exactly?"

Michael felt like a fool and stuttered, "Umm... she told me fishing. The ocean? Out past the Cape Lookout Lighthouse? Maybe?"

Michael thought, *This makes me sound dumb, but I don't know. Why am I answering a question with questions?*

The watchstander spoke again, "I need more specifics... which direction? How long ago? When was she due back?"

He grew impatient. Michael tried to beg the operator to send help and offered to get more boats out to look for them.

He said, "Ummm... I don't know if she had a plan. I'm not sure exactly when they left or were to return... the last time I talked to them was yesterday, and they planned to leave around 4 a.m..... They only go for the day. Please help us find them. Send someone, now!"

Ugh, he slammed his fist against the truck door and muttered in frustration, "Why Levi, Why Kristen? Why me?"

"Sir," said the watchstander, "It's good of you to be on the lookout for them. You've shouldered enough of the burden. We will take it from here. Your name and number, please?"

Michael answered her, hung up, leaned against Kristen's truck, and looked at the marina's open slip that should've held their boat. Several slips were vacant due to those who preferred to take their boats out before a storm.

That is a matter of extreme perspectives, Michael considered.

He then turned towards the marina's office to request help to get the word out to other mariners to be on the lookout for his friends and their kids.

At the marina's front desk, a cranky man with leathery skin lifted his unibrow as he replied.

"So let me get this straight. They went to the *most hostile* environment on earth, completely isolated themselves with *no way out*, with their *kids*, during a *hurricane*...and did not leave a float plan."

"Yup, I already called the Coast Guard," replied a sullen Michael.

"I'll lead the search, and thank you in advance for your help to get the word out," the geezer said firmly.

The man behind the desk didn't move an inch. Michael lifted his hands before him as if to say, "Do something!" The old timer dropped off his stool and ambled out the door as a tiny bell rang over his head. He took a cigar out of his mouth, cupped his hands around it, and hollered over the nearly empty marina.

"Seafarers Ahoy! There' be lost mariners! Be on the lookout for stupid and their innocent varmints."

"I meant via radio," jeered Michael.

The wise old man said, "Shoulda said so! Get specific, young man, or you'll be next..."

Michael grunted in disbelief and almost sprouted wings as he flew into action. He prepared his moored boat to set off and called in his float plan to another conscientious friend or two for good measure. Before long, he was out to fish for friends instead of mahi.

Kristen and Levi were still locked in an overnight argument while their children William, age 10, and Abigail, age 4, were down below the deck of their fishing vessel fast asleep. They were in combat over whether to call the CG for a rescue because one thought they were prepared for yet another day adrift at sea and the other not.

Levi gripped her shoulder gently and said, "Kristen, I've got this."

"I wasn't born yesterday, Levi. We're desperate since the bilge pump has stopped altogether. The meter says we've taken on water. You know I can read, don't you?"

"Okay, okay," Levi threw his hands up in surrender, "You call the Coast Guard, not me. I say we're fine."

Kristen spoke between her clenched teeth.

"We're *not* fine. Will you ask William and Abigail to row to shore in the dingy? Our cell phones don't work out here...AND the USCG might be a little busy *now* with the hurricane that blew down our necks. Why did you bring us out here anyway?"

Levi recognized she had valid points, and it was time.

He thought, *Probably past time.*

Irritated at the situation, he shrugged and turned to the radio and demonstrated to her, again, how it worked.

"I gotta go below deck and keep bailing water. Let me know what they say."

She fumbled with the dials and reminded herself to calm down and speak clearly. Kristen got ahold of the USCG watchstander on her second try.

"Thank you, Lord," she said and then exhaled deeply.

She explained their situation apologetically and gave their whereabouts with the use of her GPS on their boat. Her husband had spent the money on all the fancy devices.

Kristen thought, *Well, that's something to be thankful for.*

The CG watchstander said they would immediately launch a small boat from the closest station out of Fort Macon. The watchstander continued to ask her a couple more questions that puzzled her.

"Please give us a description of your boat?"

"Where did you leave your truck parked?"

"Do you have a friend named Michael? Over."

Finally, Kristen stopped the line of questions to ask about their specificity.

"May I ask why you want to know these things? Over."

"You've been reported missing, and a search and rescue was already launched on your behalf. Over."

Kristen was shocked. *Missing?*

"We want to be sure we've located you to cancel the SAR. Over."

SAR? Oh, Search and Rescue!

It all became clear to her then.

Michael, the truck, the timing.... Yes, indeed, they had a lot to be thankful for. And to apologize for...

Kristen's heart went out to the overworked and likely understaffed CG. She did not want to burden anyone, yet she had burdened and worried many people.

She finished the radio transmission and shouted, "Bless you, Michael."

How careless of us. I try to teach my children better than this. I constantly nag them, 'Where are you going?' How selfish to go fishing like this.... I'm surprised the CG puts up with this, well, me.

Kristen felt more than humiliated when she ended the radio conversation and assured the watchstander of their situation and need for rescue. The race for humility is easily won.

I deserve this helplessness. The point is to accept the help and learn from it. Then, help someone else to avoid making the same mistake I have.

Thank you, Lord, help is on the way.

Kristen composed herself quickly and checked on her husband's bailing ability. She asked for his forgiveness and awoke her precious children for breakfast.

"We're about to have our first and exciting CG rescue."

They were surprised and thrilled. They finished their bananas and bagels in record time while they watched and waited. They stared over the boat's bow towards the west with the glorious sun that rose in the east and warmed their strong backs.

The sunlight skimmed across the Atlantic Ocean and glared in Christian's eyes from the bright orange ball on the eastern horizon. The United States Coast Guard rescue small boat crew took off from Fort Macon northeast in gentle winds that were part of Hurricane Ian's winds that dissipated. It was hard for them to believe they had dodged one of the most significant hurricanes ever to hit the United States. The crew spoke to one another about how the family had "gone fishing." They had entered "the most hostile environment on earth and completely isolated themselves with no way out...." That had been part of a longer talk the crew had recently heard at a gathering of US Coast Guardians, Auxiliarists, and local VIP guests invited on base for maritime safety. The message had stuck, and they set out to rescue someone's bad or worst-day scenario and tried not to make fun of the family's unpreparedness.

On board were two dewatering pumps loaded by Christian. He was grateful to have something to do rather than sit and feel sorrowful about the loss of his mentor and rescuer, Petty Officer Joshua Mansoul. He doubted his decision to join the mission and was disparaged about his future. Offshore, Christian looked backward as the shoreline began to dwindle in his sight and sighed deeply. His future seemed to be dwindling, too.

Who am I kidding? I've lost another friend to the sea. Why am I in the CG?

Abigail and William were happy to be on deck with poles in their hands while their father was still hard at work. Levi's frustration seemed to increase with each trip topside with a heavy bucket of water they noticed. They stayed well out of his way. Kristen tried to distract them and directed them to keep their eyes on the horizon. A new game was born: 'Who can spot the CG first?' Beforehand, that game meant the CG would board your vessel and become a distraction and hindrance. Even when fishers knew they honestly earned a living or were having fun, when the CG boarded their vessel, it felt obtrusive. A shared experience was seeing "lights and sirens" felt oppressive until they were on for their sole benefit. Obedience to the guard rails of a moral code rarely felt like liberation until after delivered from disobedience.

Kristen was exuberant when William called out, "There they are!"

"Where?" whined Abigail, who tried to see over the deck rails.

"Oh, I got somethin' on my line!" said William, who felt a big tug.

"Bring it in now, honey. I'm going to get your dad," said Kristen.

She ran below deck, calling, "They're here, they're here."

William continued to reel in his catch.

"What are you?" he said as he pulled harder.

He discovered the pull was unique when he tugged his line, but the fish would not tug back.

He said over his shoulder, "Hey, sis, can you grab the net?"

Abigail ran for the long pole with the two-foot dip net on the end. She awkwardly held it up for William since it was longer than she was. When his catch approached the boat, he handed her the reel and scooped the net under his fish. What he beheld was a long black fin.

"What is that?" asked Abigail.

William shrugged his shoulders. He dropped it onto the deck and peered closer when he turned it over twice in his hands.

"Hmm, I guess it's some sort of a fin. It's trash, but mom said we can keep whatever we catch."

Abigail said, "Can I touch it?"

William said to her, "Sure. It looks cool to me 'cause there's some white letterin', but I ain't got a clue what man's soul means?"

Abigail giggled, "Maybe it's someone's lost sole? Get it, a lost soul?"

She kicked her heel up as high as she could toward him, though she was shoeless. William rolled his eyes at her, and she took it and dropped the heavy fin in the stern of the boat. William stowed his fishing pole as his parents had taught him and double-checked his life vest and Abigail's to ensure his sister's was on correctly. Kristen jogged back up top, gathered her children under each arm, and pointed over the water while she squinted as the sun shone brilliantly off the surface behind a Coast Guard small boat that rushed in their direction. By this point, Levi had joined them, exhausted and was decidedly glad for assistance.

The small craft with large orange floats on either side of it clearly labeled U.S. Coast Guard was warmly welcomed as it glided up and alongside the fishing vessel. Coast Guard Petty Officer 2nd Class Nathanael Danielson (Boatswain Mate, BM2), Petty Officer 2nd Class Corrie Pritchard, Fireman Micah Jesuncosky, and Seaman Christian Robbins were on the scene. There was a brief exchange of identification between the two parties. A nod was given to Christian to help load the dewatering pump aboard Levi's vessel. Radio contact was made with Sector that all was well with the vessel's occupants and about the pump's delivery. The children cautiously watched the interactions between their parents and the Coast Guard crew members. The uniformed Guardians stood heroically before them with the gift of a return to shore and hopefully an end to their parent's arguments.

While a 3rd Class Petty Officer helped set up the dewatering pump with Kristen and Levi below deck, Christian looked at the children who peered at him suspiciously. He hadn't spent much time around kids, so he didn't know what to say in the awkward silence. He gazed out over the calm water that sparkled and spoke to them.

"What are you guys out here fishing for?" he inquired.

Abigail mumbled, "Bluefish," but he couldn't hear her. He stepped forward to listen to her shy reply and saw they stepped back toward the stern, wide-eyed. They looked surprised at his movement, as if they had done something they should be in trouble about.

Christian thought, *Maybe it's my uniform?*

What they saw was the sadness in his eyes. They misunderstood that he wasn't happy to be there with them. They stood awkwardly and regarded one another.

Mom said children are exceptionally perceptive, thought Christian.

Christian understood they hadn't done anything wrong. They were only there at the mercy of their parents, who had completely forgotten what they were supposed to be doing, namely watching out for their little kids on the open ocean.

He thought, *Well, why not teach them a short lesson while we wait*?

He asked the kids, "I got a question for you. What is *going fishing?*"

The kiddos looked at him, turned to each other, and then back to him with a shrug of their shoulders.

William said, "It's catching cool fish and then eating them. Or if we get enough, we sell them to other people who like to eat them, too."

Abigail, shyer than her big brother, said, "Same."

Christian, not finished yet with his lesson, replied to them both.

"Well, the Coast Guard is here to remind you that fishing is an activity. It's not a destination. If you tell someone you're going fishing, you must also tell them *where* you are going. Fishing is a verb *and* a noun."

Abigail squinted and looked up at him with questions in her eyes.

She said, "What is a ...verb?"

William punched her in the arm and said all knowingly, "It's an action, silly. You'll learn all 'dat when you're in the 3rd grade."

She pulled back, "Ouch!"

"That's right," said Christian, "It's a *where* not just *what*."

He smiled then at their antics for the first time in days. Christian looked up and around the boat deck. Out of the corner of his eye, he saw a long, black, and undeniable rescue swimmer's fin. Before his bewildered eyes, he reread the word MANSOUL several times. It was standard CG format of block format, white letters, four inches high. Christian stumbled back a whole step and almost fell overboard. He gasped and directed his gaze challengingly at the children.

He spoke to them too roughly, "Where did you get that?" as he pointed at the fin.

The children were frozen in fear. They, too, took a step backward in fear. Abigail's eyes pooled with tears. William looked at the fin and back to the Guardian, whose face had changed so quickly at the sight of his catch.

He stammered, "Uh, I... I just fished it out. I didn't do nothin' with it."

Stark realization hit Christian with the total weight of unfulfilled hope.

An indication of where he is. A glimmer of hope in the loss of my hero. Unbelievable.

Christian's eyes went wide with surprise, and he dropped to his knees because the breath had been stolen from his lungs. After he realized that he had inadvertently scared the children, he began with an apology. His face had softened, and he looked at them intently from his knees.

"Hey guys, I'm sorry I reacted so strongly, but I have a friend with that name. I'd like to have it..."

Could it belong to him? It has got to be his!

"When exactly did you fish it out of the water?" he asked them.

Abigail pointed her finger up at her big brother's face and shook it. She still felt like she was in trouble. She wiped her tears with the back of her hand and snuffed back the snot in her nose.

She spat, "He's the one who did it. Blame him."

Then she put both hands on her hips like she had seen her mother do many times. William looked at her; then he looked at Christian with fear and guilt he did not understand.

He said, "Sir, I just pulled it out of the water when you was' comin' up, but she helped me with the net."

William threw his hands up in surrender and glared at Abigail as a traitor. They still felt like they were being accused of something they had done wrong. They dropped their heads in shame. Christian knew he had misstepped to gain their confidence in him and knowledge. He spoke with exaggerated kindness to encourage them and release their fears.

He said, "Oh, wow, great job! A team effort to help me out so much!"

"May I have a good look at it?"

Christian moved toward the fin as if it was alive and about to jump overboard. He stood and inched his way across the deck, still in shock. He picked up the fin, still in disbelief that he held such an important, sacred relic and yet a piece of equipment. It was heavier than he expected, both in his hands and heart. He knew every rescue swimmer had personalized fins and that they were marked individually. Each was distinguished by name and whatever else was within Coast Guard policy. No one would lose this fin with this name unless it had been Joshua himself.

Could it be?

How far were they precisely from where he was last seen days ago?

Christian's mind ran wild. He spun around and jumped towards the ladder and his crewmates. He hollered down below deck to his Petty Officer in charge.

"BM2 Danielson, I need you up here quick!"

Christian said, "313 Nautical miles, 2.6 days at sea, 5 knots."

"Anything is possible, right BM2?" he continued.

Danielson nodded in the affirmative. He knew he was beside himself with the joy of such an essential piece of equipment. Christian clutched the fin to his chest. More than that, it was that he'd found hope. Christian felt he'd taken a deep breath of fresh air for the first time in three days. His rescue as a surfer years before had given him the same feel when he entered the Jayhawk cabin after his near drowning. The glorious salty wind pressed their faces as they faced the open sea and raced northward with eyes wide for any sign of life.

After the news was reported, the CG small boat crew had installed the pump in record time. They sent the family directly back to Morehead City and promised a tour of their facility for the kiddos' part in the SAR. Christian had shaken William's hand like a man and saluted him. He gently hugged Abigail. She was all smiles when she realized the joy she had brought the whole crew.

The newly found swimmer's fin found not far from the southern North Carolina shore was an amazement to all. The watchstander, located in Sector North Carolina in Wilmington, spread the word of the find to a multitude of mariners out to sea to search for the CG's most precious lost treasure. The urgent marine information broadcast carried an especially crucial message. Their search was renewed and in a different area. The Coast Guard called all available vessels to search for a person in the water (PIW) from Virginia Beach to Charleston, South Carolina. The CG had kept their searches ongoing, but private citizens also wanted to take up the mission. Mariners knew the CG and swimmers like Mansoul protected them in their recreation and vocations. Even the Navy in the area pitched in to send out a pararescue crew out of Norfolk to survey the shorelines.

The CG members and Joshua's family received the news with tempered joy. Already left in disbelief for days, they were too stunned to speak. Maria didn't have more tears to shed, so she waited and watched the mission in awe. The emotional turmoil left them afraid of yet another wave of emotive upheaval. Several of Joshua's closest friends volunteered eagerly with the command to step up and search in any available aircraft or vessel of the CG. Air Crews launched from Air Station Elizabeth City, including several Jayhawks and a C-130 Hercules. Everyone knew any pair of sharp eyes was imperative and appreciated to help rescue their loved one without any location beacon. Planes and helicopters were relaunched at an undeniably heavy rate to save one of their own. Up and down the coast, beachcombers and clean-up crews swept their eyes from the collection of shells and trash toward the lost soul.

Sector North Carolina had instructed the 29-foot Response Boat Christian was on to begin an immediate SAR mission. In Latin, the US Coast Guard Sector North Carolina's motto was *Aliorum Vitae Supra*

Nostram, which translates to English as 'Their Lives Above Ours.' He had been happy to see that when he arrived just a few weeks ago. He looked at his watch. It was 10 a.m., and Christian did the math.

He's been missing for 60 hours. Hang on, Mansoul.

Christian was a Seaman, a non-rate in the CG, but he knew he felt like he had the responsibility of a Captain as he braced his stance along with his crew that surveyed the water along the southern end of the Outer Banks. They searched for hours. The small boat crew watched in amazement as boats filed out of harbors to help with the search, and the sky filled with C-130s, Civil Air Patrol aircraft, Air Force Auxiliarists, and Jayhawks. All joined in a sophisticated search pattern back and forth over the open water for hundreds of hope-filled miles.

Christian was motivated to pause and remember on their slow, agonized search. He recalled Joshua's radiant face. He remembered his crooked teeth behind a meek smile. He remembered their last conversation about how excited he was to have braces on his teeth. Christian, who had fought his parents over braces, was ashamed of his immaturity. In many ways, Joshua had personified what it was to put first things first.

The mission was to put others first.

Christian closed his eyes temporarily. He knew full well he would never find Joshua with his eyes closed. Even with his eyes open, he knew the CG was at a miracle stage of rescue. He savored his deep and steadfast friendship with the man who rescued him physically and emotionally.

That had been a miracle.

Until that moment, Christian had never seen it that way. He resolved to follow Joshua's mission unreservedly if he was found that day. If one had been given him, then he would expect another. He decisively wanted to be like him all his days and follow him. The freedom he felt was like a burden lifted from his frame he didn't know he had carried. The fierce wind from the boat's powerful engines pushed against him as they flew across the water. Christian leaned into them. Christian opened his eyes with a deep sigh. The first thing he saw over the horizon was the Cape Lookout Lighthouse.

Christian hollered over the sound of the boat engines, "BM2, has anyone looked for Mansoul at the lighthouses?"

Petty Officer 2nd Class Corrie Pritchard radioed the same question to the watchstander.

She replied, "Should be empty. Closed for the duration of the hurricane and under construction. Let's check it out, though."

Up and down the Graveyard of the Atlantic stood old sentinels of the sea. Historic lighthouses mostly gave tourists beautiful vistas to see the sea. Christian had taken field trips in school and family vacations up and down the Outer Banks to see the most significant and scenic. His favorite was Cape Hatteras Lighthouse, which had been moved intact, with no small effort, inland to keep it from being washed into the Atlantic. It was the tallest brick lighthouse in the U.S. and had a black and white candy cane stripe.

"In daylight, Joshua would've known where he was if he had seen the familiar lighthouses, and at night, he surely would've seen the lights," Christian explained to his peers in the boat.

He realized he boasted in his friend, Joshua, but could not help himself as his apprehension grew.

Christian added, "This guy could've easily swum the twelve miles to shore, which is how far out the light shines. I know it."

His crew mates listened intently to him over the wave action the boat accelerated through as they neared shore. They had no idea Mansoul had saved Christian's life, but they were all impressed at his passionate persistence in this endeavor. The easily distinguished Cape Lookout Lighthouse grew more prominent as they approached it. It wore a distinct black diamond pattern on a white background. It was the hardest to reach from land due to the requirement of a boat to get to it. Christian hadn't been there more than twice in his life due to the necessary arrangement of a ferry in season. It was hours from his home in Southern Shores, North Carolina, where he grew up.

And where I almost died.

Christian wished he had been back since he arrived in Morehead City a month ago. Christian had no boat to get there alone, but they were in one with the CG and closed in fast. His heart rate increased, as did his faith in the mission. BM2 Corrie Pritchard agreed it was worth a stop to look vigilantly and gave the directions to investigate since they were so close and had jurisdiction on the remote island. A Jayhawk also neared overhead on a lap in their renewed coastal search pattern. Christian could feel its rotors in his chest as they thumped from far away.

Or is that my heartbeat?

He yearned to know: *Can Joshua hear and feel us?*

Chapter 29

SKY RULERS

The Jayhawk's co-pilot, Captain Ruth Kodesh, said, "Let's plan to put down somewhere near the lighthouse. I prefer to stay off the sand."

The aircraft commander, Lt. Commander Kyle Paulson, retorted, "Captain, there's sand everywhere!"

He added, "If we even get near that lighthouse, we'll sandblast it and everything nearby."

The CG crew was on high alert after a watchstander called for them to assess the Cape Lookout National Seashore. They flew as low as they dared to without blasts of sand to scorch the earth. The aqua crystal waters that lapped the shore enticed them. They could see birds take flight and dolphins under the surface. They flew over dozens of unoccupied cabins, old buildings, a lighthouse, and the wild horses that still occupied the island's remote wilderness. The aircraft commander stationed in ECity had purposefully been paired with the co-pilot, who, although more experienced as a pilot, was from a different base. She had come TDY for hurricane relief and volunteered for the SAR of the CG swimmer she fondly remembered at AHRS. They could hardly tear their eyes away from the Cape Lookout lighthouse painted with its distinctive black-and-white diagonal checkers or 'diamond' pattern.

"Every day, the light flashes once every 15 seconds as the two aerobeacons rotate," said Jordan.

The mech was Jordan Roi, a longtime friend of Joshua's. She had volunteered for every mission the CG would put her on and refused to give up hope for the recovery of her lost friend. Others had tried to dissuade her from her passion. They had said she would be of more comfort to Joshua's grief-stricken mother. Jordan was singularly focused on the mission to find Joshua. Jordan stubbornly refused to dwell on the exchanges that the mission had become a recovery effort by day three.

Jordan already knew she wanted to write a book about all her experiences with Joshua. He was different than any other human she'd ever known. How this experience turned out would be the decisive factor. His story had to be told, and the mission had to be explained so everyone would want to be rescued. This new evidence about a piece of Joshua's equipment found so close by gave her an unexpected jolt of determination. She expressed her excitement to her crew.

"I will never stop the search of these beaches. Please fly as close as you're able."

The mech, Jordan, continued over the intercom and chatted away into her communications system, "The lighthouse has been here since 1873 and was originally manned by the lighthouse keeper, and later his family assumed the duty. The US made the Life Saving Service in 1848. Some of these old camps ahead and behind us are what's left."

Whether it was nervousness or idle chatter, Jordan clamored on. She leaned so far forward that her helmet pressed the glass. She loved the anticipation when she flew, but she knew for the first time she felt unreserved desperation. This SAR was personal.

She asked, "Can we fly with the door open, and I can get a better look, please?"

Jordan had never been the foremost fan of riding harnessed inside the door while in forward flight, but she knew she'd do whatever that day to find what she was desperate for. The rescue swimmer with her, Ruakh, nodded vigorously. Once it was okayed, he flopped onto his stomach in excitement after they cautiously pulled the cabin door open.

He said, "Don't be scared, let's get closer!"

Underneath them was a Cape Lookout dock for CG small boats to check on the light at the end of the island, where it hooked towards the shore. They saw a USCG small boat headed around the end of the island for it. They all knew the lighthouses still served an essential role for mariners headed up the U.S. coast. Due to Hurricane Ian's close brush with the Carolinas, the National Seashore had briefly closed to tourists over the weekend.

"Is anyone officially allowed on the island today?" asked Jordan.

As the Jayhawk circled the lighthouse, the old Keeper's Quarters, and outbuildings, the crew held their breaths as their eyes searched for any sign of life.

"There, between the lighthouse and the old Keeper's Quarters, we may be able to touch down," said Kyle, the co-pilot.

Jordan continued her irksome long Park Ranger tour since she'd been stationed in ECity nearby for years beforehand.

"On July 14, 2003, the Coast Guard transferred the tower and remaining property to the National Park Service to allow the lighthouse to be opened for public climbs. We still maintain the light itself. The Keepers' Quarters serves as a museum. It gives visitors a glimpse into the lives of Lighthouse Keepers and Surfmen of the US

Life-Saving Service. The museum is open from 9:00 AM to 5:00 PM, seven days a week during the spring, summer, and fall."

Jordan, the most talkative crew member the crew had ever experienced, had nearly exasperated them with her non-stop small talk. Her crew understood her conversant chit-chat was a demonstration of her heightened eagerness.

Ruakh interrupted her, "Are we there yet?"

Jordan punched him in the arm mischievously but in good humor.

Kyle said, "Boardwalks are everywhere!"

With a swimmer's composed virtue, Ruakh added, "Put me down, and I can help direct you in. I want to investigate that campfire."

"Campfire? WHERE?!" exclaimed Jordan.

"Is that a good plan, Lt. Commander?" said Captain Kodesh.

"Agreed," answered Lt. Commander Kyle Paulson, joyful for the interruption and proclamation.

Christian and his entire boat crew in their 29-foot vessel came around the end of the island called Lookout Bight. It was a formidable navigational hazard with tides and sands that often shifted. They used more precision and speed than he'd ever experienced. He had previously asked permission to run ashore to search around the lighthouse. He still clutched the fin that was emblazoned with MANSOUL.

I feel like a kid with my blanket. I just can't let it go, Christian muttered to himself.

He realized he was irritated by the helicopter's noise as it hovered overhead. It was so much louder than their boat. He wanted to get to the lighthouse first for some reason.

He thought, *Whenever a Jayhawk gets this close, it sounds like the heavens are ripped open over us. And yet, it's comforting to me.*

The Jayhawk descended in front of them, much nearer to the Lighthouse and precisely where he wanted to be. Christian realized the jealousy he felt rose within him due to the aircraft's speed on scene.

So much for hearing anyone calling out for help over that noise... but two are better than one.

The small boat slowed, and the back end tipped up and rocked them forward as the swell of the boat's wake shoved them toward shore. Christian did his best not to stumble. He'd worked hard to gain the sea legs that every boat crew member seemed to have but himself. Christian decided he did want to be an Airman as soon as possible. Now that he was in the surface CG, he was even more determined to be an aviator. The surface guys were hardy, and his respect for them grew daily. A sky ruler rescued him, and he wanted to become one. His heart was set on it.

I'd give anything to find Joshua...alive. But will I be determined to be a swimmer if my rescuer is lost?

The blue sky, sandy shore all around them, and dancing seagulls on the wind were a welcome sight.

Christian instantly thought, *Is that smoke I smell, or fuel?*

The vessel's commander focused on the CG pier they were headed towards, and the others prepared for their duties to perform at the dock. The only exception was Christian, who gazed intently at the shoreline. There in front of them on the island's leeward side was the smoke of a campfire that wafted up to the heavens.

"A fire on a closed island. That's illegal!" shouted Christian.

He turned to look at BM2 Pritchard with a look of question. He turned back to the beach to look again and grabbed a pair of binoculars that were always at the ready. He focused, and there was a figure. A bare-chested man wrapped in a brightly colored beach towel wore dark sunglasses and a broad beach hat. He sat low in a white beach lounge chair. He uncomfortably raised one arm with an open palm that faced forward. It looked like he expected them. He did not fear reprisal for his misdemeanor of an unauthorized fire on CG property.

Micah yelled, “Where did he come from?” with disbelief to his crew.

They all acknowledged there was no boat of any kind nearby. The crew was trained to assess details before any approach to situations of uncertainty. The crew stood attentive and discussed how they would confront the stranger.

“He’s a bold one...to build a fire right in front of our dock,” said Corrie.

“Please, let’s not let this guy waste our time. We need to search for our own,” said Christian.

“Maybe he’s seen something,” said Nathanael, “or someone.”

The CG helicopter had landed just out of sight beyond the Lighthouse Museum, closer to the lighthouse. The helicopter engines quieted, and the small boat motored slowly closer to the shoreline. It was directed towards the dock as its reduced power lowered the sound obstruction.

“Good ...morning!” called the beach bum with great effort.

With apparent strain in his raspy voice, the beach bum stood with great effort and called out to them specifically.

“Did you ...bring anything ...for breakfast?” he added.

The crew looked at one another and scoffed at the outrageous man. The boat was just shy of the shoreline, about 50 yards. However, the dock was further down the beach, about 200 yards farther away. The crew was determinedly focused and stood at the ready for their prescribed duties in preparation for disembarkation, except for Christian.

He stood captivated by the oddity of the otherworldly figure and the circumstances of his unauthorized presence.

"No," shouted Christian back.

Corrie spoke to the crewmembers, "Let's be cautious. He might be high."

"Mooring, starboard," quipped Nathanael at the helm.

The bum cupped his hands around his mouth and hollered in pain as loud and as clearly as he could with an indication of a hoarse throat.

"It's me! You leave a Guardian on his own and see what happens."

He gestured with one arm raised and a thumb up. His voice was croaky and almost unintelligible. The crew looked at one another with confusion.

"You remembered me!" the beach bum hollered again to them.

With no more deliberation, Christian leaped from the front of the boat into the water and popped to the surface. He howled with delight. He resembled a child still fully dressed and dragged his uniformed body and boots through the water. He swam the last twenty-five yards to shore frantically. The crew made way for the dock and expeditiously moored it according to USCG standards. They were shocked at Christian's action and ran for the bum and Christian, unsure of who they had found. The signal the man had given was a CG signal, "Ready to be hoisted."

"Could it *really* be him?" Nathanael shouted with glee.

Ruakh, the swimmer, and Jordan approached the campfire from between the museum and the lighthouse 200 yards away. They appeared from behind a small dune and regarded the riotous scene. They stood in disbelief with sweat that dripped from their brows in the hot September sun. The run in the sand, especially with heavy boots, was a challenge. The heat in Jordan's flight suit and Ruakh's short wet suit was brutal, with helmets still on. They lowered their eye shades over their eyes to survey the scene under a full orange sun that glared overhead. A beachcomber was doubled over in joyous amusement near his unauthorized campfire.

Jordan said, "What is this?"

She spun around to the swimmer at her side with incredulity, "How did he get here?"

Ruakh exhaled heavily and turned to her, "You don't recognize our man?"

He smirked and pushed her ahead, "I said, 'Don't be afraid!'" and took off in a jog.

Jordan's eyes went wide, and she, too, turned and flung herself forward. She ran down the dune towards the water's edge and nearly lost her coordinated steps in the sand. She no longer cared about protocol and tore at her helmet's chin strap. She had to see if it was her treasured friend dressed as a beach loiterer. When Christian came up the beach soaked to the skin and threw himself toward Joshua, Jordan also charged from behind him with a loud shout.

Joshua Mansoul raised tall and looked up towards the sky. He painfully tossed his large sun hat skyward in the likeness of commencement celebrations. He cautiously lifted and extended his stiff arms, still in agony, and opened them to shoulder height on either side. Without a word, he welcomed their crushed embraces with joy. When their heads met his chest in an embrace, they felt him breathe on them. They inhaled the salty air deeply and wiped their fresh tears away. They could only laugh and cry in an interwoven moment of miraculous celebration encircled in their rescued rescuer's arms.

Jordan looked up at him with earnest tears that still flowed from her eyes and said, "Such good news! I cannot wait to tell somebody."

Christian added, “I believed!”

Joshua added in a rough and scratchy voice, “Rescue Checklist part two, we must complete.”

Chapter 30

A SURVIVOR'S GIFT

Hours later, a jubilant reunion was held at Naval Medical Center Portsmouth in Norfolk, Virginia. Joshua's crew, who had become family, his family, and a superior officer, stood around his hospital bed, still in awe. He struggled to speak due to the frailty of his condition. His heart overflowed. The mission had been a success. Down the hall was Mayim, who also recovered from his death-defying ordeal at the hands of his foolish father. Joshua looked forward to the moment when they would meet face-to-face.

Joshua whispered, "I'd like us to find and meet Kimberly, our new friend, and make her an honorary Guardian or an Auxiliarist. She left and wrote me a survivor's gift and letter."

Tears of joy had dried and flowed again intermittently, but spirits had never been higher in that room, in the CG community, and around the world. He extended a wrinkled piece of paper from his cracked and bloated hand. Maria, his mother, took the note and read it aloud to the Guardians closely around them. They each leaned in to hear about the factors that contributed to Joshua's presence now in their midst. Joshua rested on the soft pillow and closed his eyes to listen to the dedication again.

Maria read, "Welcome to the Keeper's Station. The NPS (National Park Service) makes us leave when you need us the most. Use these things all up, dearheart. They're all yours, for keeps. We'll be right back in a jiffy after the storm blows over to rescue you ourselves, so sit tight and make yourself at home. Unless the CG finds you first, that is. We love those kids. Faith, Hope, and Love, -Keeper's Quarters Docents Kimberly (and Max)"

Joshua continued his rescue story as softly as possible as if they were all in a library. A liter of warm fluid continued to drip slowly into this arm. A blood pressure cuff, oxygen monitor, and heart rate display vigilantly monitored him. He took a sip of water from a straw over his burnt lips, now covered with Vaseline. He was barely recognizable, though a light white hospital blanket covered him. His face and neck still glowed red from the vicious sunburn he had received on the water's surface the previous two days. His shiny braces peeked through his lips, which were blistered and bled. His listeners knew they dared not ask him to speak long.

Joshua spoke carefully, "She packed me this beach bag of stuff left over from the season. She stowed it on the covered front porch of the lighthouse Keeper's Quarters, where I found it tied to the door. I think I washed up on shore very early this morning. Exhausted but glad to be alive again, I must have slept for a few hours in the sand while the tide rolled out. I began to shiver uncontrollably in my wetsuit and awoke thankful to be on the ground, under brilliant stars and you sky rulers that hovered out of sight."

Joshua paused when his nurse, Olivia, entered the room with a fresh pitcher of cold water. She smiled from ear to ear behind her mask. Her eyes crinkled at the edges and gave away her joyous spirit. She was particularly grateful to be the nurse on duty for her miracle patient. Her dark curls bounced as she walked around them. She set the pitcher down after she refilled the cup Maria held. She motioned to all the visitors, even the highest-ranked one, and used her authority to speak.

"Don't stay long and wear him out much more than he is already. He's mine now."

The group chuckled and resigned themselves to a shorter visit than they wanted. Olivia left them in privacy. Everyone waited with bated breath for his words.

"I am so grateful to the Commandant to be here again with you. My last memories were of sky rulers' rotors and engines that beat around me, searched, and waited over the hellish underworld I was adrift in. I don't recall all that happened. The Guardian's light atop the lighthouse just drew me back, and the sound of you, who remembered me, urged me forward. The next thing I remember was that the sun's light faithfully poured over me."

One lone tear streaked its way down Joshua's face. It wasn't of sadness. It was pent-up joy and relief. Maria dabbed at the tear and then wiped her own away. She looked around the room and saw no dry face inside. In the long silence afterward, she held up a cup for Joshua to take another sip of water painfully. She dabbed at his lips with Vaseline on a long Q-tip to salve the wounds. He needed a minute to recover.

Joshua continued, "When I awoke, I knew I needed water foremost and then shade. I've never been so thirsty. I thought the gift shop would have water if I could make it. I didn't want to break in, but I knew I was a dead man walking ... to my surprise, right there on the porch was the beach bag waiting for me. It was loaded with water and food, and the campfire materials were stacked beside it. The beach stuff was a lifeline."

Joshua smirked even though it clearly hurt to do so. He took another sip of the offered water.

He continued, "Because I needed to get out of that wet suit badly. I sure hope some NPS beach camera didn't pick up my awesome nakedness."

"Look how wrinkled I am," he added.

They all laughed, and Joshua laid his head back on the pillow. His mother gave him another sip of water. He blinked heavily. Then he turned his eyes fully onto his mama,

He thought, *More wonderful than I'd dreamt of her near the end.*

Maria Mansoul smiled at her unique and extraordinary child, El Niño. She pondered in her heart that he was indeed alive again. She looked up at the men and women of the CG who stood nearby and grinned ear to ear behind their masks over their friend and co-worker with unashamed tears. Though they had doubts, the mission had not failed the past three days. Maria turned to her son but spoke to the small crowd that surrounded them.

"You need more rest, my El Niño. There is more for you to share, not everything at once."

Maria had her son back from the dead, and she savored every moment with him and treasured the experiences in her heart more than she ever had before. She stood as she assumed the responsibility of his care. She tried to protect and guard him the best she could until his recovery would be complete. They all recognized her orders ruled the day. One by one, the Guardians stepped forward to say a word to Joshua privately. The others sensed the sacredness of the moments that transpired. They were grateful for the face masks the nurses required them to wear post-Covid. The masks shielded some of their exhaustion, demonstrated in tumultuous emotions of relief, joy, and disbelief. The upheaval that the Covid pandemic caused to the CG and the entire Earth was enormous. It was an excellent situation to be in a mask and so joyful since they frequently caused so much division.

In turn, they gave each other personal space for a moment at his bedside. Shoulder to shoulder the presence of the least and the greatest had made for quite a sight for Joshua to behold. Eleazar, the Commandant of the Coast Guard, went first and then took his leave. The rest swayed back and forth on their tired feet as they waited their turn to say in their own words, “We will always remember you.” Christian, the Seaman, was now dressed in a dry and borrowed physical training uniform and unexpectedly followed the Commandant. The mech, Jordan, who still brushed the sand from her flight suit and bit into the side of her cheek to keep her tears at bay, followed him. Kodesh, Paulson, and Ruakh pulled at their reverent, yet barely controlled, joyous tears in the corner of their eyes and were last to bid him adios. They all swayed back and forth on their tired feet as they waited their turn to say in their own words, “We will always remember you.”

The USCG Band proudly played the upbeat, historic, and beloved Coast Guard Marching Song. It was August 4th, the birthday of the US Coast Guard, and a significant celebration and honorary appreciation banquet was being held for a crowd of about 500 inside an aircraft hangar. This many people hadn’t been assembled on CG property since before the COVID pandemic, so it was well attended and had several featured presentations, guests, and VIPs.

“We’re always ready for the call,
We place our trust in Thee.
Through surf and storm and howling gale,
High shall our purpose be.
“Semper Paratus” is our guide,
Our fame, our glory too.

To fight to save or fight and die,
Aye! Coast Guard we are for you!"

The familiar strains ended on a robust and accentuated note, and almost all sang lustily. The Master of Ceremonies (MC) asked the crowd to find seats. The room quieted, and a boy, age 11, was invited to the microphone. He wore a button-down shirt with a bow tie, which he tugged repeatedly. He wasn't used to such formal attire. His sandy brown hair and blue eyes swept over the large crowd as he stepped up on a step stool to reach the microphone, just as he had practiced. Nervously, he reached for the microphone and looked at the sea of faces who regarded him. Everyone understood it must have been an overwhelming ocean to face alone on stage as a youngster.

The child said, "Hi, my name is William, and I want to be a rescue swimmer like my heroes when I grow up."

He pointed at Joshua on the front row and gestured to others nearby he had just met that day. William glanced at his prepared talk on the podium in front of him. Then he looked up to find his parents, who gave him a thumbs up.

"So, there I was...it was a dark and stormy night. Haha, naw, I'm just kiddin' with ya'll. Last year during Ian, we'd gone out fishin' in September, and I caught a real rescue swimmer fin. My mom says I need to tell you *where* I was fishing ... 34°North 76°West, 'cuz fishin' ain't a place you go to..."

Laughter tittered through the crowd. They appreciated the reminder and cautionary lesson. The crowd quieted to encourage the boy to continue. Joshua scanned the crowd behind him to see his brothers' faces a few rows behind him. His mother sat next to them as a special guest of the CG. James' eyes met his eyes, twinkling with delight as they remembered a similar story when Joshua retold his version of what had happened the previous September. Joshua was so very proud that James was just about to begin his career in the CG as well. Boot camp was just around the corner, and Joshua was not as proud of any other accomplishment of his own as of having his flesh and blood follow him into the mission. They would serve their papa's aspirations together in Spirit, wherever the CG may send them. He smiled as William continued his story, and Joshua and James refocused.

William had gone on, "Well, about that same time, a fella named Christian from the Coast Guard was helpin' us with a dewaterin' pump. We sure was in a fix. Well, he spied my catch and took it. It was the CG fin named Mansoul. The truth is, he made me some kind of upset, but he wanted it way worse than I did, I could tell. But I wanted it bad, too. Who steals a fellas catch?"

The crowd laughed with the boy and knew he was a born storyteller. William left his notes and began to tell his story with gusto.

"Here's the good news. The fella, Christian, with my help o'course, found his rescue swimmer friend, and he's sittin' right there," he pointed at Joshua again.

"Today, I got a new pair of fins all my own. I mean, well, two *real* fins, a life vest, a chem light, mask, AND a snorkel, for keeps!"

Applause erupted across the gathering of hundreds of dignitaries, USCG personnel, families, and the U.S. Secretary of State. The MC approached the podium. The boy refused to step down and continued to speak to his parents' trepidation. His planned comments had already been said. The MC stood warily at the boy's side as he continued his unplanned remarks.

"My sister and me were *real* afraid until my mom reminded me that the Coast Guard never stops workin' night and day. No holidays, no weekends, *every* day of the year, always, like God. They have since

1790, and I hope all ya'll never quit, or we'll all be in a big fix. I say my prayers every night like Mama taught me, and you'd better say yours. Be sure to include the part I do that we just sang about to 'Place your trust in Thee.' I asked my Mama what that meant, and she said, '"Thee" is just another word for you.' But I noticed today it's capitalized, and my teacher said if it's capitalized, then it's proper, like a certain *you*.... So, folks, pray to the You, capital Y. O. U," he gestured with a pointed finger upward, "that will save you," he pointed emphatically towards them all. I know I did, and so did Christian and Joshua." He gestured to each of the men as he named them for emphasis, "That makes them my heroes."

William grinned at the men in the front row, who were bigger than life to him. He wanted to follow them and become just like them in so many ways. The crowd, primarily uniformed service members, felt they could neither applaud nor disapprove in the US government facility near the nation's capital. The child had given them a greater appreciation of their robust USCG service song. The orders of the child settled over them as William stepped down from the podium and walked off the stage to his parents, who beamed on the front row. His little sister fist-bumped him as he took his seat. She snuggled her new little CG stuffed dog, a black lab named Onyx.

The MC removed the stepstool and was so humbled and moved by the boy's sincerity that he could not speak his prepared words.

He said, "Thank you, William."

The crowd understood and empathized with the man and waited momentarily as he continued to clear his throat. A weighty silence filled the room, and a sudden breeze blew over the crowd from where a back door was propped open. It was a welcome disruption as some guests began to fan themselves and perhaps their consciences from the hangar's heat.

A recently retired Captain Paz sat adjacent to Petty Officer 1st Class Mansoul. He turned to her with his broad smile and displayed his evenly and flawlessly distributed teeth. She winked at him. He closed his mouth and licked the front of his new straight teeth behind his lips without braces. He bowed his head and waited as they all did for the decorum of the occasion to continue as planned. Flags began to ripple as the wind continued to blow where it pleased.

The MC introduced the Senator from North Carolina, Ric McCollins, as he approached the same podium. The Senator began his remarks with the same sweet coastal Carolina drawl William had used but in a more refined and dignified manner found in the state capital region of Raleigh.

The Senator nodded, grinned broadly, and began, "Ladies and gentlemen, I am so proud of the USCG and its presence in our great state of Nooorth Care'o-lina," as if it had been his idea to locate them there.

Senator Ric McCollins continued for a long while about the beauty of the state of North Carolina and specifically the Outer Banks until the onlookers wondered if this had become a commercial for the NC state visitor's guide. He, at long last, mentioned that he particularly wanted the folks who volunteered their time to stay at the Lighthouses and work with the National Park System to be recognized. He invited Ms. Kimberly and Mr. Max to the platform.

Senator McCollins said, "Although they are natives of Murphy in the mountains of Western North Carolina, it had always been her dream to operate a lighthouse or at least live in one voluntarily for a few weeks."

He added, "Ya'll are welcome to visit our fine state of North Care'olina and volunteer at any of our parks or even join one of our staff ..."

He tacked on as an afterthought, "As soon as you retire from the Guardin' business, that is. We need you savin' us 'til then."

The crowd laughed politely at his infomercial conclusion while Kimberly used the handrail to pull herself carefully onto the platform. She made her way slowly toward the podium, aided by her husband, Max, who looked uncomfortable on stage. She shook hands with her Senator and laid either hand on the podium frame. She pushed herself on her tiptoes to see Joshua on the other side.

"There you is, young man. You look terrific in that dashin' uniform. All youin's do!" she gestured across the crowd.

They muffled their laughter at her quaint Appalachian accent from the Smoky Mountains of the Carolinas. This became more colorful, and collectively, they leaned forward in their seats.

"It is my distinct hon'or (it sounded like 'on or') to accept this nice Guard membership from Sector North Carolina. I am truly over the moon, I am. The highest hon'or was gettin' to be at the Keepers' Quarters, which serves as a museum that gives visitors a glimpse into the lives of Lighthouse Keepers and Surfmen of the US Life-Saving Service. The birthday of the Coast Guard is a great day to remember our surfmen and their families of the good ole days. The museum is open from 9 AM to 5 PM, seven days a week durin' the spring, summer, and fall. Except for hurr'icanes."

Everyone laughed with her when Ms. Kim paused for dramatic effect. She drew the crowd in further with her dialect, slow and softened speech.

"When the Mr. and I," she nodded towards Max, who stood shyly beside her, "arrived at Harker's Island Cape Lookout National Seashore. It was a beautiful day. Glorious. Simply divine. The Visitors Center Ferry took us to our dream work vacation and casually made mention' that the ferry service was weather de-pen-dent. I looked at my Max and asked him what *ever* could *that* mean? He says to me, "Ain't always runn'in', I 'spose.'"

The crowd chortled with them both. She slapped the podium at her humorous remembrance.

She continued, "I says to him that ain't right. Folk's is goin' need that ferry when the weather ain't good! And you know what my man says? "'S'pose that's what the Coast Guard's for."

The crowd roared with laughter, hooted, and cheered despite the formality of the occasion. Max smiled from ear to ear and visibly relaxed among his newfound friends.

"We just nestl'd right down and enjoyed every bit of the time we shared with the vacationers, biologists, and lost souls' wanderin' those pretty beaches. The lighthouse is closed for repairs nowadays, but it'll be fix'd up right quick, we been told.

As another natural storyteller, Ms. Kimberly paused for a dramatic effect and looked directly at William and Abigail. She wanted the children to remember her words especially.

"So, there we were," she winked at William, "In the middle of our work-cation when old hurricane Ian made us skedaddle. As I was a packin' my bags, somethin' occurred to me. When the old timers wrecked on the Carolina shores, they had the US Life Saving Service; an open home, a dry blanket, and a warm *far* (fire) to warm themselves near. I was told to git, so I packed one more bag. I left it sheltered and tied to the front door 'for we left. Good thing, too. Lord knows where we'd all be today if He hadn't prompted me to. I says a prayer of thanks for a lovely place to come today with all ya'll and for any mariner needin' the lighthouses and their keepers. Thank ye."

The silence in the vast room was palpable. Most present knew about the minor saving grace the woman had demonstrated, but none dared diminish the importance that everyone played in the rescue of one of their own. She drew on their energy and leaned towards them to share the rest of her story.

"Next thing I knows is this youngin' Joshua phones us up and says he's got some good news. He done found my tote and my note! He says it helped bring him back to life. Truth be told, days like today help save us all. We need each other—more than ever. The mission was never just for one person. It ain't about you. It's about all ya'll. Youngin' Joshua said the swimmer shop wanted to offer me fins and a snorkel like 'ol Willy mentioned earlier," she gestured to little William and his family.

She shook her head with disbelief and then looked dramatically at Max, and he shrugged his shoulders. The onlookers were rapt with attention and giggled with her. Every mind pictured the sweet older couple with the same gear of a rescue swimmer with hilarity.

"I says, Lordy, I don't do none of that in my Western Carolina home. Youin's keep that junk. Just let me see ya'll in you uniforms.' Bam, here we are! I wanna have me a picture made with some of you's so I can git home and tell all the world about today. The gift weren't no 'thing'. It was in the offer'n up the rescue. My joy was when I knew it had been rightly received and remembered."

She pounded the lectern joyfully and paused with a wide grin. Applause broke out and filled the hangar. She winked at her husband, who stood beside her and shifted nervously from one foot to another. He motioned to his watch to wrap it up.

"I thank ya for includin' us in youin's birthday party and the Guard's business of savin'. We must guard one another's souls all our days. That is for sure. Let's have us some cake. And I brought nana-puddin', too."

Ms. Kimberly pointed at William and his sister Abigail, who waved excitedly back. The crowd came to its feet with appreciation for the heartfelt words of the speaker. The MC motioned the next speaker with a nod. The follow-on speaker went to the platform and shook Kim and Max's hands enthusiastically while he was introduced to the crowd. He paused and collected his emotions before he began to speak, and the crowd quieted. The newest Commandant of the USCG, in his brilliant tropical blue uniform and gold stripes up the sleeves that dazzled under the spotlights, inclined his head towards Joshua Mansoul.

Commandant Eleazar spoke, "I'd like to ask Petty Officer 1st Class Joshua Mansoul to come forward to receive his Distinguished Flying Cross, the nation's highest flying-achievement military decoration."

Joshua was humble as he stepped forward carefully in his Class A uniform before a silent audience to receive his medal for 'heroism while participating in an aerial flight.' He made his way to the side of the Commandant on the platform and stood rigidly with precision. Before an ocean of well-wishers, Joshua was stunned briefly by the compassionate looks of appreciation of strangers and the many of those he knew by name. His gaze passed from his Mama, Maria, to his little brothers, who had become grown men, friends from his CG tours, and acquaintances he'd made his whole life. He found mothers and sons reunited like Mayim, Christian, and others, too many to name. There were many onlookers, but his eyes searched for the face of the man he wanted most desperately to share the day.

The MC announced, "Ladies and Gentlemen, please rise for the presentation of the Distinguished Flying Cross. Attention to orders. Petty Officer 1st Class Joshua Mansoul distinguished himself in selfless sacrifice with survivors on 30th September 2022. Exemplifying the Coast Guard's core values of honor, respect, and devotion to duty, he put himself in great danger when he knowingly entered a hostile environment during Hurricane Ian..."

After the MC finished the citation, he returned the floor to Commandant Eleazar, who shared his perspective on the CG's responsiveness.

Eleazar said, "AST1 Mansoul attempted to rescue two survivors at dusk and was lost at sea in the churning Atlantic Ocean for approximately sixty hours. He honorably facilitated one survivor's eventual rescue due to his heroic swim and rescue into a life raft in formidable sea conditions during Hurricane Ian. After locating each survivor, he heroically and respectfully negotiated with a hostile survivor. He steadied the life raft, and all were inside. Unfortunately, one survivor did not consent and put himself in harm's way, knocking Mansoul sightless from behind. Both men were later retrieved from the life raft. One is deceased; the other is present today. After being stripped of his life-saving technology, Mansoul endured storm and gale-force winds for the remaining two days alone at sea. His tenacity to the swimmer's mission, 'so others may live,' is exemplary to us all. We exist to leave the confines of our safety and security to find the lost. Our nation is a better community to live in and serve due to the lived-out core values of honor, respect, and devotion to duty."

The Commandant paused briefly and regarded the room at full attention to be sure he had their full attentiveness to his words.

He continued, "Everyone knows the scariest place in the universe is to be alone in a vast ocean and desperate for rescue. When he put one finless foot in front of the other finless foot, Petty Officer 1st Class Joshua Mansoul persevered in his devotion to duty as he made his way forward through a sea of stars in the sky and chaos of waves below. He knew it would be a long night alone, let alone two. He was never alone; the mission was never foiled, though, for a time, it looked bleak. When some were ready to plan the funeral, I was ready to welcome Joshua home. The mission continued and continues ceaselessly. Under my watch and yours, it will always continue. May we all follow, answer, and remember the example of Petty Officer 1st Class Joshua Mansoul."

The Commandant concluded his remarks and shifted his gaze over the crowd in earnestness for those who would obey his command. The two men faced each other and saluted one another in a moment of deep respect and profound introduction to the awarding of the Distinguished Flying Cross.

After the speech, Joshua finally found the familiar face he was desperate for with round spectacles, a slight tremor, and shameless tears that streamed down his face. Jones was now in a wheelchair and seated on the platform's far side, dressed in an oversized blue jacket with a CG orange tie. Pinned to his dark coat was his prized Distinguished Flying Cross. The two men looked at each other with soulful recognition and deep respect. They knew a deep and principal secret. Those who humbled themselves before their rescuers would live; if not, they would face peril. Others would die to themselves, lost to the eyes of the world, and yet genuinely live. Joshua's wide grin of perfectly aligned white teeth escaped after the applause that thundered like a Jayhawk helo through him.

The award was presented, and the medal was placed over Joshua's heart on his uniform to another sizeable standing ovation. Joshua refused any photo without other Guardians with him. He mainly wanted photos with the crew that both took him to the scene and the other that assisted him three days later from shore. More photos were taken with his family that flanked him on either side. Joshua was certain to have a photo taken with Jones and the Commandant for a remarkable gesture of affection for his hero.

The Commandant offered the podium to Joshua to make his remarks afterward. Joshua stepped lightly to the podium and gathered his thoughts briefly before he dove into the sea of familiar and unfamiliar faces to share his story.

"*Deo Juvante,* 'With God's help.' On the horizon, I made out the dim flash of repeated light that would anchor my soul and eventually welcome me home. The darkness could not shut out the light. I wanted to find respite from the storm but could not do it alone. When my eyes regained their sight, they began to swing back and forth over the sea of hostility: tumultuous weather, thrashing waves, shark-infested waters, dehydration, hypothermia, and the march of time that was relentless as my life slipped away. When midday became midnight, I was tempted to entertain despair without hope. However, I realized guardianship was what I did, who I am, and who I wanted to be remembered for. It was better for me to suffer for doing good. My suffering would not compare to the glory of a life well lived and given sacrificially to fulfill the mission and motto, "So others may live." We just sang the song, which I continued to mumble to myself over the waves that threatened to pull me under."

Joshua, with uncharacteristic bravado, launched into a rousing rendition of the CG song,

"Our fame, our glory too.
To fight to save or fight and die,
Aye! Coast Guard we are for you!"

"After so long in the water, in exhaustion, I laid back in my flotation collar and surrendered to the unseen forces. The sun rose, and then there was evening, and there was morning again. The sea currents swirled about me, and the waves and breakers swept over me. I felt the promised Spirit of unity we hold tightly to every day; it held me up when I could no longer hold myself. Into that Spirit, I gave myself over. From the east, a wind had come. I must have ridden the wind over the waves that gathered in swells headed towards the Carolina shore. Like sea glass washed ashore, broken and redeemed for a new purpose, I was given new life. It seems I was spat onto shore, much like the prophet of old, Jonah, glad to be alive once more..."

Joshua scanned over the crowd and found Jonah's face from the night of his perilous duty. Jonah was as sober as many were glad. After Jonah's words of shame that night, the young mech had suffered more than most of the crew when Joshua had been lost in the sea. The gaze they shared was meant to heal their relationship. Joshua, in his death and restoration to life, had forgiven Jonah and Nabal for their faults and disbelief.

Joshua continued, "Today, you have bestowed upon me some measure of fame for which I am grateful, but it is not my glory. I needed a miracle of epic proportions to live for another day during that tragic time. I required an inexplicably strong east wind and the buoyancy of my Coast Guard-approved flotation device."

They crowd of Guardians snickered and Joshua grinned and took a breath along with everyone else as they raptly listened.

"I slipped away in the surf, storm, and howling gale. Not everyone is saved physically, but everyone can be prepared to be rescued if they know I am and we are out there and willing to give our lives for them. I thought of the many survivors who perhaps waited as I did when no rescue appeared: when the float plan wasn't made, when the communication was broken, when survivors didn't know how or where to ask for help... or when the rescue eventually came supernaturally. The Coast Guard was there for them if only they had been prepared. We have always been there for them. You were there for me and searched for me in the darkest night. I thought of my Papa and those who wore the Distinguished Flying Cross. Would I be rescued like one of those many have given their lives for?"

Joshua's eyes beheld Jones briefly before he scanned the crowd again.

"You remembered me. I stand here in a long, ancient line of heroes and heroines on the mission to give themselves selflessly. Let us all share the mission to follow, answer, and remember our callings. I will bear this cross humbly because I know my resurrection is a gift for the sake of others. I glory only in the mission of us all, for it bears the authority to do this and more than we ever thought imaginable for all of humanity."

Joshua focused on the few people he knew had been with him his whole life who were most thrilled at his deliverance. The speech went on to recount for the world who had ears to hear the way his rescuers had assisted him when his body had given up. His eyes met with Christian, who wore his uniform and sported his shiny new AST wings. Those wings were confirmation that the terrible days behind them both had been redeemed. New opportunities for living abundantly had sprung up where suffering had bonded them. His eyes met those of Jordan, who busily took meticulous notes. Benjamin, Caleb, and comrades from all his days in the CG had been sat near the front. They celebrated his admiration as theirs. The mission, they all knew, was forever a collaborative effort.

Joshua continued, "...and due to the diligence of the US Life Saving Service, the Coast Guard ethos to protect, defend, and save, we have been tested and proven genuine. Where will your help come from? We are, *Semper Paratus.*"

Joshua took his seat to applause and another standing ovation. The MC spoke again from the podium.

"Ladies and Gentlemen, please be seated. Thank you to all our Senators, distinguished guests, service members, friends, and family, and you who have made this Coast Guard Birthday a celebration of all our achievements. Your presence with us today is the culmination of a mission that knows no bounds, holds no fear, and exemplifies selfless devotion to duty. May the testimony of our history, countless souls rescued, and mystery of selflessness in action continue upon our shoulders as we keep the watch."

The MC looked over the crowd as a steady breeze blew through the hangar, flags unfurled, and a small child whimpered somewhere to be comforted.

"Allow me to ask my friend and Coast Guard Chaplain to quote from a favorite letter in closing."

The Chaplain of the Coast Guard approached the platform, opened an essential document of correspondence, and spoke, "From another Guardian of souls, Petros, from a different place and era, but it has never been truer for us he shares a survivor's gift. Hear this, you who are ready to hear, 'If with heart and soul you're doing good, do you think you can be stopped? Even if you suffer for it, you're still better off. Don't give the opposition a second thought. Through thick and thin, keep your heart's attention in adoration before Christ, your Master. Be ready, *Semper Paratus*, to speak up and tell anyone who asks why you're living the way you are, and always with the utmost courtesy. Keep a clear conscience before God so that when people throw mud at you, none of it will stick. They'll end up realizing that they're the ones who need a bath. It's better to suffer for doing good, if that's what God wants, than to be punished for doing bad. That is what Christ did definitively; suffered because of others' sins, the Righteous One for the unrighteous ones. He went through it all- was put to death and then made alive to bring us to God.'"

DEDICATION

With thanksgiving for my Captain and to Coast Guardsmen
and their families past, present, and future.

SHOUT OUTS AND ACKNOWLEDGEMENTS

My sincerest appreciation goes to my immediate family for their encouragement, sacrifices, and steadfast support of my callings to them and the Trinity. To them belong my heart, soul, mind, and strength.

I'd like share my gratitude with my parents and all the saints who have believed in how the Trinity could use even me and applaud my feeble attempts at love. My loving extended family, who have inspired me to create and take an audacious risk, I am in your debt forever.

"Friends are the family we chose for ourselves..."

Beside and among them are my remarkable friends, with whom I am grateful beyond measure. To those who took the time to read rough drafts, converse about these topics, share their skills, and walk this journey with me, you have done the heavy work, and I am indebted to you.

My friends have helped shape my life in countless ways in abiding friendship over our current season in the mountains, Coast Guard and Air Force years. I am and will forever be grateful for those in my educational decades at Asbury, Purdue, Wawasee, and in my formative years of childhood when I learned about the power of a great story.

To my dear Church families, who have been at the crossroads of my life, you have given me an enriched experience and more vital witness.

I have a better story to tell because of you. Your addition to the Mission has been essential, and your graciousness humbles me.

Lastly, I'm tremendously humbled by you, the reader, the reason I have written. I am deeply grateful for your gift of time and attention, the best expression of your love. We may not yet be family, but how I long to add you to the adventure in the co-mission of the Trinity: to love my neighbors (that's you) as myself. I wrote this novel for you to know how much "Thee" Supreme Author(ity) delights in rescue, especially of you.

ABOUT THE AUTHOR

After she graduated from Space Academy, Purdue University, Asbury Seminary, and Air Force Chaplain School, the author discerned it was time to write. The Coast Guard mission was supreme for composing a book about a few of her favorite people, places, and things. This debut novel has been prepared for with grand adventures around the globe. Amy Sheffield, her husband, and their children are grateful for their existence, time on the water and in the mountains, and steadfast fellowship with the Trinity.

AFTERWORD

Here is a brief word about the origin of this labor of love. Captain Maria-Paz Smith, United States Public Health Service (Retired), asked me to share a prayer at her retirement ceremony. She is a dear friend and was a co-worker with my husband at USCG Base Elizabeth City, NC. I began to search for the words to honor the Godly woman I knew her to be. She is to me, as Dr. Tim Mackie ascribed, "A human fully alive to God is a human empowered, connected to, and influenced by God's ruakh (Spirit)." I was humbled to pray for her as I knew her to be a strong prayer warrior and an astute dentist in the U.S. Coast Guard.

In a quick online search, I found the CG motto, *Semper Paratus,* in the Holy Writ on only one occasion. It's in the letter attributed to Peter, the follower and protégé of Jesus. 1 Peter chapter 3, verse 15 says, "...*Always be prepared* to give an answer for the hope that you have..." More valid words could not have been likened to Dr. Maria-Paz Smith. The spoken prayer on that memorable day of May has been lost to time. My Public Health Dentist friend, Maria-Paz, had serendipitously challenged me to answer for the hope we shared with anyone, family, and friends. As of this writing in Nov. of '23, we invite you to answer, too.

What has not been lost to time is my astonishment in further study. I found that with the help of two more public health dentists nearly 100 years ago, Captain Francis Saltus Van Boskerck, USCG, put his words to music in the remote region of Alaska. In the far reaches of the Alaska Territory, the Coast Guard Marching Song was born on a borrowed piano. The upbeat tune includes the lyrics, 'High Shall our purpose Be' and 'We place our trust in Thee.' This also renewed my quest to live *Semper Paratus* and always be prepared to assist others to answer for their hope.

While I have meditated on this subject for years, it has been a persistent companion that, like a great friend, has not left me alone. I listened intently to stories about how survivors had astonishingly refused rescue. Treasured CG friends are remarkable men and women who represent core values and selflessness and, at times, have faced rejection of a CG rescue and the subsequent devastation. Their shared witnesses could not be disregarded. My study included these formative and wise words shared with permission from Mario Vittone, USCG AST (Retired), "I realized that what we did for a living, most of the time, was to try and save people from themselves. That case changed me more than any other and convinced me that the last great gains to be made in maritime safety involved the way people thought about boating. The realization that prevention saves more lives than response is what made me change professions from rescuer to writer and teacher. We didn't find the kids on that search, though we kept looking until we ran low on fuel and had to head back to base. We were the last to look before the search was called off. The place is still there, and I'm going to keep doing my best to change the way boaters think about it, and about all the places where they're out on boats."

Incredulous of the profound nature these accounts of CG crew members had upon me, I began to pull together the allegory of the rescue mission of the CG to that of Jesus' rescue mission to humanity. I have always had a fondness for the parables of Jesus, the allegorical tales of Lewis' *Chronicles of Narnia*, the profound truths in Bunyan's *Pilgrim's Progress*, and the importance of story for every life and culture. "For me, reason is the natural organ of truth; but imagination is the organ of meaning." --C.S. Lewis

I then, in obedience, began to write the novel you hold in your hands. Much like Mario, I want to change how people think about boating. However, I would like to challenge how they understand their souls being rescued by "Joshua" could make a rescue story possible for all of humanity. My audacious quest is to follow Him, as did Petros, Captain Van, Maria-Paz, my spouse, and many remarkable others who shared their rescue stories with me. I've not courageously leaped into an untamed ocean on your behalf, but I am in the spiritual sense. My rescue would never have happened if the ancients and my ancestors hadn't shared their stories. We are entrusted to rescue once we have been rescued. Share your story, too. If you think no one wants to listen, please write to me. I desire to be *Semper Paratus* for you.

If you're interested in a deeper dive into the mission of the US Coast Guard, I'll try to connect you to someone who knows more about their mission. Perhaps you may be interested in discussing an inside look at the specific call to "So Others May Live." If you're interested in the mission of the rescue of humanity, I'd be honored to have that conversation with you. There are nuances in this novel that I'd be delighted to share regarding the names, spiritual foundations, and references to the whole unified story that leads to "Joshua." Write to me, and I'll joyfully share those thoughts for further exploration and a richer understanding.

For instance, allow me to put a toe into the water about what I mean to explore the names. The name used by most English-speaking people today, Jesus, is an English transliteration of a Germanic version, of a Latin transliteration, of a Greek transliteration of an initially Hebrew name, that is simply Yeshua. In Hebrew, the name Yeshua translates to Yahweh is salvation. Yehoshua is a derivation of yeho (meaning God) and shua (meaning to deliver or save). **Joshua** comes from "Yehoshua" and **means "God is deliverance."**

We who have joined the co-mission of Father (Papa), Son (Joshua), and Spirit (Ruakh) desire everyone to be always prepared to live out these words and have an answer for their hope in "Joshua" with gentleness and respect. The allegorical heart of this book is before you, and so is the application for all to meet their Rescuer. Therefore, I remind you to prepare your rescue checklist with these questions for your quest in this extraordinary and adventuresome life.

Will you follow?
What is your answer?
Will you remember?

REVIEWS PLEASE

Thank you for reading my book!

Please leave a great review if you liked it and share the book! Thank you for taking your most valuable gift, your time, to read and participate in its life. As a self-published author, it's never too late to make corrections! Please take two minutes now to leave a helpful review of what you thought of the book on Amazon or Goodreads.

You can leave your comments at these places:

Amazon
Goodreads
Facebook: Rescue Checklist Part 1

Or You may correspond with me at:
rescuechecklist@gmail.com

Made in the USA
Columbia, SC
09 September 2024

42032512R00297